Dear Reader,

Those of you who are familiar with my books know that Ireland is one of my favorite places to visit, in real life and in fiction. It's a country of dramatic cliffs and quiet fields. One of myth and magic and legend. In Jewels of the Sun, I've borrowed from some of those myths and created my own legend.

It could have happened.

I'd like you to meet the Gallaghers of Ardmore: Aidan, Shawn, and Darcy, who run the local pub in this pretty seaside village in the county of Waterford. Not far from the village is a cottage, a place of magic where a lonely American woman comes to explore her roots and her heart.

She won't be alone in the house, for there is another lonely woman in residence. She just happens to be a ghost.

With the help of a faerie prince who loved well if not wise, Aidan Gallagher of Ardmore and Jude Frances Murray from Chicago will find their place, and take the first step toward breaking a hundred-year spell.

I'd like to take you back to Ireland with me, through the doors of Gallagher's Pub where the fire's burning low and the pints are waiting. I have a story to tell you.

Nora Roberts

HOMEPORT

"*Homeport* is vintage Roberts. The prose is taut, the story is well researched, and the bodice-ripping sex scenes (minus the bodice) are steamy. Roberts, whose last bestseller was *Sanctuary*, is fond of titles that suggest refuge. After flirting with danger, that is just what her heroine hopes to find—a home, herself, and the man of her dreams."

—*People*

"Roberts will certainly continue her prolific track record of bestsellers with this newest work . . . just the right combination of romance, humor . . . an amazingly varied cast of family characters, and a cliff-hanger (literally) of an ending. . . . Sure to please Roberts's legions of fans."

—*Library Journal*

"In all her writing, Roberts is known for her wry humor . . . keeps pushing the envelope of the romance form . . . the Joyce Carol Oates of the romance."

—*Publishers Weekly*

"Nora Roberts is a prolific writer whose quality of work has never diminished. With *Homeport*, the author again delivers a marvelous story, gratifying from beginning to end."

—*Rocky Mountain News*

JEWELS
OF THE SUN

NORA ROBERTS

JOVE BOOKS, NEW YORK

JEWELS OF THE SUN

A Jove Book / published by arrangement with
the author

PRINTING HISTORY
Jove edition / November 1999

The Penguin Putnam Inc. World Wide Web site address is
http://www.penguinputnam.com

ISBN: 0-515-12677-2

A JOVE BOOK®
Jove Books are published by The Berkley Publishing Group,
a division of Penguin Putnam Inc.,
375 Hudson Street, New York, New York 10014.
JOVE and the ''J'' design
are trademarks belonging to Penguin Putnam Inc.

PRINTED IN THE UNITED STATES OF AMERICA

10 9 8 7 6 5 4 3 2 1

For Ruth Ryan Langan

Come away! O, human child!
To the woods and waters wild,
With a fairy hand in hand,
For the world's more full of weeping than
you can understand.

—W. B. YEATS

JEWELS
OF THE SUN

ONE

OBVIOUSLY, WITHOUT QUESTION, she'd lost her mind.

Being a psychologist, she ought to know.

All the signs were there, had been there, hovering and humming around her for months. The edginess, the short temper, the tendency toward daydreaming and forgetfulness. There'd been a lack of motivation, of energy, of purpose.

Her parents had commented on it in their mild, you-can-do-better-Jude way. Her colleagues had begun to glance at her, covertly, with quiet pity or unquiet distaste. She'd come to detest her job, resent her students, find a dozen petty faults with her friends and her family, her associates and superiors.

Every morning the simple task of getting out of bed to dress for the day's classes had taken on the proportions of scaling a mountain. Worse, a mountain she had absolutely no interest in seeing from a distance, much less climbing.

Then there was the rash, impulsive behavior. Oh, yes,

that was the final tip-off. Steady-as-she-goes Jude Frances Murray, one of the sturdiest branches on the family tree of the Chicago Murrays, sensible and devoted daughter of Doctors Linda and John K. Murray, quit her job.

Not took a sabbatical from the university, not asked for a few weeks' leave, but quit, right in the middle of the semester.

Why? She didn't have the faintest idea.

It had been as much a shock to her as to the dean, to her associates, to her parents.

Had she reacted in this manner two years before when her marriage had shattered? No, indeed. She'd simply continued her routine—her classes, her studies, her appointments—without a hitch, even while shuffling in the lawyers and neatly filing the paperwork that symbolizes the end of a union.

Not that there'd been much of a union, or a great deal of hassling for the lawyers to legally sever it. A marriage that had lasted just under eight months didn't generate a great deal of mess or trouble. Or passion.

Passion, she supposed was what had been missing. If she'd had any, William wouldn't have left her flat for another woman almost before the flowers in her bridal bouquet had faded.

But there was no point in brooding over it at this late date. She was what she was. Or had been what she was, she corrected. God only knew what she was now.

Maybe that was part of it, she mused. She'd been on some verge, had looked down at the vast, dark sea of sameness, of monotony, of tedium that was Jude Murray. She'd pinwheeled her arms, scrambled back from the edge—and run screaming away.

It was so unlike her.

Thinking about it gave her such sharp palpitations she

wondered if she might be having a heart attack just to cap things off.

AMERICAN COLLEGE PROFESSOR FOUND DEAD
IN LEASED VOLVO

It would be an odd obituary. Perhaps it would make it into the *Irish Times*, which her grandmother so loved to read. Her parents would be shocked, of course. It was such an untidy, public, *embarrassing* kind of death. Completely unsuitable.

Naturally, they'd be heartbroken as well, but overall they would be puzzled. What in the world was the girl thinking of, going off to Ireland when she had a thriving career and a lovely condo on the lakeside?

They would blame Granny's influence.

And, of course, they would be right, as they had been right since the moment she'd been conceived in a very tasteful mating precisely one year after they'd married.

Though she didn't care to imagine it, Jude was certain that her parents' lovemaking was always very tasteful and precise. Rather like the well-choreographed and traditional ballets they both so enjoyed.

And what was she doing, sitting in a leased Volvo that had its stupid wheel on the stupid wrong side of the car and thinking about her parents having sex?

All she could do was press her fingers to her eyes until the image faded away.

This, she told herself, was just the sort of thing that happened when you went crazy.

She took a deep breath, then another. Oxygen to clear and calm the brain. As she saw it, she now had two choices. She could drag her suitcases out of the car, go inside the Dublin airport and turn the keys back in to the leasing agent with the carrot-red hair and the mile-wide smile, and book a flight home.

Of course she had no job, but she could live off her stock portfolio very nicely for quite some time, thank you. She also no longer had a condo, as she'd rented it to that nice couple for the next six months, but if she did go home she could stay with Granny for a while.

And Granny would look at her with those beautiful faded blue eyes full of disappointment. *Jude, darling, you always get right to the edge of your heart's desire. Why is it you can never take that last step over?*

"I don't know. I don't know." Miserable, Jude covered her face with her hands and rocked. "It was your idea I come here, not mine. What am I going to do in Faerie Hill Cottage for the next six months? I don't even know how to drive this damn car."

She was one sob away from a crying jag. She felt it flood her throat, ring in her ears. Before the first tear could fall, she let her head roll back, squeezed her eyes tight shut, and cursed herself. Crying jags, temper tantrums, sarcasm, and otherwise rude behavior were merely various ways of acting out. She'd been raised to understand it, trained to recognize it. And she would not give in to it.

"On to the next stage, Jude, you pathetic idiot. Talking to yourself, crying in Volvos, too indecisive, too goddamn paralyzed to turn on the ignition and just go."

She huffed out another breath, straightened her shoulders. "Second choice," she muttered. "Finish what you started."

She turned the key and, sending up a little prayer that she wouldn't kill or maim anyone—including herself—on the drive, eased the car out of Park.

She sang, mostly to keep herself from screaming every time she came to one of the circles on the highway that the Irish cheerfully called roundabouts. Her brain would fizzle, she'd forget her left from her right, visualize plowing the Volvo into half a dozen innocent bystanders, and belt out whatever tune jumped into her terrified brain.

On the route south from Dublin to County Waterford, she shouted show tunes, roared out Irish pub songs, and at a narrow escape outside the town of Carlow, screeched out the chorus of ''Brown Sugar'' loud enough to make Mick Jagger wince.

After that it calmed down a bit. Perhaps the gods of the traveler had been shocked enough by the noise to step back and stop throwing other cars in her path. Maybe it was the influence of the ubiquitous shrines to the Blessed Virgin that populated the roadside. In either case, the driving smoothed out and Jude began, almost, to enjoy herself.

Roll after roll of green hills shimmered under sunlight that glowed like the inside of seashells and spread back and back into the shadows of dark mountains. The hulk of them rambled against a sky layered with smoky clouds and pearly light that belonged in paintings rather than reality.

Paintings, she thought, as her mind wandered, so beautifully rendered that when you looked at them long enough you felt yourself slipping right into them, melting into the colors and shapes and the scene that some master had created out of his own brilliance.

That was what she saw, when she dared take her eyes off the road. Brilliance, and a terrible, stunning beauty that ripped the heart even as it soothed it again.

Green, impossibly green, the fields were broken by rambling walls of rough hedges or lines of stunted trees. Spotted cows or shaggy sheep grazed lazily in them, figures on tractors putted over them. Here and there they were dotted with houses of white and cream where clothes flapped on lines and flowers burst with wild and careless color in the dooryards.

Then wonderfully, inexplicably, there would be the ancient walls of a ruined abbey, standing proud and broken against the dazzling field and sky as if waiting for its time to come round again.

What would you feel, she wondered, if you crossed the field and walked up the smooth and slick steps left standing in those tumbling stones? Would you—could you—feel the centuries of passing feet that had trod those same steps? Would you, as her grandmother claimed, be able to hear— if only you listened—the music and voices, the clash of battles, the weeping of women, the laughter of children so long dead and gone?

She didn't believe in such things, of course. But here, with this light, with this air, it seemed almost possible.

From the ruined grandeur to the charmingly simple, the land spread out and offered. Thatched roofs, stone crosses, castles, then villages with narrow streets and signs written in Gaelic.

Once she saw an old man walking with his dog on the side of the road where the grass grew tall and a little sign warned of loose chippings. Both man and hound wore little brown hats that she found absolutely charming. She kept that picture in her mind a long time, envying them their freedom and the simplicity of their routine.

They would walk every day, she imagined. Rain or shine, then go home to tea in some pretty little cottage with a thatched roof and a well-tended garden. The dog would have a little house of his own, but would most usually be found curled at his master's feet by the fire.

She wanted to walk those fields with a devoted dog, too. Just to walk and walk until she felt like sitting. Then to sit and sit until she felt like standing. It was a concept that dazzled her. Doing what she wanted when she wanted, at her own pace and in her own way.

It was so foreign to her, that simple, everyday freedom. Her great fear was to finally find it, nip the silvered edge of it with her fingertips, then bungle it.

As the road wound and ribboned around the coast of Waterford, she caught glimpses and stretches of the sea, blue silk against the horizon, turbulent green and gray as it spewed against a wide, sandy curve of beach.

The tension in her shoulders began to slide away. Her hands relaxed a bit on the wheel. This was the Ireland her grandmother had spoken of, the color and drama and peace of it. And this, Jude supposed, is why she'd finally come to see where her roots had dug before being ripped free and replanted across the Atlantic.

She was glad now she hadn't balked at the gate and run back to Chicago. Hadn't she managed the best part of the three-and-a-half-hour drive without a single mishap? She wasn't counting the little glitch at that roundabout in Waterford City where she'd ended up circling three times, then nearly bashing into a car full of equally terrified tourists.

Everyone had escaped without harm, after all.

Now she was nearly there. The signs for the village of Ardmore said so. She knew from the careful map her grandmother had drawn that Ardmore was the closest village to the cottage. That's where she would go for supplies and whatever.

Naturally, her grandmother had also given her an impressive list of names, people she was supposed to look up, distant relatives she was to introduce herself to. That, Jude decided, could wait.

Imagine, she thought, not having to talk to anyone for several days in a row! Not being asked questions and being expected to know the answers. No making small talk at faculty functions. No schedule that must be adhered to.

After one moment of blissful pleasure about the idea, her

heart fluttered in panic. What in God's name was she going to *do* for six months?

It didn't have to be six months, she reminded herself as her body tensed up again. It wasn't a law. She wouldn't be arrested in Customs if she went back after six weeks. Or six days. Or six hours, for that matter.

And as a psychologist, she should know her biggest problem lay in struggling to live up to expectations. Including her own. Though she accepted that she was much better with theories than action, she was going to change that right now, and for as long as she stayed in Ireland.

Calm again, she switched on the radio. The stream of Gaelic that poured out had her goggling, poking at the buttons to find something in English, and taking the turn into Ardmore instead of the road up Tower Hill to her cottage.

Then, as soon as she realized her mistake, the heavy skies burst open, as if a giant hand had plunged a knife into their heart. Rain pounded the roof, gushed over her windshield while she tried to find the control for the wipers.

She pulled over to the curb and waited while the wipers gaily swished at the rain.

The village sat on the southern knob of the county, kissing the Celtic Sea and Ardmore Bay. She could hear the thrash of water against the shore as the storm raged around her, passionate and powerful. Wind shook the windows, whined threateningly in the little pockets where it snuck through.

She'd imagined herself strolling through the village, familiarizing herself with it, its pretty cottages, its smoky, crowded pubs, walking the beach her grandmother had spoken of, and the dramatic cliffs, the green fields.

But it had been a lovely, sun-washed afternoon, with villagers pushing rosy-cheeked babies in carriages and flirty-eyed men tipping their caps to her.

She hadn't imagined a sudden and violent spring storm bringing wild gusts of wind and deserted streets. *Maybe no one even lives here*, she thought. Maybe it was a kind of Brigadoon and she'd fumbled in during the wrong century.

Another problem, she told herself, was an imagination that had to be reeled in with distressing regularity.

Of course people lived here, they were just wise enough to get the hell out of the rain. The cottages were pretty, lined up like ladies with flowers at their feet. Flowers, she noted, that were getting a good hard hammering just now.

There was no reason she couldn't wait for that lovely sun-washed afternoon to come back down to the village. Now she was tired, had a bit of a tension headache, and just wanted to get inside somewhere warm and cozy.

She eased away from the curb and crept along in the rain, petrified that she would miss the turn yet again.

She didn't realize she was driving on the wrong side of the road until she narrowly missed a head-on collision. Or, to be perfectly accurate, when the oncoming car missed her by swerving around her and blasting the horn.

But she found the right turn, which she reminded herself should have been impossible to miss, given the stone spear of the great round tower that topped the hill. Through the rain it lanced up, guarding the ancient and roofless cathedral of Saint Declan and all the graves, marked with stones that tipped and tilted.

For a moment she thought she saw a man there, wearing silver that glinted dully, wetly in the rain. And straining to see, she nearly ran off what there was of a road. Nerves didn't make her sing this time. Her heart was pounding too violently to allow it. Her hands shook as she inched along, trying to see where he was, what he was doing. But there was nothing but the great tower, the ruins, and the dead.

Of course there hadn't been anyone there at all, she told

herself. No one would stand in a graveyard in the middle of a storm. Her eyes were tired, playing tricks. She just needed to get somewhere warm and dry and catch her breath.

When the road narrowed to little more than a muddy track bordered on both sides by man-high hedgerows, she considered herself well lost and hopeless. The car jerked and bumped over ruts while she struggled to find some place to turn around and head back.

There was shelter in the village, and surely someone would take pity on a brainless American who couldn't find her way.

There was a pretty little stone wall covered with some sort of bramble that would have been picturesque at any other time, then a skinny break that turned out to be someone's excuse for a driveway, but she was too far past it when she realized what it was and was terrified to attempt backing up and maneuvering in the mud.

The road climbed, and the ruts became second cousin to ditches. Her nerves were fraying, her teeth clicking audibly as she negotiated another bump, and she seriously considered just stopping where she was and waiting for someone to come along and tow her all the way back to Dublin.

She groaned aloud with relief when she saw another break. She turned in with a coat of paint to spare, then simply laid her forehead against the wheel.

She was lost, hungry, tired, and had to pee rather desperately. Now she was going to have to get out of the car in the pouring rain and knock on a stranger's door. If she was told the cottage was more than three minutes away, she'd have to beg for the use of a bathroom.

Well, the Irish were known for their hospitality, so she doubted that whoever answered the door would turn her away to relieve herself in the hedgerows. Still, she didn't want to appear wild-eyed and frantic.

She tipped down the rearview mirror and saw that her eyes, usually a calm and quiet green, were indeed a bit wild. The humidity had frizzed her hair so that it looked as though she had some wild, bark-colored bush on her head. Her skin was dead pale, a combination of anxiety and fatigue, and she didn't have the energy to dig out her makeup and try to repair the worst of it.

She tried a friendly smile that did manage to convince the dimples to flutter in her cheeks. Her mouth was a little too wide, she thought, just as her eyes were a little too big, and the attempt was much closer to a grimace than a grin.

But it was the best she could do.

She grabbed her purse and shoved open the car door to meet the rain.

As she did, she caught a movement in the second-story window. Just a flutter of curtain that had her glancing up. The woman wore white and had pale, pale hair that tumbled in lush waves over her shoulders and breasts. Through the gray curtain of rain, their eyes met briefly, no more than an instant, and Jude had the impression of great beauty and great sadness.

Then the woman was gone, and there was only the rain.

Jude shivered. The windy wet cut clean to the bone, and she sacrificed her dignity by loping to the pretty white gate that opened into a tiny yard made glorious by the rivers of flowers flowing on either side of a narrow white walk.

There was no porch, only a stoop, but the second story of the cottage pitched over it and provided much welcome cover. She lifted a brass knocker in the shape of a Celtic knot and rapped it against a rough wooden door that looked thick as a brick and was charmingly arched.

While she shivered and tried not to think of her bladder,

she scanned what she could from under her shelter. It was like a doll's house, she thought. All soft white with forest-green trim, the many-paned windows flanked by shutters that looked functional as well as decorative. The roof was thatched, a charming wonder to her. A wind chime made up of three columns of bells sang musically.

She knocked again, more sharply now. Damn it, I know you're in there, and tossing manners aside, she stepped out in the rain and tried to peer through the front window.

Then she leaped back guiltily when she heard the friendly *beep-beep* of a horn.

A rusty red pickup with an engine that purred like a contented cat pulled in behind her car. Jude dragged dripping hair out of her face and prepared to explain herself when the driver popped out.

At first she took it to be a trim and tiny man with scarred, muddy boots, a filthy jacket, and worn work pants. But the face that beamed at her from under a dung-brown cap was definitely female.

And very nearly gorgeous.

Her eyes were as green as the wet hills surrounding them, her skin luminous. Jude saw tendrils of rich red hair tumbling out of the cap as the woman hurried forward, managing to be graceful despite the boots.

"You'd be Miss Murray, then. That's fine timing, isn't it?"

"It is?"

"Well, I'm running a bit behind today, as Mrs. Duffy's grandson Tommy stuffed half his building blocks down the loo again, then flushed away. It was a hell of a mess altogether."

"Hmmm," was all Jude could think to say as she wondered why she was standing in the rain talking to a stranger about blocked toilets.

"Can't you find your key?"

"My key?"

"To the front door. Well, I've mine, so we'll get you in and out of the wet."

That sounded like a wonderful idea. "Thank you," Jude began as she followed the woman back to the door. "But who are you?"

"Oh, I beg your pardon, I'm Brenna O'Toole." Brenna shot out a hand, gripped Jude's and shook briskly. "Your granny told you, didn't she, that I'd have the cottage ready for you?"

"My gran—the cottage?" Jude huddled under the overhang. "My cottage? This is my cottage?"

"It is, yes, if you're Jude Murray from Chicago." Brenna smiled kindly, though her left brow had arched. "You'll be more than a bit tired by now, I'll wager, after your trip."

"Yes." Jude rubbed her hands over her face as Brenna unlocked the door. "And I thought I was lost."

"Appears you're found. *Ceade mile failte,*" she said and stepped back so Jude could enter first.

A thousand welcomes, Jude thought. She knew that much Gaelic. And it felt like a thousand when she stepped into the warmth.

The foyer, hardly wider than the outside stoop, was flanked on one side by stairs polished by time and traffic. An arched doorway to the right led to the little living area, pretty as a picture with its walls the color of fresh biscuits, honey-toned trim, and lace curtains warmly yellowed with age so that everything in the room looked washed by the sun.

The furniture was worn and faded, but cheerful with its blue and white stripes and deep cushions. The gleaning tables were crowded with treasures—bits of crystal, carved figures, miniature bottles. Rugs were scattered colorfully over the wide-planked floor, and the stone fireplace was already laid with what Jude thought must be hunks of peat.

It smelled earthy, and of something else faint and floral.

"It's charming, isn't it?" Jude pushed at her hair again as she turned a circle. "Like a playhouse."

"Old Maude, she liked pretty things."

Something in the tone had Jude stopping her circle, to look back at Brenna's face. "I'm sorry, I didn't know her. You were fond of her."

"Sure, everyone loved Old Maude. She was a grand lady. She'll be pleased you're here, looking after the place. She wouldn't want it standing alone and empty. Should I show you about, then? So you have your bearings."

"I'd appreciate it, but first I'm desperate for the bathroom."

Brenna let out a quick laugh. "A long ride from Dublin. There's a little powder room right off the kitchen. My dad and I put it in for her out of a closet only three years back. Straight that way it is."

Jude didn't waste any time exploring. "Little" was exactly the word for the half bath. She could have rapped her elbows on the side walls by crooking her arms and lifting them. But the walls were done in a pale, pretty rose, the white porcelain gleamed from fresh scrubbing, and there were sweetly embroidered fingertip towels hung neatly on the rack.

One glance in the oval mirror over the sink told Jude that yes, she looked every bit as bad as she'd feared. And though she was of average height and build, beside the fairylike Brenna she felt like a galumphing Amazon.

Annoyed with herself for the comparison, she blew her frizzed bangs off her brow and went back out.

"Oh, I would have gotten those."

Already the efficient Brenna had unloaded her luggage and hauled it into the foyer. "You've got to be ready to drop after your travels. I'll get your things upstairs. I imagine you'll want Old Maude's room, it's pleasant, then we'll put the kettle on so you can have some tea and I'll start your fire. It's a damp day."

As she spoke she carried Jude's two enormous suitcases up the stairs as if they were empty. Wishing she'd spent more time in the gym, Jude followed with her tote, her laptop, and her portable printer.

Brenna showed her two bedrooms, and she was right—Old Maude's, with its view of the front gardens, was the more pleasant. But Jude got only a hazy impression, for one look at the bed and she succumbed to the jet lag that dropped into her body like a lead weight.

She only half listened to the cheerful, lilting voice explain about linens, heat, the vagaries of the tiny fireplace in the bedroom as Brenna set the peat to light. Then she followed as if walking through water as Brenna clattered downstairs to put on tea and show her how the kitchen operated.

She heard something about the pantry being freshly stocked and how she should do her marketing at Duffy's in the village when she needed supplies. There was more—stacks of peat outside the back door, as Old Maude had preferred it, but wood as well in case she herself preferred that, and how the telephone had been hooked back up again and how to light the fire in the kitchen stove.

"Ah, there, now, you're asleep on your feet." Sympathetic, Brenna pressed a thick blue mug into Jude's hands. "Take that on up with you and have a lie-down. I'll start the fire down here for you."

"I'm sorry. I can't seem to focus."

"You'll do better after some sleep. My number's here

by the phone if you're needing anything. My family's barely a kilometer from here, my mother and dad and four sisters, so if there's anything you need, you've only to call or come by the O'Tooles'.''

"Yes, I—four sisters!''

Brenna laughed again as she led Jude back down the hall. "Well, my dad kept hoping for a boy, but that's the way of it. Surrounded by females, he is, even the dog. Up you go, now."

"Thank you so much. Really, I'm not usually so . . . vague."

"Well, it's not every day you fly over the ocean now, is it? Do you want anything before I go?"

"No, I . . ." She leaned on the banister, blinked. "Oh, I forgot. There was a woman in the house. Where did she go?"

"A woman, you say? Where?"

"In the window." She swayed, nearly spilled the tea, then shook her head clear. "There was a woman in the window upstairs, looking out when I got here."

"Was there now?"

"Yes. A blond woman, young, very lovely."

"Ah, that would be Lady Gwen." Brenna turned, slipped into the living room, and lit the stack of peat. "She doesn't show herself to just everyone."

"Where did she go?"

"Oh, she's still here, I imagine." Satisfied that the peat had caught, Brenna rose, brushed off the knees of her trousers. "She's been here three hundred years, give or take. She's your ghost, Miss Murray."

"My what?"

"Your ghost. But don't trouble yourself about her. She won't be after harming you any. Hers is a sad tale, and a story for another time, when you're not so tired."

It was hard to concentrate. Jude's mind wanted to shut down, her body to shut off, but it seemed important to clear up this one point. "You're trying to say the house is haunted?"

"Sure and it's haunted. Didn't your granny tell you?"

"I don't believe she mentioned it. You're telling me you believe in ghosts."

Brenna lifted her brow again. "Well, did you see her or didn't you? There you are," she said when Jude merely frowned. "Have yourself a nap, and if you're up and about later, come on down to Gallagher's Pub and I'll buy you your first pint."

Too baffled to concentrate, Jude merely shook her head. "I don't drink beer."

"Oh, well now, that's a bloody shame," Brenna said, sounding both shocked and sincere. "Well, good day to you, Miss Murray."

"Jude." She murmured it and could do nothing but stare.

"Jude, then." Brenna flashed her gorgeous smile and slipped out the door into the rain.

Haunted, Jude thought, as she started up the stairs with her head circling lazily several inches over her shoulders. Fanciful Irish nonsense. God knew, her grandmother was full of fairy stories, but that's all they were. Stories.

But she'd seen someone . . . hadn't she?

No, the rain, the curtains, the shadows. She set down the tea that she'd yet to taste and managed to pull off her shoes. There weren't any ghosts. There was just a pretty house on a charming little hill. And the rain.

She fell facedown on the bed, thought about dragging the spread over her, and tumbled into sleep before she could manage it.

•　•　•

And when she dreamed, she dreamed of a battle fought on a green hill where the sunlight flashed on swords like jewels, of faeries dancing in the forest where the moonlight lay as tears on the leaves, and of a deep blue sea that beat like a heart against the waiting shore.

And through all the dreams, the one constant thing was the sound of a woman's quiet weeping.

TWO

WHEN JUDE WOKE it was full dark, and the little peat fire had burned down to tiny ruby lights. She stared at them, her eyes bleary with sleep, her heart leaping like a wild stag in her throat as she mistook the embers for watching eyes.

Then her memory snapped into place, her mind cleared. She was in Ireland, in the cottage where her grandmother had lived as a girl. And she was freezing.

She sat up, rubbing her chilled arms, then fumbled for the bedside lamp. A glance at her watch made her blink, then wince. It was nearly midnight. Her recovery nap had lasted close to twelve hours.

And, she discovered, she was not only cold. She was starving as well.

She puzzled over the fire a moment. Since it seemed basically out and she didn't have a clue how to get it going again, she left it alone and went down to the kitchen to hunt up food.

The house creaked and groaned around her—a homey sound, she told herself, though it made her want to jump and look over her shoulder. It wasn't that she was thinking about, even considering the ghost Brenna had spoken of. She just wasn't particularly used to homey sounds. The floors of her condo didn't creak, and the only red glow she might come across was the security light on her alarm system.

But she would get used to her new surroundings.

Brenna was as good as her word, Jude discovered. The kitchen was well stocked with food in the doll-size fridge, in the narrow little pantry. She might be cold, she mused, but she wouldn't starve.

Her first thought was to open a can of soup and buzz it up in the microwave. So with can in hand, she turned around the kitchen and made a shocking discovery.

There was no microwave.

Well, Jude thought, *that's a problem.* Nothing to do but rough it with saucepan and stove, she supposed, then hit the next dilemma when she realized there was no automatic can opener.

Old Maude had lived not only in another country, Jude decided as she pushed through drawers, but another century.

She managed to use the manual can opener that she found, and put the soup in a pan on the stove. After choosing an apple from the bowl on the kitchen table, she walked to the back door and opened it to a swirling mist, soft as silk and wet as rain.

She could see nothing but the air itself, the pale gray layers of it shifting over the night. There was no form, no light, only the wisps and shapes the mist chose to make of itself. Shivering, she took one step out and was instantly cloaked in it.

The sense of solitude was immediate and complete, deeper than any she'd ever known. But it wasn't frightening or sad, she realized as she held an arm out and watched the mist swallow her hand to the wrist. It was oddly liberating.

She knew no one. No one knew her. Nothing was expected of her, except what she asked of herself. For tonight, one wonderful night, she was absolutely alone.

She heard a kind of pulse in the night, a low, drumming beat. Was it the sea? she wondered. Or was it just the mist breathing? Even as she started to laugh at herself, she heard another sound, quiet and bright, a tinkling music.

Pipes and bells, flutes and whistles? Enchanted by it, she nearly left the back stoop, nearly followed the magic of the sound into the fog like a dreamer walking in sleep.

Wind chimes, she realized, with another little laugh, a bit nervous around the edges now. It was only wind chimes, like the pretty bells at the front of the house. And she must still be half asleep if she'd considered dancing out of the house at midnight and wandering through the fog to follow the sound of music.

She made herself step back inside, firmly shut the door. The next sound she heard was the hiss of the soup boiling over.

"Damn it!" She rushed to the stove and switched off the burner. "What's wrong with me? A twelve-year-old could heat up a stupid can of soup, for God's sake."

She mopped up the mess, burned the tips of two fingers, then ate the soup standing up in the kitchen while she lectured herself.

It was time to stop bumbling around, to yank herself back in line. She was a responsible person, a reliable woman, not one who stood dreaming into the mist at midnight. She spooned up the soup and ate it mechanically, a duty to her body with none of the foolish pleasure a midnight snack allowed.

It was time to face why she'd come to Ireland in the first place. Time to stop pretending it was an extended holiday during which she would explore her roots and work on papers that would cement the publishing end of her not very stellar university career.

She'd come because she'd been mortally afraid she was on the verge of some kind of breakdown. Stress had become her constant companion, gleefully inviting her to enjoy a migraine or flirt with an ulcer.

It had gotten to the point where she wasn't able to face the daily routine of her job, to the point where she neglected her students, her family. Herself.

More, worse, she admitted, where she was coming to actively dislike her students, her family. Herself.

Whatever the cause of it—and she wasn't quite ready to explore that area—the only solution had been a radical change. A rest. Falling apart wasn't an option. Falling apart in public was out of the question.

She wouldn't humiliate herself, or her family, who'd done nothing to deserve it. So she had run—cowardly, perhaps, but in some odd way the only logical step she'd been able to think of.

When Old Maude had graciously passed on at the ripe old age of a hundred and one, a door had opened.

It had been smart to walk through that door. It had been responsible to do so. She needed time alone, time to be quiet, time to reevaluate. And that was exactly what she was going to do.

She did intend to work. She would never have been able to justify the trip and the time if she hadn't had some sort of plan. She intended to experiment with a paper that combined her family roots and her profession. If nothing else, documenting local legends and myths and conducting a psychological analysis of their meaning and purpose would keep her mind active and give her less time for brooding.

She'd been spending entirely too much time brooding. An Irish trait, her mother claimed, and the thought of it made Jude sigh. The Irish were great brooders, so if she felt the need to indulge from time to time, she'd picked the best place in the world for it.

Feeling better, Jude turned to put her empty bowl in the dishwasher and discovered there wasn't one.

She chuckled all the way upstairs to the bedroom.

She unpacked, meticulously putting everything away in the lovely creaky wardrobe, the wonderful old dresser with drawers that stuck. She set out her toiletries, admired the old washbasin, and indulged in a long shower standing in the claw-foot tub with the thin plastic curtain jangling around her on its tarnished brass hooks.

She dived into flannel pajamas and a robe before her teeth started chattering, then got down to the business of lighting bricks of peat. Surprised at her success, she lost twenty minutes sitting on the floor with her arms wrapped around her knees, smiling into the pretty glow and imagining herself a contented farmer's wife waiting for her man to come in from the fields.

When she snapped back from her daydream she went off to explore the second bedroom and consider its potential as an office.

It was a small room, boxlike, with narrow windows facing front and side. After some deliberation, Jude chose to set up facing south so she could see the rooftops and church steeples of the village and the broad beach that led down to the sea.

At least, she assumed that would be the view once daylight broke and the fog lifted.

The next problem was what to set up on, as the little room had no desk. She spent the next hour hunting up a suitable table, then hauling that from the living room up the stairs and placing it exactly in the center of the window before she hooked up her equipment.

It did occur to her that she could write on the kitchen table, by the cozy little fire with the wind chimes singing to her. But that seemed too casual and disorganized.

She found the right adaptor for the plug, booted up, then opened the file that she intended to be a daily journal of her life in Ireland.

April 3, Faerie Hill Cottage, Ireland
  I survived the trip.

She paused a moment, laughed a little. It sounded as though she'd been through a war. She started to delete it, start again. Then she stopped herself. No, the journal was only for herself, and she would write what came into her mind, as it came.

The drive from Dublin was long, and more difficult than I'd imagined. I wonder how long it will take me to grow used to driving on the left. I doubt I ever will. Still, the scenery was wonderful. None of the pictures I've seen begin to do the Irish countryside justice. To say it's green isn't enough. Verdant somehow isn't right either. It, well, shimmers is the best I can do.

The villages seem charming, and so unbelievably tidy that I imagined armies of elves slipping in every night to scrub the sidewalks and polish the buildings.

I saw a bit of the village of Ardmore, but it was pouring

rain by the time I arrived, and I was too tired to form any real impressions other than that habitual tidiness and the charm of the wide beach.

I came across the cottage by sheer accident. Granny would call it fate, of course, but it was really just blind luck. It's so pretty sitting here on its little hill with flowers flooding right up to the front door. I hope I can care for them properly. Perhaps they have a bookstore in the village where I'll find books on gardening. In any case, they're certainly thriving now, despite the damp chill in the air.

I saw a woman—thought I saw a woman—at the bedroom window, looking out at me. It was an odd moment. It seemed that our eyes actually met, held for a few seconds. She was beautiful, pale and blond and tragic. Of course it was just a shadow, a trick of the light, because there was no one here at all.

Brenna O'Toole, a terrifyingly efficient woman from the village, pulled up right after me and took things over in a way that was somehow brisk and friendly—and deeply appreciated. She's gorgeous—I wonder if everyone here is gorgeous—and has that rough, mannish demeanor some women can adopt so seamlessly and still be perfectly female.

I imagine she thinks I'm foolish and inept, but she was kind about it.

She said something about the house being haunted, which I imagine the villagers say about every house in the country. But since I've decided to explore the possibility of doing a paper on Irish legends, I may research the basis for her statement.

Naturally, my time clock and my system are turned upside down. I slept the best part of the day away, and had a meal at midnight.

It's dark and foggy out. The mist is luminous and

somehow poignant. I feel cozy of body and quiet in my mind.

It's going to be all right.

She sat back, let out a long sigh. Yes, she thought, it was going to be all right.

At three A.M., when spirits often stir, Jude huddled in bed under a thick quilt with a pot of tea on the table and a book in her hand. The fire simmered in the grate, the mist slid across the windows. She wondered if she'd ever been happier.

And fell asleep with the light burning and her reading glasses slipping down her nose.

In the daylight, with the rain and mist whisked away by the breeze, her world was a different place. The light glowed soft and turned the fields to an aching green. She could hear birds, which reminded her that she needed to dig out the book she'd bought on identifying species. Still, at the moment it was so nice just to stand and listen to that liquid warbling. It didn't seem to matter what bird was singing, so long as it sang.

Walking across the thick, springy grass seemed almost like a sacrilege, but it was a sin Jude couldn't resist.

On the hill beside the village, she saw the ruin of the once grand cathedral dedicated to Saint Declan and the glorious round tower that ruled over it. She thought briefly of the figure she'd thought she'd seen there in the rain. And shivered.

Foolish. It was just a place, after all. An interesting and historical site. Her grandmother, and her guidebook, had told her about the ogham inscriptions inside and the Romanesque arcading. She would go there and see for herself.

And to the east, if memory served, beyond the cliff hotel, was the ancient Saint Declan's Well with its three stone crosses and stone chair.

She would visit the ruins, and the well, climb the cliff path, and perhaps walk around the headland one day soon. Her guidebook had assured her the views were spectacular.

But today she wanted quieter, simpler things.

The waters of the bay shimmered blue as they flowed into the deeper tones of the sea. The flat, wide beach was deserted.

Another morning, she thought, she would drive to the village just to walk alone on the beach.

Today was for rambling over the fields, just as she'd imagined, away from the village with her eyes on the mountains. She forgot she'd only meant to check on the flowers, to orient herself to the area just around the cottage before she attended to practical matters.

She needed to arrange for a phone jack in the spare bedroom so she could access the Net for research. She needed to call Chicago and let her family know she was safe and well. Certainly she needed to go into the village and find out where she could shop and bank.

But it was so glorious out, with the air gentle as a kiss, the breeze just cool enough to clear the last of the travel fatigue from her mind, that she kept walking, kept looking until her shoes were wet from the rain-soaked grass.

Like slipping into a painting, she thought again, one animated with the flutter of leaves, the sounds of birds, the smell of wet, growing things.

When she saw another house it was almost a shock. It was nestled just off the road behind the hedgerows and rambled front, back, and sideways as if different pieces of it had been plopped down carelessly on a whim. And somehow it worked, she decided. It was a charming combination of stone and wood, juts and overhangs with flowers rioting in both the front yard and the back. Beyond the gardens in the rear was a shed—what her grandmother would have called a cabin—with tools and machines tumbling out the door.

In the driveway she saw a car, covered with stone-gray paint, and looking as though it had come off the assembly line years before Jude had been born.

A big yellow dog slept, in a patch of sunlight in the side yard, or she assumed it slept. It was on its back with its feet in the air like roadkill.

The O'Tooles' house? Jude wondered, then decided it must be so when a woman came out the back door with a basket of laundry.

She had brilliant red hair and the wide-hipped, sturdy frame that Jude would imagine in a woman required to carry and birth five children. The dog, proving she was alive, rolled over to her side and thumped her tail twice as the woman marched to the clothesline.

It occurred to Jude that she'd never actually seen anyone hang clothes before. It wasn't something even the most dedicated of housewives tended to do in downtown Chicago. It seemed like a mindless and thereby soul-soothing process to her. The woman took pegs from the pocket of her apron, clamped them in her mouth as she bent to take a pillowcase from the basket. Snapped it briskly, then clamped it to the line. The next item was dealt with in the same way and shared the second peg.

Fascinating.

She worked down the line, without any obvious hurry, with the yellow dog for company, emptying her basket while what she hung billowed and flapped wetly in the breeze.

Just another part of the painting, Jude decided. She would title this section *Country Wife*.

When the basket was empty, the woman turned to the facing line and unhooked clothes already hanging and dry, folding them until her basket was piled high.

She cocked the basket on her hip and walked back into the house, the dog prancing behind her.

What a nice way to spend the morning, she thought.

And that evening, when everyone came home, the house would smell of something wonderful simmering in the kitchen. Some sort of stew, Jude imagined, or a roast with potatoes browned from its juices. The family would all sit around the table, one crowded with bowls and plates wonderfully mismatched, and talk about their day and laugh and sneak scraps to the dog, who begged from under the table.

Large families, she thought, must be a great comfort.

Of course, there was nothing wrong with small ones, she added, immediately feeling guilty. Being an only child had its advantages. She'd gotten all her parents' attention.

Maybe too much of their attention, a little voice murmured in her ear.

Considering that voice very rude, she blocked it out and turned to return to her cottage and do something practical with her time.

Because she felt disloyal, she immediately phoned home. With the time difference she caught her parents before they left for work, and squashed her guilt by chatting happily, telling them she was rested, enjoying herself, and looking forward to this new experience.

She was well aware that they both considered her impulsive trip to Ireland a kind of experiment, a quick forty-five-degree turn from the path she'd been so content to pursue for so long. They weren't against it, which relieved her. They were just puzzled. She had no way to explain it to them, or to herself.

With family on her mind, she placed another call. There was no need to explain anything to Granny Murray. She simply knew. Lighter of heart, Jude filled her grandmother in on every detail of the trip, her impressions, her delight with the cottage while she brewed a pot of tea and made a sandwich.

"I just had a walk," she continued, and with the phone braced on her shoulder, set her simple lunch on the table. "I saw the ruins and the tower from a distance. I'll have a closer look later."

"It's a fine spot," Granny told her. "There's a lot to feel there."

"Well, I'm very interested in seeing the carvings and the arcading, but I didn't want to wander that far today. I saw the neighbor's house. It must be the O'Tooles'."

"Ah, Michael O'Toole. I remember him when he was just a lad—a quick grin Mick had and a way of talking you out of tea and cakes. He married that pretty Logan girl, Mollie, and they had five girls. The one you met, Brenna, she'd be the oldest of the brood. How's she faring, pretty Mollie?"

"Well, I didn't go over. She was busy with laundry."

"You'll find no one's too busy to take a moment, Jude Frances. Next time you're roaming you stop in and pay your respects to Mollie O'Toole."

"I will. Oh, and Gran?" Amused, she smiled as she sipped her tea. "You didn't tell me the cottage was haunted."

"Sure and I did, girl. Haven't you listened to the tapes, or read the letters and such I gave you?"

"No, not yet."

"And you're thinking there goes Granny again, with her

make-believe. You just go through the things I sent along with you. The story's there about Lady Gwen and her faerie lover.''

''Faerie lover?''

''So it was said. The cottage is built on a faerie hill with its raft, or palace, beneath, and she waits for him still, pining because she turned off happiness for sense, and he losing it for pride.''

''That's sad,'' Jude murmured.

''Well, it is. Still, it's a good spot, the hill, for looking inside yourself to your heart's desire. You look inside yours while you're there.''

''Right now I'm just looking for some quiet.''

''Take as much of it as you need, there's plenty to go around. But don't stand back too long and watch the rest of the world. Life's so much shorter than you think.''

''Why don't you come out, Gran, stay here with me?''

''Oh, I'll come back, but this is your time now. Pay attention to it. You're a good girl, Jude, but you don't have to be good all the time.''

''So you're always telling me. Maybe I'll find some handsome Irish rogue and have a reckless love affair.''

''It wouldn't hurt you any. Put flowers on Cousin Maude's grave for me, will you, darling? And tell her I'll come see her when I'm able.''

''I will. I love you, Gran.''

Jude didn't know where the time went. She'd meant to do something productive, had really intended to go out to play with the flowers for a few minutes. To pick just a handful to put in the tall blue bottle she'd found in the living room. Of course she'd picked too many and needed another bottle. There didn't seem to be an actual vase in the house. Then it had been such fun sitting on the stoop arranging them and wishing she knew their names that she'd whiled away most of the afternoon.

It had been a mistake to carry the smaller squat green bottle up to her office to put on the table with her computer. But she'd only meant to lie down for a minute or two. She'd slept for two solid hours on top of the little bed in her office, and woke up groggy and appalled.

She'd lost her discipline. She was lazy. She'd done nothing but sleep or piddle for more than thirty hours now.

And she was hungry again.

At this rate, she decided as she foraged for something quick in the kitchen, she'd be fat, slow, and stupid in a week.

She would go out, drive down to the village. She'd find a bookstore, the bank, the post office. She'd find out where the cemetery was so that she could visit Old Maude's grave for her grandmother. Which is what she should have done that morning. But this way it would be done and she could spend the next day going through the tapes and letters her grandmother had given her to see if there was a paper in them.

She changed first, choosing trim slacks, a turtleneck, and a blazer that made her feel much more alert and professional than the thick sweater and jeans she'd worn all day.

She attacked her hair—"attack" was the only term she could use to describe what she had to do to tame it into a thick, bound tail when all it wanted to do was frizz up and spring out everywhere at once.

She was cautious with makeup. She'd never been handy with it, but the results seemed sufficient for a casual tour of the village. A glance in the mirror told her she didn't look like a day-old corpse or a hooker, both of which could and had happened on occasion.

Taking a deep breath, she headed out to attempt another

session with the leased car and the Irish roads. She was behind the wheel, reaching for the ignition when she realized she'd forgotten the keys.

"Ginkgo," she muttered as she climbed back out. "You're going to start taking ginkgo."

After a frustrated search, she found the keys on the kitchen table. This time she remembered to turn a light on, as it might be dark before she returned, and to lock the front door. When she couldn't remember if she'd locked the back one, she cursed herself and strode around the cottage to deal with it.

The sun was drifting down in the west and through its light a thin drizzle was falling when she finally put the car in reverse and backed slowly out into the road.

It was a shorter drive than she remembered, and a much more scenic one without rain lashing at the windshield. The hedgerows were budded with wild fuchsia in drops red as blood. There were brambles with tiny white flowers that she would learn were blackthorn and friesia hazed and yellow with spring.

As the road turned she saw the tumbled walls of the cathedral on the hill and the spear of the tower lording over the seaside village.

No one walked there.

Eight hundred years they had stood. That, Jude thought, was a wonder of its own. Wars, feast and famine, through blood and death and birth, the power remained. To worship and to defend. She wondered if her grandmother was right, and if so, what one would feel standing in their shadow on soil that had felt the weight of the pious and the profane.

What an odd thought, she decided, and shook it off as she drove into the village that would be hers for the next six months.

THREE

INSIDE GALLAGHER'S PUB the light was dim and the fire lively. That's how the customers preferred it on a damp evening in early spring. Gallagher's had been serving, and pleasing, its customers for more than a hundred and fifty years, in that same spot, by providing good lager or stout, a reasonable glass of whiskey that wasn't watered, and a comfortable place to enjoy that pint or glass.

Now when Shamus Gallagher opened his public house in the Year of Our Lord 1842, with his good wife, Meg, beside him, the whiskey might have come cheaper. But a man has to earn his pence and his pound, however hospitable he may be. So the price of the whiskey came dearer than once it had, but it was served with no less a hope of being enjoyed.

When Shamus opened the pub, he'd sunk his life's hopes and his life's savings into it. There had been more thin times than thick, and once a gale wind had whipped over the sea and lifted the roof clean off and carried it to Dungarvan.

Or so some liked to say when they'd enjoyed more than a glass or two of the Irish.

Still, the pub had stood, with its roots dug into the sand and rock of Ardmore, and Shamus's first son had moved into his father's place behind the old chestnut bar, then his son after him, and so forth.

Generations of Gallaghers had served generations of others and had prospered well enough to add to the business so more could come in out of the damp night after a hard day's work and enjoy a pint or two. There was food as well as drink, appealing to body as well as soul. And most nights there was music too, to appease the heart.

Ardmore was a fishing village and so depended on the bounty of the sea, and lived with its capriciousness. As it was picturesque and boasted some fine beaches, it depended on the tourists as well. And lived with their capriciousness.

Gallagher's was one of its focal points. In good times and bad, when the fish ran fast and thick or when the storms boiled in and battered the bay so none dared venture out to cast nets, its doors were open.

Smoke and fumes of whiskey, steam from stews and the sweat of men had seeped deep into the dark wood, so the place forever carried the smell of living. Benches and chairs were covered in deep red with blackened brass studs to hold the fabric in place.

The ceilings were open, the rafters exposed, and many was the Saturday night when the music was loud enough that those rafters shook. The floor was scarred from the boots of men, the scrape of chair and stool, and the occasional careless spark from fire or cigarette. But it was clean, and four times a year, needed or not, it was polished glossy as a company parlor.

The bar itself was the pride of the establishment, a rich, dark chestnut bar that old Shamus himself had made from a tree folks liked to say had been lightning-struck on Midsummer's Eve. In that way it carried a bit of magic, and those who sat there felt the better for it.

Behind the bar, the long mirrored wall was lined with bottles for your pleasure. And all were clean and shiny as new pennies. The Gallaghers ran a lively pub, but a tidy one as well. Spills were mopped, dust was chased, and never was a drink served in a dirty glass.

The fire was of peat because it charmed the tourists, and the tourists often made the difference between getting by and getting on. They came thick in the summer and early fall to enjoy the beaches, sparser in winter and at the dawn of spring. But they came nonetheless, and most would stop in at Gallagher's to lift a glass, hear a tune, or sample one of the pub's spiced meat pies.

Regulars trickled in soon after the evening meal, as much for conversation or gossip as for a pint of Guinness. Some would come for dinner as well, but usually on a special occasion if it was a family. Or if it was a single man, because he was tired of his own cooking, or wanted a bit of a flirt with Darcy Gallagher, who was usually willing to oblige.

She could work the bar or the tables and the kitchen as well. But the kitchen was where she least liked to be, so she left that to her brother Shawn when she could get away with it.

Those who knew Gallagher's knew it was Aidan, the eldest, who ran the show now that their parents seemed bent on staying in Boston. Most agreed he seemed to have settled down from his wanderlust past and now tended the family pub in a manner that would have made Shamus proud.

For himself, Aidan was content in where he was, and what he did. He'd learned a great deal of himself and of life during his rambles. The itchy feet were said to come from the Fitzgerald side, as his mother had, before she married, traveled a good bit of the world, with her voice paying the fare.

He'd strapped on a knapsack when he was barely eighteen and traveled throughout his country, then over into England and France and Italy and even Spain. He'd spent a year in America, being dazzled by the mountains and plains of the West, sweltering in the heat of the South, and freezing through a northern winter.

He and his siblings were as musical as their mother, so he'd sung for his supper or tended bar, whichever suited his purposes at the time. When he'd seen all he longed to see, he came home again, a well-traveled man of twenty-five.

For the last six years he'd tended the pub and lived in the rooms above it.

But he was waiting. He didn't know for what, only that he was.

Even now, as he built a pint of Guinness, drew a glass of Harp, and tuned in with one ear to the conversation in case he was obliged to comment, part of him sat back, patient and watchful.

Those who looked close enough might see that watchfulness in his eyes, eyes blue as a lightning bolt under brows with the same dark richness as the prize bar where he worked.

He had the rawboned face of the Celts, with the wild good looks that the fine genes of his parents had blended, with a long, straight nose, a mouth full and shamelessly sensual, a tough, take-a-punch chin with just a hint of a cleft.

He was built like a brawler—wide of shoulder, long of arm, and narrow of hip. And indeed, he had spent a good portion of his youth planting his fists in faces or taking them in his own. As much, he wasn't shamed to admit, for the fun of it as for temper.

It was a matter of pride that unlike his brother, Shawn, Aidan had never had his nose broken in battle.

Still, he'd stopped looking for trouble as he'd grown from boy to man. He was just looking, and trusted that he'd know what it was when he found it.

When Jude walked in, he noticed—first as a publican, and second as a man. She looked so tidy, with her trim jacket and bound-back hair, so lost with her big eyes scanning the room as a doe might consider a new path in the forest.

A pretty thing, he thought, as most men do when they see an attractive female face and form. And being one who saw many faces in his career, he noted the nerves as well that kept her rooted to the spot just inside the door as if she might turn and flee at any moment.

The look of her, the manner of her, captured his interest and a low and pleasant hum warmed his blood.

She squared her shoulders, a deliberate move that amused him, and walked to the bar.

"Good evening to you," he said as he slid his rag down the bar to wipe up spills. "What's your pleasure?"

She started to speak, to ask politely for a glass of white wine. Then he smiled, a slow, lazy curving of lips that inexplicably set her insides a fluttering and turned her mind into a buzzing mess of static.

Yes, she thought dimly, everyone was gorgeous here.

He seemed in no particular hurry for her answer, only

leaned comfortably on the bar, bringing that truly wonderful face closer to hers, cocking his head and his brow at the same time.

"Are you lost, then, darling?"

She imagined herself melting, just sliding onto the floor in a puddle of hormones and liquid lust. The sheer embarrassment of the image snapped her back to herself. "No, I'm not lost. Could I have a glass of white wine? Chardonnay if it's available."

"I can help you with that." But he made no move to, just then. "You're a Yank, then. Would you be Old Maude's young American cousin come to stay in her cottage awhile?"

"Yes. I'm Jude, Jude Murray." Automatically she offered her hand and a careful smile that allowed her dimples a brief appearance in her cheeks.

Aidan had always had a soft spot for dimples in a pretty face.

He took her hand, but didn't shake it. He only held it as he continued to stare at her until—she swore she felt it—her bones began to sizzle. "Welcome to Ardmore, Miss Murray, and to Gallagher's. I'm Aidan, and this is my place. Tim, give the lady your seat. Where are your manners?"

"Oh, no, that's—"

But Tim, a burly man with a mass of hair the color and texture of steel wool, slid off his stool. "Beg your pardon." He shifted his gaze from the sports event on the television over the end of the bar and gave her a quick, charming wink.

"Unless you'd rather a table," Aidan added as she continued to stand and look mildly distressed.

"No, no, this is fine. Thank you." She climbed onto the stool, trying not to tense up as she became the center of attention. It was what troubled her most about teaching, all those faces turned to hers, expecting her to be profound and brilliant.

He finally released her hand, just as she expected it to dissolve in his, and took the pint glass from under the tap, to slide it into welcoming hands. "And how are you finding Ireland?" he asked her as he turned to take a bottle of wine from the mirrored shelf.

"It's lovely."

"Well, there's no one here will disagree with you on that." He poured her wine, looking at her rather than the glass. "And how's your granny?"

"Oh." Jude was amazed that he'd filled the glass perfectly without so much as a glance at it, then set it precisely in front of her. "She's very well. Do you know her?"

"I do, yes. My mother was a Fitzgerald and a cousin to your granny—third or fourth removed, I'm thinking. So, that makes us cousins as well." He tapped a finger on her glass. "*Slainte,* cousin Jude."

"Oh, well . . . thank you." She lifted her glass just as the shouting started from the back. A woman's voice, clear as church bells, accused someone of being a bloody, blundering knothead with no more brains than a turnip. This was answered, in irritated male tones, that he'd rather be a bleeding turnip than dumb as the dirt it grew in.

No one seemed particularly shocked by the shouts and curses that followed, nor by the sudden crash that had Jude jolting and spilling a few drops of wine on the back of her hand.

"That would be two more of your cousins," Aidan explained as he took Jude's hand yet again and efficiently dried it. "My sister, Darcy, and my brother, Shawn."

"Oh. Well, shouldn't someone see what's the matter?"

"The matter with what?"

She only goggled as the voices in the back rose.

"You throw that plate at my head, you viper, and I swear to you, I'll—"

The threat ended on a vicious curse as something crashed against the wall. Seconds later, a woman swung out of the door behind the bar, carrying a tray of food and looking flushed and satisfied.

"Did you nail him, Darcy?" someone wanted to know.

"No, he ducked." She tossed her head, sending a cloud of raven-black hair flying. Temper suited her. Her Kerry blue eyes snapped with it, her generous mouth pouted. She carried the tray with a sassy twitch of hip to a family of five crowded at a low table. And when she served, bending down to catch whatever the woman at the table murmured to her, she threw back her head and laughed.

The laughter suited her just as well as the temper, Jude noted.

"I'll be taking the price of the plate out of your pay," Aidan informed her when she strolled over to the bar.

"That's fine, then. Worth every penny, more if I'd hit the mark. The Clooneys are needing two more Cokes, a ginger ale and two Harps—a pint and a glass."

Aidan began to fill the order. "Darcy, this is Jude Murray from America, come to stay in Old Maude's cottage."

"Pleased to meet you." The temper was quickly replaced by a lively interest in Darcy's eyes. The pout gave way to a quick and dazzling smile. "Are you settling in well?"

"Yes, thank you."

"It's Chicago, isn't it, where you're from? Do you love it there?"

"It's a beautiful city."

"And loaded with fine shops and restaurants and the like. What do you do in Chicago, for your living?"

"I teach psychology." *Taught,* Jude thought, but that was too hard to explain, especially since attention had once again focused on her.

"Do you, now? Well, and that's very handy." Darcy's beautiful eyes gleamed with humor, and just a touch of malice. "Perhaps you could examine my brother Shawn's head when you've time. There's been something wrong with it since birth."

She picked up the tray of drinks Aidan nudged toward her, then grinned at him. "And it was two plates. I missed both times, but I nearly caught him at the ear the second round."

She sauntered off to serve drinks and take orders from the tables.

Aidan exchanged glasses for pounds, set another two under the taps for building, then lifted a brow at Jude. "Is the wine not to your taste?"

"What?" She glanced down, noting that she'd barely sipped at it. "No, it's nice." She drank to be polite, then smiled so her dimples fluttered shyly to life again. "Lovely, actually. I was distracted."

"You needn't worry about Darcy and Shawn. Shawn's fast on his feet, true enough, but our sister's an arm like a bullet. If she'd meant to hit him, she likely would have."

Jude made a noncommittal sound as someone in the front corner began to play a tune on a concertina.

"I've cousins in Chicago." This came from Tim, who continued to stand behind her, waiting patiently for his second pint. "The Dempseys, Mary and Jack. You wouldn't happen to know them?"

"No, I'm sorry." Jude shifted on her stool, tipped her face up to his.

"Chicago's a big place. My cousin Jack and I were boys together, and he went over to America to work with his uncle on his mother's side, in a meat-packing plant. Been there ten years now and complains bitter about the wind and the winters, but makes no move to come back home.''

He took the pint from Aidan with a thanks and slid the coins for it over the bar. ''Aidan, you've been to Chicago, haven't you?''

''Passed through, mostly. The lake's a sight, and seems big as the sea. The wind coming off it's like knives through the skin and into the bone. But you can get a steak there, if memory serves, that will make you weep with gratitude that God created the cow.''

He was working as he spoke, filling another order for his sister's tray, keeping the taps going, opening a bottle of American beer for a boy who looked as if he should still be sucking on milk shakes.

The music picked up, a livelier pace now. When Darcy lifted the tray from the bar this time, she was singing in a way that made Jude stare with admiration and envy.

Not just at the voice, though it was stunning enough with its silver-bright clarity. But at the kind of ease of self that would allow someone to simply break into song in public. It was a tune about dying an old maid in a garret, which Jude concluded from the glances of the males in the room, ranging from the Clooney boy of about ten to an ancient skeleton of a man at the farthest end of the bar, was a fate Darcy Gallagher would never face.

People joined in the chorus, and the taps began to flow more quickly.

The first tune blended into a second, with barely a change of rhythm. Aidan picked up the lyrics, singing of the betrayal of the woman wearing the black velvet band so smoothly that Jude could only stare. He had a voice as rich as his sister's and as carelessly beautiful.

He pulled a pint of lager as he sang, then winked at her

as he slid it down the bar. She felt heat rush into her face—the mortification of being caught openly staring—but she trusted the light was dim enough to mask it.

She picked up her glass, hoping she looked casual, as if she often sat in bars where song broke out all around her and men who looked like works of art winked in her direction. And discovered her glass was full. She frowned at it, certain that she'd sipped away at least half the wine. But as Aidan was halfway down the bar and she didn't want to interrupt his work or the song, she shrugged and enjoyed the full glass.

The door of what she assumed was the kitchen swung open again. She could only be grateful that no one was paying attention to her, because she was sure she goggled. The man who came through it looked as though he'd stepped out of a movie set—some film about ancient Celtic knights saving kingdoms and damsels.

He had a loose and lanky build that went well with the worn jeans and dark sweater. His hair was black as night and wove its way over the collar of the sweater. Eyes a dreamy lake blue sparkled with humor. His mouth was like Aidan's, full and strong and sensual, and his nose was just crooked enough to spare him from the burden of perfection.

She noted the nick on his right ear and assumed this was Shawn Gallagher, and that he hadn't ducked quite quickly enough.

He moved gracefully across the room to serve the food he carried on the tray. Then, in a lightning move that made Jude catch her breath and prepare for the battle, he grabbed his sister, yanked her to face him, then spun her into a complicated dance.

What kind of people, Jude wondered, could swear at each other one minute, then dance around a pub together laughing the next?

The patrons whistled and clapped. Feet pounded. The dance whirled close enough to Jude for her to feel the breeze of spinning bodies. Then when it stopped, Darcy and Shawn cozily embraced and grinned at each other like fools.

After he'd kissed his sister smartly on the mouth, he turned his head and studied Jude in the friendliest of manners. "Well, who might this be, come out of the night and into Gallagher's?"

"This is Jude Murray, cousin to Old Maude," Darcy told him. "This is my brother Shawn, the one in dire need of your professional help."

"Ah, Brenna told me she'd met you when you arrived. Jude F. Murray, from Chicago."

"What's the 'F' for?" Aidan wanted to know.

Jude swiveled her head to look at him, found it was just a little light. "Frances."

"She saw Lady Gwen," Shawn announced, and before Jude could swivel her head back again, the pub had gone quiet.

"Did she, now?" Aidan wiped his hands on his cloth, set it aside, then leaned on the bar. "Well, then."

There was a pause, an expectant one. Fumbling, Jude tried to fill it. "No, I just thought I'd seen . . . it was raining." She picked up her glass, drank deeply, and prayed the music would start again.

"Aidan's seen Lady Gwen, walking the cliffs."

Jude stared at Shawn, then back at Aidan. "You've seen a ghost," she said in carefully spaced words.

"She weeps as she walks and as she waits. And the sound of it stabs into your heart so it bleeds from the inside out."

Part of her simply wanted to ride on the music of his

voice, but she blinked, shook her head. "But you don't actually believe in ghosts."

He lifted that handsome eyebrow again. "Why wouldn't I?"

"Because . . . they don't exist?"

He laughed, a rich and rolling sound, then solved the mystery of her never empty glass by topping off the wine. "I'll be wanting to hear you say that after living here another month. Didn't your granny tell you the story of Lady Gwen and Carrick of the faeries?"

"No. Well, actually, I have a number of tapes she made for me, and letters and journals that deal with legends and myths. I'm, ah . . . considering doing a paper on the subject of Irish folklore and its place in the psychology of the culture."

"Isn't that something." He didn't trouble to hide his amusement, even when he saw the frown cloud over her face. To his mind she had as pretty a pout as he'd ever seen. "You've come to a good place for material for such a fine project."

"You should tell her about Lady Gwen," Darcy put in. "And other stories, Aidan. You tell them best."

"I will, then, another time. If you're interested, Jude Frances."

She was miffed, and she realized with some distress, just a little drunk. Mustering her dignity as best she could, she nodded. "Of course. I'd like to include local color and stories in my research. I'd be happy to set up appointments—at your convenience."

His smile came again, slow, easy. Devastating. "Oh, well, we're not so very formal around here. I'll just come around one day, and if you're not busy, I'll tell you some stories I know."

"All right. Thank you." She opened her purse, started

to get out her wallet, but he laid a hand over hers.

"There's no need to pay. The wine's on the house, for welcome."

"That's very kind of you." She wished she had a clue as to just how much welcome she'd put into her bloodstream.

"See that you come back," he said when she got to her feet.

"I'm sure I will. Good night." She scanned the room, since it seemed polite to make it a blanket statement, then looked back at Aidan. "Thank you."

"Good night to you, Jude Frances."

He watched her leave, absently getting a glass as another beer was called for. A pretty thing, he thought again. And just prim enough, he decided, to make a man wonder what it would take to relax her.

He thought he might enjoy taking the time to find out. After all, he had a wealth of time.

"She must be rich," Darcy commented with a little sigh.

Aidan glanced over. "Why do you say that?"

"You can tell by her clothes, all simple and perfect. The little earrings she had on, the hoops, those were real gold, and the shoes were Italian or I'll marry a monkey."

He hadn't noticed the earrings or the shoes, just the overall package, that understated and neat femininity. And being a man, he had imagined loosening that band she'd wrapped around her hair and setting it free.

But his sister was pouting, so he turned and flicked a finger down her nose. "She may be rich, Darcy my darling, but she's alone and shy as you never are. Money won't buy her a friend."

Darcy pushed her hair back over her shoulder. "I'll go by the cottage and see her."

"You've a good heart."

She grinned and picked up her tray. "You were looking at her bum when she left."

He grinned back. "I've good eyes."

After the last customer wandered his way home, and the glasses were washed, the floor mopped, and the doors locked, Aidan found himself too restless for sleep, or a book, or a glass of whiskey by his fire.

He didn't mind that last hour of the day spent alone in his rooms over the pub. Often he treasured it. But he treasured just as much the long walks he was prone to take on nights where the sky was thrown open with stars and the moon sailed white over the water.

Tonight he walked to the cliffs, as they were on his mind. It was true enough what his brother had said. Aidan had seen Lady Gwen, and more than once, standing high over the sea, with the wind blowing her pale hair behind her like the mane of a wild horse and her cloak billowing, white as the moon overhead.

The first time, he'd been a child and initially had been filled with excited terror. Then he'd been moved beyond measure by the wretched sound of her weeping and the despair in her face.

She'd never spoken, but she had looked at him, seen him. That he would swear on as many Bibles as you could stack under his hand.

Tonight he wasn't looking for ghosts, for the spirit memory of a woman who'd lost what she loved most before she'd recognized it.

He was only looking for a walk in the air made chilly by night and sea, in a land he'd come back to because nowhere else had ever been home.

When he climbed up the path he knew as well as the

path from his own bed to his bath, he sensed nothing but the night, and the air, and the sea.

The water beat below, its endless war on rock. Light from the half moon spilled in a delicate line over black water that was never quite calm. Here he could breathe, and think the long thoughts he rarely had time for in the day-to-day doing of his work.

The pub was for him now. And though he'd never expected the full weight of it, it sat well enough on his shoulders. His parents' decision to stay in Boston rather than to remain only long enough to help his uncle open his own pub and get it over the first six months of business hadn't come as that much of a surprise.

His father had missed his brother sorely, and his mother had always been one for moving to a new place. They'd be back, not to live, perhaps, but they would be back to see friends, to hold their children. But Gallagher's Pub had been passed on from father to son once again.

Since it was his legacy, he meant to do right by it.

Darcy wouldn't wait tables and build sandwiches forever. He accepted that as well. She stored her money away like a squirrel its nuts. When she had enough to content her, she'd be off.

Shawn was happy enough for the moment to run the kitchen, to dream his dreams and to have every other female in the village pining over him. One day he would stumble over the right dream, and the right woman, and that would be that as well.

If Aidan intended Gallagher's to go on—and he did— he would have to think about finding himself a woman and going about the business of making a son—or a daughter, for that matter, as he wasn't so entrenched in tradition he couldn't see passing what he had on to a girl.

But there was time for that, thank Jesus. After all, he was

only thirty-one, and he didn't intend to marry just for responsibility. There would be love, and passion, and the meeting of minds before there were vows.

One of the things he'd learned on his travels was what a man could settle for, and what he couldn't. You could settle for a lumpy bed if the alternative was the floor, and be grateful. But you couldn't settle for a woman who bored you or failed to stir your blood, no matter how fair her face.

As he was thinking that, he turned and looked out over the roll of land, over to the soft rise where the white cottage sat under the sky and stars. There was a thin haze of smoke rising from the chimney, a single light burning against the window.

Jude Frances Murray, he thought and found himself bringing her face into his mind. What are you doing in your little house on the faerie hill? Reading a good book perhaps, one with plenty of weight and profound messages. Or do you sneak into a story with fun and foolishness when no one's around to see?

It's image that worries you, he mused. That much he'd gotten from the hour or so she'd spent on one of his stools. What are people thinking? What do they see when they look at you?

And while she was thinking that, he mused, she was absorbing everything around her that she could see or hear. He doubted she knew it, but he'd seen it in her eyes.

He thought he would take some time to find out what he thought of her, what he saw in her, and what was real.

She'd already stirred his blood with those big sea goddess eyes of hers and that sternly bound hair. He liked her voice, the preciseness of it that seemed so intriguingly at odds with the shyness.

What would she do, pretty Jude, he wondered, if he was to ramble over now and rap on her door?

No point in frightening her to death, he decided, just because he was restless and something about her had made him want.

"Sleep well, then," he murmured, sliding his hands into his pockets as the wind whirled around him. "One night when I go walking it won't be to the cliffs, but to your door. Then we'll see what we see."

A shadow passed the window, and the curtain twitched aside. There she stood, almost as if she'd heard him. It was too far away for him to see more than the shape of her, outlined against the light.

He thought she might see him as well, just a shadow on the cliffs.

Then the curtain closed again, and moments later, the light went out.

FOUR

RELIABILITY, JUDE TOLD herself, began with responsibility. And both were rooted in discipline. With this short lecture in her head, she rose the next morning, prepared a simple breakfast, then took a pot of tea up to her office to settle down and work.

She would not go outside and take a walk over the hills, though it was a perfectly gorgeous day. She would not wander out to dream over the flowers, no matter how pretty they looked out the window. And she certainly wasn't going to drive into the village and spend an hour or two roaming the beach, however compelling the idea.

Though many might consider her notion of exploring the legends handed down from generation to generation in Ireland a flighty idea at best, it was certainly viable work if approached properly and with clear thinking. The oral storytelling art, as well as the written word, was one of the cornerstones in the foundation of culture, after all.

She couldn't bring herself to acknowledge that her most

hidden, most secret desire was to write. To write stories, books, to simply open that carefully locked chamber in her heart and let the words and images rush out.

Whenever that lock rattled, she reminded herself it was an impractical, romantic, even foolish ambition. Ordinary people with average skills were better off contenting themselves with the sensible.

Researching, detailing, analyzing were sensible, things she'd been trained to do. Things, she thought with only a whisper of resentment, she'd been expected to do. The subject matter she'd selected was rebellion enough. So she would explore the psychological reason for the formation and perpetuation of the generational myths particular to the country of her ancestors.

Ireland was ripe with them.

Ghosts and banshees, pookas and faeries. What a rich and imaginative wonder was the Celtic mind! They said the cottage stood on a faerie hill, one of the magic spots that hid the gleaming raft below.

If memory served, she thought the legend went that a mortal could be lured, or even snatched, into the faerie world below the hill and kept there for a hundred years.

And wasn't that fascinating?

Seemingly rational, ordinary people on the cusp of the twenty-first century could actually make such a statement without guile.

That, she decided, was the power of the myth on the intellect, and the psyche.

And it was strong enough, powerful enough, that for a little while, when she'd been alone in the night, she'd almost—almost believed it. The music of the wind chimes and the wind had added to it, she thought now. Songs, she mused, played by the air were meant to set the mind dreaming.

Then that figure standing out on the cliffs. The shadow of a man etched against sky and sea had drawn her gaze and caused her heart to thunder. He might have been a man waiting for a lover, or mourning one. A faerie prince weaving magic into the sea.

Very romantic, she decided, very powerful.

And of course—obviously—whoever it had been, whoever would walk wind-whipped cliffs after midnight, was lunatic. But she hadn't thought of that until morning, for the punch of the image had her sighing and shivering over it into the night.

But the lunacy, for lack of a better word, was part of the charm of the people and their stories. So she would use it. Explore it. Immerse herself in it.

Revved, she turned to her machine, leaving the tapes and letters alone for the moment, and started her paper.

They say the cottage stands on a faerie hill, one of the many rises of land in Ireland under which the faeries live in their palaces and castles. It's said that if you approach a faerie hill, you may hear the music that plays in the great hall of the castle under the deep green grass. And if you walk over one, you take the risk of being snatched by the faeries themselves and becoming obliged to do their bidding.

She stopped, smiled. Of course that was all too lyrical and, well, *Irish* a beginning for a serious academic paper. In her first year of college, her papers had been marked down regularly for just that sort of thing. Rambling, not following the point of the theme, neglecting to adhere to her own outlines.

Knowing just how important grades were to her parents, she'd learned to stifle those colorful journeys.

Still, this wasn't for a grade, and it was just a draft. She'd clean it up later. For now, she decided, she would just get her thoughts down and lay the foundation for the analysis.

She knew enough, from her grandmother's stories, to give a brief outline of the most common mythical charac-ters. It would be her task to find the proper stories and the structure that revolved around each character of legend and then explain its place in the psychology of the people who fostered it.

She worked through the morning on basic definitions, often adding a subtext that cross-referenced the figure to its counterpart in other cultures.

Intent on her work, she barely heard the knocking on the front door, and when it registered she blinked her way out of an explanation of the Pisogue, the Irish wise woman found in most villages in earlier times. Hooking her glasses in the neck of her sweater, she hurried downstairs. When she opened the door, Brenna O'Toole was already walking back to her truck.

"I'm sorry to disturb you," Brenna began.

"No, you're not." How could a woman wearing muddy work boots intimidate her? Jude wondered. "I was in the little room upstairs. I'm glad you stopped by. I didn't thank you properly the other day."

"Oh, it's not a problem. You were asleep on your feet." Brenna stepped away from the gate, walked back toward the stoop. "Are you settling in, then? You have all you need?"

"Yes, thanks." Jude noticed that the faded cap Brenna squashed down over her hair carried a small winged figure pinned just over the bill. More faeries, Jude thought, and found it fascinating that such an efficient woman would wear one as a charm.

"Ah, would you like to come in, have some tea?"

"That would be lovely, thanks, but I've work." Still,

Brenna seemed content to linger on the little garden path. "I only wanted to stop and see if you're finding your way about, or if there's anything you'd be needing. I'm back and forth on the road here a time or two a day."

"I can't think of anything. Well, actually, I wonder if you can tell me who I contact about getting a telephone jack put into the second bedroom. I'm using it as an office, and I'll need that for my modem."

"Modem, is it? Your computer?" Now her eyes gleamed with interest. "My sister Mary Kate has a computer as she's studying programming in school. You'd think she'd discovered the cure for stupidity with the thing, and she won't let me near it."

"Are you interested in computers?"

"I like knowing how things work, and she's afraid I'll take it apart—which of course I would, for how else can you figure out how a thing works, after all? She has a modem as well, and sends messages to some cousins of ours in New York and friends in Galway. It's a marvel."

"I suppose it is. And we tend to take it for granted until we can't use it."

"I can pass your need on to the right party," Brenna continued. "They'll have you hooked up sooner or later." She smiled again. "Sooner or later's how 'tis, but shouldn't be more than a week or so. If it is, I can jury-rig something that'll do you."

"That's fine. I appreciate it. Oh, and I went into the village yesterday, but the shops were closed by the time I got there. I was hoping to find a bookstore so I could pick up some books on gardening."

"Books on it." Brenna pursed her lips. Imagine, she thought, needing to read about planting. "Well, I don't know where you'd find such a thing in Ardmore, but you could likely find what you're looking for over in Dungarvan or into Waterford City for certain. Still, if you want to know something about your flowers here, you've only to ask my mother. She's a keen gardener, Ma is.''

Brenna glanced over her shoulder at the sound of a car. ''Well, here's Mrs. Duffy and Betsy Clooney come 'round to say welcome. I'll move my lorry out of your street so they can pull in. Mrs. Duffy will have brought cakes,'' Brenna added. ''She's famed for them.'' She waved cheerfully to the two women in the car. ''Just give a shout down the hill if you've a need for something.''

''Yes, I—'' Oh, God, was all Jude could think, don't leave me alone with strangers. But Brenna was hopping back in her truck.

She zipped out with what Jude considered a reckless and dashing disregard for the narrow slot in the hedgerows or the possibility, however remote, of oncoming traffic, then squeezed fender to fender with the car to chat a moment with the new visitors.

Jude stood mentally wringing her hands as the truck bumped away down the road and the car pulled in.

''Good day to you, Miss Murray!'' The woman behind the wheel had eyes bright as a robin's and light brown hair that had been beaten into submission. She wore it in a tight helmet of waves under a brutal layer of spray. It glinted like shellack in the sun.

She popped out of the car, ample breasts and hips plugged onto short legs and tiny feet.

Jude pasted a smile on her face and dragged herself toward the garden gate like a woman negotiating a walk down death row. As she rattled her brain for the proper greeting, the woman yanked open the rear door of the car, chattering away to Jude and to the second woman, who stepped out of the passenger side. And, it seemed, to the world in general.

"I'm Kathy Duffy from down to the village, and this is Betsy Clooney, my niece on my sister's side. Patty Mary, my sister, works at the food shop today or she'd've come to pay her respects as well. But I said to Betsy this morning, why if she could get her neighbor to mind the baby while the two older were in school, we'd just come on up to Faerie Hill Cottage and say good day to Old Maude's cousin from America."

She said most of this with her rather impressive bottom, currently covered by the eye-popping garden of red poppies rioting over her dress, facing Jude as she wiggled into the back of the car. She wiggled out again, face slightly flushed, with a covered cake dish and a beaming smile.

"You look a bit like your grandmother," Kathy went on, "as I remember her from when I was a girl. I hope she's well."

"Yes, very. Thank you. Ah, so nice of you to come by." She opened the gate. "Please come in."

"I hope we gave you time enough to settle." Betsy walked around the car, and Jude remembered her from the pub the night before. The woman with her family at one of the low tables. Somehow even that vague connection helped.

"I mentioned to Aunt Kathy that I saw you at the pub last night, at Gallagher's? And we thought you might be ready for a bit of a welcome."

"You were with your family. Your children were so well behaved."

"Oh, well." Betsy rolled eyes of clear glass green. "No need to disabuse you of such a notion so soon. You've none of your own, then?"

"No, I'm not married. I'll make some tea if you'd like," she began as they stepped inside the front door.

"That would be lovely." Kathy started down the hall,

obviously comfortable in the cottage. "We'll have a nice visit in the kitchen."

To Jude's surprise, they did. She spent a pleasant hour with two women who had warm ways and easy laughs. It was simple enough to judge that Kathy Duffy was a chatterbox, and not a little opinionated, but she did it all with great good humor.

Before the hour was over, Jude's head swam with the names and relations of the people of Ardmore, the feuds and the families, the weddings and the wakes. If there was something Katherine Anne Duffy didn't know about any soul who lived in the area during the last century, well, it wasn't worth mentioning.

"It's a pity you never met Old Maude," Kathy commented. "For she was a fine woman."

"My grandmother was very fond of her."

"More like sisters than cousins they were, despite the age difference." Kathy nodded. "Your granny, she lived here as a girl after she lost her parents. My own mother was friends with the pair of them, and both she and Maude missed your granny when she married and moved to America."

"And Maude stayed here." Jude glanced around the kitchen. "Alone."

"That's the way it was meant. She had a sweetheart, and they planned to marry."

"Oh? What happened?"

"His name was John Magee. My mother says he was a handsome lad who loved the sea. He went for a soldier during the Great War and lost his life in the fields of France."

"It's sad," Betsy put in, "but romantic too. Maude never loved another, and she often spoke of him when we came to visit, though he'd been dead nearly three-quarters of a century.''

"For some," Kathy said with a sigh, "there's only one. None comes before and none after. But Old Maude, she lived happy here, with her memories and her flowers.''

"It's a contented house," Jude said, then immediately felt foolish. But Kathy Duffy only smiled and nodded again.

"It is, yes. And those of us who knew her are happy one of her own is living here now. It's good you're getting around the village, meeting people and acquainting yourself with some of your kin.''

"Kin?"

"You're kin to the Fitzgeralds, and there are plenty of them in and around Old Parish. My friend Deidre, who's in Boston now, was a Fitzgerald before she married Patrick Gallagher. You were at their place last night.''

"Oh, yes." Aidan's face immediately swam into Jude's mind. The slow smile, the wildly blue eyes. "We're cousins of some sort.''

"Seems to me your granny was first cousin to Deidre's great-aunt Sarah. Or maybe it was her great-granny and they were second cousins. Well, hardly matters. Now the oldest Gallagher lad''—Kathy paused long enough to nibble on one of her cakes—"you had your eye on him at one time, didn't you, Betsy?''

"I might have glanced his way a time or two, when I was a lass of sixteen." Betsy's eyes laughed over her cup. "And he might've glanced back as well. Then he went off on his rambles, and there was my Tom. When Aidan Gallagher came back . . . well, I might have glanced again, but only in appreciation for God's creation.''

"He was a wild one as a lad, and there's a look about him that says he could be again." Kathy sighed. "I've always had a soft spot for a wild heart in a man. Have you no sweetheart in the States, then, Jude?''

''No.'' She thought briefly of William. Had she ever considered her husband her sweetheart? ''No one special.''

''If they're not special, what would the point be?''

No point at all, Jude thought later when she showed her guests to the door. She couldn't claim he'd been her great love, as John Magee had been to Maude. They hadn't been special to each other, she and William.

They should have been. And for a time, he'd been the focus of her life. She'd loved him, or had believed she loved him. Damn it, she'd wanted to love him and had given him her best.

But it hadn't been good enough. It was mortifying knowing that. Knowing how easily, how thoughtlessly he'd broken still fresh vows and dismissed her from his life.

But neither, she could admit, would she have grieved for him for seventy years if he'd died in some heroic or tragic fashion. The fact was, if William had died in some freak accident, she could have been the stalwart widow instead of the discarded wife.

And how horrible it was to realize she'd have preferred it that way.

What had hurt more? she wondered now. The loss of him or the loss of her pride? Whichever was true, she wouldn't allow such a thing to happen again. She wouldn't simply fall in line—into marriage, then out again, because it was asked of her.

This time around, she would concentrate on herself, and being on her own.

Not that she had anything against marriage, she thought as she loitered outside. Her parents had a solid marriage, were devoted to each other. It might not have had that cinematic, wildly passionate scope some imagined for themselves, but their relationship was a fine testament to a partnership that worked.

Perhaps she'd pretended she would have something near to that with William, a quiet and dignified marriage, but it hadn't hit the mark. And the fault was hers.

There was nothing special about her. She was more than a little ashamed to admit that she'd simply become a habit to him, part of his routine.

Meet William for dinner Wednesday night at seven at one of three favored restaurants. On Saturday, meet for a play or a film, followed by a late supper, followed by tasteful sex. If both parties are agreeable, extend evening to a healthy eight hours' sleep, followed by brunch and a discussion of the Sunday paper.

That had been the pattern of their courtship, and marriage had simply slipped into the scheme of it.

And it had been so easy, really, to end the pattern altogether.

But God, *God*, she wished she'd done the ending. That she'd had the guts or the flair for it. A torrid affair in a cheap motel. Moonlighting as a stripper. Running away to join a motorcycle gang.

As she tried to imagine herself slithering into leather and hopping on the back of a motorcycle behind some burly, tattooed biker named Zero, she laughed.

"Well, now, sure that's a fair sight for a man on an April afternoon." Aidan stood at the break in the hedgerows, hands comfortably in his pockets, grinning at her. "A laughing woman with flowers at her feet. Now some might think, being where we are, that they'd stumbled across a faerie come out to charm the blossoms to blooming."

He strolled toward the gate as he spoke, paused there. And she was certain she'd never seen a more romantic picture in her life than Aidan Gallagher with his thick, rich hair ruffled by the breeze, his eyes a clear, wild blue, standing at the gate with the distant cliffs at his back.

"But you're no faerie, are you, Jude Frances?"

"No, of course not." Without thinking she lifted a hand to make sure her hair was still tidy. "I, ah, just had a visit from Kathy Duffy and Betsy Clooney."

"I passed them on the road when I was walking this way. They said you had a nice hour over tea and cakes."

"You walked? From the village?"

"It's not so very far if you like to walk, and I do." She was looking just a bit distressed again, Aidan mused. As if she wasn't quite sure what to do about him.

Well, he supposed that made them even. But he wanted to make her smile, to watch her lips curve slow and shy and her dimples come to life.

"Are you going to ask me into your garden or would you rather I just kept walking?"

"No, sorry." She hurried to the gate and reached for the latch just as he did. His hand closed over hers, warm and firm, so they lifted the latch together.

"What were you thinking of that made you laugh?"

"Oh, well . . ." Since he still had her hand, she found herself backing up. "Just something foolish. Mrs. Duffy left some cakes, and there's still tea."

He couldn't recall ever having seen a woman so spooked just by speaking to him. But he couldn't say that her reaction was entirely displeasing. Testing, he kept her hand in his, continued forward as she walked back.

"And I imagine you've had your fill of both for now. Truth is, I need the air from time to time, so I go on what people call Aidan's rambles. Unless you're in a hurry to go back in, we could just sit on your stoop awhile."

His free hand reached out, pressed her hip and stopped her retreat. "You're about to step on your flowers," he murmured. "A shame it would be to crush them underfoot."

"Oh." Cautious, she edged away. "I'm clumsy."

"I wouldn't say so. A bit nervy is all." Despite the odd pleasure of seeing her flustered, he had an urge to smooth those nerves away and put her at ease.

With his fingertips curled to hers, he shifted, turned her with such fluid grace she could only blink to find herself facing the other way. "I wondered," he went on as he led her toward the stoop, "if you're interested in hearing the stories I know. For your paper."

"Yes, very much." She let out a relieved breath and lowered herself to the stoop. "I started on it this morning— the paper—trying to get a feel for it, formulate an outline, the basic structure."

She wrapped her arms around her knees, then tightened them as she glanced over and saw him watching her. "What is it?"

He lifted a brow. "It's nothing. I'm listening. I like listening to you. Your voice is so precise and American."

"Oh." She cleared her throat, stared straight ahead again as if she had to keep a close eye on the flowers so they didn't escape. "Where was I . . . the structure of it. The different areas I want to address. The fantasy elements, of course, but also the social, cultural, and sexual aspects of traditional myths. Their use in tradition as entertainment, as parables, as warnings, in romance."

"Warnings?"

"Yes, mothers telling children about bog faeries to keep them from wandering into dangerous areas, or relating tales of evil spirits and so forth to influence them to behave. There are as many—more actually—grotesque legends as there are benevolent ones."

"Which do you prefer?"

"Oh, well." She fumbled a little. "Both, I suppose, depending on the mood."

"Do you have many?"

"Many what?"

"Moods. I think you do. You have moody eyes." *There*, he thought, *that's made her look in my direction again.*

Those long, liquid pulls started up again in her belly, so she looked away again. Quickly. "No, actually, I'm not particularly moody. Anyway, hmmm. You have babies being snatched from their cradles and replaced with changelings, children devoured by ogres. In the last century we've changed passages and endings in fairy tales to happy-ever-after, when in reality their early forms contained blood and death and devouring. Psychologically, it mirrors the changes in our cultures, and what parents want their children to hear and to believe."

"And what do you believe?"

"That a story's a story, but happy-ever-after is less likely to give a child nightmares."

"And did your mother tell you stories of changelings?"

"No." The idea of it had Jude laughing. "But my grandmother did. In a very entertaining fashion. I imagine you tell an entertaining one, too."

"I'll tell you one now, if you've a mind to walk down to the village with me."

"Walk?" She shook her head. "It's miles."

"No more than two." Suddenly he wanted very much to walk with her. "You'll work off Mrs. Duffy's cakes, then I'll feed you supper. We have beggarman's stew on the menu tonight, and it sits well. I'll see you get a ride home after a bit."

She slid her gaze toward him, then away again. It sounded wonderfully spontaneous, just stand up and go, no plans, no structure. Which, of course, was exactly why it wouldn't do.

"That's tempting, but I really should work a little longer."

"Then come tomorrow." He took her hand again, drawing her to her feet as he rose. "We have music at Gallagher's of a Saturday night."

"You had music there last night."

"More," he told her. "And a bit more . . . structured you'd say, I suppose. Some musicians from Waterford City, the traditional sort. You'll enjoy it and you can't write about Ireland's legends, can you, without its music? So come down to the pub tomorrow night, and I'll come to you on Sunday."

"Come to me?"

He smiled again, slow, deliberate, delightful. "To tell you a story, for your paper. Will Sunday in the afternoon do for you?"

"Oh, yes, that would be fine. Perfect."

"Good day to you, then, Jude Frances." He strolled to the gate, then turned. His eyes were bluer, more intense when they met hers, held hers. "Come on Saturday. I like looking at you."

She didn't move a muscle, not when he turned to open the gate, not when he walked through and down to the road. Not even after he was well beyond the high hedge and away.

Looking at her? What did he mean by that? Exactly.

Was that some sort of casual flirtation? His eyes hadn't looked casual, she thought as she began to pace up and down the narrow path. Of course, how would she know, really, when this was only the second time she'd seen him?

That was probably it. Just an offhand, knee-jerk flirtation

from a man used to flirting with women. More, when you considered the situation, a friendly remark.

" 'I'd like to see you in the pub on Saturday, come on by,' " she murmured. "That's all he meant. And damn it all to hell and back, why do I have to pick everything apart?"

Annoyed with herself, she strode back into the house, closed the door firmly. Any sensible woman would have smiled at him when he'd said it, flirted back a little. It was a harmless, even conditioned response. Unless you were a neurotic tight-ass.

"Which, Jude F. Murray, is exactly what you are. A neurotic tight-ass. You couldn't just open your idiot mouth and say something like, 'I'll see what I can do. I like looking at you, too.' Oh, no, you just stand there like he'd shot you between the eyes."

Jude stopped, holding up both hands, shutting her eyes. Now she wasn't just talking to herself. She was scolding herself as if she were two different people.

Taking deep breaths, she calmed herself and decided she really wanted another of those little frosted cakes, just to take the edge off.

She marched into the kitchen, ignoring the prissy little voice in her head that told her she was compensating with oral gratification. Yeah, so what? When some gorgeous man she barely knew had her hormones erupting, she was damn well going to comfort herself with sugar.

She snatched up a cake with pale pink frosting, then whirled around at the loud thud against the back door. At the sight of the hairy face and long teeth, she cut loose with a squeal and the cake sailed up, bounced off the ceiling, then landed with a plop—frosting side down—at her feet.

It took her only the amount of time the cake was airborne to realize it wasn't a monster at the back door but a dog.

"Jesus! Jesus Christ, what's with this country? Every two minutes something's coming to the door." She dragged her fingers through her hair, setting curls free, then she and the dog eyed each other through the glass.

She had big brown eyes, and Jude decided they looked hopeful rather than aggressive. Her teeth were showing, true, but her tongue was lolling out, so what choice did they have? Huge paws had already smeared the glass with mud, but when she let out a friendly woof, Jude caved.

As she moved to the door, the dog disappeared. But there she was when Jude opened it, sitting politely on the back stoop, thumping her tail and gazing up at her.

"You're the O'Tooles' dog, aren't you?"

She seemed to take this for an invitation and shoved her way in to clomp around the kitchen, spreading mud. Then she did Jude the favor of cleaning up the dropped cake before walking to the fire and sitting on her haunches again.

"I didn't feel like starting the fire in here today." She walked over, holding out her hand to see what the dog would do about it. When she sniffed it politely, then gave it a nudge with her nose so it landed on her head, Jude laughed.

"Clever, aren't you?" Obligingly, she scratched between her ears. She'd never had a dog, though her mother had two ill-tempered Siamese cats that were pampered like royalty.

She imagined the dog had visited Old Maude regularly, had curled up by the kitchen fire and kept the old woman company from time to time. Did dogs feel grief when a friend had died? she wondered, then remembered she'd yet to keep her promise to take flowers to Maude's grave.

She'd inquired about the location in the village the night before. Maude was buried east of the village, above the sea, beyond the path that ran near the hotel, and back to the ruins and the oratory and the well of Saint Declan.

A long and scenic walk, she mused.

On impulse, Jude pulled the flowers she'd put on the kitchen counter out of their bottle, then cocked her head at the dog.

"Want to go visit Old Maude?"

The dog gave another woof, got to her feet, and as they walked out the back door together, Jude wondered who was leading whom.

It felt very rural and rustic. As she hiked over hills with the yellow dog, flowers in her hand for an ancestor's grave, Jude imagined it as part of her weekly routine. The Irish country woman with her faithful hound, paying respects to a distant cousin.

It would be something she would make a habit—well, if she actually had a dog and really lived here.

It was soothing, being out in the air and the breeze, watching the dog race off to sniff at God knew what, catching all those glorious signs of spring in the blooming hedges, the quick dart and trill of a bird.

The sea rumbled. The cliffs brooded.

As she approached the steeply gabled oratory, the sun shot through the clouds and splashed over the grass and the stone. The three stone crosses stood, casting their shadows, with the well holding its holy water under them.

Pilgrims had washed there, she remembered from her guidebook. And how many, she wondered, had secretly poured a bit of water on the ground for the gods, hedging their bets?

Why take chances, she thought with a nod. She'd have done both herself.

It was a peaceful place, she thought. And a moving one

that seemed to understand life and death, and what connected them.

The air seemed warmer, almost like summer despite the wind, with the fragrance of flowers that scattered through the grass and lay on the dead suddenly wild and sweet. She heard the hum of bees and birdsong, the sound of it clear and musical and ripe.

The grass grew tall and green and just a little wild over uneven ground. A handful of small, rough stones, she noted, that marked ancient graves settled into it. And with them, the single new. Old Maude had chosen to be buried here, nearly alone, on a hill that looked over the gameboard-neat village, the blue skirt of sea, and the roll of green that led to mountain.

Tucked into a stone shelf in the ruins was a long plastic pot filled with deep red flowers. The sight of them touched Jude's heart.

So often people forgot, she thought. But not here. Here, people remembered, and honored those memories with flowers for the dead.

"Maude Alice Fitzgerald," the simple marker read. "Wise Woman" had been carved under her name, and below that the dates of her long, long life.

It was an odd epitaph, Jude mused as she knelt beside the gentle slope. There were flowers there already, a tiny clutch of early violets just beginning to fade. Jude lay her bouquet beside them, then sat back on her heels.

"I'm Jude," she began, "your cousin Agnes's granddaughter. The one from America. I'm staying in your cottage for a while. It's really lovely. I'm sorry I never met you, but Granny used to talk about the times you spent together, in the cottage. How you were happy for her when she married and went to America. But you stayed here, at home."

"She was a fine woman."

With her heart leaping into her throat, Jude jerked her head up and looked into deep blue eyes. It was a handsome face, young and smooth. He wore his black hair long, nearly to his shoulders. His mouth tipped up at the corners in a friendly fashion as he stepped closer to face Jude across the grave.

"I didn't hear you. I didn't know you were here."

"One walks soft on a holy place. I don't mean to frighten you."

"No." Only half to death, she thought. "You just startled me." She pushed at the hair the wind had loosened and sent dancing around her face. "You knew Maude?"

"Sure and I knew Old Maude, a fine woman as I said who lived a rich and generous life. It's good that you're bringing flowers to her, for she favored them."

"They're hers, out of her garden."

"Aye." His smile widened. "That makes them all the better." He laid his hand on the head of the dog that sat quietly at his side. Jude saw a ring glint on his finger, some deep blue stone that winked in a heavy setting of silver. "You've waited a long time to come to your beginnings."

She frowned at him, blinking against the sun, which seemed stronger now, strong enough to make her vision waver. "Oh, you mean to come to Ireland. I suppose I have."

"It's a place where you can look into your heart and see what matters most." His eyes were like cobalt now. Intense, hypnotic. "Then choose," he told her. "Choose well, Jude Frances, for 'tisn't only you who'll be touched by it."

The scent of flowers, grass, earth whirled in her head until she felt drunk from it. The sun blinded her, shooting up fiery facets that burned and blurred. The wind rose, a sudden, dazzling burst of energy.

She would have sworn she heard pipes playing, rising notes flying on that fast wind. "I don't know what you mean." Woozy, she lifted a hand to her head, closed her eyes.

"You will."

"I saw you, in the rain." Dizzy, she was so dizzy. "On the hill with the round tower."

"That you did. We've been waiting for you."

"Waiting? Who?"

The wind stilled as quickly as it had risen, and the music faded away into silence. She shook her head to clear it. "I'm sorry. What did you say?"

But when she opened her eyes again, she was alone with the quiet dead and the big yellow dog.

FIVE

AIDAN DIDN'T OBJECT to paperwork. He bloody well hated
it.

But three days a week, rain or shine, he spent an hour
or more at the desk in his upstairs rooms laboring over
orders and overhead, payroll and profits.

It was a constant relief to him that there was a profit.
He'd never concerned himself overmuch with money before Gallagher's had been passed into his hands. And he
often wondered if that was part of the reason his parents
had pushed it there. He'd had a fine time living from hand
to mouth when he'd traveled. Scraping by, or just scraping.
He hadn't saved a penny or felt the need to.

Responsibility hadn't precisely been his middle name.

After all, he'd grown up comfortable enough, and certainly he'd worked his share during his childhood and ad-
olescence. But mopping up, serving pints, and singing a
tune was a far cry from figuring how much lager to order,
what percentage of breakage—thank you very much, sister

Darcy—the business could bear, the juggling of numbers into ledgers, and the calculation of taxes.

It gave him a headache every blessed time, and he had no more love for sitting inside with books than he had for having a tooth pulled, but he learned.

And as he learned, he realized the pub meant more to him because of it. Yes, parents were clever creatures, he decided. And his knew their son.

He spent time on the phone with distributors trying to wangle the best price. That he didn't mind so much, as it was a bit like horse trading. And something he discovered an aptitude for.

It pleased him that musicians from Dublin, from Waterford, from as far away as Clare and Galway were not only willing but pleased to do a turn at Gallagher's. He took pride in knowing that in his four years at the head of it, he'd helped polish the pub's reputation as a place for music.

And he expected the summer season, when the tourists flowed in, to be the best they'd had.

But that didn't make the adding and subtracting any less a chore.

He'd thought about a computer, but then he'd have to learn the goddamn thing. He could admit, without shame, that the very idea of it frightened him beyond speech. When he broached the idea to Darcy, that she could perhaps learn the ins and outs of it, she'd laughed at him until tears ran down her pretty cheeks.

He knew better than to ask Shawn, who wouldn't think to change a lightbulb if he was reading in the dark.

He wasn't about to hire the chore out, not when Gallagher's had managed its own since the doors had opened. So it was either continue to labor with pencil and adding machine or gather the courage to face technology.

He imagined Jude had knowledge of computers. He

wouldn't mind having her teach him a thing or two. He'd certainly enjoy, he thought with a slow smile, returning the favor in a different area altogether.

He wanted his hands on her. He'd already wondered what he would find in taste, in texture, in that lovely wide mouth of hers. It had been some time since a woman had put this hum in his blood, and he was enjoying the anticipation of it, the wondering of it.

She put him in mind of a young mare not quite sure of her legs. One who shied at the approach of a man even as she hoped for a nice, gentle stroke. It was an appealing combination, that hesitant manner with the clever mind and educated voice.

He hoped she would come that evening, as he'd asked her.

He hoped she'd wear one of her neat outfits, with her hair tidied back so he could imagine the pleasure of mussing her up.

If Jude had had a clue where Aidan's thoughts were traveling, she would never have found the courage to leave the cottage. Even without that added complication, she'd changed her mind about going half a dozen times.

It would be impolite not to after she'd been asked.

It would look as if she expected his time and attention.

It was simply a nice way to spend a friendly evening.

She wasn't the type of woman who spent evenings in bars.

Her own vacillation irritated her so much she decided to go on principle for one hour.

She dressed in stone-gray slacks and jacket, jazzing them up with a vest with thin burgundy stripes. It was Saturday night after all, she thought, and added silver earrings that dangled cheerfully. There would be music, she remembered, as she toyed with going crazy and adding a pair of thin silver bangle bracelets.

She had a secret and passionate love affair with jewelry.

As she slipped the bangles on her wrist, she thought of the ring the man in the cemetery had worn. That flash of sapphire in deeply carved silver, so out of place in the quiet countryside.

He'd been so odd, she thought now, coming and going so quietly it was almost as if she'd dreamed him. But she remembered his face and voice very clearly, as clearly as that sudden burst of scent, the quick kick of wind and the dizziness.

Just a sugar crash, she decided. All those cakes she'd eaten had leaped into her system and then away, leaving her momentarily giddy.

She shrugged it off, leaning forward to the mirror to make sure she hadn't smeared her mascara. She would probably see him again, in the pub tonight or when she took flowers to Maude the next time.

With her bracelets jangling cheerfully and giving her confidence, she headed downstairs. She remembered her keys before she got all the way to the car this time, which she considered good progress. Just as she considered it a good sign that her palms didn't sweat while she negotiated the road in the dark.

Pleased with herself, anticipating a quiet and enjoyable evening, she parked at the curb just down from Gallagher's. Smoothing her hair as she went, she walked to the door, breathed in, pulled it open.

And was nearly knocked back again by the blast of music.

Pipes, fiddle, voices, then the wild roar of the crowd on the chorus of ''Whiskey in the Jar.'' The rhythm was so fast, so reckless it was a blur of sound and that sound grabbed her, yanked her inside, then surrounded her.

This wasn't the dark, quiet pub she'd stepped into before. This one was crowded with people, spilling over at the low tables, jammed into the bar, milling about with glasses full and glasses empty.

The musicians—how could only three people make such a sound?—were shoehorned into the front booth, taking the space over in their workingmen's clothes and boots as they played like demon angels. The room smelled of smoke, yeast, and Saturday-night soap.

For a moment she wondered if she'd walked into the wrong place, but then spotted Darcy, her glorious cloud of dark hair tied back with a sassy red ribbon. She carried a tray loaded with empty glasses, bottles, overflowing ashtrays while she flirted skillfully with a young man whose face was as red as her ribbon with embarrassed delight and whose eyes were filled with desperate admiration.

Catching Jude's eye, Darcy winked, then gave the infatuated young man a pat on the cheek and nudged her way through the crowd. "Pub's lively tonight. Aidan said you'd be coming in and to keep an eye out for you."

"Oh . . . that was nice of him, of you. I wasn't expecting so . . . much."

"The musicians are favored around here, and they draw a good crowd."

"They're wonderful."

"They play a fine tune, yes." Darcy was more interested in Jude's earrings, and wondered where she'd bought them and what the price might have been. "Here now, just keep in my wake and I'll get you to the bar safe enough."

She did just that, winding and wending, nudging now and then with a laugh and a comment addressed to this one or that one by name. She headed for the far end of the bar, where she slipped her tray through bodies to the order station.

"Good evening, Mr. Riley, sir," Darcy said to the ancient man at the very last stool.

"Good evening to you as well, young Darcy." He spoke in a reedy voice, smiled at her out of eyes that looked half blind to Jude as he sipped his thick, dark Guinness. "If you marry me, darling, I'll make you a queen."

"Then marry we will Saturday next, for a queen I deserve to be." She gave him a pretty kiss on his papery cheek. "Will Riley, let the Yank here have your seat next to your grandda."

"Pleasure." The thin man hopped off the stool and beamed a smile at Jude. "You're the Yank, then. Sit down here, next to me grandda, and we'll buy you a pint."

"The lady prefers wine." Aidan, the glass already in his hand, stepped into her vision and offered it.

"Yes. Thank you."

"Well, then, put it on Will Riley's tab, Aidan, and we'll drink to all our cousins across the foam."

"That I'll do, Will." He spread that slow smile over Jude, said, "Stay awhile, won't you?" Then moved off to work.

She stayed awhile. Because it seemed polite, she drank toasts to people she'd never heard of. Because it required little effort on her part, she had a conversation with both Rileys about their relations in the States and their own visits there—though she knew she disappointed them both when she admitted she'd never been to Wyoming and seen an actual cowboy.

She listened to the music, because it was wonderful. Tunes both familiar and strange, both rousing and heartbreaking flowed through and over the crowd. She let herself hum when she recognized the song and smiled when old Mr. Riley piped out words in his thin voice.

"I was sweet of heart on your cousin Maude," Mr. Riley told Jude. "But she was only for Johnny Magee, rest his soul." He sighed deep and sipped his Guinness in the same fashion. "And one day when I went to her door with my hat in my hand once again, she told me I'd marry a lass with fair hair and gray eyes before the year was out."

He paused, smiling to himself as if, Jude thought, looking backward. She leaned closer to hear him over the thunder of music. "And before a month had passed I met my Lizzie, with her fair hair and gray eyes. We were married in June and had nearly fifty years together before she passed on."

"That's lovely."

"Maude, she knew things." His faded eyes looked into Jude's. "The Good People often whispered in Maude's ear."

"Did they?" Jude said, amused now.

"Oh, aye, and you being her blood, they may come whispering in yours. See that you listen."

"I'll do that."

For a time they sipped companionably and listened to the music. Then tears filmed Jude's eyes when Darcy slipped her arm around the old man's bony shoulders and matched her glorious voice to his on a song of endless love and loss.

When she saw Brenna pouring whiskey and pulling the taps behind the bar, Jude smiled. For once the cap was missing, and Brenna's mass of red curls tumbled down as they chose.

"I didn't know you worked here."

"Oh, now and again, when there's need. What's your pleasure there, Jude?"

"Oh, this is Chardonnay, but I really shouldn't—"

But she was talking to Brenna's back and before she knew it the woman had turned around and filled her glass again. "Weekends can be busy at Gallagher's," Brenna went on. "And I'll lend a hand over the summer season as well. It's fine music tonight, isn't it?"

"It's wonderful."

"And how's it all going then, Mr. Riley, my darling?"

"It's going well, pretty Brenna O'Toole. And when are you going to be my bride and stop my heart from aching?"

"In the merry month of May." Smoothly, she replaced his empty pint with a full one. "Watch this rogue, mind you, Jude, or he'll be after toying with your affections."

"Take the other end, will you, Brenna?" Aidan slipped behind her, tugged on her bright hair. "I've a mind to work down here so I can flirt with Jude."

"Ah, there's another rogue for you. The place is full of them."

"She's a pretty one," Mr. Riley put in and Aidan winked at Jude.

"Which one of them, Mr. Riley, sir?"

"All of them." Mr. Riley wheezed out a laugh and slapped his thin hand on the bar. "Sure and I've never seen a female face that wasn't pretty enough for a pinch. The Yank here has witchy eyes. You mind your step, Aidan lad, or she'll put a spell on you."

"Maybe she has already." He cleared glasses, put them in the sink under the bar, got fresh ones for the tap. "Have you been out of a midnight, Jude Frances, picking moonflowers and whispering my name?"

"I might," she heard herself say, "if I knew which were moonflowers."

This made Mr. Riley laugh so hard she feared he'd topple off his stool. Aidan only smiled, served his pints, took the coin. Then he leaned close, watched her eyes go wide and her lips tremble apart in surprise. "I'll point out the moon-flowers for you, the next I come to call."

"Well. Hmmm." So much for snappy repartee, she decided, and gulped down some wine.

Either the wine, or the intimacy of the look he sent her, went straight to her head. She decided she would have to approach both with a bit more caution and respect. This time when Aidan lifted the bottle, she shook her head and put her hand over her glass.

"No, thanks. I'll just have water now."

"You want the fizzy sort?"

"Fizzy? Oh, yes, that would be nice."

He brought it to her in a short glass with no ice to speak of. She sipped it, watching as he set two more glasses under taps and began the methodical process of building a Guinness.

"It takes an awfully long time," she said more to herself than him, but he glanced over, one hand still maneuvering the taps.

"Only as long as it takes to make it right. One day, when you're in the mood for it, I'll build you a glass and you'll see what you're missing by sipping that French business there."

Darcy swung back to the bar, set down her tray. "A pint and a half, Smithwick, pint of Guinness and two glasses of Jameson's. And when you're done there, Aidan, Jack Brennan's come to his limit."

"I'll see to it. What time do you have, Jude Frances?"

"Time?" She stopped staring at his hands—they were so quick and clever—and glanced down at her watch. "Lord, it's after eleven. I had no idea." Her hour had stretched into nearly three. "I need to get back."

Aidan gave her an absent nod, a great deal less than she'd

hoped for, and filled his sister's order while Jude searched for the money to pay for her drinks.

"My grandson's paying." Mr. Riley laid a fragile hand on her shoulder. "He's a good lad. You put your money away, darling."

"Thank you." She offered a hand to shake, then found herself charmed when the old man lifted it to his lips. "I enjoyed meeting you." She slid off her stool, sent a smile to the younger Riley. "Both of you."

Without Darcy to clear the path, getting to the door was a little more problematic than getting to the bar had been. When she got there, her face was flushed from the heat of bodies, and her blood dancing to the hot lick of the fiddle.

She considered it one of the most entertaining evenings of her life.

Then she stepped outside into the cool night air. And saw Aidan just as he ducked under the violent swing of an arm the width of a tree trunk.

"Now, Jack," he said in reasonable tones as a giant of a man with shocking red hair bunched hamlike fists again. "You know you don't want to hit me."

"I'll do it! I'll break your interfering nose this time, by Jesus, Aidan Gallagher. Who are you to tell me I can't have a fucking drink in the fucking pub when I've a fucking mind to?"

"You're well and truly pissed, Jack, and you need to go home now and sleep it off."

"Let's see if you can sleep this off."

He charged, and while Aidan prepared to pivot and easily avoid the bull rush, Jude let out a short scream of alarm. It took only that to distract Aidan enough to have Jack's wild punch connect.

"Well, hell." Aidan wiggled his jaw, blew out a breath

as Jack's lumbering charge sent the man sprawling face-down on the sidewalk.

"Are you all right?" Terrified, Jude rushed over, skirting the sprawled form that was approximately the size of a capsized ocean liner. "Your mouth's bleeding. Does it hurt? This is awful." She fumbled in her bag for a tissue as she stuttered.

Aidan was irritated enough to tell her the blood was as much her fault for screaming as it was Jack's for throwing the punch. But she looked so pretty and distressed, and was already dabbing at his painfully cut lip with the tissue.

He started to smile, and as that hurt like twice the devil, he winced.

"Oh, what a bully! We need to call the police."

"For what?"

"To arrest him. He attacked you."

Sincerely shocked, Aidan gaped at her. "Now, why would I want to have one of my oldest friends arrested just for bloodying my lip?"

"Friend?"

"Sure. He's just nursing a broken heart with whiskey which is foolish but natural enough. The lass he thought he loved went off with a Dubliner, two weeks ago last Wednesday, so he's taken to drinking out his sorrows the past few days, then causing a ruckus. He doesn't mean anything by it."

"He hit you in the face." Perhaps if she said it slowly, clearly, the meaning would get through. "He said he was going to break your nose."

"That's only because he's tried to break it before and hasn't found success. He'll be sorry for it in the morning, nearly as sorry as he'll be because his aching head won't just roll off his shoulders and leave him in peace."

Aidan did smile now, but cautiously. "Were you worried for me, darling?"

"Apparently I shouldn't have been." She said it primly and balled up the bloody tissue. "As you appear to enjoy brawling in the street with your friends."

"Was a time I enjoyed brawling in the street with strangers, but with maturity I prefer my friends." He reached out, as he'd been wanting to, and toyed with the ends of her bound-back hair. "And I thank you for having concern for me."

He stepped forward. She stepped back.

And he sighed. "One day you won't have quite so much room to back away. And I won't have poor drunk Jack at me feet to deal with."

Philosophically he bent down and, to Jude's astonishment, picked up the enormous semiconscious man and swung him handily over his shoulder.

"Is that you, then, Aidan?"

"Aye, Jack."

"Did I break your nose?"

"No, you didn't, but you bloodied my lip a bit."

"Fucking Gallagher luck."

"There's a lady present, you knothead."

"Oh. Begging pardon."

"You're both ridiculous," Jude decided and turned away to march to her car.

"Jude, my darling?" Aidan grinned, hissed as his lip split again. "I'll see you tomorrow, say at half-one." He only chuckled when she continued to walk, heels clicking briskly, then turned to give him a fulminating look as she got into her car.

"Is she gone now?" Jack wanted to know.

"She's going. But not far," Aidan murmured as she drove decorously down the street. "No, she won't go far."

•　　•　　•

Men were baboons. Obviously. Jude shook her head, tapped her finger on the wheel in a disapproving manner as she drove home. Drunken brawls on the street were not amusing pastimes, and anyone who thought they were was in dire need of therapy.

God, he'd made her feel like an idiot. Standing there grinning at her while she dabbed at the blood on his mouth and babbled. An indulgent grin, she thought now, from the big, strong man to the foolish, fluttery female.

Worse, she had been foolish and fluttery. When Aidan had tossed that enormous man over his shoulder as if he was a bag of feathers, her stomach had definitely fluttered. If she hadn't tightened up that very instant and stalked away, she might well have whimpered in admiration.

Mortifying.

And had he been the least bit embarrassed at getting a fist planted in his face in front of her? No, indeed. Had he blushed to introduce the drunken fool at his feet as an old and close friend? No, he had not.

He was very likely behind the bar again right this minute, entertaining his customers with the story, making them laugh over her scream of alarm and trembling hands.

Bastard.

She sniffed once, and felt better for it.

By the time she pulled in the drive she'd convinced herself that she'd behaved in a scrupulously dignified and reasonable manner. It was Aidan Gallagher who'd been the fool.

Moonflowers, indeed. She slammed the door of her car sharply enough to send the echo ringing down to the valley.

After huffing out another breath and smoothing down her hair, she headed for the gate. And when her gaze was drawn up, she saw the woman in the window.

"Oh, God."

The blood drained out of her head. She felt each individual drop of it flow out. Moonlight shimmered gently on the pale fall of hair, on the white cheeks, against the deep green eyes.

She was smiling, a beautiful, heart-wrenching smile that hooked Jude's soul and all but ripped it out.

Gathering courage, she shoved the gate back and ran for the door. When she yanked it open it occurred to her that she'd neglected to lock it. Someone had gone in while she'd been in the pub, she told herself. That was all.

Her knees trembled as she dashed up the stairs.

The bedroom was empty, as was every other room when she hurried through the house. All that was left was the faint sighing scent of woman.

Uneasy, she locked the doors. And when she was in her bedroom again, she locked that as well from the inside.

After she undressed and huddled in bed, she left the light burning. It was a long time before she slept. And dreamed of jewels bursting out of the sun and tumbling through the sky to be caught in a silver bag by a man riding a winged horse white as snowfall.

They swooped out of the sky, over the fields and mountains, the lakes and rivers, the bogs and the moors that were Ireland. Across the battlements of castles and the humble thatched roofs of cottages, with the white wings of the horse singing against the wind.

They came to a flashing stop, hooves striking ground at the front of the cottage on the hill with its white walls and deep-green shutters and flowers spilling from the door.

She came out to him, her hair the palest of golds around her shoulders, her eyes green as the fields. And the man, with hair as dark as hers was light, wearing a silver ring centered with a stone no less brilliant than his eyes, leaped from the horse.

He walked to her and spilled the flood of jewels at her feet. Diamonds blazed in the grass.

"These are my passion for you," he told her. "Take them and me, for I would give you all I have and more."

"Passion isn't enough, nor are your diamonds." Her voice was quiet, contained, and her hands stayed folded at her waist. "I'm promised to another."

"I'll give you all. I'll give you forever. Come away with me, Gwen, and a hundred lifetimes I'll give you."

" 'Tisn't fine jewels and lifetimes I want." A single tear slipped down her cheek, as bright as the diamonds in the grass. "I can't leave my home. Won't change my world for yours. Not for all your diamonds, for all your lifetimes."

Without a word, he turned from her and mounted his horse. And as they rose up into the sky, she walked away into the cottage, leaving the diamonds on the ground as if they were no more than flowers.

And so they became flowers and covered the ground with fragrance, humble and sweet.

SIX

Jude awoke to the soft, steady patter of rain and the vague memory of dreams full of color and motion. She was tempted to snuggle under the covers and slide back into sleep, to find those dreams again. But that seemed wrong. Overindulgent.

More productive, she decided, to create and maintain a routine. A rainy Sunday morning could be spent on basic housekeeping chores. After all, she didn't have a cleaning service here in Ardmore as she had in Chicago.

On some secret level she actually looked forward to the dusting and mopping, the little tasks that would in some way make the cottage hers. She supposed it wasn't very sensible of her, but she actually enjoyed rooting through the cleaning supplies, selecting her rags and cloths.

She spent a pleasant portion of the morning dusting and rearranging the knickknacks Old Maude had scattered all over the house. Pretty painted fairies, elegant sorcerers, intriguing chunks of crystal had homes on every tabletop and shelf. Most of the books leaned toward Irish history and folklore, but there were a number of well-worn paperbacks tucked in.

Old Maude had liked to read romance novels, Jude discovered, and found the idea wonderfully sweet.

Rather than a vacuum, Jude unearthed an old-fashioned upright sweeper, and hummed along with its squeaky progress over rug and wood.

She scrubbed down the kitchen and found a surprising glow of satisfaction when chrome and porcelain gleamed. Gaining confidence as she went, she wielded her polishing cloth in the office next. She would get to the boxes in the tiny closet soon, she promised herself. Perhaps that evening. And she'd ship off to her grandmother anything that seemed worthwhile or sentimental enough to keep.

She stripped the bed in her room, gathered the rest of the laundry. She found it slightly embarrassing that she'd never done laundry before in her life. But surely it couldn't be that complex a skill to learn. It occurred to her that she should have started the wash before she started the cleaning, but she'd remember that next time.

In the cramped room off the kitchen, she found the basket, which she realized she should have taken upstairs in the first place, and dumped the laundry in it.

She also discovered there was no dryer. If she wasn't mistaken, that meant she had to hang clothes out on a line. And though watching Mollie O'Toole as she did so had been enjoyable, doing it herself, for herself, would be a little more problematic.

She'd just have to learn. She *would* learn, Jude assured herself. Then, clearing her throat, she took a hard look at the washing machine.

Hardly new, it had a spray of rust spots over the white surface. The controls were simple. You got cold water or hot, and she assumed if you wanted something clean, you used hot and plenty of it. She read the instructions on the box of detergent and followed them meticulously. The sound of water pouring into the tub made her beam with accomplishment.

To celebrate she put on the kettle for tea and treated herself to a handful of cookies from the tin.

The cottage was tidy. *Her* cottage was tidy, she corrected. Everything was in place, the laundry was going so . . . Now there was no excuse not to think about what she'd seen the night before.

The woman at the window. Lady Gwen.

Her ghost.

There was no reasonable way to deny she'd seen that figure twice now. It had been too clear. So clear she knew she could, even with her rudimentary skills, sketch the face that had watched her from the window.

Ghosts. They weren't something she'd been brought up to believe in, though part of her had always loved the fancy of her grandmother's tales. But unless she had suddenly become prone to hallucinations, she'd seen a ghost twice now.

Could it be she'd tumbled off the edge of the breakdown that had been so worrying her when she left Chicago?

But she didn't feel so unsteady now. She hadn't had a tension headache or a queasy stomach or felt the smothering weight of oncoming depression in days.

Not since she'd stepped over the threshold of Faerie Hill Cottage for the first time.

She felt . . . good, she decided after a quick mental check. Alert, calm, healthy. Even happy.

So, she thought, either she'd seen a ghost and such things did exist, which meant readjusting her thinking to quite an extent . . .

Or she'd had a breakdown and the result of it was contentment.

She nibbled thoughtfully on another cookie and decided she could live with either situation.

At the knock on the front door she quickly brushed crumbs from her sweater and glanced at the clock. She had no idea where the morning had gone, and she had deliberately put Aidan's promised visit out of her head.

Apparently he was here now. That was fine. They'd work in the kitchen, she decided, shoving pins back into her hair as she walked down the hall to the door. Despite her initial, well, chemical reaction to him, her interest in him was purely professional. A man who fought with drunks on the street and flirted so outrageously with women he barely knew had no appeal to her whatsoever.

She was a civilized woman who believed in using reason, diplomacy, and compromise to solve disputes. She could only pity someone who preferred using force and bunched fists.

Even if he did have a beautiful face and muscles that just *rippled* when put into use.

She was much too sensible to be blinded by the physical.

She would record his stories, thank him for his cooperation. And that would be that.

Then she opened the door, and he was standing in the rain, his hair gleaming with it, his smile warm as summer and just as lazy. And she felt about as sensible as a puppy.

"Good day to you, Jude."

"Hello." It was a testament to his effect on her that it took her a full ten seconds to so much as notice the enormous man beside him clutching flowers in his huge hand. He looked miserable, she noted, the rain dripping off the bill of his soaked cap, his wide face pale as moonlight, his truck-grill shoulders slumped.

He only sighed when Aidan rammed an elbow hard into his ribs.

"Ah, good day to you, Miss Murray. I'm Jack Brennan. Aidan here tells me I behaved badly last night, in your presence. I'm sorry for that and hope to beg your pardon."

He shoved the flowers at her, with a pitiful look in his bloodshot eyes. "I'd had a bit too much of the drink," he went on. "But that's no excuse for using strong language in front of a lady—though I didn't know you were there, did I?" He said that with a slide of his eyes toward Aidan and a mutinous set to his mouth.

"No." She kept her voice stern, though the wet flowers were so pathetic they melted her heart. "You were too busy trying to hit your friend."

"Oh, well, sure Aidan's too fast for me to plant a good one on him when I'm under the influence, so to speak." His lips curved, for just a moment, into a surprisingly sweet smile, then he hung his great head again. "But despite circumstances being what they were, it's no excuse for behaving in such a manner in front of a lady. So I'm after begging your pardon and hoping you don't think too poorly of me."

"There now." Aidan gave his friend a hearty slap on the back. "Well done, Jack. Miss Murray's too kindhearted to hold a grudge after so pretty an apology." He looked back at her, as if they were sharing a lovely little joke. "Aren't you, Jude Frances?"

Actually she was, but it irritated her to be so well pegged. Ignoring Aidan, she nodded at Jack. "I don't think poorly of you, Mr. Brennan. It was very considerate of you to come by and bring me flowers. Would you like to come in and have some tea?"

His face brightened. "That's kind of you. I wouldn't mind—"

"You've got places to go, Jack."

Jack's brows drew together. "I don't. Particularly."

"Aye, you do. This and the other. You take my car and be about it. You'll remember I told you Miss Murray and I have business to tend to."

"All right, then," he muttered. "But I don't see how one bloody cup of tea would matter. Good day, Miss Murray." Shoulders hunched, cap dripping, he lumbered back to the car.

"You might have let him come in out of the rain," Jude commented.

"You don't seem to be in any great hurry to ask me in out of it." Aidan angled his head as he studied her face. "Maybe you hold a grudge after all."

"You didn't bring me flowers." But she stepped back to let him come inside and drip.

"I'll see that I do next time. You've been cleaning. The house smells of lemon oil, a nice, homey scent. If you get me a rag, I'll wipe up this wet I'm tracking in to your nice, clean house."

"I'll take care of it. I have to go up and get my tape recorder and so forth. We'll work in the kitchen. You can just go ahead back."

"All right, then." His hand closed over hers, making her frown. Then he slipped the flowers out of her fingers. "I'll put these in something for you so they don't look quite so pitiful."

"Thank you." The stiffly polite tone was the only defense she could come up with against six feet of wet, charming male in her hallway. "I'll only be a minute."

She was barely longer than that, but when she walked into the kitchen he already had the flowers in one of Maude's bottles and was handily brewing a pot of tea.

"I started a fire there in your hearth to take the chill off. That all right, then?"

"Of course." And she tried not to be annoyed that every one of the tasks he'd done took her three times as long to accomplish. "Have a seat. I'll pour the tea."

"Ah, it needs to steep a bit yet."

"I knew that." She mumbled it as she opened a cupboard for cups and saucers. "We make tea in America, too." She turned back, set the cups on the table, then hissed out a breath. "Stop staring at me."

"Sorry, but you're pretty when you're all flustered and your hair's falling down."

Mutiny ripe in her eyes, she jammed pins back in violently enough to drill them into her scalp. "Perhaps I should make myself clear. This is an intellectual arrangement."

"Intellectual." Wisely he controlled the grin and kept his face sober. "Sure it's a fine thing to have an interest in each other's minds. You've a strong one, I suspect. Telling you you're pretty doesn't change that a bit, does it?"

"I'm not pretty and I don't need to hear it. So if we can just get started?"

He took a seat because she did, then cocked his head again. "You believe that, don't you? Well, now, that's interesting, on an intellectual level."

"We're not here to talk about me. My impression was that you have a certain skill as a storyteller and are familiar with some of the myths and legends particular to this area."

"I know some tales." When her voice went prim that way it just made him want to lap at her, starting anywhere at all. So he leaned back in his chair. If it was intellectual she wanted, he figured they could begin with that . . . then move along.

"Some you may know already, in one form or another.

The oral history of a place may shift here and there from teller to teller, but the heart of it remains steady. The shape-shifter is told one way by the Native Americans, another by the villagers of Romania, and still another by the people of Ireland. But the same threads weave through.''

While she continued to frown, he lifted the pot to pour the tea himself. ''You have Santa and Father Christmas and Kris Kringle—one may come down the chimney, another fills shoes with candy, but the basis of the legend has its roots in the same place. Because it does, time after time, country after country, the intellect comes to the conclusion that the myth has its core in fact.''

''You believe in Santa Claus.''

His eyes met hers as he set the pot down again. ''I believe in magic, and that the best of it, the most true of it, is in the heart. You've been here some days now, Jude Frances. Have you felt no magic?''

''Atmosphere,'' she began, and turned her recorder on. ''The atmosphere in this country is certainly conducive to the forming of myths and the perpetuation of them, from paganism with its small shrines and sacrifices to the gods, Celtic folklore with its warnings and rewards and the addition of culture seeded in through the invasions of the Vikings, the Normans, and so on.''

''It's the place,'' Aidan disagreed. ''Not the people who tried to conquer it. It's the land, the hills and rock. It's the air. And the blood that seeped into all of it in the fight to keep it. 'Tis the Irish who absorbed the Vikings, the Normans, and so on, not the other way around.''

There was pride there that she understood and respected. ''The fact remains that these people came to this island, that they mated with the women here, passed down their seed, and brought with them their superstitions and beliefs. Ireland absorbed them, too.''

"Which came first, the tale or the teller? Is that part of your study then?"

He was quick, she thought. A sharp mind and a clever tongue. "You can't study one without studying the other. Who tells and why, as much as what's told."

"All right, I'll tell you a story that was told to me by my grandda, and to him by his father, and his by his for as far back as any knows, for there have been Gallaghers on this coast and in these hills for longer than time remembers."

"The story came down paternally?" Jude interrupted and was met with that quirked brow. "Very often stories come down the generations through the mother."

"True enough, but the bards and harpists of Ireland were traditionally male, and it's said one was a Gallagher who wandered to this place singing his stories for coin and ale, that he saw some of what I'll tell you with his own eyes, heard the rest from the lips of Carrick, prince of the faeries, and from that told the story himself to all who cared to listen."

He paused, noting the amused interest in Jude's eyes. Then began. "There was a maid known as Gwen. She was of humble birth but a lady in her heart and in her manner. She had hair as pale as winter sunlight, and eyes as green as moss. Her beauty was known throughout the land, and though she carried herself with pride, for she had a slim and pleasing form, she was a modest maid who, as her blessed mother had died in the birthing of her, kept the tidy cottage for her aging father. She did as she was bid and what was expected and was never heard to complain. Though she was seen, from time to time, walking on the cliffs of an evening and staring out over the sea as if she wished to grow wings and fly."

As he spoke, a silent stream of sunlight shimmered

through the rain, through the window, to lie quietly on the table between them.

"I can't say what was in her heart," Aidan continued. "Perhaps this is something she didn't know herself. But she kept the cottage, cared for her father, and walked the cliffs alone. One day, when she was taking flowers to the grave of her mother, for she was buried near the well of Saint Declan, she met a man—what she thought was a man. He was tall and straight, with dark hair waving to his shoulders and eyes as blue as the bluebells she carried in her arms. By her name he called her, and his voice was like music in her head and set her heart to dancing. And in a flash like a lightning strike, they fell in love over her dear mother's grave with the breeze sighing through the tall grass like faeries whispering."

"Love at first sight," Jude commented. "It's a device often used in fables."

"Don't you believe that heart recognizes heart?"

An odd and poetic way to put it, she thought, and was glad she'd have the question recorded. "I believe in attraction at first sight. Love takes more."

"You've had the Irish all but drummed out of you," he said with a shake of his head.

"Not so much I don't appreciate the romance of a good story." She sent him a smile, a hint of dimples. "What happened next?"

"Well, however heart recognized heart, it was not the simple matter of a maid and a man taking hands and joining lives, for he was Carrick, the faerie prince who lived in the silver palace under the hill where her cottage sat. She feared a spell, and she doubted both his heart and her own. And more her heart yearned, more she doubted, for she'd been taught to beware of the faeries and the rafts where they gathered."

His voice, rising and falling like music on the words, lulled Jude into propping her elbows on the table, resting her chin on her fists.

"Even so one night, when the moon was ripe and full, Carrick lured Gwen from the cottage and onto his great winged horse to fly with her over the land and the sea and show her the wonders he would give her if only she would pledge to him. His heart was hers and all he had he would give her.

"And it happened that her father, wakeful with aches in his bones, saw his young Gwen swirl out of the sky on the white winged horse with the faerie prince behind her. In his fear and lack of understanding he thought only to save her from the spell he was sure she was under. So he forbade her to have truck with Carrick again, and to ensure her safety he betrothed her to a steady young man who made his living on the water. And Lady Gwen, a maid with great respect for her father, dutifully tucked her heart away, ceased her walking, and prepared to be wed as was bid her."

Now, the little slash of sunlight that danced across the table between them vanished, and the kitchen plunged into gloom lit only by the simmering fire.

Aidan kept his eyes on Jude's, fascinated by what he saw in them. Dreams and sadness and wishes.

"On first hearing, Carrick gave way to a black temper and sent the lightning and thunder and wind to whip and crash over the hills and down to the sea. And the villagers, the farmers and fishermen trembled, but Lady Gwen sat quiet in her cottage and saw to her mending."

"He could have just taken her into the raft," Jude interrupted, "and kept her for a hundred years."

"Ah, so you know something of how it's done." Those blue eyes warmed with approval. "True enough he could have snatched her away, but in his pride he wanted her to come to him willing. In this way the gentry aren't so very different from ordinary people.''

He angled his head, studying her face. "Would you rather be snatched up and away without a choice or romanced and courted?''

"Since I don't think one of the Good People is going to come along and do either in my case, I don't have to decide. I'd rather know what Carrick did.''

"All right, then, I'll tell you. At dawn Carrick mounted his winged horse and flew up to the sun. He gathered fire from it, formed dazzling diamonds from it, and put them in a silver sack. And these flaming and magic jewels he brought to her at her cottage. When she went out to meet him, he spilled them at her feet, and said to her, 'I've brought you jewels from the sun. These are my passion for you. Take them, and me, for I will give you all I have, and more.' But she refused, telling him she was promised to another. Duty held her and pride him as they parted, leaving the jewels lying among the flowers.''

"And so they became flowers.''

When Jude shuddered, Aidan reached for her hand. "Are you cold, then?''

"No.'' She forced a smile, deliberately freed her hand and picked up her tea, sipping slowly to soothe away the flutter in her throat.

She knew the story. She could see it, the magnificent horse, the lovely woman, the man who wasn't a man, and the fiery blaze of diamonds on the ground.

She had seen it, all of it, in her dreams.

"No, I'm fine. I think my grandmother must have told me some version of this.''

"There's more yet.''

"Oh." She sipped again, made an effort to relax. "What happened next?"

"On the day she married the fisherman, her father died. It was as if he'd held on to his life, with all its pains, until he was assured his Gwen was safe and cared for. So, her husband moved into the cottage, and left her before the sun rose every day to go out and cast his nets. And their life settled into a contentment and order."

When he paused, Jude frowned. "But that can't be all."

Aidan smiled, sampled his tea. Like any good storyteller, he knew how to change rhythm to hold interest. "Did I say it was? No, indeed, it's not all. For you see, Carrick, he could not forget her. She was in his heart. While Gwen was living her life as was expected of her, Carrick lost his joy in music and in laughter. One night, in great despair, he mounted his horse once again and flew up to the moon, gathering its light, which turned to pearls in his silver bag. Once more he went to her, and though she carried her first child in her womb, she slipped out of her husband's bed to meet him.

" 'These are tears of the moon,' he told her. 'They are my longing for you. Take them, and me, for I will give you all I have, and more.' Again, though tears of her own spilled onto her cheeks, she refused him. For she belonged to another, had his child inside her, and would not betray her vow. Once more they parted, duty and pride, and the pearls that lay on the ground became moonflowers.

"So the years passed, with Carrick grieving and Lady Gwen doing what was expected of her. She birthed her children, and took joy in them. She tended her flowers, and she remembered love. For though her husband was a good man, he had never touched her heart in its deepest chambers. And she grew old, her face and her body aging, while her heart stayed young with the wistful wishes of a maid."

"It's sad."

" 'Tis, yes, but not yet over. As time is different for faeries than for mortals, one day Carrick mounted his winged horse and flew out over the sea, and dived deep, deep into it to find its heart. There, the pulse of it flowed into his silver bag and became sapphires. These he took to Lady Gwen, whose children had children now, whose hair had gone white and whose eyes had grown dim. But all the faerie prince saw was the maid he loved and longed for. At her feet, he spilled the sapphires. 'These are the heart of the sea. They are my constancy. Take them, and me, for I will give you all I have, and more.'

"And this time, with the wisdom of age, she saw what she had done by turning away love for duty. For never once trusting her heart. And what he had done, for offering jewels, but not giving her the one thing that may have swayed her to him."

Without realizing it, Aidan closed his fingers over Jude's on the table. As they linked together, that little sunbeam danced back.

"And that it was the words of love—rather than passion, rather than longing, even rather than constancy—she'd needed. But now she was old and bent, and she knew as the faerie prince couldn't, not being mortal, that it was too late. She wept the bitter tears of an old woman and told him that her life was ended. And she said that if he had brought her love rather than jewels, had spoken of love rather than passion, and longing and constancy, her heart might have won over duty. He had been too proud, she said, and she too blind to see her heart's desire.

"Her words angered him, for he had brought her love, time and again, in the only way he knew. And this time before he walked away from her, he cast a spell. She would wander and she would wait, as he had, year after year, alone and lonely, until true hearts met and accepted the gifts he had offered her. Three times to meet, three times to accept before the spell could be broken. He mounted and flew into the night, and the jewels at her feet again became flowers. She died that very night, and on her grave flowers sprang up season to season while the spirit of Lady Gwen, lovely as the young maid, waits and weeps for love lost.''

Jude felt weepy herself and oddly unsettled. ''Why didn't he take her away then, tell her it didn't matter?''

''That's not the way it happened. And wouldn't you say, Jude Frances, that the moral is to trust your heart, and never turn away from love?''

She caught herself, and realizing she'd been too wrapped up in the tale, even as her hand was in his, drew back. ''It might be, or that following duty provides you with a long, contented life if not a flashy one. Jewels weren't the answer, however impressive. He should have looked back to see them turn into flowers—flowers she kept.''

''As I said, you've a strong mind. Aye, she kept his flowers.'' Aidan flicked a finger over the petals in the bottle. ''She was a simple woman with simple ways. But there's a bigger point to the tale.''

''Which would be?''

''Love.'' Over the blooms, his eyes met hers. ''Love, whatever the time, whatever the obstacles, lasts. They're only waiting now for the spell to run its course, then she'll join him in his silver palace beneath the faerie hill.''

She had to pull herself out of the story and into the reasoning, she reminded herself. The analysis. ''Legends often have strings attached. Quests, tasks, provisions. Even in folklore the prize rarely comes free. The symbolism in this one is traditional. The motherless maid caring for her aging father, the young prince on a white horse. The use of the elements: sun, moon, sea. Little is said about the man she married, as he's only a vehicle used to keep the lovers apart.''

Busily making notes, she glanced up, saw Aidan studying her thoughtfully. ''What?''

''It's appealing, the way you shift back and forth.''

''I don't know what you mean.''

''When I'm telling it to you, you're all dreamy-eyed and going soft, now here you are, sitting up straight and proper, all businesslike, putting pieces of the story that charmed you into little compartments.''

''That's precisely the point. And I wasn't dreamy-eyed.''

''I'd know better about that, wouldn't I, as I was the one looking at you.'' His voice warmed again, flowed over her. ''You've sea goddess eyes, Jude Frances. Big and misty green. I've been seeing them in my mind even when you're not around. What do you think of that?''

''I think you have a clever tongue.'' She got up, without a clue what she intended to do. For lack of anything else, she carried the teapot back to the stove. ''Which is why you tell a very entertaining story. I'd like to hear more, to coordinate them with those from my grandmother and others.''

She turned back around, jolted when she realized he was standing just behind her. ''What are you doing?''

''Nothing at the moment.'' *Ah, boxed you in now, haven't I?* he thought, but kept his voice easy. ''I'm happy enough to tell you tales.'' Smoothly, he rested his hands on the edge of the stove on either side of her. ''And if you've a mind to, you can come into the pub on a quiet night and find others who'll do the same.''

''Yes.'' Panic was beating bat wings in her stomach. ''That's a good idea. I should—''

''Did you enjoy yourself last night? The music?''

''Mmmm.'' He smelled of rain, and of man. She didn't

know what to do with her hands. "Yes. The music was wonderful."

"Is it that you don't know the tunes?" He was close now, very close, and could see a thin ring of amber between the silky black of her pupils and the misty green of the iris.

"Ah, I know some of them. Do you want more tea?"

"I wouldn't mind it. Why didn't you sing then?"

"Sing?" Her throat was bone-dry, a desert of nerves.

"I had my eye on you, most of the time. You never sang along, chorus or verse."

"Oh, well. No." He really had to move. He was taking all her air. "I don't sing, except when I'm nervous."

"Is that the truth, then?" Watching her face, he moved in, sliding his body into an amazing fit against hers.

She knew what to do with her hands now. They lifted quickly to brace against his chest. "What are you doing?"

"I've a mind to hear you sing, so I'm making you nervous."

She managed a stuttering laugh, but when she tried to shift she only succeeded in pressing more firmly against him. "Aidan—"

"Just a little nervous," he murmured and lowered his mouth to nip gently at her jaw. "You're trembling." Another nip, teasing and light. "Easy now, I'm after stirring you up, not frightening you to death."

He was doing both. Her heart was rapping against her ribs, ringing in her ears. While he slowly nibbled his way over her jaw, her hands were trapped against the solid wall of his chest. And she felt marvelously weak and female.

"Aidan, you're . . . This is . . . I don't think—"

"That's fine, then, a fine idea. Let's neither of us think for just a minute here."

He caught her bottom lip—the wide, soft wonder of it—between his teeth. She moaned, quiet; her eyes clouded, dark. A spear of pure and reckless lust shot straight to his loins.

"Jesus, you're a sweet one." His hand lifted from the stove, fingers skimming over her collarbone. As he held her where he wanted her, he took her mouth. Sampling, then savoring, then wallowing in the taste of her.

Even as she slid toward surrender, he used his teeth to make her gasp. And went deeper than he'd intended.

Still she trembled, putting him in mind of a volcano poised to erupt, a storm ready to strike. Her hands remained trapped between them, but her fingers gripped his shirt now and held fast.

She heard him murmur something, a whisper against the wall of sound that was her blood raging. His mouth, so hot, so skilled, his body, so hard, so strong. And his hands, light as moth wings on her face. She could do nothing but give, and give, even as some shocking, unrecognizable part of her urged her to take.

And when he drew away it was as if her world tilted and spilled her out.

He kept his hands on her face, waited for her eyes to open, focus. He'd intended only to taste, to enjoy the moment. To see. But it had gone beyond intentions into something just out of his control. "Will you let me have you?"

Her eyes were huge, glazed with confusion and pleasure. And nearly brought him to his knees. He didn't particularly care for the sensation.

"I . . . what?"

"Come upstairs and lie with me."

Shock came a bare instant before she simply nodded her head. "I can't. No. This is completely irresponsible."

"Is there someone in America who has a hold on you?"

"A hold?" Why wouldn't her brain function? "Oh. No, I'm not involved with anyone." The sudden gleam in Aidan's eyes had her straining back. "That doesn't mean I'm going to just . . . I don't sleep with men I barely know."

"At the moment, I feel we know each other pretty well."

"That's a physical reaction."

"You're damn right." He kissed her again, hard and hot.

"I can't breathe."

"I'm having a bit of trouble with that myself." It was against his natural instincts, but he stepped away. "Well, what do we do about this, then, Jude Frances? Analyze it on an intellectual level?"

His voice might have carried the musical lilt of Ireland, but it could still slash. Because she wanted to wince, she straightened her shoulders. "I'm not going to apologize for not jumping into bed with you. And if I prefer to function on an intellectual level, it's my business."

He closed his mouth before the snarl escaped, then jammed his hands in his pockets and paced up and down the tiny room. "Do you always have to be reasonable?"

"Yes."

He stopped, eyed her narrowly, then to her complete confusion, threw back his head and laughed. "Damn it, Jude, if you'd shout or throw something, we could have a nice bloody fight and end it wrestling on the kitchen floor. And, speaking for myself, I'd feel a hell of a lot more satisfied."

She allowed herself a quiet breath. "I don't shout or throw things or wrestle."

He lifted a brow. "Ever?"

"Ever."

His grin came fast this time, a flash of humor and challenge. "I bet I can change that." He stepped toward her, shaking his head when she backed away. He caught a loose strand of her hair and tugged. "Will you wager on it?"

"No." She tried a hesitant smile. "I don't gamble either."

"You walk around with a name like Murray, then tell me you don't gamble. It's a disgrace you are to your blood."

"I'm a testament to my breeding."

"I'll put my money on the blood every time." He rocked back on his heels, considering her. "Well, I'd best start back. A walk in the rain'll clear my head."

She steadied herself as he took his jacket from the hook. "You're not angry?"

"Why would I be?" His gaze whipped to hers, bright and intense. "You've a right to say no, haven't you?"

"Yes, of course." She cleared her throat. "Yes, but I imagine a number of men would still be angry."

"I'm not a number of men, then, am I? And, added to that, I mean to have you, and I will. It doesn't have to be today."

He flashed her another grin when her mouth fell open, then walked to the door. "Think of that, and of me, Jude Frances, until I get my hands on you again."

When the door closed behind him, she stood exactly where she was. And though she did think of that, and of him, and of all the pithy, lowering, brilliant responses she should have made, she thought a great deal more of what it had been like to be held against him.

SEVEN

I'M COMPILING STORIES, Jude wrote in her journal, *and find the project even more interesting than I'd expected. The tapes my grandmother sent bring her here. While I'm listening to them, it's almost as if she's sitting across from me. Or, sweeter somehow, as if I were a child again and she had come by to tell me a bedtime story.*

She prefaces her telling of the Lady Gwen tale by stating she'd never told me this story. She must be mistaken, as portions of it were very familiar to me while Aidan was relating it to me.

Logically, I dreamed of it because the memory of the story was in my subconscious and being in the cottage tripped it free.

Jude stopped typing, pushed back, drummed her fingers. Yes, of course, that was it. She felt better now that she'd written it down. It was exactly the exercise she always gave to her first-year students. Write down your thoughts on a certain problem or indecision, in conversational style, without filters. Then sit back, read, and explore the answers you've found.

So why hadn't she documented her encounter with Aidan in her journal? She'd written nothing about the way he'd caged her between the stove and his body, the way he'd nibbled on her as she were something tasty. Nothing about how she felt or what she thought.

Oh, God. Just the memory of it had her stomach flipping.

It was part of her experience, after all, and her journal was designed to include her experiences, her thoughts and feelings about them.

She didn't want to know her thoughts and feelings, she reminded herself. Every time she tried to think about it in a reasonable manner, those feelings took over and turned her mind to mush.

"Besides, it's not relevant," she said aloud.

She huffed out a breath, rolled her shoulders, and put her fingers back on the keys.

It was interesting to note that my grandmother's version of the Lady Gwen tale was almost exactly the same as Aidan's. The delivery of each was defined by the teller, but the characters, details, the tone of the story were parallel.

This is a clear case of well-practiced and skilled oral tradition, which indicates a people who respect the art enough to keep it as pure as possible. It also indicates to me, psychologically, how a story becomes legend and legend becomes accepted as truth. The mind hears, again and again, the same story with the same rhythm, the same tone, and begins to accept it as real.

I dream about them.

Jude stopped again, stared at the screen. She hadn't meant to type that. The thought had slipped into her mind and down through her fingers. But it was true, wasn't it? She dreamed about them almost nightly now—the prince on the winged white horse who looked remarkably like the man she'd met at Maude's grave. The sober-eyed woman whose face was a reflection of the one she thought she'd seen—had seen, Jude corrected, in the window of the cottage.

Her subconscious had given them those faces, of course. That was perfectly natural. The events in the story were said to have happened at the cottage where she lived, so naturally the seeds had been planted and they bloomed in dreams.

It was nothing to be surprised by or concerned about.

Still, she decided she was in the wrong mood for journal entries or exercises and turned off the machine. Since Sunday she'd kept very close to the cottage—to work, she assured herself. Not because she was avoiding anyone. And though the work was satisfying her, fueling her in a way, it was time to get out.

She could drive into Waterford for some supplies and those gardening books. She could explore more of the countryside, instead of just roaming the hills and fields near her house. Surely the more she drove, the more comfortable she'd be with driving.

Solitude, she reminded herself, was soothing. But it could also become stifling. And it could make you forgetful, she decided. Hadn't she had to look at the calendar that morning just to figure out if it was Wednesday or Thursday?

Out, she told herself while she hunted up her purse and her keys. Explore, shop, see people. Take photographs, she added, stuffing her camera in her purse, to send to her grandmother with the next letter home.

Maybe she would linger and treat herself to a nice dinner in the city.

But the minute she stepped outside, she realized it was here she wanted to linger, right here in the pretty garden with her view of the green fields and the shadowy mountains and wild cliffs.

What harm would it do to spend just half an hour weeding before she left? Okay, she wasn't dressed for weeding, but so what? Did she or did she not know how to do her own laundry now?

Except for the sweater she'd managed to shrink to doll size, that little experiment had come off very well.

So she didn't know a weed from a daisy. She had to learn, didn't she? She just wouldn't yank anything that looked pretty.

The air was so soft, the light so lovely, the clouds so thick and white.

When the yellow dog bounded up to dance at her gate, she gave in. Just half an hour, she promised herself as she walked over to let her in.

Jude delighted the dog with strokes and scratches until she all but dissolved at Jude's feet in a puddle of devotion.

"Caesar and Cleo never let me pet them," she murmured, thinking of her mother's snobbish cats. "They have too much dignity." Then she laughed as the dog sprawled on her back to expose her belly. "You just don't have any dignity at all. That's what I like about you."

She'd made a mental note to include dog treats on her supply list when Brenna's pickup bumped along the road and zipped into her drive.

"Well, you've met Betty, then."

"Is that her name?" Jude hoped her grin wasn't as foolish as it felt on her face as the dog nuzzled her nose into her hand. "She's very friendly."

"Oh, she has a fondness for the ladies, particularly." Folding her arms on the open window, Brenna rested her chin there. She wondered why the woman seemed embarrassed to have been caught petting a dog. "So you're fond of dogs, are you?"

"Apparently."

"Whenever she wears out her welcome, you just shove her out the gate, and she'll head home. Our Betty knows a soft touch, and she doesn't mind taking advantage."

"She's wonderful company. But I suppose I'm keeping her from your mother."

"She's more on her mind than Betty's presence at the moment. Refrigerator's out again. I'm heading down to kick it for her. Haven't seen you at the pub this week."

"Oh. No, I've been working. I haven't really been out."

"But you're heading off today." She nodded her head toward Jude's purse.

"I thought I'd drive into Waterford, hunt up those gardening books."

"Oh, now there's no need to go all that way, unless you're set on it. Come down the house and talk to my mother while I'm banging on the icebox. She'd enjoy that, and it'd keep her from badgering me with questions."

"She wouldn't be expecting company. I wouldn't want to—"

"Door's always open." The woman was so interesting, Brenna thought. And hardly said more than one short string of words at a time unless you bumped and nudged at her. If anyone could pry bits and pieces out of her, to Brenna's mind, it was Mollie O'Toole.

"Come on, hop in," she added, then whistled for the dog.

Betty yapped once, cheerfully, then bounded to the truck and leaped neatly into the back.

Jude searched for a polite excuse, but everything that came to mind seemed stilted and rude. Smiling weakly, she latched the gate and walked around the truck to the passenger side. "You're sure I won't be in the way."

"Not a bit of it." Pleased, Brenna beamed at her, waited until she climbed in, then roared backward out of the drive.

"God!"

"What?" Brenna slammed on the brakes, forcing Jude to slap her hands on the dash before her face plowed into it. She hadn't had time to fasten her seat belt.

"You . . . ah." Regulating her breathing, Jude hastily dragged the belt around her. "You don't worry that a car might be coming?"

Brenna laughed, a rollicking sound, then gave Jude a friendly pat on the shoulder. "There wasn't, was there? Don't fret, I'll keep you in one piece. Those are lovely shoes," she added. Though Brenna didn't see how they'd be as comfortable as a stout pair of boots. "Darcy wagers you wear shoes made in Italy. Is that the truth?"

"Um . . ." With a vague frown, Jude stared down at her neat black flats. "Yes, actually."

"She's a keen eye for fashion, Darcy does. Loves looking through the magazines and such. Dreamed through them even when we were girls together."

"She's beautiful."

"Oh, she is, yes. The Gallaghers are a fine, handsome family."

"It's odd that such attractive people aren't involved with anyone. Particularly." Even as she said it, casually as she could, she cursed herself for prying.

"Darcy has no interest, never has, in the local lads. Above a bit of flirting, that is. Aidan—" She jerked a shoulder. "Seems married to the pub since he came back, else the man is very discreet. Shawn . . ."

A frown marred Brenna's brow as she whipped the truck into the drive at her house. "He doesn't look hard enough at what's in front of his face, if you're asking me."

The dog leaped out of the truck and raced around the back of the house.

The frown vanished as Brenna hopped out. "If you're of a mind to do some shopping in Waterford City, or Dublin, Darcy's your girl. Nothing she likes better than wandering the shops and trying on clothes and shoes and playing at the paints and powders. But if your stove's acting up, or you find a leak in your roof—" She winked as she led Jude to the front door. "You give me a call."

There were flowers here, snugged together in color and shape into a lovely blanket outside the door, trailing and tangling up a trellis, spilling happily out of pots of simple red clay.

They seemed to grow as they chose, yet there was a tidiness, an almost ruthless neatness, Jude thought, to the entrance of the house. The stoop was scrubbed so clean it looked adequate as a table for major surgery. And Jude felt herself wince when Brenna carelessly left dirt from her boots over its surface.

"Ma!" Brenna's voice rang out, down the pretty hallway, up the angled staircase, as a fat gray cat slid out of a doorway to wind around her boots. "I've brought company."

The house smelled female, was Jude's first thought. Not just the flowers, or the polish, but the underlying scent of women—perfume, lipstick, shampoo—the sort of candy-coated fragrance young women and girls often carried with them.

She remembered it from college, and wondered if that

was why her stomach clutched. She'd been so miserably awkward and out of place among all those recklessly confident females.

"Mary Brenna O'Toole, I'll let you know when my hearing's gone, and then you can shout at me." Mollie came down the hallway, tugging off a short pink apron.

She was a sturdy-looking woman, no taller than her daughter but certainly wider. Her hair was only slightly less brilliant than Brenna's but quite a bit tidier. She had a plump, pretty face with an easy smile and friendly green eyes that beamed welcome even before she held out her hand.

"So you brought Miss Murray to see me. You've the look of your granny, a dear woman she is. I'm happy to meet you."

"Thank you." The hand that clasped Jude's was strong and hard from a lifetime of making a home. "I hope I'm not catching you at a bad time."

"Not at all. If it's not one thing than for sure it's another around the O'Tooles'. Come in and sit in the parlor, won't you? I'll fix us some tea."

"I don't want to put you to any trouble."

"Of course you're not." Mollie gave her a comforting squeeze on the shoulder as she might to any of her girls if they felt out of place. "You'll keep me company while the lass here is in the kitchen, banging and cursing. Brenna, I'm telling you just as I'll tell your dad when I get hold of him. It's time that refrigerator was hauled out of my house and another brought in."

"I can fix it."

"And so both of you say, time and time again." She shook her head as she led Jude into the front parlor with its company chairs and fresh flowers. "It's a cross to bear, Miss Murray, having those that are handy with things in your life, for nothing ever gets tossed away. It's always 'I can fix it,' or 'I have a use for it.' Make Miss Murray at home, Brenna, while I see to the tea. Then you can have at it.''

"Well, I *can* fix it," Brenna mumbled when her mother was out of earshot. "And if I can't it's good for parts, isn't it?''

"Parts of what?''

Brenna glanced back, focused on Jude again and grinned. "Oh, for this and for that, or else for the other thing entirely. So I hear Jack Brennan came to beg your pardon with a fistful of posies Sunday last.''

"Yes, he did." Jude perched on her chair and looked with some envy at the way Brenna slouched comfortably in hers. "He was very sweet and embarrassed. Aidan shouldn't have made him do it.''

"It was one way to pay Jack back for the fat lip.'' Twinkling now, she shifted in her chair, hooking one booted ankle over the other. "How did he manage it? It's a rare thing for a fist slowed by whiskey to land on Aidan Gallagher.''

"It was my fault, I suppose. I called out—'' Screamed, Jude thought in self-disgust. "I must have distracted him and then he had a fist in his face, and his head was snapping back, his mouth bleeding. I've never seen anything like it.''

"Haven't you?'' Fascinated, Brenna pursed her lips. Even in a female household, she'd grown up with the stray fist flying. It would often be her own. "Don't they have the occasionally donnybrook in Chicago?''

It was a word that made Jude smile, and think for some reason of baseball. "Not in my neighborhood,'' she murmured. "Does Aidan often have fistfights with his customers?''

"No, indeed, though he started his own fair share of

brawls once upon a time. These days if someone's reached his limit and is feeling a bit frisky, Aidan talks them around it. Most don't want to push him in any case. Gallaghers are known for their dark moods and black temper.''

''Unlike the O'Tooles,'' Mollie said dryly as she carted in a tea tray. ''Who are of a sunny nature night and day.''

''That's the truth.'' Brenna leaped up and planted a loud kiss on her mother's cheek. ''I'll see to your fridge, Ma, and have it working like new for you.''

''Hasn't worked like new since Alice Mae was born, and she's fifteen this summer. Go on then before the milk sours. She's a good girl, my Brenna,'' Mollie went on when Brenna strolled out. ''All my girls are. Will you have some biscuits with your tea, Miss Murray? I baked yesterday.''

''Thank you. Please call me Jude.''

''I will, then, and you call me Mollie. It's nice to have a neighbor in Faerie Hill Cottage again. Old Maude would be pleased you've come as she wouldn't want the house sitting lonely. No, none for you, you great lump.'' Mollie addressed this to the cat who leaped onto the arm of her chair. She nudged him off again, but not before scratching his ears.

''You have a wonderful house. I like looking at it when I'm walking.''

''It's a hodgepodge, but it suits us.'' Mollie poured the tea into her good china cups, smiling as she set the pot down again. ''My Mick was always one for adding a room here and a room there, and when Brenna was big enough to swing a hammer, why the two of them ganged up on me and did whatever they liked to the place.''

''With so many children, you'd need room.'' Jude accepted the tea and two golden sugar cookies. ''Brenna said you have five daughters.''

''Five that sometimes seems like twenty when the lot of

them are running around tame. Brenna's the oldest, and her father's apple. My Maureen's getting married next autumn, and driving us all mad with it and her squabbles with her young man, and Patty's just gotten herself engaged to Kevin Riley and will, I'm sure, be putting us through the same miseries as Maureen is before much longer. Then my Mary Kate's at the university in Dublin, studying computers of all things. And little Alice Mae, the baby, spends all her time with animals and trying to talk me into taking in every broken-winged bird in County Waterford.''

Mollie paused. ''And when they're not here, underfoot, I miss them something terrible. As I'm sure your mother's missing you with you so far from home.''

Jude made a noncommittal sound. She was sure her mother thought of her, but actively miss her? She couldn't imagine it, not with the schedule her mother kept.

''It—'' Jude broke off, goggling as harsh, vicious curses erupted from the rear of the house.

''Damn you to fiery hell, you bloody, snake-eyed bastard. I've a mind to drop your worthless hulk off the cliffs myself.''

''Brenna takes after her dad in other aspects as well,'' Mollie continued, topping off the tea with a serene grace as her daughter's curses and threats were punctuated by banging and crashing. ''She's a fine, clever girl, but a bit short of temper. So, she tells me you've an interest in flowers.''

''Ah.'' Jude cleared her throat as the cursing continued. ''Yes. That is, I don't know much about gardening, but I want to keep up the flowers at the cottage. I was going to buy some books.''

''That's fine, then. You can learn a lot from books, though for Brenna she'd rather be tied facedown on a hill of ants than have to read about the workings of a thing.

Prefers to rip it apart for herself. Still, I've a bit of a hand with a garden myself. Maybe you'd like to take a walk around with me, take a look at what I've done. Then you could tell me what it is you've a need to know."

Jude set down her cup. "I'd really like that."

"Fine. Let's leave Brenna alone so she can raise the roof without us worrying it'll crash down on our heads." She rose, hesitated. "Could I see your hands?"

"My hands?" Baffled, Jude held them out, found them firmly gripped.

"Old Maude had hands like yours. Of course, they were old and troubled with the arthritis, but they were narrow and fine, and I imagine her fingers were long and straight and slender like yours when she was young. You'll do, Jude." Mollie held her hands a moment longer, met her eyes. "You've good hands for flowering."

"I want to be good at it," Jude said, surprising herself.

And Mollie's eyes warmed. "Then you will be."

The next hour was sheer delight. Shyness and reserve melted away as Jude fell under the spell of the flowers and Mollie's innate patience.

Those feathery leaves were larkspur that Mollie said would bloom in soft and showy colors, and the charming bicolored trumpets were columbine. Dancing around as they chose were flowers with odd and charming names like flax and pinks and lady's mantel and bee balm.

She knew she'd forget names, or mix them up, but it was a wonder to be shown which bloomed in spring, what would flower in summer. What was hardy and what was delicate. What drew the bees and the butterflies.

She didn't feel foolish asking what she was certain were almost childishly basic questions. Mollie would just smile or nod and explain.

"Old Maude, we would trade back and forth, a clump

or a cutting or some seeds. So most of what I have here, you have at the cottage. She liked romantic flowers, and me the cheerful. So between us we ended up with both. I'll walk up your way one day, if you wouldn't mind, and take a look to see if there's something you need to be doing that you're not.''

''I'd appreciate that so much, especially knowing how busy you are.''

Mollie cocked her head; her face was bright, as cheerful as her gardens. ''You're a nice girl, Jude, and I'd enjoy spending some time with you now and again over the gardens. And you've a pretty bit of polish on you. I wouldn't mind seeing some of it rub off on my Brenna. She's a wide heart and a clever mind, but she's rough on the edges.''

Mollie's gaze drifted over Jude's shoulder, and she sighed. ''Speaking of it. Have you finally killed the beast, then, Mary Brenna?''

''It was a struggle, a battle of sweat and tears, but I won.'' Brenna swaggered around the side of the house. There was a smear of grease on her cheek and a dry crust of blood over her left knuckles. ''It'll run for you now, Ma.''

''Damn it, girl, you know I've my heart set on a new one.''

''Ah, that one's years left in it.'' Cheerfully, she kissed her mother's cheek. ''I've got to get on now. I've promised to go by and see to fixing the windows in Betsy Clooney's house. Do you want to ride back with me, Jude, or would you rather stay awhile?''

''I should get back. I really enjoyed myself, Mollie. Thank you.''

''You come back whenever you want a bit of company.''

''I will. Oh, I left my purse inside. I'll just run in and get it, if that's all right.''

"Go right on." Mollie waited until the door shut. "She's thirsty," she murmured.

"Thirsty, Ma?"

"For doing. For being. But she's afraid to drink too fast. It's wise to take things in small sips, but once in a while . . ."

"Darcy thinks Aidan has his eye on her."

"Oh, is that so?" Amused, Molly turned to wiggle her eyebrows at her daughter. "That would be some fine and fast drinking now, wouldn't it?"

"Darcy told me she once spied on him while he was courting the Duffy girl, and when he'd finished kissing the lass, she staggered like a drunk."

"Darcy's no business spying on her brothers," Mollie said primly, then slid her gaze back to Brenna. "Which Duffy girl? Tell me later," she added quickly when Jude came out again.

"So you had a nice visit then," Brenna began when they slid back into the truck.

"Your mother's wonderful." On impulse, Jude swiveled to wave as Brenna pulled out of the drive with her usual speed and enthusiasm. "I'll never remember half of what she told me about gardening, but it's a good start."

"She'll like having you to talk with. Patty has a hand with flowers, but she's got her head in the clouds over Kevin Riley these days and spends most of her time sighing and looking moony."

"She's awfully proud of you and your sisters."

"That's part of a mother's job."

"Yes, but it doesn't always glow out of them," Jude decided. "You're probably used to it, so you don't really notice, but it's a lovely thing to see."

"Being what you are," Brenna mused, "you pay more

attention to such things. Do you learn that, or do you just have it in you?''

''I suppose it's both—like the way I noticed that she was proud you'd been able to fix the refrigerator, even though she was hoping you couldn't.''

Brenna turned her head to laugh into Jude's eyes. ''Nearly didn't manage it this time, frigging temperamental heap. But the thing is, my dad's wheeled a deal for a brand-new one, oh, and a beauty it is, too. But we can't seal the bargain and have it delivered for another week or two. So if we're to keep the pleasure of the surprise, that wheezing son of a bitch has to last a bit longer.''

''That's so lovely.'' Jude embraced the idea of it, then tried to imagine her mother's reaction if she and her father surprised her with a new refrigerator.

Bafflement, Jude imagined, and not a little insult. Amused by the idea, she chuckled. ''If I gave my mother a major appliance as a gift, she'd think I'd lost my mind.''

''But then, your mother's a professional woman, as I recall.''

''Yes, she is, and she's wonderful at her job. But your mother's a professional woman, too. A professional mother.''

Brenna blinked, then her eyes gleamed with amused pleasure. ''Oh, she'll like that one. I'll be sure to save that for the next time she's ready to kick my ass over something. Well, look here at what's strolling up the road, handsome as two devils and just as dangerous.''

Even as Jude's lovely relaxation sprang into one sticky ball of tension, Brenna was braking at the narrow drive of the cottage and leaning out to call to Aidan.

''There's a wild rover.''

''Never, no more,'' he said with a wink, then took the hand she'd laid on the window to examine the skinned knuckles. "What have you done to yourself now?"

"Bloody bastard refrigerator took a bite out of me."

He clucked his tongue, lifted the scrape to his lips. But his gaze drifted to Jude. "And where are you two lovely ladies bound for?"

"I'm just bringing Jude back from a visit with my mother, and I'm off to Betsy Clooney's to bang on her windows."

"If you or your dad has the time tomorrow, the stove at the pub's acting up and Shawn's sulking over it."

"One of us'll have a look."

"Thanks. I'll just take your passenger off your hands."

"Have a care with her," Brenna said as he walked around the truck. "I like her."

"So do I." He opened the door, held out a hand. "But I make her nervous. Don't I, Jude Frances?"

"Of course not." She started to climb out, then ruined the casual elegance she'd hoped for by jerking back again because she'd forgotten to unhook her seat belt.

Before she could fumble with it, Aidan released it himself, then simply nipped her by the waist and lifted her down. Since that tangled her tongue into knots, she didn't manage to thank Brenna again before that young woman, with a wave and a grin, took the truck barreling down the road.

"Drives like a demon, that girl." With a shake of his head, Aidan released Jude, only to take her hands. "You haven't been down to the pub all week."

"I've been busy."

"Not so busy now."

"Yes, actually, I should—"

"Invite me in and fix me a sandwich." When she simply gaped at him, he laughed. "Or failing that, go walking with me. It's a fine day for walking. I won't kiss you unless you want me to, if that's what's worrying you.''

"I'm not worried.''

"Well, then.'' He lowered his head, got within an inch of his pleasure when she stumbled back.

"That's not what I meant.''

"I was afraid of that.'' But he eased away. "Just a walk then. Have you been up to Tower Hill to look at the cathedral?''

"No, not yet.''

"And with your curious mind? Then we'll walk that way, and I'll tell you a story for your paper.''

"I don't have my recorder.''

Slowly, he lifted one of the hands he still held and brushed his lips over the knuckles. "Then I'll make it a simple one, so you remember it.''

EIGHT

HE WAS RIGHT about the day. It was a perfect one for walking. The light glowed like the inside of a pearl. Luminous, with a slight sheen of damp. She could see, over the hills and fields rolling toward the mountains, a thin and silvery curtain that was certainly a line of rain.

Sunlight poured through it in beams and ripples, liquid gold through liquid silver.

It was the kind of day that begged for rainbows.

The breeze was just a teasing shimmer on the air, fluttering leaves growing toward their summer ripeness and surrounding her with the scent of green.

He held her hand with the careless, loose-fingered grip of familiarity and made her feel simple.

Relaxed, at ease, and simple.

Words rolled off his tongue to charm her.

"Once, it's said, there was a young maid. Fair as a dream was her face, with skin white and clear as milk and hair black as midnight, eyes blue as a lake. More than her beauty was the loveliness of her manner, for a kind maid was she. And more than her manner was the glory of her voice. When she sang, the birds stilled to listen and the angels smiled.''

As they climbed the hill, the sea began to sing as backdrop, or so it seemed, to his story.

"Many's the morning her song would carry over the hills, and the joy of it rivaled the sun,'' he continued, and tugged her along the path. As they walked on, the breeze turned to wind and danced merrily over sea and rock.

"Now the sound of it, the pure joy of it, caught the ear and the envy of a witch.''

"There's always a catch,'' Jude commented and made him chuckle.

"Sure and there's a catch if the story's a good one. Now this witch had a black heart and the powers she had she abused. She soured the morning milk and caused the nets of the fisherfolk to come up empty. Though she could use her arts to disguise her vile face into beauty, when she opened her mouth to sing, a frog's croaking was more musical. She hated the maid for her gift of song, and so cast a spell on her and rendered her mute.''

"But there was a cure—involving a handsome prince?''

"Oh, there was a cure, for evil should always be confounded by good.''

Jude smiled because she believed it. Despite all logic, she believed in the happy-ever-after. And such things seemed more than merely possible here, in this world of cliffs and wild grass, of sea with red fishing trawlers streaming over deep blue, of firm hands clasped warm over hers.

They seemed inevitable.

"The maid was doomed to silence, unable to share the joy in her heart through her songs, as the witch trapped it inside a silver box and locked it with a silver key. Inside the box, the voice wept as it sang.''

"Why are Irish stories always so sad?"

"Are they?" He looked sincerely surprised. "It's not sad so much as . . . poignant. Poetry doesn't most usually spring from joy, does it, but from sorrows.''

"I suppose you're right.'' She brushed absently at her hair as the wind tugged tendrils free. "What happened next?''

"Well, I'll tell you. For five years the maid walked these hills and the fields, and the cliffs as we walk them now. She listened to the song of the birds, the music of the wind in the grass, the drumbeat of the sea. And these she stored inside her, while the witch hoarded the joy and passion and purity of the maid's voice inside the silver box, so only she could hear it.''

As they reached the top of the hill with the shadow of the old cathedral, the sturdy spear of the round tower, Aidan turned to Jude, whisked her hair back from her face with his fingers. "What happened next?" he asked her.

"What?"

"Tell me what happened next.''

"But it's your story.''

He reached down to where little white flowers struggled to bloom in the cracks of tumbled rocks. Picking one, he slid it into her hair. "Tell me, Jude Frances, what you'd like to happen next.''

She started to reach up for the flower, but he caught her hand, lifted a brow. After a moment's thought, she shrugged. "Well, one day a handsome young man rode over the hills. His great white horse was weary, and his armor dull and battered. He was lost and injured from battle, and a long way from home.''

She could see it, closing her eyes. The woods and shadows, the wounded warrior longing for home.

"As he moved into the forests, the mists swirled in so he could hear nothing but the labored breathing of his own heart. With each beat counted, he understood he came closer to the last.

"Then he saw her, coming toward him through the mists like a woman wading through a silver river. Because he was ill and in need, the maid took him in and tended his wounds in silence, nursed him through his fevers. Though she was unable to speak to comfort him, her gentleness was enough. So they fell in love without words, and her heart almost burst from the need to tell him, to sing out her joy and her devotion. And without hesitation, without regret, she agreed to go with him to his home far away and leave behind her own, her friends and family and that part of herself locked tight in a silver box."

Because she could see it, feel it, even as she spoke, Jude shook her head, moved through the tilted gravestones to lean back against the round tower. The bay swept out below, a spectacular blue where the red boats bobbed, but she was caught in the story.

"What happens next?" she asked Aidan.

"She mounted the horse with him," he continued, picking up the threads she'd left for him as if they'd been his own. "Bringing with her only her faith and her love, and asking for nothing but his in return. And at that moment, the silver box, still clutched in the greedy hands of the witch, burst open. The voice trapped inside flew out, a golden stream that winged its way over the hills and into the heart of the maid. And as she rode off with her man, her voice, more beautiful than ever, sang out. And the birds stilled to listen, and the angels smiled again."

Jude sighed. "Yes, that was perfect."

"You've a way with telling a story."

The words thrilled her, rocked her, then made her feel shy all over again. "No, not really. It was easy because you'd started it."

"You filled in the middle part, and in a lovely way that makes me think not all the Irish has been drummed out of you after all. There now," he murmured, pleased. "You've a laugh in your eyes and a flower in your hair. Let me kiss you now, will you, Jude Frances?"

She moved fast. Caution, she told herself, sometimes had to be quick. Ducking under his arm, she scooted around him. "You'll make me forget why we walked here. I've read about round towers, but I've never seen one up close."

Patience, Gallagher, he thought, and tucked his thumbs in his pockets. "Someone was always trying to invade and conquer the jewel of Ireland. But we're still here, aren't we?"

"Yes, you're still here." She turned a slow circle, studying hill and cliff and sea. "It's a wonderful spot. It feels old." She stopped, shook her head. "That sounds ridiculous."

"Not at all. It does feel old—and sacred. If you listen well, you can hear the stones sing of battle and of glory."

"I don't think I have the ear for singing stones." She wandered, skirting the carved markers, the graves laden with flowers, and picked her way over the rough ground. "My grandmother told me she used to come up here and sit. I bet she heard them."

"Why didn't she come with you?"

"I wanted her to." She brushed her hair back as she turned to face him. He fit here, she thought, with the old and the sacred, with the songs of battle and glory.

Where, she wondered, did she fit?

She walked inside the old ruin where the sky soared

overhead for a roof. "I think she's teaching me a lesson—how to be Jude in six months or less."

"And are you learning?"

"Maybe." She traced her fingers over the ogham carving, and for a moment, just a moment, felt them tingle with heat.

"What does Jude want to be?"

"That's too general a question, with too many simple answers like happy, healthy, successful."

"Aren't you happy?"

"I . . ." Her fingers danced over the stones again, dropped away. "I wasn't happy teaching, in the end anyway. I wasn't good at it. It's discouraging not to be good at what you've chosen as your life's work."

"Your life is far from done, so you've more than time enough to choose again. And I'll wager you were better at it than you decided to believe."

She glanced up at him, then began to walk out again. "Why would you think so?"

"Because in the time I've spent with you I've listened to you, and learned."

"Why are you spending time with me, Aidan?"

"I like you."

She shook her head again. "You don't know me. If I haven't figured myself out yet, you can't know me."

"I like what I see."

"So it's a physical sort of attraction."

That quick brow quirked again. "And is that a problem for you, then?"

"Yes, actually." But she managed to turn and face him. "One I'm working on."

"Well, I hope you work fast because I want the pleasure of you."

Her breath clogged and had to be released slowly and

deliberately. "I don't know what to say to that. I've never had a conversation like this in my life, so obviously I don't know what to say to that, except something that's bound to sound incredibly stupid."

He frowned as he stepped toward her. "Why would it sound stupid if it's what you're thinking?"

"Because I have a habit of saying stupid things when I'm nervous."

He slipped the flower stem deeper into her hair as the wind wanted to tug it free again. "I thought you sang when you were nervous."

"One or the other," she muttered, moving backward to keep what she thought was a safe distance.

"You're nervous now?"

"Yes! God!" Knowing she was close to stuttering, she held her hands up to hold him off. "Just stop. I've never had anything tie me up like this. Instant attraction. I said I believe in it, and I do, but I've never felt it before. I have to think about it."

"Why?" It was a simple matter to reach out, grab her by the wrists, and tug her forward against him. "Why not just act on it when you know it'll feel good? Your pulse is jumping." His thumbs skimmed over her wrist. "I like feeling it leap like that, seeing your eyes go cloudy and dark. Why don't you kiss me this time and see what happens next?"

"I'm not as good at it as you are."

Now he laughed. "Jesus, woman, you're quite the package. Let me decide for myself if you're good at it or not. Come on and kiss me, Jude. Whatever happens next is up to you."

She wanted to. Wanted to feel his mouth against hers again, the shape and texture and flavor of it. Just now his lips were curved, and the light of fun was in his eyes. Fun, she thought. Why couldn't it just be fun?

With his fingers still lightly braceleting her wrists, she leaned toward him. And he watched her. She rose onto her toes, still his eyes stayed on hers. Tilting her head just slightly, she eased up to brush her lips over his.

"Do it again, why don't you?"

So she did, mesmerized when his eyes stayed open, compelling hers to do the same. She lingered longer this time, brushing left, then right. Fascinating. Experimenting, she scraped her teeth lightly, over his bottom lip and heard her own quiet sound of pleasure as from a great distance.

His eyes were so blue, as vivid as the water that stretched to the horizon. It seemed her world turned that single, marvelous color. Her heart began to pound, her vision to blur as it had that first time at Maude's grave.

She said his name, just one sigh, then threw her arms around him.

The jolt rocked him to the soles of his feet, the sudden heat, the abrupt burst of power that whipped out of her and snaked around him like rope.

His hands streaked up, over her hips, her back, into her hair to grip hard and fast. The kiss changed from a coy brush and nibble to a wild war of tongues and teeth and lips where body strained to body and pulse thundered against pulse.

In that warm cascade of sensation, she lost herself. Or perhaps she found the Jude that had been trapped inside her—like a voice locked in a silver box.

Later, she would swear she heard the stones sing.

She buried her face in the curve of his neck and gulped in the scent of him like water.

"This is too fast." Even as she said it she locked her

arms around him. "I can't breathe, I can't think. I can't believe what's going on inside my body."

He gave a weak laugh and nuzzled her hair. "If it's anything to what's going on inside mine, we're likely to explode any second here. Darling, we could be back at the cottage in minutes, and I'd have you in bed in the blink of an eye. I promise you we'd both feel a good deal better for it."

"I'm sure you're right, but I—"

"Can't go quite that fast, or you wouldn't be Jude."

Though it cost him, he drew her back to study her face. More than pretty, he thought now, but solid as well. Why was it, he wondered, she didn't seem to know just how pretty or just how solid she was?

Because she didn't, more time and more care were needed.

"And I like Jude, as I've said before. You need some courting."

She couldn't say if she was stunned, amused, or insulted. "I certainly don't."

"Oh, but you do. You want flowers and words, and stolen kisses and walks in soft weather. It's romance Jude Frances wants, and I'm the one to give it to you. Well, now, look at that face." He caught her by the chin as an adult might a sulky child, and she decided insult won. "You're pouting now."

"I certainly am not." She would have jerked her face free, but he tightened his grip, then leaned down and kissed her firm on the mouth.

"I'm the one who's looking at you, sweetheart, and if that's not a fine pout, I'm a Scotsman. It's that you're thinking I'm making fun of you, but I'm not, or not much anyway. What's wrong with romance then? I'd like some myself."

His voice went warm and rich, like whiskey by the fire. "Will you give me long looks and warm smiles from across the room, and the brush of your hand on my arm? A hot, desperate kiss in the shadows? A touch"—he skimmed his fingertips over the curve of her breast and all but stopped her heart—"in secret?"

"I didn't come here looking for romance."

Hadn't she? he thought. With her myths and legends and tales. "Looking or not, you'll have it." On that score his mind was made up. "And when I make love with you, the first time, it'll be long and slow and sweet. That's a promise. Walk back with me now, before the way you're looking at me makes me break that promise as soon as I've made it."

"You just want to be in charge. In control of the situation."

He took her hand again in the friendliest and most annoying of manners. "I suppose I'm accustomed to being so. But if you want to take over and seduce me, darling Jude, I can promise to be weak and willing."

She laughed, damn it, before she could stop herself. "I'm sure we both have work to do."

"But you'll come see me," he continued as they walked. "You'll sit and have a glass of wine in my pub so I can look at you and suffer."

"God, you're Irish," she whispered.

"To the bone." He lifted her hand and nipped her knuckle. "And Jude, by the way, you're damn good at kissing."

"Hmmm," was the safest response she could think of.

But she went to the pub, and sat and listened to stories. Over the next days as spring took a firmer hold on Ardmore, Jude could often be found at the pub for an hour or two in the evening, or the afternoon. She listened, recorded, took notes. And as the word spread, others with stories came to tell them, or to be entertained by them.

She filled tapes and reams of pages and dutifully transcribed and analyzed them at her computer while she sipped at what was becoming her habitual cup of tea.

If sometimes she dreamed herself into the stories of romance and magic, she thought it harmless enough. Even useful if she stretched things a bit. After all, she could understand the meanings and the motives all the better if the stories and the actions in them became more personal.

It wasn't as if she was going to waste time actually writing it that way. An academic paper had no room for fancies or fantasies. She was only exploring until she found the core of her thesis, then she'd tidy up the language and delete the ramblings.

What the hell are you going to do with it, Jude? she asked herself. What do you really think you're going to do even if you polish and perfect and hammer it until it's dry as dust? Try to have it published in some professional journal absolutely no one reads for pleasure? Use it to try to kick off a lecture tour?

Oh, the idea of that happening, however remote the possibility, felt like an entire troop of Boy Scouts tying knots in her stomach.

For an instant she nearly buried her face in her hands and gave in to despair. Nothing was ever going to come of this paper, this project. It was self-defeating to believe differently. No one was ever going to stand around at a faculty function and discuss the insights and interests of Jude F. Murray's paper. Worse, she didn't want them to.

It was no more than a kind of therapy, a way to pull her back from the edge of a crisis she couldn't even identify.

What good had all those years of study and work accomplished if she couldn't even find the right terms for her own crises?

Poor self-esteem, bruised ego, a lack of belief in her own femininity, career dissatisfaction.

But what was under all of that? Really under it. Blurred identity? she mused. Maybe that was part of it. She'd lost herself somewhere along the line until whatever was left, whatever she'd been able to recognize, had been so pale, so unattractive, that she'd run from it.

To what?

Here, she thought and was more than a little surprised to realize that her fingers were racing over the keyboard, her thoughts were speeding out of her head and onto the page.

I ran here, and here I feel somehow more real, certainly more at home than I ever did in the house William and I bought, or the condo I moved into after he'd grown tired of me. Certainly more at home than in the classroom.

Oh, God, oh, God, I hated the classroom. Why couldn't I ever admit it, just say it out loud? I don't want to do this, don't want to be this. I want something else. Nearly anything else would do.

How did I become such a coward, and worse, so pitifully boring? Why do I, even now with no one to answer to but myself, question this project when it pleases me so much? When it gives me such satisfaction. Can't I, just for this little piece of time, indulge myself with something that doesn't have any solid, guaranteed-practical purpose or goal?

If it's therapy, it's time I let it work. It's not doing any harm. In fact, I think—I hope—it's doing me some good. I feel attracted to the writing. That's an odd term to use, but it fits. Writing attracts me, the mystery of it, the way words fit together on a page to make an image or a point or just to be there, sounding.

Seeing my own words on the page is thrilling. There's a wonderful kind of conceit in reading them, knowing they're mine. Part of that terrifies me because it's so incredibly exciting. For so much of my life I've turned away, backed away, hidden away from anything that's frightening. Even when it is thrilling as well.

I want to feel substantial again. I yearn for confidence. And under it all, I have a deep and nearly crushed-out delight in the fantastic. How it was nearly crushed and by whom isn't really important. Not now that I find the glimmer of it's still there, inside me. Enough of a glimmer for me to be able to write, at least in secret, that I want to believe in the legends, in the myths, in the faeries and the ghosts. What harm is there in that? It can't possibly hurt me.

No, she thought, leaning back again, resting her hands in her lap. Of course it can't hurt me. It's harmless and it makes me wonder. It's been too long since I really let myself wonder.

Letting out a long breath, she closed her eyes and felt nothing but the sweetness of relief. "I'm so glad I came here," she said aloud.

She rose to look out the window, satisfied that she'd used her writing to fight off the threat of despair. Her days here, nights here, were soothing some threatening storm inside her. These little moments of joy were precious.

She turned away from the window, wanting the air and the outdoors. There she would ponder the other aspect of her new life.

Aidan Gallagher, she thought. Gorgeous, somehow exotic, and inexplicably interested in solid, sensible Jude F. Murray. Talk about the fantastic.

Perhaps the time spent with Aidan wasn't quite so sooth-

ing, she admitted, though she was careful enough to arrange
things so they were never alone. Still, the lack of privacy
didn't stop him from flirting, from indulging himself in
those long looks he'd spoken of, or the slow, secret smiles,
the lazy brush of a hand over her arm, her hair, her cheek.

And what was wrong with that? she asked herself as she
carried a fresh bouquet of flowers over the hill to Maude's
grave. Every woman was entitled to a flirtation. Maybe,
unlike the blossoms in her hand, she was a slow bloomer,
but better late than never.

She badly wanted to bloom. The idea of it was as thrilling, as frightening, as exciting as writing.

Wasn't it wonderful to discover that she *liked* being
flirted with, being looked at as if she was pretty and desir-
able. For God's sake, if she stayed in Ireland the full six
months, she'd be thirty before she saw Chicago again, so
it was high time she felt pretty, wasn't it?

Her own husband had never flirted with her. And if memory served, his highest compliment on her appearance had
been telling her she looked quite nice.

"A woman doesn't want to be told she looks nice," Jude
muttered as she sat down beside Maude's grave. "She
wants to be told she's beautiful, sexy. That she looks outrageous. It doesn't matter if it's not true." She sighed and
laid the flowers against the headstone. "Because for the
moment, when the words are said and the words are heard,
it's perfect truth."

"Then may I say you're as lovely as the flowers you
carry on this fine day, Jude Frances."

She looked up quickly and into the bold blue eyes of the
man she'd met once before in this same spot. Eyes, she
thought uneasily, that she so often saw in dreams. "You
move quietly."

"It's a place for a quiet step." He crouched down with

the soft grass and bright flowers adorning Maude's grave between them.

The water of the ancient well murmured like a pagan chant.

"And how are you faring in Faerie Hill Cottage?"

"Very well. Do you have family here?"

His bright eyes clouded as they skimmed over the stones and high grass. "I have those I remember, and who remember me. I once loved a maid and would have offered her everything I had. But I forgot to offer her my heart first and last. Forgot to give her the words."

When he looked up, his expression was more quizzical than confident. "Words are important to a woman, aren't they?"

"Words are important, to everyone. When they're not said, they leave holes." Deep, dark holes, Jude thought now, where doubts and failures breed. Unsaid words were as painful as slaps.

"Ah, but if the man you'd married had said them to you, you wouldn't be here today, would you now?" When she blinked at him in shock, he only smirked. "He wouldn't have meant them, so they would have just been convenient lies. You already know he wasn't the one for you."

A little lick of fear worked up her spine. No, not fear, she realized, breathless. A thrill. "How do you know about William?"

"I know about this, and I know about that." He smiled again, easily. "I wonder why you take upon yourself the blame for something that wasn't your doing. But then, women have always been a charming puzzle to me."

She supposed her grandmother had spoken to Maude, and Maude to this man, though she didn't care for the fact that her personal life, and embarrassments, had been discussed over the teapot by strangers. "I can't imagine that my marriage and its failure is of particular interest to you.''

If the cold chill in her voice affected him, his breezy shrug didn't show it. "Well, I've always been a selfish sort, and in the long scheme of things what you've done and do may have bearing on what I most want. But I apologize if I've offended you. As I said, women are puzzles to me.''

"I suppose it doesn't matter.''

"It does as long as you let it. I wonder if you would answer a question for me?''

"Depends on the question.''

"It seems a simple one to me, but again, it's a woman's perspective I'm wanting. Would you tell me, Jude, if you'd rather a handful of jewels, such as this . . .''

He turned over an elegant hand, and mounded in it was the blinding brilliance of diamonds and sapphires, the aching gleam of creamy pearls.

"My God, how—''

"Would you take them as they're offered from the man who knows he holds your heart, or would you rather the words?''

Dazzled, she lifted her head. The fire and spark still sheened her vision, but she saw how dark, how fiercely intent was his gaze as he studied her. She said the first thing that came into her head, because it seemed the only thing.

"What are the words?''

And he sighed, long and deep, his proud shoulders slumping, his eyes going soft and sad. "So it's true, then, they matter so much. And these . . .''

He opened his fingers and let the shimmer, the fire, the glow of the stones sift through and sprinkle over the grave. "Are nothing but pride.''

She watched, her breath coming short, her head going light, as the jewels melted into puddles of color, and those puddles sprang into simple young flowers.

"I'm dreaming," she said softly, while her head reeled. "I've fallen asleep."

"You're awake if you'll let yourself be." He spoke sharply now, with an impatience ripe and ready. "Look beyond your nose for a change, woman, and listen. Magic is. But its power is nothing beside love. It's a hard lesson I've learned, and a long time it's taken me to learn it. Don't make the same mistake. More than your own heart lies on the line now."

He got to his feet while she stood frozen. On his hand the stone he wore shot sparks, and it seemed his skin began to glow.

"Finn save me, I've to depend on a mortal to begin it all, and a Yank at that. Magic is," he said again. "So look at it, and deal with it."

He shot her one last look of smoldering impatience, lifted both hands toward the sky in a sweeping gesture of drama. And vanished into the air.

Dreaming, she thought giddily as she staggered to her feet. Hallucinating. It was all the time she was spending listening to fairy tales, all the time she spent alone in the cottage reviewing them. She'd told herself they were harmless, but obviously they'd pushed her over some edge.

She stared down at the grave, the new flowers in their colorful dance over the mound. When a flash caught her eye, she bent down, reached carefully among the pretty petals, and plucked out a diamond as big as a quarter.

Real, she thought, struggling to steady her breathing. She could see it, feel the shape and the cold heat it held inside.

She was either crazy, or she'd just had her second conversation with Carrick, prince of the faeries.

Shivering, she rubbed her free hand over her face. Okay, either way she was crazy.

Then why did she feel so damn good?

She walked slowly, fingering the priceless jewel as a child might a pretty stone. She needed to write it all down, she decided. Carefully, concisely. Exactly how he'd looked, what he'd said, what had happened.

And after that, she would try to get some sort of perspective on it. She was an educated woman. Surely she would find a way to make sense of it all.

When she came down the slope toward her cottage, she saw the little blue car in the drive and Darcy Gallagher just getting out.

Darcy was wearing jeans and a bright red sweater. Her hair tumbled down her back like wild black silk. One glance had Jude sighing with envy even as she cautiously tucked the diamond into the pocket of her slacks.

To once, she thought—just once—look that carelessly gorgeous, that absolutely confident. She fingered the jewel absently and thought it would be worth the price of diamonds.

Darcy spotted her and shaded her eyes with the flat of one hand while she waved with the other. "There you are. Out for a walk, are you? It's a fine day for it, even if they're calling for rain tonight."

"I've been visiting Maude." *And I talked to a faerie prince who left me a diamond that could probably buy a small Third World country before he vanished into thin air.* With a weak smile, Jude decided she'd keep that little bit of information to herself.

"I just went a couple rounds with Shawn and took a drive to cool off." Darcy skimmed her gaze over Jude's shoes, casually, she hoped, to try to gauge how close in size they were to what she wore herself. The woman, Darcy thought, had fabulous taste in shoes. "You're looking a bit pale," she noted when Jude walked closer. "Are you all right?"

"Yes, I'm fine." Self-consciously, she pushed at her hair. The breeze had teased strands out of the band. Which, she thought, would make her look unkempt rather than wonderfully tousled like Darcy. "Why don't we go in and have some tea?"

"Oh, that would be nice, but I've got to get back. Aidan'll already be cursing me." She smiled then, a dazzle of charm. "Maybe you'd like to come back with me for a time, and then he'd be distracted with you and forget to skin my ass for walking out."

"Well, I . . ." No, she thought, she didn't think she was up to dealing with Aidan Gallagher when her head was already light. "I really should work. I have notes to go over."

Darcy pursed her lips. "You really enjoy it, don't you? Working."

"Yes." Surprise, surprise, Jude thought. "I enjoy the work I'm doing now very much."

"If it was me, I'd find any excuse in the world to avoid working." Her brilliant gaze scanned the cottage, the gardens, the long roll of hill. "And I'd die of loneliness out here all by myself."

"Oh, no, it's wonderful. The quiet, the view. Everything."

Darcy shrugged, a quick gesture of discontent. "But then you've got Chicago to go back to."

Jude's smile faded. "Yes. I have Chicago to go back to."

"I'm going to see it one day." Darcy leaned back against her car. "All the big cities in America. All the big cities everywhere. And when I do, I'll be going first class, make no mistake." Then she laughed and shook her head. "But for now, I'd best be getting back before Aidan devises some hideous punishment for me."

"I hope you'll come back when you have more time."

Darcy shot her that dazzling look again as she climbed into her car. "I've the night off, thank the Lord. I'll come by with Brenna later, and we'll see what kind of trouble we can get you in. You make me think you could use a bit of trouble."

Jude opened her mouth without a clue how to respond, but was saved the trouble when Darcy gunned the motor and shot out into the road with scarcely more care than Brenna took.

NINE

THERE ARE THREE *maids,* Jude wrote, as she nibbled on a shortbread biscuit, *and each represents some particular facet of traditionally held views of womanhood. In some tales two are wicked and one good, as in the Cinderella myth. In others, the three are blood sisters or fast friends, poor and orphaned or caring for one sickly parent.*

Some variations have one or more of the female characters possessing mystical powers. In nearly all, the maidens are beautiful beyond description. Virtue, i.e., virginity, is vital, indicating that innocence of physical sexuality is an essential ingredient to the building of legend.

Innocence, a quest, monetary poverty, physical beauty. These elements repeat themselves in a number of perpetuated tales that become, over generations, legends. The interference, for good or ill, of beings from the otherworld— so to speak—is another common element. The mortal or mortals in the story have a moral lesson to learn or a reward to glean from their selfless behavior.

Almost as often simple beauty and innocence are equally rewarded.

Jude sat back and closed her eyes. She struck out there, didn't she? Since she wasn't beautiful or innocent, had no particular power or skill, it didn't look like she was going to be whisked away into a fairy tale with a happy ending.

Not that she wanted to be. The mere idea of coming face-to-face with the inhabitants of a faerie hill or a sky castle, or a witch, wicked or otherwise, made her shaky.

Shaky enough, she admitted, to imagine jewels turning into flowers. Warily, she slipped her hand into her pocket and pulled the bright stone out to examine it yet again.

Just glass, she assured herself, beautifully faceted certainly, sparkling like sunlight. But glass.

It was one thing to accept that she was sharing the cottage with a three-hundred-year-old ghost. That had been leap enough. But she could reason that out as there had been studies on that particular phenomenon, documentation. Parapsychology wasn't universally accepted, but some very reputable scientists and respected minds believed in the energy forms that laymen called ghosts.

So she could deal with that. She could rationalize what she had seen with her own eyes.

But elves and faeries and . . . whatever. No. Saying you wanted to believe and stating you *did* believe were two different matters. That was when the indulgence of it all stopped being harmless and became a psychosis.

There were no handsome faeries wandering the hills, visiting graveyards to hold philosophical discussions, then becoming annoyed with people who happened by.

And those nonexistent faeries didn't go around tossing priceless jewels at strange American women.

Since logic didn't seem to apply to the situation, she had

to assume that her imagination, always a bit of a problem, had tipped out of control.

All she had to do was yank it back on track, do her work. It was very possible she'd had some sort of episode. A fugue state during which she'd incorporated various elements from her research. The fact that she felt almost ridiculously healthy didn't enter into it. The stress of the past few years could have caught up with her, and while her body was fine, her mind could be suffering.

She should go to a good neurologist and have a full workup to rule out a physical problem.

And visit a reputable jeweler to have the diamond—the glass, she corrected herself—examined.

The first idea frightened her and the second depressed her, so she defied logic and put both notions on hold.

Just for a few days, she promised herself. She would do the responsible thing, but not quite yet.

All she wanted to do was work, to pour herself into the stories. And she would resist the urge to wander down to the pub, to spend the evening pretending not to watch Aidan Gallagher. She'd stay at home with her papers and notes, then drive into Dublin in a few days and find both jeweler and doctor.

She'd shop, buy books, do a bit of sight-seeing.

One solid evening of work, she told herself. After that, she would take a few days to explore the countryside and the cities, the villages and the hills. She'd take a logical step back from the stories she was gathering and studying, and that would help her with her own perspective before she went to Dublin.

At the knock on the front door her fingers fumbled on the keys of the computer. And her heart jumped. Aidan, was her first thought, and that alone irritated her. Of course it wasn't Aidan, she told herself, even as she dashed to the mirror to check her hair. It was well after eight, and he'd be busy at the pub.

Still, when she hurried downstairs to answer, her heart was beating just a little fast. She opened the door and barely had time to blink.

"We brought food." Brenna strolled in, a brown grocery sack propped on her hip. "Biscuits and crisps and chocolate."

"And best of all, wine." Darcy clinked the three bottles she carried as she casually booted the door closed behind her.

"Oh. Well . . ." Jude hadn't taken Darcy seriously, hadn't been able to think of a reason either she or Brenna would want to come over. But they were already heading toward the kitchen in a flurry of movement and chatter.

"Aidan tried to have me work another shift tonight to make up for walking out today. I told him to bugger it," Darcy said cheerfully as she set the wine on the counter. "The man'd have me chained to the taps if I wasn't fast on my feet. We'll need a corkscrew."

"There's one in the—"

"Got it," Brenna interrupted and simply shot a quick grin at Jude as she plucked it out of the drawer. "You should've seen the black looks Aidan sent us when we left the pub. 'Why can't you fetch her down and drink here,' he wants to know, grumbling and muttering all the while."

"Then he sees I'm taking three bottles," Darcy continued, rooting out glasses while Brenna opened the wine. "And he's blathering on about how Jude Frances doesn't have much of a head for spirits and we're not to get you sick. Like you were some puppy we were going to give too many table scraps to on the sly. Men are such pea-brains."

"Now that's a fine thing to drink to first off." With a flourish, Brenna poured three glasses. "To the tiny brains of the male of the species," she stated, thrusting a glass at Jude and lifting her own.

"Bless them every one," Darcy added and drank. Then her eyes sparkled brilliantly at Jude, who'd done little more than stare. "Drink up, darling, then we'll sit around and discuss the highs and lows of our sex lives just to get better acquainted."

Jude took one long gulp, blew out a breath. "I won't have a great deal to contribute to that area of discussion."

Darcy laughed, a throaty sound of amusement. "Aidan's after changing all that, now, isn't he?"

Jude opened her mouth, shut it again, then decided the best thing to do with it was drink after all.

"Don't tease her so, Darcy." Brenna ripped open the bag of potato chips and dug in. Then winked. "We'll get her drunk first, then pry it all out of her."

"When she's drunk I'm going to talk her into letting me try on all her clothes."

They were talking so fast, Jude couldn't keep up. "My clothes?"

"You've wonderful clothes." Darcy dropped into a chair. "We're not that far from coloring and size, so I'm thinking some may fit me well enough. What size shoe do you wear?"

"Shoe?" Jude looked down blankly at the half boots she wore. "Um, seven and a half, medium."

"That's American sizing, let me think . . ." Darcy shrugged, sipped. "Well, close enough, take those off and let me see how they work on me."

"Take my shoes off?"

"Your shoes, Jude." Darcy's eyes twinkled as she slipped off her own. "A couple more drinks and we'll try on the trousers."

"You may as well," Brenna advised around another

mouthful of potato chips. "She's a demon about clothes, our Darcy, and she'll hound you to death about it."

Feeling as mystified as she had by Maude's graveside that afternoon, Jude sat and took off her shoes.

"Oh!" Darcy stroked the boot like an indulgent mother her child's cheek. "They're like butter, aren't they?" She looked up, her face stunning and filled with sheer female delight. "This is going to be fun."

"So he has it in his head that because I let him take me to dinner a time or two, and let him stick his tongue in my mouth, which was not nearly as exciting as he thought it was, that I'd be pleased and proud to strip naked and let him bounce on me. Sex is a fine pastime," Darcy continued as she licked chocolate from her fingers. "But half the time or more, you're better off just painting your nails and watching the telly."

"Maybe it's the men you let lap at you." Brenna gestured with her wineglass. "They're all so dazzled they end up fumbling. What you need, Darcy my girl, is a man who's as bone-deep cynical and self-absorbed and vain as you are yourself."

Jude choked on her wine, certain the insult would cause an argument, but Darcy merely smiled craftily. "And when I find him, and providing he's rich as Midas, I'll wrap him tidily around this finger here." She held up her right index finger. "And allow him to treat me like a queen."

Brenna snorted, reached for more chips. "And the moment he does, he'll bore you to tears. Darcy's a perverse creature," she told Jude. "That's what we love about her. Now me, I'm a simple, straightforward sort. I'm after a man who'll look me straight in the eye, see what and who I am . . ." She drank, snickered. "Then fall to his knees and promise me everything."

"They never see what you are." Shocked, Jude glanced around to see who'd spoken, then realized she had.

"Don't they?" Brenna wanted to know, lifting her brow as she topped off Jude's glass yet again.

"They see a reflection of their own perception. Whore or angel, mother or child. Depending on their view, they're compelled to protect or conquer or exploit. Or you're a convenience," she murmured. "Easily discarded."

"And you say I'm cynical," Darcy said with a smirk for Brenna. "Have you been discarded then, Jude?"

There was a pleasant buzz in her blood, a lovely spin in her head. The logical part of her said it was the wine. But the heart of her, the needy heart, said it was the company. Girls. She'd never had a foolish girl night in her life.

She picked up a chip, examined it, nibbled, sighed. "Three years ago next June I was married."

"Married?" Both Brenna and Darcy leaned closer.

"Seven months later, he came home and calmly told me he was very sorry, but he was in love with someone else. He thought it best for all parties involved if he moved out that night, and we filed for divorce immediately."

"Why, the cad!" In sympathy, Brenna poured wine all around. "The bastard!"

"Not really. He was honest about it."

"Fuck honesty. I hope you skinned him." Darcy's eyes sparkled with malice. "Hardly more than six months into marriage and he's in love with someone else? The snake barely waited long enough to change the sheets on the marriage bed. What did you do about it?"

"Do?" Jude's brows drew together. "I filed for divorce the next day."

"And took him for everything he had."

"No, of course not." Sincerely shocked at the notion,

she gaped at Darcy. "We just each took what was ours. It was very civilized."

Because Darcy appeared to have been struck speechless, Brenna took up the torch. "If you're asking me, civilized divorces are why there are so many bloody marriages that end in it. Me, I'd rather a good fight, screaming and broken crockery, fists flying. If I loved a man enough to vow to be part of him for life, I'd damn well make him pay in blood and flesh if he threw me over."

"I didn't love him." The minute the words were out, Jude's mouth dropped open. "I mean—I don't know if I loved him. My God, that's just awful, that's horrible! I just realized it. I have no idea if I loved William at all."

"Well, I say he was a bastard and you should have kicked his ass, then set it out for the dogs, love or not." Darcy selected one of Mollie O'Toole's homemade brownies and bit into it with gusto. "I promise you this—in fact, I take an oath on it here and now—whatever man I'm with, whenever I'm with him, it'll be me who ends it. And if he should try to close it off before I'm ready, he'll pay for it the rest of his days."

"Men don't leave women like you," Jude put in. "You're the kind of woman they leave me for." She caught her breath. "I didn't mean—I only meant—"

"Don't worry yourself. I think there was a compliment in there." And being more pleased than offended, Darcy patted Jude's arm. "And I'm also thinking if your tongue's that loose, you've had enough wine that you'll let me play with your clothes. Let's take all this upstairs."

Jude didn't know what to make of it. Perhaps it was because she'd never had any sisters to casually raid her closet. None of her friends had shown particular interest in her wardrobe, other than the usual comments on a new jacket or suit.

She'd never considered herself especially fashion-wise and tended to lean toward classic lines and good fabrics.

But from the muffled sounds coming from where Darcy's head was buried in the armoire, Jude's wardrobe had taken on the sheen of Aladdin's treasure.

"Oh, just look at this jumper! It's cashmere." Darcy yanked out a hunter-green turtleneck and pleasured herself by rubbing it against her cheek.

"It's a good layering piece," Jude began, then watched openmouthed as Darcy stripped off her own sweater.

"Might as well make yourself comfortable." Brenna stretched out on the bed, crossed her ankles, and sipped her wine. "She'll be a while at this."

"Soft as a baby's bum." Darcy all but cooed as she posed in front of the mirror. "Gorgeous, but the color's a bit deep for me. More you, I'm thinking, Brenna." Cheerfully, she stripped it off and tossed it on the bed. "Give it a look."

Absently, Brenna fingered the sleeve of the sweater. "Got a nice feel to it."

Lowering herself to the bed, Jude watched Darcy try on a cream-colored silk blouse. "Ah, there's more in the other bedroom."

Darcy's head came up like a wolf scenting sheep. "More?"

"Yes, um, lighter-weight clothes and a couple of cocktail things I brought along in case—"

"Be right back."

"Now you've done it." Brenna spoke in dire tones as Darcy dashed out of the room. "You'll never be rid of her now." Setting her wine aside, she flipped open the buttons of her shirt. As a delighted squeal was emitted from the next room, Brenna rolled her eyes and tugged the sweater over her head.

"Oh, this is lovely." Surprised by the pleasure the soft wool brought to her skin, Brenna got up to take a look in the mirror. "The way it fits, it almost looks as if I have tits."

"You have a wonderful figure."

Though she'd never be accused of vanity, Brenna twisted and turned in the mirror. "Be nice to have breasts, though. My sister Maureen got mine, I think. I should have had the breasts, by right as the oldest."

"You need a decent bra," Darcy claimed as she came back in a black cocktail dress and carrying a heap of clothes. "Make use of what God gave you instead of letting it flop about. Jude, this dress is brilliant, but you really need to whack an inch or two off the hem."

"I'm taller than you."

"Hardly a bit. Here, put it on and let's have a look."

"Well, I—" But Darcy was already wriggling out of it. Faced with a woman holding out a little black number while dressed in bra and panties, Jude took the dress. She took a deep gulp to swallow her modesty and stripped.

"I knew you had good legs," Darcy said with a nod of approval. "Why are you after hiding them in a dress like this? Needs a good inch off, don't you think, Brenna?" Still half naked, Darcy knelt down and folded up the hem, pursing her lips as she studied the result. "Inch and a half, and you wear it with those spiky black shoes with the open toes. You'll be a killer."

She nodded, then got up to try on a pair of gray pipestem trousers. "Just put the dress over there, and I'll hem it for you."

"Oh, really, you don't have to—"

"As payment," Darcy said with a wicked gleam, "for you letting me borrow your clothes."

"Darcy's a fine hand with a needle," Brenna assured

her. "You don't have to worry." Getting into the spirit, she found a charcoal blazer and topped the sweater with it.

"Try this vest to jazz it up," Jude suggested and dug out one with tiny checks in green and burgundy.

"You've a good eye." Darcy beamed approval and added to it by giving Jude a quick one-armed hug. "Now, Brenna, you finish that with a really short excuse for a skirt and men'll be falling all over you."

"I don't want them falling all over me. You just have to boot them out of the way again."

"When enough of them fall, you just climb over their prone bodies and go on to the next." Darcy found a suit in slate blue and wiggled into the skirt. "You are going to give Aidan a tumble, aren't you, Jude?"

"A tumble?"

"Skirt needs to be lifted here, too. A tumble," she continued. "You haven't slept with him yet, have you?"

"I—" She stepped back to pick up her wine again. "No. No, I haven't."

"Didn't think so." Darcy swiveled to check the line of the jacket from the back. "Figured you'd have more a gleam in your eye if you'd wrestled with him." Experimenting, she scooped her hair up, turning this way and that, and imagined borrowing those pretty silver dangles she'd seen Jude wear on her ears. "You're going to sleep with him, aren't you?"

"Darcy, you twit, you're embarrassing her."

"Why?" Darcy let her hair fall so she could choose from two pairs of bone-colored heels. "We're all of us female and none of us virgins. Nothing wrong with sex, is there, Jude?"

Don't blush, Jude ordered herself. You will *not* blush. "No, of course not."

"Aidan's supposed to be damn good at it, too." She

laughed when Jude gulped down more wine. "So, when you do the deed with him, Brenna and I would appreciate some of the details as, at the moment, neither of us has a particular man we're after tumbling with ourselves."

"Talking about sex is the next best thing to having it." Brenna spotted a striped shirt in the armoir and pulled it out. "Of the three of us, you look most likely to be having it in the foreseeable future. The closest I've come in nearly a year is when I had to punch Jack Brennan for copping a feel last New Year's Eve—and I'm still not sure he wasn't just reaching for another pint as he claimed to be."

Discarding the shirt, she sat down in her underwear and poured more wine.

"I, for one, know when a man's reaching for me or for his beer." Darcy cocked her head in the mirror. She looked rather elegant, she thought. Like a lady who had lovely places to go and wonderful things to do. "What do you wear a suit like this for, Jude?"

"Oh, for meetings, lectures, luncheons."

"Luncheons." Darcy sighed and did a slow turn. "In some fancy restaurant or ballroom, with waiters in white jackets."

"And this week's miserable chicken surprise," Jude answered with a smile. "Along with the most tedious luncheon speaker the committee could dig up."

"That's just because you're used to them."

"So used to them, I'd live happily with the knowledge I never have to attend another. I was a poor academic."

"Were you now?" Brenna topped off Jude's wine before reclaiming her own sweater.

"Terrible. I hated planning courses, having to know the answers, and judging papers. On top of that, the politics and the protocol."

"Then why did you do it?"

Distracted, Jude glanced back at Darcy. The woman was so confident, Jude thought, so completely comfortable with herself even as she stood there in a cotton bra and another woman's skirt. How could anyone so sure of who and what she was understand what it was not to know. Just not to know.

"It was expected," Jude said at length.

"And did you always do what was expected?"

Jude let out a long breath and picked up her wine again. "I'm afraid so."

"Well, now." Swept along by affection, Darcy grabbed Jude's face in her hand and kissed her. "We'll fix that."

By the time the second bottle of wine was emptied, the bedroom was a disaster. Brenna had the wit to start a fire, then to hunt up cheese and biscuits. She sat on the floor, vaguely disappointed that Jude's shoes were too big for her. Not that she had any place to wear them, but they were awfully smart.

Jude lay sprawled on the bed, her head propped on her fists as she watched Darcy try on endless variations of outfits. The goofy expression on her own face made Jude wonder if she were drunk or just soft in the head.

Every now and then she gave a quiet hiccough.

"The first time," Darcy was saying, "was with Declan O'Malley and we swore we would love each other ever and a day. We were sixteen and fumbling at it. We did it on a blanket on the beach one night when we both snuck out of the house. And let me tell you, there's nothing a bit romantic about rolling around on the sand, even when you are sixteen and stupid as a turnip."

"I think it's sweet," Jude said dreamily, imagining the moonlight and the crash of waves and two young bodies gleaming with love and discovery. "What happened to Declan O'Malley?"

"Well, forever and a day lasted about three months for the pair of us, and we went on to other things. Two years back he got Jenny Duffy in trouble, so they married and have a second daughter to go with the first. And seem happy enough."

"I'd like to have children." Jude rolled over to find her wine. It had begun to taste like ambrosia. "When William and I discussed it—"

"Discussed it, did you?" Brenna put in, and as guardian of the bottle, took Jude's glass to refill it.

"Oh, yes, in a very logical, practical, and civilized manner. William was always civilized."

"I think William needed a boot in the arse." Brenna handed the glass back, ducking so the wine that slopped as Jude laughed missed splashing on her hair.

"His students call him Dour Powers. That's his name, William Powers. Of course, being a modern professional woman, I kept my own name, so I didn't have all that fuss with the divorce. Anyway . . . what was I saying?"

"How civilized Dour Powers is."

"Oh, yes. William decided that we'd wait five to seven years. Then, if circumstances were acceptable, we would discuss having a child again. If we decided to go ahead with it, we would research and choose the proper day care, preschool facilities, and once we knew the sex of the child, we'd determine which educational plan to put into action straight up to college."

"College?" Darcy turned. "Before the baby's born?"

"William was very forward-thinking."

"For a man with his head up his bum."

"He's probably not as bad as I'm making him out to be." Jude frowned into her wine. "Probably. He's much happier with Allyson.'' To her shock, tears sprang to her eyes. ''He just wasn't happy married to me.''

''The bastard.'' Swamped with sympathy, Darcy abandoned the closet and sat on the bed to wrap an arm around Jude's shoulders. ''He didn't deserve you.''

''Not for a bloody minute,'' Brenna agreed, patting Jude's knee. ''Stuffy, stub-nosed, philandering bastard. You're a hundred times better than any Allyson.''

''She's blond,'' Jude said with a sniffle. ''And has legs up to her ears.''

''Blond from a bottle, I'll wager,'' Darcy said staunchly. ''And you have wonderful legs. Gorgeous legs. I can't keep me eyes off them.''

''Really?'' Jude swiped a hand under her nose.

''They're fabulous.'' Brenna gave Jude's calf a bolstering stroke. ''He's probably going to bed each night steeped in regret for losing you.''

''Oh, hell.'' Jude exploded. ''He was a boring son of a bitch. Allyson's welcome to him.''

''He probably can't even get her off,'' said Darcy, and Jude snorted with glee.

''Well, I certainly never heard the angels sing. This is great.'' She rubbed the heels of her hands over her face to dry it. ''I never had friends to come over and get drunk and toss my clothes around before.''

''You can count on us.'' Darcy gave her a hard squeeze.

Sometime during the third bottle of wine, Jude told them about what she'd seen—thought she'd seen—in the old cemetery.

''It comes down through the blood,'' Darcy said with a knowing nod. ''Old Maude had the sight, and it's often she talked to the Good People.''

''Oh, come on.''

Darcy only lifted one elegant brow at Jude's comment. "And this from the woman who's just described two meetings with a faerie prince."

"I never said that. I said I met this odd man twice. Or thought I did. I'm afraid I have a brain tumor."

Brenna grimaced at the very idea. "Nonsense. You're healthy as a horse."

"If not that, if there's no physical cause, then I'm just crazy. I'm a psychologist," she reminded them. "Well, I was one, a mediocre one, but still, I have enough training to recognize the symptoms of a serious mental disfunction."

"Why should that be?" Brenna demanded. "As far as I can tell, you're the most sensible of women. My ma thinks because of that, and your ladylike manner, you'll be good for me." Cheerfully, Brenna gave Jude a light punch on the shoulder. "And despite that I like you anyway."

"You really do, don't you?"

"Of course I do, and so does Darcy, and not just for your fine clothes."

"Of course I don't just like our Jude for her clothes." Darcy's tone radiated insult at the very idea. "I like her for her baubles, too." With that, she collapsed in laughter. "I'm joking. Sure we like you, Jude. You're fun to be with and a wonderful puzzle to listen to half the time."

"That's so nice." Her eyes welled up again. "It's so nice to have friends, especially when you're either dying of brain cancer or acting like a raving lunatic."

"You're neither. You saw Carrick of the faeries," Brenna announced. "Wandering the hills above his raft until Lady Gwen joins him."

"Do you really believe that?" It seemed possible now, in a way it hadn't—a way she hadn't let it—only a few hours before. "Believe in faerie forts and ghosts and spells that last centuries? You're not just saying that to make me feel better?"

"I'm not, no." Wrapped in Jude's thick robe, Brenna dipped into what was left of the chocolate. "I believe in lots of things until it's proved otherwise. So far as I know, no one's ever proved there absolutely aren't faerie forts under the hills hereabouts, and people say there are more often than not."

"Yes!" Even blurred by wine, Jude's enthusiasm was ripe as she slapped Brenna on the shoulder. "Exactly my point. Legends are perpetuated, and often take on the sheen of truth by the repetition. Arthur of history becomes Arthur of legend with additions of magic swords and Merlin. Vlad the Destroyer becomes a vampire. The wise women, the healers, of villages become witches, and so on. The human tendency to expound, to extrapolate, to garnish with fantasy to make a tale more entertaining in turn makes the tale a legend that certain groups then take into their culture as fact."

"Just listen to her. She sure talks fancy and fine." Darcy, delighted to be wearing one of the cashmere sweaters, pursed her lips in thought. "And I'm sure, Jude darling, there's something in what you just said that's profound and miraculous, even for one who claims to have been a mediocre psychologist. But it sounds like bullshit to me at the moment. Did you or did you not see Carrick of the faeries this very day?"

"I saw someone. He didn't tell me his name."

"And did this someone vanish into the air before your very eyes?"

Jude scowled. "It seemed he did, but—"

"No, no buts, just the facts. That's how it's done, isn't it, logically speaking? If he talked to you, he wants something from you, as I haven't heard of him talking to anyone but Old Maude in my lifetime. Have you, Brenna?''

"No, I can't say as I have. Were you frightened of him, Jude?''

"No, of course not.''

"That's good, then. I think you'd know if he meant to cause you harm or mischief. I think he's just lonely and wanting his lady beside him. Three hundred years,'' she said longingly. "It's a kind of comfort to know love can last.''

"You're such a romantic, Brenna.'' Darcy yawned and curled up in a chair. "Love lasts easy as long as there's yearning. Put the two of them together, and it's just as like they'd be sniping and snarling at each other in six months' time.''

"You've just never had a man courageous enough to take a good hold of your heart.''

Darcy shrugged and snuggled down. "And I don't intend to ever give one the chance. Holding theirs keeps you on top of things. Let them get a grip on yours, and you're sunk.''

"I think I'd like to be in love.'' Jude's eyes drifted shut. "Even if it hurt. You couldn't feel ordinary if you were in love, could you?''

"No, but you can surely feel stupid,'' Brenna muttered, and Jude laughed lightly as she slipped into sleep.

TEN

TINY DANCERS WEARING sturdy clogs were doing a brisk step-toe inside Jude's head when she woke. She could count the beats, each little shuffle-stomp-kick against her temples. It was more baffling than unpleasant, and her eyes twitched as she cautiously opened them.

Hissed at the light, closed, then much more cautiously slitted them open again.

Clothes were everywhere. At first she thought there'd been some sort of violent storm, a kind of Dorothy out of Oz tornado that had swooped in and swirled her things every which way around the room.

That would have explained why she was lying crosswise, half naked, and facedown on the bed.

At a soft snuffling sound beneath the bed she caught her breath, then it came fast. She imagined rodents at best; at worst she was sure it was one of those maniacal little dolls that come to life and carry knives and like to slash at people's hands and feet if they're unwary enough to let them hang over the bed at night.

She'd had nightmares about those hideous dolls since childhood and never, ever let any part of her hang over the bed. Just in case.

Whatever was down there, she was alone with it and had to defend herself. Fortunately, there happened to be a navy suede pump on her pillow. Without questioning the why of that, Jude gripped the shoe like a weapon and steadied herself

With gritted teeth, she crawled closer to the edge of the bed, peered over, and prepared to do what had to be done.

Brenna was on the floor, wrapped like a mummy in Jude's thick robe, with her head pillowed on a stack of sweaters and an empty wine bottle at her feet.

Jude stared, squeezed her eyes tightly shut, then popped them open to stare again.

The evidence was there, she thought. It was irrefutable. Wine bottles, glasses, empty bowls, scattered clothes.

She hadn't been invaded by rodents or evil dolls. She had hosted a drunken party.

The snicker snuck up on her, and she quick had to bury her face in the tangled sheets for fear of waking Brenna up and then having to explain why she was hanging over the bed and laughing like a loon.

Oh, wouldn't her friends, relations, and associates be shocked if they could see the morning-after here? Holding her aching stomach, she rolled over and stared happily at the ceiling. The entertaining she'd done in Chicago had always involved scrupulously planned dinners or get-togethers, with the background music as carefully selected as the proper wine.

And if anyone had one too many, it was always dealt with discreetly. The hostess never passed out on the bed, no, indeed, but graciously saw each of her guests to the door, then responsibly tidied up the disarray.

She'd never had anyone curl up to sleep on her floor, and she'd never awakened the next morning with what was surely a hangover.

She liked it.

She liked it so much that she wanted to write about it in her journal right away. She climbed out of bed, wincing, then grinning when her head pounded. Her very first hangover. It was marvelous!

She tiptoed out, thrilled at the thought of noting it all down in her journal. Then she'd have a shower, and make coffee. Make a huge breakfast for her guests.

Guests, she remembered abruptly. Where in the world was Darcy?

Jude had her answer the minute she stepped into her little office. The lump under the covers on the little bed was bound to be Darcy, which meant the journal entry would have to wait a bit longer.

No matter, Jude thought, amused and delighted that her new friends had felt at home enough to settle in for the night. Despite her aching head, she all but danced into the shower.

It had been the best night of her life. She didn't care how pathetic that sounded, she thought as she ducked her head under the hot spray. It had been wonderful—the talk and the laughter, the foolishness. These two interesting women had come to her, enjoyed her, made her feel part of what they had together.

A friendship. Just as easy as that. And none of it had hinged on where she'd gone to school, what she did for a living, where she'd grown up. It was all about who she was, what she had to say, how she felt.

And not a little to do with her wardrobe, she added with

a giggle. But her clothes were a reflection of who she was, weren't they? At least a reflection of how she saw herself. And why shouldn't she be flattered that a beautiful woman like Darcy Gallagher admired her clothes?

Still smiling, she stepped out to dry off, then took a couple of aspirin out of the medicine cabinet. She wrapped the towel around her, figuring she could find something to wear just by cruising her bedroom floor, then with her hair a dripping mass of curls she stepped out into the hall.

Her first shriek could have cracked glass—it certainly scored her throat and caused her abused head to reel. The second came out more like a yip as she clutched at the towel and gaped at Aidan.

"Sorry to startle you, darling, but I did knock—front and back—before letting myself in."

"I was—I was in the shower."

"So I see." And what a treat for the eyes she was, he decided, with her all pink and damp and her hair dripping in wet ropes about her shoulders. A dense, glossy brown it was against that pink and white skin.

It took all a man's will not to just step forward and take a bite somewhere.

"You—you can't just come in."

"Well, the back door was unlocked, as back doors usually are hereabouts." He continued to smile, to look directly into her eyes. Though it was tempting—more than tempting—to let his gaze go wandering. "And I saw Brenna's lorry parked in your street, so I figured she and Darcy were still here. They are still here, aren't they?"

"Yes, but—"

"I need to fetch Darcy. She has the lunch shift today and she tends to forget such matters."

"We're not dressed."

"I've seen that for myself, darling, and I've tried not to

comment on it overly. But since you mention it, I'd like to say you're looking lovely this morning. Fresh as a rose and . . .'' He stepped a little closer and sniffed at her. ''Twice as fragrant.''

''How's a body to sleep with all that yammering going on!'' Jude jolted as Brenna's voice erupted from the bedroom. ''Kiss her, for sweet Christ's sake, Aidan, and stop talking her ear off.''

''Well, now, I was working my way along to it.''

''No!'' The squeal was so foolish, Jude immediately wished to be buried alive. The best she could do was dash to the bedroom and snatch up a sweater. Before she'd pushed her way through the piles for trousers, Aidan had come in behind her.

''Mother of God, what secret female ritual results in this?''

''Jesus, Aidan, put a cork in it, will you? Me head's falling off me shoulders.''

He crouched down beside the tangle of red hair. ''You know wine gives you a bad head, lass, if you overindulge.''

''There wasn't any beer,'' Brenna muttered.

''Then what's a body to do, after all? I brought along the Gallagher Fix.''

''Did you?'' She rolled, turning her white face and bleary eyes up to him and grasping at his hand. ''Truly? God bless you, Aidan. The man's a saint, Jude. A saint, I tell you. There should be a monument to him in the square of Ardmore.''

''When you get yourself on your feet, crawl down to the kitchen. I brought a jug along just in case.'' He gave Brenna a light kiss on the forehead. ''Now where's my sister?''

''She's in my office, the second bedroom,'' Jude told

him with what she hoped was cool dignity as she clutched the clothes to her breast.

"Is there much breakable in there?"

"I beg your pardon?"

Aidan straightened. "Just pay no mind to the screams and crashes. I'll do my best to keep the property damage to a minimum."

"What does he mean by that?" Jude hissed the question at Brenna the moment he was out of the room, even as she rushed to drag on the slacks.

"Oh." Brenna yawned hugely. "Just that Darcy doesn't wake cheerful."

At the first scream, Brenna clutched her head and moaned. Shocked, Jude yanked the sweater over her head and rushed toward the sound of the thumps and curses.

"Get your hands off me, you blackhearted baboon. I'll kick your ass from here to Tuesday."

"It's your ass that'll be kicked if you don't get it out of bed and to work, my girl."

If the words and the vicious tone in which they were delivered had shocked her, it was nothing to the visual impact. Jude burst into the room in time to see Aidan, his face grim and set, drag Darcy, dressed in nothing but her bra and panties, from the bed to the floor.

"Why, you brute! Stop that this minute!" Driven to protect her new friend, Jude leaped forward. The order and the movement managed to distract Aidan just long enough for Darcy to ball her fist, bare her teeth, and deliver a short-armed punch straight to his crotch.

Jude wasn't sure the sound he made was human. Torn between yet another layer of shock and a wave of pure female amusement that she wasn't the least bit proud of, she watched Aidan crumple to his knees and Darcy fall on him like a she-wolf.

"Ouch. Jesus! Bloody hell!" He did what he could to defend himself as his sister thumped, yanked, and bit exactly as he'd taught her, and still wheezing from that first blow, he finally managed to pin her.

"One of these days, Darcy Alice Mary Gallagher, I'm going to forget you're a female and plant one on you."

"Go ahead, you great bully." She thrust out her chin, blew her hair out of her eyes. "Plant one now."

"I'd likely break my hand on that face of yours. However pretty it is, it's stretched over a skull made of rock."

Then they were grinning at each other, and he was rubbing his hand over her face with what surely was as much affection as exasperation. Jude just kept staring as they got to their feet.

"Put some clothes on, you shameless hussy, and get in to work."

Darcy pushed at her tumbled hair and didn't seem in the least bothered by the recent tumble. "Jude, can I borrow the blue cashmere jumper?"

"Um, yes, of course."

"Oh, you're a sweetheart, you are." She danced by, giving Jude a peck on the cheek. "Don't worry, I'll tidy up what I can before I go."

"Oh, well, that's all right. I'll make coffee."

"That would be lovely. Tea even better if you have it."

"Coffee?" Aidan said when Darcy had sauntered out the door. "I think you owe me a cup at least."

"Owe you?"

He stepped toward Jude. "That's the second time you've distracted me in battle and caused me to take a blow I'd have dodged otherwise. Oh, and very well you might bite your cheek to hold back the grin, but I see your eyes laughing clear enough."

"I'm sure you're mistaken." Jude looked deliberately aside. "But I'll make the coffee."

"And how's your head faring this morning?" he asked as he followed her out and down the stairs.

"It's fine."

He lifted a brow. "No ill effects due to squeezing a bit too much of the grape?"

"Maybe a little headache." She was too proud of it to be embarrassed. "I took some aspirin."

"I've better than that for you." He rubbed a hand casually over the back of her neck, miraculously hitting just the spot that made her want to purr, then moved to the counter as they entered the kitchen. The jar he picked up was filled with some dark and dangerous-looking red liquid.

"Gallagher's Fix. It'll set you up right and tight."

"It looks awful."

"Not a half-bad taste all in all, though some say it needs a bit of acquiring." He took a glass from the cupboard. "When a man serves drinks for a living, he's honor-bound to have a cure for the morning after."

"It's only a little headache." She studied the glass he poured dubiously.

"Then drink only a little, and I'll fix you some breakfast."

"You will?"

"A bit of this, a bit of that, and a little lie-me-down." He nudged the glass on her. She was a bit pale and her eyes were shadowed. He wanted to cuddle her until she felt herself again. "You'll wake up forgetting you had a hedonistic orgy last night."

"It wasn't an orgy. There weren't any men."

He grinned, fast and bright. "Next time invite me. Here now, sip a little and start the coffee, and some tea as well. I'll see to the rest."

It seemed like a nice connection to the evening to have a handsome man cooking breakfast in her kitchen. That was one more thing that had never happened to her before.

It was amazing, she thought, just how quickly, and how completely, a life could change. Jude sipped carefully, found the brew more tolerable than expected. Drinking the rest, she put on the kettle.

"Jude, you've no sausage. You've no bacon."

The quiet shock in his voice amused her. "No, I don't really eat it."

"Don't eat it? How do you cook breakfast?"

Because the shock wasn't so quiet now, she couldn't resist fluttering at him. Imagine, she thought, flirting before breakfast. "Usually by putting a piece of whole wheat bread in the toaster and pressing down the little lever."

"A single piece of toast?"

"And a half a grapefruit or a cup of whatever fresh fruit I have on hand. But now and then, I confess, I go wild and have an entire bagel with low-fat cream cheese."

"And this is what a sensible person calls breakfast?"

"Yes, a healthy one."

"Yanks," Aidan shook his head, as he took out eggs. "Why is it you think you'll live forever and why do you want to, I'd like to know, when you deny yourselves so many of the basic pleasures in life?"

"Somehow I manage to get through day after day without gnawing on greasy pig meat."

"A little testy in the morning, are we? Well, you wouldn't be if you'd eat a proper breakfast. But we'll do what we can for you."

She turned, prepared to snarl at him, but with the hand that wasn't holding the eggs, he cupped the back of her neck and nudged her up against him, then nipped her bottom lip. Before she'd recovered from that, he was following up the quick bite with a long, soft kiss that drained what few thoughts were left in her head.

"Do you have to do that before breakfast?" Brenna complained.

"Aye." Aidan ran that wonderful hand down Jude's spine, then up again. "And after, if I have my way about it."

"Bad enough you come in, stomping about and waking a body up." Scowling, and wearing the robe she'd wrapped herself in the night before, Brenna headed straight for the jar and poured some Gallagher's Fix into a glass. Gulping it down, she eyed Aidan narrowly. "Are you making breakfast then?"

"I'm about to. You're looking a bit peaked this morning, Mary Brenna. Do you want a kiss as well?"

She sniffed, then grinned at him. "I wouldn't mind it."

He obliged her by putting the eggs aside and stepping up to lift her off the floor by her elbows. When she whooped, he planted a loud, smacking kiss on her lips. "There you have it, and some roses back in your cheeks as well."

"That's from two punches of a fix by Gallagher," she said and made him laugh.

"We aim to please. Is my sister still on her feet?"

"She's in the shower, and still cursing you. As I would be if you weren't so free with your kisses."

"If God didn't want a woman's lips to be kissed, he wouldn't have made them so easy to reach. Are there potatoes in the larder, Jude?"

"I think—yes."

Free with his kisses? She'd been warmly entertained watching the easy and affectionate byplay, but now she stood worrying about just what "free with his kisses" meant while Aidan scrubbed off some potatoes and put them in a pot to boil. Did that mean he just went around scooping up women with both hands? He certainly had the charm for it.

The skill for it.

The looks for it.

What did it matter? They didn't have what anyone would call a relationship. She didn't want a relationship. Not really.

She just wanted to know if she was one of a pack, or if—for once—she was something more special. Just once something special to someone.

"Where have you gone off dreaming?" Aidan asked her.

Jude jerked back, ordered herself not to flush. "Nowhere." She busied herself with the coffee and tried not to feel odd when Brenna rummaged through the cupboards for plates and flatware.

She'd never had people make themselves so easily at home in her house. It surprised her to realize she liked it. It made her feel a part of something friendly and simple.

It didn't matter if Brenna was efficient enough to intimidate a well-programmed robot. It didn't matter if Darcy was so beautiful every other woman looked dull by comparison.

It didn't even matter if Aidan kissed a hundred women before breakfast every day of the week.

Somehow within a few short weeks, they were her friends. And they didn't appear to expect her to be anything but what she was.

It was a small but precious miracle.

"Why don't I smell bacon cooking?" Darcy demanded as she strolled in.

"Jude didn't have any," Aidan told her.

Jude beamed as Darcy helped herself to coffee. "I'll get some. For next time."

• • •

The feeling stayed with her all day, the warmth and quiet joy of it. Over breakfast she made plans to drive to Dublin and shop with Darcy, to have Sunday dinner at the O'Tooles', and she scheduled another storytelling session with Aidan.

She wasn't asked to come down to the pub that evening. It was understood that she would. And that was so much better. When you were part of something, she reflected, you didn't need to be asked.

The kitchen smelled of fried potatoes and coffee. The wind chime outside the door sang in the breeze. As she rose to get more coffee, she spotted Betty outside running wildly after a bounding rabbit over hills sprinkled with wildflowers.

Jude imprinted it all on her mind, promising herself she'd take the moment out again when she was feeling low or lonely.

Later, when she was alone and settling down to work, it seemed to her the house still held all that warmth and energy. So she wrote in her journal:

It's odd that I never realized this is so much what I want. A home. A place where people I enjoy and who enjoy me will come when they like. Will feel comfortable and easy. Maybe it wasn't solitude I was looking for after all when I so rashly flew to Ireland. It was what I've had over these last hours. Companionship, laughter, foolishness, and well, romance.

I suppose I didn't realize it because I never let myself really wish for it. Now without even the wish, here it is.

That's a kind of magic, isn't it? Every bit as much as faeries and spells and winged horses. I'm accepted here, not for what I do, or where I come from, or where I went to school. I'm accepted for who I am. For who, more importantly, I'm finally letting myself become.

When I have dinner at the O'Tooles' I won't be shy or feel awkward. I'll have fun. When I go shopping with Darcy I'm determined to buy something extravagant and useless. Because it'll be fun.

And when next Aidan comes through my garden gate, I may take him as a lover. Because I want him. Because he makes me feel something I've never felt before. Outrageously and completely female.

And because, damn it, it'll be fun.

With a satisfied nod she switched documents and settled back to review some of her work. Scanning the screen, sifting through written notes, she slid into the routine of research and analysis. She was deep into the study of a story on a crofter's changeling when her phone rang.

With her mind circling the crofter's dilemma, she picked up the receiver. "Yes? Hello."

"Jude. I hope I'm not interrupting your work."

Jude blinked at the screen and tuned in to her mother's voice. "No, nothing important. Hello, Mother. How are you?"

"I'm very well." Linda Murray's voice was cultured and smooth, and just a little cool. "Your father and I are about to take advantage of the end of the semester. We're going to New York for a few days to attend an exhibit at the Whitney and see a play."

"That's nice." It made her smile, thinking how much her parents enjoyed each other's company. A perfect meeting of minds. "You'll enjoy that."

"Very much. You're welcome to fly in and join us if you like, if you've had enough of country living."

A perfect meeting of minds, Jude thought again. And

she'd never quite been able to mesh with that lovely unity. "I appreciate the offer, but I'm fine. I really love it here."

"Do you?" There was faint surprise in the tone. "You always took after your grandmother, who sends her love, by the way."

"Send mine right back to her."

"You're not finding the cottage a bit too rustic?"

Jude thought of her initial reaction—no microwave, no electric can opener—and grinned to herself. "I have everything I need. There are flowers blooming outside the windows. And I'm starting to recognize some of the birds."

"That's nice. You do sound rested. I hope you're planning on spending some time in Dublin while you're there. They're supposed to have marvelous galleries. And of course you'll want to see Trinity College."

"As a matter of fact, I'm going to Dublin for the day next week."

"Good. Good. A little respite in the country is all well and good, but you don't want your mind to stagnate."

Jude opened her mouth, shut it again, then took a long breath. "I'm working on my paper now, as a matter of fact. I'm finding no end of material here. And I'm learning to garden."

"Really? That's a lovely hobby. You sound happy, Jude. I'm so glad to hear it. It's been too long since you sounded happy."

Jude closed her eyes and felt the burgeoning resentment fade away. "I know you've been worried about me, and I'm sorry. I really am happy. I suppose I just needed to get away for a while."

"I'll admit both your father and I were concerned. You seemed so listless and dissatisfied."

"I suppose I was both."

"The divorce was hard on you. I understand that, better

I think, than you knew. It was so sudden and so final, and it took all of us by surprise.''

"It certainly took me by surprise," Jude said dryly. "It shouldn't have. Wouldn't have if I'd been paying attention."

"Perhaps not," Linda said, and Jude winced at her mother's easy agreement. "But that doesn't change the fact that William wasn't the man any of us thought he was. And that's one of the reasons I called, Jude. I felt it would be better if you heard this from me rather than through the gossip mill or some letter from an acquaintance."

"What is it?" Something inside her belly clenched. "Is it about William? Is he ill?"

"No, quite the contrary. He appears to be thriving."

Jude gaped at the sudden and undisguised bitterness in her mother's voice. "Well, that's fine."

"You have a more forgiving nature than I do," Linda snapped back. "I'd prefer it if he'd contract some rare debilitating disease or at least go bald and develop a facial twitch."

Stunned as much by the uncharacteristic violence in her mother's voice as by the sentiment, Jude burst out laughing. "That's terrible! I love it! But I had no idea you felt that way about him."

"Your father and I did our best to maintain a polite front, to make things easier for you. It couldn't have been comfortable for you, facing your mutual friends and colleagues. You remained dignified. We were proud of you."

Dignity, Jude mused. Yes, they'd always found pride in her dignity. So how could she have disappointed them by going into wild rages or having public snits? "I appreciate that."

"I think it showed enormous strength, the way you held your head up. And I can only imagine how much it cost you to do so. I suppose leaving your position at the university and going away like this was necessary. To rebuild.''

"I didn't think you understood."

"Of course we did, Jude. He hurt you."

As simple as that, Jude realized and felt her eyes sting. Why hadn't she trusted her family to stand behind her? "I thought you blamed me."

"Why in the world would we blame you? Honestly, your father actually threatened to strike William. It's so rare for that Irish blood to surface, and it took quite some doing to calm him down again."

Jude tried to imagine her dignified father plowing into the dignified William. But it would not compute. "I can't tell you how much better that makes me feel."

"I never said anything because you seemed so determined to keep it all civilized. And I hope this doesn't upset you, but I don't want you to hear it from some other source."

Jude's belly seized up again. "What is it?"

"William and his new wife are taking advantage of semester's end as well. They're going to the West Indies for a couple of weeks. Of all places. William is cheerfully telling anyone who'll listen that they want this exotic holiday before they have to settle in. Jude, they're expecting a baby in October."

Whatever had clutched in her belly sank, dropped through clean to her toes. "I see."

"The man's acting like a fool about it. He actually has a copy of the sonogram and is showing it off like a family photo. He bought her this gaudy emerald ring to celebrate. He's behaving as if she's the first woman to conceive."

"I'm sure he's just very happy."

"I'm glad you can take it well. For myself, I'm infuri-

ated. We have several mutual friends and this, well, glee
of his, is very awkward in social situations. You'd think he
would show more tact.''

Linda paused, obviously to get her temper under control.
When she spoke again, it was gently. "He wasn't worth a
moment of your time, Jude. I'm sorry I didn't realize that
before you married him."

"So am I," she murmured. "Please don't worry about
it, Mother. It's history. I'm just sorry it's embarrassing for
you."

"Oh, I can manage. As I said, I didn't want you to hear
it from someone else. I can see now I needn't have been
concerned that you'd be upset or hurt again. Honestly, I
wasn't sure you were completely over him. I'm relieved
you're so sensible. As always."

"Yes, sensible Jude," she said, even as something hot
lodged in her throat. "Absolutely. In fact, be sure to give
him my best wishes the next time you see him."

"I'll do that. I really am glad you're happy, Jude. Your
father or I will be in touch once we're back from New
York."

"Good. Have a wonderful time. Give Father my love."

"I will."

When she hung up, Jude felt paralyzed. Frozen. Her skin
was chilled, her blood frigid. All the warmth and pleasure,
the simple delight that had carried over from the morning
iced up in what she assumed was despair.

William flying off to some charming island in the West
Indies with his pretty new wife. Sliding into sparkling blue
water, strolling along sugar-white sand under a full moon
with hands clasped and eyes dreamy.

William giddy over the prospect of fatherhood, bragging
about his pretty pregnant wife, poring through baby books
with Allyson, compiling lists of names. Pampering the

mother-to-be with emerald rings and flowers and lazy Sunday mornings in bed with freshly squeezed orange juice and croissants.

She could visualize it perfectly, a curse of her well-honed imagination. The characteristically buttoned-down William, gleefully nuzzling the lovely Madonna as they lounged on the beach. The usually reserved William telling perfect strangers about the upcoming blessed event.

The notoriously frugal William shelling out the price of an emerald ring. A gaudy one.

The bastard.

She snapped the pencil she held in two, heaved both parts at the wall. It wasn't until she'd leaped out of her chair, knocking it to the floor with a resounding crash, that she realized it wasn't despair she felt. It was fury. Blazing, blistering fury.

Her breath came in pants, her fists were clenched. There was nothing to pound on, nothing to beat senseless. The rage building inside her was so black, so fierce, she looked around wildly for somewhere to put it before it exploded out of her chest.

She had to get out, to move, to breathe, before the force of anger came out in a scream that shattered every window in the cottage. Blindly she whirled toward the door and raced out, down the stairs, out of the house.

She ran over the hills until she couldn't catch her breath, until her sides stung and her legs trembled. A soft rain began to fall through the sunshine, sparkling the air and dewing the grass. The wind came up strong and sounded like a woman weeping. Through it, like a whisper, was the music of pipes.

Finding herself on the path to Ardmore, Jude continued to walk.

ELEVEN

A RAINY EVENING at the pub had people snuggled into their chairs and doing as much dreaming as talking. Young Connor Dempsey played wistful tunes on the squeeze-box while his father sipped his Smithwick's and discussed the state of the world with his good friend Jack Brennan.

Since Jack's heart was mending now, he paid as much attention to the conversation as he did his own beer.

From behind the bar, Aidan kept an eye on him nonetheless. Jack and Connor Dempsey Senior often disagreed on the state of the world and occasionally felt the need to use their fists to bring the point home.

Aidan understood the need well enough, but he didn't care to have the debate rage in his place.

He checked the progress of the football game on the bar set now and then. Clare was outscoring Mayo and he gave them a quick mental cheer, as he had a small wager on the outcome.

He anticipated a quiet night and wondered if he could

call upon Brenna to cover for him. He had an urge to see if Jude would like another meal with him. In a restaurant this time, with flowers and candles on the table and a nice straw-colored wine in pretty glasses.

It would be the sort of thing she was more accustomed to, he imagined, than scrambled eggs and fried potatoes dished up in her own kitchen.

Shy and sweet she might be, but she was a sophisticated woman. City-bred and upper class. The men she was used to would take her to the theater and fancy restaurants. They would wear ties and well-cut suits and talk of literature and cinema in weighty tones.

Well, he wasn't exactly ignorant, was he? He read books and enjoyed films. He'd traveled more than most and had seen great art and architecture firsthand. He could hold his own against any Chicago dandy in conversation.

When he caught himself scowling, he shook his head. What was he doing, for Christ's sake, setting himself up in competition with some imaginary man? It was pathetic the way he couldn't seem to hold three thoughts in his head unless one of them centered on Jude Murray.

It was likely just sexual frustration, he decided. He hadn't slid his hands over a woman's body in a considerable amount of time. Every time he imagined doing so, it was Jude's body under his hands. And thanks to that morning, he had a much clearer picture of just what that body of hers included.

All that soft white skin that tended to show a rosy flush so easily. Long, slim legs, and a tiny, sexy mole just at the rise of her left breast. She had such pretty shoulders, shoulders that just seemed to cry out for the trail of a man's lips.

The way she shied, then melted when he touched her. Was it any wonder he was fixated on her? A man would have to be dead a decade not to be stirred.

A part of him—one that he wasn't particularly proud of—wished he could just charm her into bed and be done with it. Release and relief and a pleasure for both of them. Another part admitted, just a bit uneasily, that he was just as fascinated by her mind and her manner as he was by the package wrapped around it.

Quiet and shy, tidy and polite. She just made a man want to keep rubbing away at the sheen of composure until he found everything that lay hidden beneath.

The door opened. Aidan glanced over casually, then he looked again, eyes widening in something close to shock.

Jude stepped in. No, it was more a stalking. She was wet down to the skin, her hair wild and dripping around her shoulders. Her eyes were dark, and though he told himself it was a trick of the light, they looked dangerous. He would have sworn they sent off sparks as she strode up to the bar.

"I'd like a drink."

"You're soaking wet."

"It's raining, and I've been walking in it." Her voice was clipped with an undertone of heat. She shoved at her wet, heavy hair. She'd lost her band somewhere along the run. "That's the usual result. Can I have a drink or not?"

"Sure, I've the wine you like. Why don't you take it over by the fire there, and warm yourself a bit. And I'll get you a towel for your hair."

"I don't want the fire. I don't want a towel. I want whiskey." She issued it like a challenge and dropped a fisted hand on the bar. "Here."

Her eyes still made his think of a sea goddess, but it was a vengeful one now. He nodded slowly. "As you like."

He got out a short glass and poured two fingers of Jameson's into it. Jude snatched it up, tossed it back like water. Her breath exploded out of the sudden fire dead center of her chest. Her eyes watered but stayed hot.

A wise man, Aidan kept his face carefully blank. "You're welcome to go upstairs to my rooms if you'd like to borrow a dry shirt."

"I'm fine." Her throat felt as if someone had raked hot needles down it, but there was a rather pleasant little fire simmering in her gut now. She set the glass back down on the bar, nodded to it. "Another."

Experience had him leaning casually on the bar. With some you could empty the bottle and no one was the worse for it. With others you nudged them out the door before they bent their elbow once too often. And there were some who needed to pour out their troubles more than they needed the publican to pour the whiskey.

He recognized which he was dealing with here. Added to that, if a glass and a half of wine gave her a buzz, two shots of whiskey would put her under. "Why don't you tell me what the trouble is, darling?"

"I didn't say there was any trouble. I said I wanted another glass of whiskey."

"Well, you won't get one here. But I'll make you some tea and a seat by the fire."

She drew in a breath, then let it out with a shrug. "Fine, forget the whiskey."

"There's a lass." He patted the fist still bunched on his bar. "Now you go and sit, and I'll bring you tea. Then you can tell me what's the matter."

"I don't need to sit." She tossed her wet hair out of her face, then leaned forward as he was. "Come closer," she ordered. When he obliged and their faces were only inches apart, she took a handful of his shirt. She spoke clearly, concisely, but still had the wit to keep her voice low. "Do you still want to have sex with me?"

"I beg your pardon?"

"You heard me." But it gave her a dark thrill to repeat

herself. "Do you want to have sex or not?"

Even as his nerves jangled, he went hard. It was beyond his power to control either reaction. "Right this minute?"

"What's wrong with now?" she demanded. "Does everything have to be planned and patterned and tied up in a damn bow?"

She forgot to keep her voice down this time, and several heads turned and eyebrows wiggled. Aidan laid a hand over the one still clutching his shirt and patted gently.

"Come on back in the snug, why don't you, Jude?"

"In the what?"

"Come on, back here." He patted her hand again, then pried her fingers off. With a gesture he pointed out a door at the end of the bar. "Shawn, come out here and man the bar for a moment, would you?"

He lifted the flap at the end of the bar so Jude could pass through, then nudged her through the door.

The snug was a small, windowless room furnished with two sugan chairs that had been his grandmother's and a table his father had made that wobbled just enough to be endearing. There was an old globe lamp that Aidan switched on, and a decanter of whiskey that he ignored.

The snug was a place designed for private conversations and private business. He couldn't think of anything more private than dealing with the woman he'd been fantasizing about asking him if he wanted to have sex.

"Why don't we—" "Sit down" was what he'd intended to say, but his mouth was too busy being devoured by hers. She had his back up against the door, her hands fisted in his hair, and her lips hotly, hungrily fastened on his.

He managed one strangled groan, then lost himself in the pleasure of being attacked by a wet and willful woman. She was pressed against him. Jesus, plastered against him, and her body was like a furnace. He wondered that her clothes didn't simply steam away.

Her heart was racing, or maybe it was his. He felt the frantic, nervous beat pound and pitch between them. She smelled of the rain and tasted of his whiskey, and he wanted her with a fervor that was like a sickness. It crawled through him, clawed at him, reeled in his head, burned in his throat.

Dimly, he heard his brother's voice, an answering laugh, the faint tune played by a young boy. And he remembered, barely, where they were. Who they were.

"Jude. Wait." The blood was roaring in his head as he tried to ease her back. "This isn't the place."

"Why?" She was desperate. She needed something. Him. Anything. "You want me. I want you."

Enough that he would easily imagine reversing their positions and mounting her where they stood like a stallion covering a ready mare. With fire in the blood, and no heart at all.

"Stop now. Let's catch our breath here." He stroked a hand over her hair, a hand that was far from steady. "Tell me what's the matter."

"Nothing's the matter." Her voice cracked and proved her a liar. "Why does something have to be the matter? Just make love with me." Her hands shook as she fought with the buttons of his shirt. "Just touch me."

Now he did reverse positions, pressed her against the door and firmly took her face in his hands to lift it. Whatever his body was telling him, his heart and mind gave different orders. He was a man who preferred following the heart.

"I might touch, but I'll never reach you if you don't tell me what's troubling you."

"There's nothing troubling me," she hissed at him. Then burst into tears.

"Oh, there now, darling." It was less worrisome to comfort a woman than to resist one. Gently, he gathered her in, cradled her against his chest. "Who hurt you, *a ghra?*"

"It's nothing. It's stupid. I'm sorry."

"Of course it's something, and not stupid at all. Tell me what's made you sad, *mavourneen.*"

Her breath hitched, and desolate, she pressed her face into his shoulder. It was solid as a rock, comforting as a pillow. "My husband and his wife are going to the West Indies and having a baby."

"What?" The word came out like a bullet as he jerked her back. "You've a husband?"

"Had." She sniffled, and wished her head could be on his shoulder again. "He didn't want to keep me."

Aidan took two long breaths, but his head still reeled as though he'd swallowed a bottle of Jameson's. Or been clobbered by one. "You were married?"

"Technically." She fluttered a hand. "Do you have a handkerchief?"

Staggered, Aidan dug in his pocket, handed it to her. "I think we'll start back at some beginning, but we'll get you some dry clothes and some hot tea before you catch a chill."

"No, I'm all right. I should—"

"Just be quiet. We'll go upstairs."

"I'm a mess." She blew her nose savagely. "I don't want people to see me."

"There's no one out there who hasn't shed a few tears of their own, and some right here in this pub. We'll go out and through the kitchen and up."

Before she could argue, he took her arm and pulled her to the door. Then even as the first wave of embarrassment hit, he continued to pull her, into the kitchen, where Darcy looked over in surprise.

"Why, Jude, whatever's the matter?" she began, then closed her mouth as Aidan gave a quick shake of his head and nudged Jude up a narrow staircase.

He opened a door at the head of it and stepped into his small, cluttered living room. "The bedroom's through there. Take whatever works best for you, and I'll put on the tea."

She started to thank him, apologize, something, but he was already moving through a low doorway. There was enough tension in his wake to bow her spirits even lower.

She stepped into the bedroom. Unlike the living room, it was neat as a pin and sparsely furnished. She wished she had the time, and the right, to poke about a bit. But she moved quickly to the little closet, giving herself time only to scan the single bed with its navy cover, the tall chest of drawers that looked old and comfortably worn at the hinges, the faded rug over an age-darkened wood floor.

She found a shirt, as gray as her mood. While she changed she studied the walls. There he had indulged in his romantic side, she thought. Posters and prints of far-away places.

Street scenes of Paris and London and New York and Florence, stormy seascapes and lush islands. Towering mountains, quiet valleys, mysterious deserts. And of course, the fierce cliffs and gentle hills of his own country. They were tacked up edge to edge, like a fabulous, eccentric wallpaper.

How many of those places had he been? she wondered. Had he been to them all, or had he places still to go?

She let out a huge sigh, not caring that the sound was ripe with self-pity, and carrying her wet sweater, went back into the living room.

He was pacing, and stopped when she came in. She was dwarfed by his shirt and looked small and miserable and not nearly up to dealing with the emotions swinging around inside him. So he said nothing, not yet, merely took her sweater and carried it into the bath to hang over the shower rod and drip.

"Sit down, Jude."

"You've every right to be angry with me, coming in this way, behaving as I did. I don't know how to begin to—"

"I wish you'd be quiet for a minute." He snapped it at her, telling himself when she winced that he wasn't made of stone. Then he stalked into the kitchen to deal with the tea.

She'd been married, was all he could think. That was quite a detail she'd neglected to mention.

He'd thought her to have had little experience with men, and here she'd been married and divorced and was obviously still pining for the bastard.

Pining for some fancy man in Chicago who wasn't true enough to keep his vows, and all the while Aidan Gallagher had been pining for her.

If that wasn't enough to burn your ass, what was?

He poured the tea strong and black and added a healthy drop of whiskey to his own.

She was standing when he came back, the fingers of her hands twisted together. Her damp hair curled madly, and her eyes were drenched. "I'll go downstairs and apologize to your customers."

"For what?"

"For making a scene."

He set the cups down and drew his brows together to study her with as much bafflement as irritation. "What do I care about that? If we don't have a scene in Gallagher's once a week we wonder why. Will you sit down, damn it, and stop looking at me as if I was about to take a strap to you?''

He sat after she did, then picked up his own tea. Jude sipped, burned her tongue, then hastily set her cup down again.

''Why didn't you tell me you'd been married?''

''I didn't think of it.''

''Didn't think of it?'' His cup clattered as he snapped it down on the table. ''Did it mean so little to you?''

''It meant a great deal to me,'' she returned with a quiet dignity that had him narrowing his eyes. ''It meant considerably less to the man I married. I've been trying to learn to live with that.''

When Aidan said nothing, she picked up her tea again to give herself something to do with her hands. ''We'd known each other several years. He's a professor at the university where I taught. On the surface, we had a great deal in common. My parents liked him very much. He asked me to marry him. I said yes.''

''Were you in love with him?''

''I thought I was, yes, so that amounts to the same thing.''

No, Aidan thought, it didn't amount to the same thing at all. But he let it pass. ''And what happened?''

''We—he, I should say, planned it all out. William likes to plan carefully, considering details and possible pitfalls and their solutions. We bought a house, as it's more conducive to entertaining and he had ambitions to rise in his department. We had a very small, exclusive, and dignified wedding with all the right people involved. Meaning caterers, florists, photographers, guests.''

She breathed deep and, since her tongue was already scalded, sipped the tea again. ''Seven months later, he came to me and told me he was dissatisfied. That's the word he used. 'Jude, I'm dissatisfied with our marriage.' I think I said, 'Oh, I'm sorry.' ''

She closed her eyes, let the humiliation settle along with the whiskey in her stomach. "That grates, knowing my first instinct was to apologize. He accepted it graciously, as if he'd been expecting it. No," she corrected, looking at Aidan again. "*Because* he'd been expecting it."

It was hurt he felt from her now, quivering waves of it. "That should tell you that you apologize too much."

"Maybe. In any case, he explained that as he respected me and wanted to be perfectly honest, he felt he should tell me that he'd fallen in love with someone else."

Someone younger, Jude thought now. And prettier, brighter.

"He didn't want to involve her in a sordid and adulterous affair, so he requested that I file for divorce immediately. We would sell the house, split everything fifty-fifty. As he was the instigator, he would be willing to give me first choice in any particular material possessions I might want."

Aidan kept his eyes on her face. She was composed again, eyes quiet, hands still. Too composed, to his thinking. He decided he preferred it when she was passionate and real. "And what did you do about it?"

"Nothing. I did nothing. He got his divorce, he remarried, and we all got on with our lives."

"He hurt you."

"That's what William would call an unfortunate but necessary by-product of the situation."

"Then William is a donkey's ass."

She smiled a little. "Maybe. But what he did makes more sense than struggling through a marriage that makes you unhappy."

"Were you unhappy in it?"

"No, but I don't suppose I was really happy either." Her head ached now, and she was tired. She wished she could just curl into a ball and sleep. "I don't think I'm given to great highs of emotions."

He too was drained. This was the same woman who'd thrown herself lustfully into his arms, then wept bitterly in them only moments before. "No, you're a right calm one, aren't you, Jude Frances?"

"Yes." She whispered. "Sensible Jude."

"So, being such, what set you off today?"

"It's stupid."

"Why should it be stupid if it meant something to you?"

"Because it shouldn't have. It shouldn't have meant anything." Her head snapped up again, and the glitter that came into her eyes didn't displease him in the least. "We're divorced, aren't we? We've been divorced for two years. Why should I care that he's going to the West Indies?"

"Well, why do you?"

"Because I wanted to go there!" she exploded. "I wanted to go somewhere exotic and wonderful and foreign on our honeymoon. I got brochures. Paris, Florence, Bimini. All sorts of places. We could have gone to any of them, and I would have been thrilled. But all he could talk about was—was—"

She circled her hand, as words momentarily failed her. "The language difficulties, the cultural shocks, the different germs, for God's sake."

Furious all over again, she leaped out of the chair. "So we went to Washington and spent hours—days—centuries—touring the Smithsonian and going to lectures."

He'd been fairly shocked before, but this one did it. "You went to *lectures* on your honeymoon?"

"Cultural bonding," she spat out. "That's what he called it." She threw up her hands and began to stalk around the room. "Most couples have impossibly high expectations for their honeymoon, according to William."

"And why shouldn't they?" Aidan murmured.

"Exactly!" She whirled back, her face flushed with righteous fury. "Better to meet the minds on common ground? Better to go to an environment that is recognizable? The hell with that. We should've been having crazy sex on some hot beach."

A part of Aidan was simply delighted that that hadn't occurred. "Sounds to me like you're well rid of him, darling."

"That's not the *point*." She wanted to tear her hair out, nearly did. Jude's Irish was up now, bubbling, boiling in a way that would have made her grandmother proud. "The point is, he left me, and his leaving crushed me. Maybe not my heart, but my pride and my ego, and what difference does it make? They're all part of me."

"It makes no difference at all," Aidan said quietly. "You're right. No difference."

The fact that he agreed, without a second's hesitation, only added fuel to her temper. "And now, the bastard, he's going where I wanted to go. And they're having a baby, and he's *thrilled*. When I talked about having children, he brought up our careers and lifestyles, the population, college costs, for Christ's sake. And he made a chart."

"A what?"

"A chart. A goddamn computer-generated chart, projecting our finances and health, our career status and time management over the next five to seven years. After that, he told me, if we met our goals, we could consider—just consider—conceiving a single child. But for the next several years, he had to concentrate on his career, his planned advancements, and his stupid portfolio."

Fury was a living thing now, clawing viciously at her

chest. "*He* decided when and if we would have a child. *He* decided should that eventuality take place there would be only one. If he could have managed it, he'd have decided on the sex of the projected baby.

"I wanted a family, and he gave me pie charts."

Her breath hitched, and her eyes filled again. But when Aidan rose to go to her, Jude shook her head frantically. "I thought he didn't want foreign travel and babies. I thought, well, he's just set in his ways, and he's so practical and frugal and ambitious. But that wasn't it. It wasn't it at all. He didn't want to go to the West Indies with *me*. He didn't want to make a family with *me*. What's wrong with me?"

"There's nothing wrong with you. Nothing at all."

"Of course there is." She dug out his handkerchief as her voice rose and fell and broke. "If there wasn't, I'd never have let him get away with it. I'm dull. He was bored with me almost as soon as we were married. People get bored with me. My students, my associates. My own parents are bored with me."

"That's a foolish thing to say." He went to her now, taking her arms to give her a little shake. "There's nothing dull about you."

"You just don't know me well enough yet. I'm dull, all right." She sniffled, then nodded for emphasis. "I never do anything exciting, never say anything brilliant. Everything about me is average. I even bore myself."

"Who put these ideas in your head?" He would have shaken her again, but she looked so pitiful. "Did it ever occur to you that this William with his bloody pie charts and cultural whatever it was is the boring one? That if your students weren't enthusiastic it was because teaching wasn't what you were meant to do?"

She shrugged. "I'm the common factor."

"Jude Frances, who's come to Ireland on her own, to live in a place she's never been, with people she's never met and to do work she's never done?"

"That's different."

"Why?"

"Because I'm just running away."

He felt both impatience and sympathy for her. "Boring you're not, but hardheaded you are. You could give a mule lessons. What's wrong with running away if where you were didn't suit you? Doesn't it follow you're running *to* something else? Something that does suit you?"

"I don't know." And she was too tired and achy to think it through.

"I've done some running myself. To and from. In the end I landed where I needed to be." He bent down to press a kiss to her forehead. "And so will you."

Then he drew her away, rubbed a tear from her cheek with his thumb. "Now, sit down here while I go clear up a few things in the pub. Then I'll see you home."

"No, that's all right. I can walk back."

"You'll not be walking in the rain and the dark and when you're feeling sad. Just sit and drink your tea. I won't be long."

He left her alone before she could argue, then stood on the stairs for a few minutes to get his own mind in order.

He was trying not to be angry with her for not telling him about the marriage. He was a man who took such commitments seriously, because of his faith and his own sensibilities. Marriage wasn't something you wound in and out of as you pleased, but something that cemented you.

Hers had crumbled through no fault of her own, but she should have told him. It was the principle of it.

And he'd just have to get by it, Aidan warned himself. He'd also have to do some careful treading over the sensitive areas of her that circumstance had rubbed so raw. He didn't want to be responsible for pinching where it already hurt.

Jesus, he thought, rubbing the back of his neck as he headed down to the pub. The woman was a bucket of work.

"What's the matter with Jude?" Darcy demanded the minute he stepped into the kitchen.

"She's all right. She had some news from home that upset her is all." He picked up the receiver on the wall phone to call Brenna.

"Oh, not her granny." Darcy set down the order she'd just picked up, and her eyes were full of concern.

"No, nothing like that. I'm going to call Brenna and see if she can cover for me a couple of hours. I want to drive Jude home."

"Well, and if she can't, Shawn and I will manage."

Aidan paused with the phone in his hand and smiled. "You're a sweetheart when you want to be, Darcy."

"I like her and I think she needs a bit of fun in her life. Seems to be there's been precious little up to now. And having her husband leave her for another woman before her bridal bouquet was dry is bound to—"

"Wait now—hold on a minute. You knew she was married?"

Darcy lifted a brow. "Of course." She hefted the order, sauntered toward the door with it. "It's not a secret."

"Not a secret," he muttered, then with gritted teeth dialed Brenna's number. "The whole village likely knew, but not me."

TWELVE

By THE TIME Aidan came back and they walked down to his car, Jude had time to calm down, and to review.

Mortification didn't begin to cover it. She had burst into the pub, then had sexually assaulted the man in his place of business. Perhaps in time—twenty or thirty years, she estimated—she would find that particular memory fascinating, and even amusing. But for now it was just humiliating.

Then she had compounded that by raging, weeping, blubbering, and cursing. All in all, she couldn't think of anything she might have done that could have shocked them both more unless it was stripping naked and dancing a jig on his bar.

Her mother had congratulated her on maintaining her dignity while under terrible stress. *Well, Mother,* she thought, *don't look now.*

And after all that, Aidan was driving her home because it was dark and rainy, and he was kind.

She imagined he couldn't wait to be rid of her.

As they bumped up her little road, she tried out a dozen different ways to smooth over the embarrassment, and every one sounded stilted or silly. Still, she had to say something. It would be cowardly, and rude, not to.

So she took a deep breath, then let it out in a rush.

"Do you see her?"

"Who?"

"In the window." Jude reached out, gripping his arm as she stared at the figure in the window of her cottage.

He looked up, smiled a little. "Aye. She's waiting. I wonder if time stretches out for her, or if a year is only a day."

He switched off the engine so they sat with the rain drumming until the figure faded away.

"You did see her. You're not just saying that."

"Of course I saw her, as I have before and will again." He turned his head, studied Jude's profile. "You're not uneasy, are you, staying out here with her?"

"No." Because the answer came so easily, she laughed. "Not at all. I should be, I suppose, but I'm not the least bit uneasy here, or with her. Sometimes . . ."

"Sometimes what?"

She hesitated again, telling herself she shouldn't keep him. But it was so cozy there in the warmth of the car with the rain pattering and the mists swirling. "Well, sometimes I feel her. Something in the air. Some—I don't know how to explain—some ripple in the air. And it makes me sad, because she's sad. I've seen him too."

"Him."

"The faerie prince. I've met him twice now when I've gone to put flowers on Maude's grave. I know it sounds crazy—I know I should probably see a doctor for some tests, but—"

"Did I say it sounded crazy?"

"No." She released another pent-up breath. "I guess that's why I told you, because you wouldn't say it. You wouldn't think it."

And neither did she, not any longer.

"I met him, Aidan." She shifted on her seat, her eyes bright with excitement as she faced him. "I talked to him. The first time I thought he was someone who just lived around here. But the second, it was almost like a dream or a trance or . . . I have something," she said following impulse. "I'd like to show you. I know you probably want to get back, but if you have just a minute."

"Are you asking me in?"

"Yes. I'd—"

"Then I've time enough."

They got out of the car and walked through the rain. A little nervous, she pushed at her damp hair as they stepped inside the cottage. "It's upstairs. I'll bring it down. Do you want some tea?"

"No, I'm fine."

"Just, well, wait," she said and hurried upstairs to her bedroom where she'd buried the stone among her socks.

When she came down, holding it behind her back, Aidan was already lighting the fire. The glow of it shimmered over him as he crouched by the hearth, and Jude's heart gave a pleasantly painful little lurch.

He was as handsome as the faerie prince, she thought. See the way the fire brings out the deep red tones in his hair and shifts and plays over the angles of his face, shoots gold into those wonderful blue eyes of his.

Was it any wonder she was in love with him?

Oh, God, she was in love with him! The force of it struck like a blow in the belly, nearly made her groan. How many more idiotic mistakes could she make in one single day?

She couldn't afford to fall in love with some gorgeous Irishman, to break her heart over him, to make a fool of herself. He was looking for something entirely different, and had made no pretenses about it. He wanted sex and pleasure, fun and excitement. Companionship, too, she imagined. But he didn't want some moony-eyed woman in love with him, particularly one who'd already failed at the only serious relationship she'd allowed herself.

He wanted a love affair, which was a world away from love. And if she wanted to succeed here, with him, to give herself the pleasure of a relationship with him, she would have to learn to separate the two.

She would not complicate this. She would not over-analyze this. She would not ruin this.

So when he rose and turned, she smiled at him. "It's lovely having a fire on a rainy night. Thanks."

"Then come closer to it." He held out a hand.

She was walking into the fire all right, she thought. And she wouldn't give a damn if she got burned. She crossed to him, kept her eyes on his. Slowly, she brought her hand from behind her back, spread her fingers. The diamond nestled in the center of her palm, shooting light and glory.

"Sacred heart of Jesus." Aiden stared at it, blinked. "Is that what I think it is?"

"He poured them like candy out of his bag. Jewels so bright they hurt my eyes. And I watched as they bloomed into flowers over Maude's grave. Except for this one that stayed as it was. I shouldn't believe it," she murmured, thinking as much of love as of the stone in her hand. "But here it is."

He took it from her hand to hold it in the light of the fire. It seemed to pulse, then lay quiet. "It holds every color of the rainbow. There's magic here, Jude Frances." He lifted his gaze to hers. "What will you do with it?"

"I don't know. I was going to take it to a jeweler, have it analyzed, the same way I was going to have myself analyzed. But I've changed my mind. I don't want it tested and studied and documented and appraised. It's enough just to have it, don't you think? Just to know it is. I haven't taken enough on faith in my life. I want to change that."

"That's wise. And brave. And perhaps the very reason it was given into your keeping." He took her hand, turned the palm up. After laying the stone on her palm, he curled her fingers around it. "It's for you, and whatever magic it holds. I'm glad you showed it to me."

"I needed to share it." She held the stone firmly, and though she knew it was foolish, thought she gathered courage from it. "You've been so understanding, and very patient with me. My outrageous behavior, then the way I dumped all my neuroses on you. I don't know how to repay you."

"I'm not keeping a balance sheet."

"I know. You wouldn't. You're the kindest man I know."

He managed not to wince. "Kind, is it?"

"Yes, very."

"And understanding and patient as well."

Her lips curved. "Yes."

"Like a brother might be."

She managed to keep the smile in place. "Well, I . . . hmmm."

"And are you in the habit of throwing yourself into the arms of men you think of like a brother?"

"I have to apologize for that, for embarrassing you."

"Haven't I told you that you apologize too often? Just answer the question."

"Um, well . . . Actually I've never thrown myself into anyone's arms but yours."

"Is that the truth then? Well, it's flattered I am, though you were in some distress at the time."

"Yes. Yes, I was." The stone felt like a lead weight in her hand now. She turned, grateful to have her back to him for a moment, and laid it on the mantel.

"Are you in distress at the moment?"

"No. No, thank you, I'm fine."

"Then let's try it again." He spun her around, and as her lips parted in surprise, captured them. Her body jerked, that instant of shock he always found so arousing. "Are you thinking I'm kind and patient now?" he muttered and bit lightly at the curve of her neck.

"I can't think at all."

"Good." If there was anything more potent than a woman stumbling over her own passion, he'd yet to come across it. "I like you better that way."

"I thought you'd be angry, or—"

"You're thinking again." He nibbled his way up to her temple. "I'll have to ask you to stop that."

"All right. Okay."

Her breathy agreement made him yearn. "*Mavourneen dheelish*. Let me have you tonight." His mouth came back to hers and sent her already scattered thoughts spinning. "Let it be tonight. I can't go on just dreaming of you."

"You still want me?" The stunned pleasure in her voice nearly dropped him to his knees. It humbled him, her complete lack of vanity.

"I want all there is of you. Don't ask me to go tonight."

She'd followed her heart to this place, and had found him. Now she would follow her heart again. "No." She tangled her fingers in his hair, met his mouth with all the newly discovered love and passion in her. "No, don't go."

He could have lowered her to the floor, taken her there and delighted them both in front of the fire. Neither of them was a child, and both were eager. But he remembered a promise made and scooped her up in his arms. When he saw the dazed surprise on her face, he knew it was right.

"I told you that the first time it would be slow and sweet. I'm a man of my word."

No one had ever carried her before. The romance of it was stunning, an erotic fantasy with gilt edges. Her heart-beat drummed in her ears like thunder as he carried her up the steps, down the little hall into the bedroom.

She was grateful for the dark. It would be easier not to be shy in the dark. When he sat her on the edge of the bed, she closed her eyes. Then they sprang open again when he turned on the bedside light.

"Pretty Jude," he murmured, and smiled down at her. "Just sit a moment, and I'll light the fire."

A fire, she thought. Of course, a fire would be good. She linked her hands together and tried to settle the nerves, smooth out the needs. It would add atmosphere as well as warmth. He'd want atmosphere. Oh, God, why couldn't she think of something to say? Why didn't she have some wonderful negligee or lingerie to change into and dazzle him?

Speechless, she watched him straighten from the fire once it began to flame, then begin to light the candles scattered around the room.

"I was going to call you tonight and ask you to dinner."

The idea was such a surprise, such an intriguing one, she stared. "You were?"

"That'll have to wait for another time now." He kept his eyes on her, seeing her nerves, enjoying them a bit, as he switched off the lamp again. And the room was washed in shadows and shifting light.

"I'm not very hungry."

He laughed. "I'm after changing that, right quickly then." To her complete shock, he crouched down and began to untie her shoes. "I've had an appetite for you since you first walked into the pub."

She swallowed. Hard. It was the best she could do. Then he ran a finger lightly over the arch of her bare foot and the breath strangled in her throat.

"You've pretty feet." He said it casually, with a laugh in his eyes as he lifted her foot and nibbled on her toes. The breath that had caught exploded out again, and her fingers dug like spikes into the mattress.

"But I have to admit, after seeing them this morning all damp and rosy I have a preference for your shoulders."

"My—oh . . ." He gave his attention to her other foot and wiped her brain clean. "What?"

"Your shoulders. I fancy them." Because it was true enough, he rose, and lifted Jude to her now tingling feet. "They're graceful, but they're strong." As he spoke, he unbuttoned the shirt she'd borrowed. To torment them both a little longer, he didn't remove it, but only nudged it off her shoulders so he could do as he'd imagined and trail his tongue along the curve.

"Oh, God." The sensation drizzled into her system like gold dust until everything inside her sparkled. When she gripped his hips for balance, he worked his way up the side of her neck to her jaw, like a man slowly sampling his way through a variety of dishes at a banquet.

His mouth brushed over hers, a teasing taste that stirred the juices of her own hunger. He heard it in her quiet moan and came back for a second, longer taste.

Her hands slid up his back, and she moved her body against his in a dreamy rhythm as her head fell back in surrender.

Slow, he said, and sweet. It was exactly right. With the candlelight dancing and the rain softly pattering and her own sighs filling her head, soft kisses grew longer, and deeper. It seemed her body was alive with the taste of him now, rich and male and perfect.

When he tugged his shirt off she gave a low sound of pleasure and let her hands roam over his back, knead into the muscles.

His heart leaped against hers. Those slow, hesitant strokes of her hands were maddening. Wonderful. Her mouth was so soft, so giving. And the way she shivered— nerves and anticipation—when he unhooked her slacks and let them slide to the floor flashed fresh heat into his blood. Gaelic endearments burned in his brain, tumbled off his tongue as he took his mouth over her face, down her throat, once again over those glorious shoulders until her shivers became shudders and her sighs gasps.

Slow down, slow down, he ordered himself. But how could he have known that the need for her would rear up and snap into his soul with jagged teeth? Afraid he would frighten her, he pressed his lips to the curve of her throat and just held her until the rage of it settled again.

She was floating, too tangled in sensations to note the changes of rhythm. Dreamily, she turned her head, found his mouth with hers and slid them both into the kiss. It seemed her bones were dissolving, and the pressure in her belly was glorious. Everywhere he touched, a part of her lit up.

This was making love, was all she could think. At last, this. How could she have mistaken anything else for this?

He had to have more. He slipped the shirt aside and found himself charmed by the simple white bra. To please himself, he trailed a fingertip along the top edge, circled the tiny mole.

Her legs buckled. "Aidan."

"When I saw this little dot this morning," he murmured, watching her face, "I wanted to bite you." When she only blinked at him, he grinned and flicked open the hook of her bra. "It made me wonder what other sexy little secrets you hide under those tidy clothes of yours."

"I don't have any sexy secrets."

The bra fell to the floor. Aidan lowered his gaze, watched the faint flush work over her skin and found it sinfully erotic. "You're wrong about that," he said quietly, then cupped her breasts in his hands.

There, that quick jerk of shock, and the glimmer of surprise in her eyes. Experimentally, he rubbed his thumbs over her nipples and watched those sea-green eyes blur.

"No, don't close them," he said as he lowered her to the bed. "Not yet. I want to see what my touching you does to you."

So he watched her face as he enjoyed her, as he learned the secrets she'd claimed not to have. Silky skin and tumbled hair, all smelling of rain. Soft curves, subtle dips. When his workingman's hands skimmed over her, she would quiver. And each secret he discovered was a pleasure to them both.

When he tasted her, the world slipped away until there was nothing but the rage of her own pulse and the hot glory of his mouth on her skin.

Ripe for release, she arched against his hand when he covered her. Moved against him as the ache sweetened and the sweetness became unbearable. His mouth came down on hers, catching her cry of pleasure. He gave her more, more until her breath was sobs and her body molten.

The eyes that so fascinated him were blind now, and her skin glowing and damp. It wasn't only her world that had slipped away, but his as well. She was all that was left in it.

He said her name once, then slid into her. Heat into heat,

need into need, strong and deep. Holding there, holding, until she wrapped herself around him.

Joined now, they moved together, long, slow strokes that fed the soul. Dazzled, she smiled. Light shimmered, like the brilliance of the diamond as his lips curved in response and met hers.

This, she thought, was the real magic. The most powerful. And clinging to it, she leaped off the edge of the world with him.

Candlelight fluttered. The fire hissed and rain pinged on the windows. There was a gorgeous, exciting, fascinating, and wonderfully naked man in her bed.

Jude felt like a cat who'd just been given the keys to the milking parlor.

"I'm so glad William's having a baby."

Aidan turned his head, found his face buried in her hair, and angled it away again. "What the devil does William have to do with it?"

"Oh. I didn't realize I'd said that out loud."

"It's no worse than thinking about another man when I've yet to get my breath back after loving you."

"I wasn't thinking of him like that." Appalled, she sat up, too mortified to remember she was naked. "I was just thinking that if he wasn't having a baby, my mother wouldn't have told me, and I wouldn't have gotten upset and come down to the pub and—it all led to here, to this," she finished weakly.

He still had the energy for arrogance. Lifting a brow, he said, "I'd have gotten you here eventually."

"I'm glad it was tonight. Now. Because it was so perfect. I'm sorry. It was a stupid thing to say."

"You're going to have to stop assuming every stray thought that comes out of your mouth is stupid. And since there's a logic to the pattern you just mentioned, I say we drink a toast to the timing of William's virility."

Relieved, she beamed at him. "I suppose we could, though he's not half as good in bed as you are." Instantly her cheery grin became a look of horror. "Oh, what a thing to say!"

"If you think I'm insulted by that, you're mistaken." Chuckling, Aidan sat up as well, and kissed her soundly. "I'd say it's worth another toast. To William's stupidity in not recognizing the jewel he had so she could fall into my hands."

Jude threw her arms around him, hugged hard. "No one's ever touched me the way you did. I didn't think anyone would ever want to."

"I'm already wanting to again." He nuzzled into the curve of her neck. "Why don't we go down and have that wine, and a bit of soup or whatever. Then we'll come back and start all over again?"

"I think that's a wonderful idea." She ordered herself not to feel awkward as she climbed out of bed to dress. He'd already seen all of her there was to see, so it was foolish to be shy now.

Still, she was relieved when she was covered in the borrowed shirt and her slacks. But when she reached for a band for her hair, Aidan laid a hand on her shoulder and made her jump.

"Why are you tying it back?"

"Because it's awful."

"I like it wild." He played his fingers through it. "Sort of rioting around in this lovely dense color."

"It's brown." And she'd always considered it as original as tree bark.

"So's mink, darling." He kissed the tip of her nose. "What'll we do with you, Jude Frances, if you ever take the blinders off and really look at yourself? I think you'll be a terror. Come on now and leave it be," he added and began to tug her toward the door. "I'm the one who's looking at it, after all."

She was too pleased to argue, but took a stand once they were in the kitchen. "You cooked breakfast, so I'll fix dinner," she said and got out the wine. "I'm not much of a cook, so you'll have to make do with my fallback meal."

"And what might that be?"

"Soup from a can and grilled cheese sandwiches."

"Sounds like just the trick on a rainy night." He took the wine and settled at a chair at the kitchen table. "Plus I get the pleasure of watching you make it."

"When I first saw this kitchen, I thought it was charming." She moved to the hearth and lit the fire with an ease that surprised Aidan a little. "Then I realized there wasn't a dishwasher, or a microwave, or so much as an electric can opener or coffee machine."

Laughing, she got a can of soup out of the pantry and set to opening it with her little manual opener. "I was a bit appalled, let me tell you. And I've done more in this kitchen and enjoyed what I've cooked here more than anything I ever put together in my condo. And that kitchen's state of the art. Jenn-Air range, sub-zero refrigerator."

As she spoke, she started the soup, ducked into the refrigerator for cheese and butter. "Of course, I haven't tackled anything complicated. I'm gathering the courage to try to make soda bread. It seems fairly basic, and if I don't mess it up too badly, I could work up to actually baking a cake."

"Have you a yen to bake, then?"

"I think I do." She smiled over her shoulder as she spread butter on bread. "But it's rather daunting when you've never done it before."

"You won't know if you like it unless you try."

"I know. I hate failing at things." She shook her head as she heated the skillet. "I know it's a problem. It's the reason I haven't tried a lot of the things I think about trying. I always convince myself I'll muck it up anyway, so I don't try. It comes from being an awkward child of graceful parents."

She laid the sandwiches in the skillet, pleased when they sizzled cheerfully. "But I make pretty good cheese sandwiches, so you won't starve." She turned and bumped solidly into his chest.

His mouth was on hers again. Hot, a little rough and very exciting. When he let her breathe again, he nodded. "Nothing awkward about that, or the rest of you, as far as I've seen."

Satisfied, he went back to the table and his wine.

Jude recovered in time to keep the soup from boiling over.

He stayed through the night so that she could curl warm against him. At sunrise, when the light glided through the window to shimmer on the air, he reached for her again, making lazy love to her that left her steeped in dreams.

When next she woke, he was sitting on the bed beside her, holding a cup of coffee and stroking her hair.

"Oh. What time is it?"

"Past ten, and I've ruined your reputation."

"Ten?" She sat up quickly, surprised and grateful when he handed her the coffee. "My reputation?"

"Beyond redemption now. I meant to leave at dawn so my car wouldn't be in your street. But I was distracted."

She sighed deeply. "I remember."

"There'll be talk now, about that Gallagher lad cozying up to the Yank."

Her eyes glittered. "Will there, really? How wonderful."

He laughed, tugged on her hair. "I thought somehow you might enjoy that."

"I'd like it better if I ruined your reputation. I've never ruined anyone's reputation before." She touched his face, delighted that she could, and trailed her finger down over the narrow cleft in his chin. "I could be that loose American woman who's stolen the owner of Gallagher's from under the noses of all the local ladies."

"Well, now, if you've decided to be a loose woman, I'll be back tonight after closing, and you can take unfair advantage of me."

"I'd be glad to."

"Keep a light burning for me, darling." He leaned forward to kiss her, then lingered over it long enough to make himself uncomfortable. "Bloody paperwork," he muttered. "I have to go deal with it. Miss me, will you, Jude?"

"All right."

She settled back against the pillows when he left, listened to the sound of the door closing behind him, then of his car starting.

For an hour she did nothing but sit in bed and hum.

THIRTEEN

I'M HAVING A love affair.

Jude Frances Murray is having a passionate affair with a gorgeous, charming, sexy Irishman.

I just love writing that.

I can barely resist behaving like a schoolgirl and writing his name over and over again in a notebook.

Aidan Gallagher. What a marvelous name.

He's so handsome. I know it's completely shallow to dwell on someone's physical appearance, but . . . Well, if I can't be shallow in the pages of my own journal, where can I be?

His hair is a deep, rich chestnut, and the sunlight teases out the red in it. He has wonderful eyes, a dark and brilliant blue, and when he turns them on me, just looks at me as he often does, everything inside me goes hot and soft. His is a strong face. Good bones, as Granny would say. His mouth smiles slow and easy, and there's just the slightest of clefts in his chin.

His body . . . I can hardly believe I've had it over mine, under mine. It's so hard and firm, with muscles like iron. Powerful, I suppose is the word.

My lover has a very powerful build.

I suppose that's enough wallowing in the superficial.

All right . . . done.

His other qualities are just as impressive. He's very kind and has a lively sense of humor. He listens. That's a skill in danger of being lost, and Aidan's is well honed.

His family ties are deep and strong, his work ethic admirable. I find his mind fascinating, and his skill in story-telling entertaining. The truth is, I could listen to him for hours.

He's traveled extensively, seen places I've only dreamed of seeing. Now that his parents have settled in Boston, he's taken over the family business and slipped into the role of head of the family with a calm and rather casual authority.

I know I shouldn't be in love. What Aidan and I have is a satisfying physical relationship, and a lovely and affectionate friendship. Both are precious, and should be more than enough for anyone.

But I can't help being in love with him.

I've come to realize that everything ever written about falling in love is absolutely true. The air's sweeter, the sun brighter. I don't think my feet have touched the ground in days.

It's terrifying. And it's wonderful.

Nothing I've ever experienced is like this. I had no idea I had such feelings inside me. Passionate and giddy and absolutely foolish feelings.

I know I'm the same person. I can look in the mirror and it's still me looking back. Yet somehow there seems to be more of me. It's as if pieces that were hidden or unac-knowledged have suddenly tumbled into place.

I realize the physical and emotional stimuli, the charge of endorphins and . . . oh, the hell with that. This doesn't need to be analyzed and slotted. It just has to be.

It's so outrageously romantic, the way he walks to my cottage at night. Coming through the gloom or the moonlight to knock at my door. He brings me wildflowers or seashells or pretty stones.

He does things to my body I've only read about. Oh, God, reading has definitely taken second place.

I feel wanton. I have to laugh at myself. Jude Frances Murray has a sex drive. And it shows no signs of abating.

I've never had so much fun in my entire life.

I had no idea romance could be fun. Why didn't someone tell me?

When I look in the mirror, I feel beautiful. Imagine that. I feel beautiful.

Today I'm picking Darcy up and we're going to Dublin to shop. I'm going to buy extravagant things for no reason at all.

The Gallagher house was old and lovely and sat on the edge of the village, up a steep little hill and facing the sea. If Jude had asked, she would have been told that Shamus's son, another Aidan, had built the house there the same year he married.

The Gallaghers didn't make their living on the sea, but they enjoyed the look of it.

Other generations had added bits and pieces to the house over the years, as money and time had allowed. And now that there were many rooms, most of them had a view to the sea.

The house itself was dark wood and sand-colored stone that seemed to be cobbled together in no particular style. Jude found it intriguing and unique. It was two stories, with a wide front porch that needed a coat of paint and a narrow stone walk worn by traffic. Its windows were in diamond-shaped panes she imagined were the devil to keep clean.

She thought it was caught somewhere between grand and quaint, with just enough of both. And with the light morning fog just burning off around it, it held a bit of mystery as well.

She wondered what it had been like for Aidan to grow up there, in the big, rambling house, a stone's throw from the beach and cozy enough to the village to have swarms of friends.

The gardens needed work, to Jude's newly experienced eye, but they had a nice, wild way about them.

A lean black cat stretched out on the walkway gave Jude a steely stare out of golden eyes as she approached. Hoping he wouldn't take a swipe at her, she crouched down tentatively to scratch between his ears.

He rewarded the attention by narrowing those eyes and letting out a purr that rumbled like a freight train.

"That's Bub." Shawn stood in the front doorway and shot Jude a grin. "Short for Beelzebub, as he's a devil of a cat by nature. Come in and have some tea, Jude, for if you're expecting Darcy to be ready on time, you don't know her."

"There's no hurry."

"That's a good thing, as she'll primp an hour just to run out for a quart of milk. God knows how long she'll be admiring herself for a trip to Dublin."

He stepped back to let Jude in, then tossed a shout over his shoulder toward the stairs. "Jude's here, Darcy, and she says to get your vain ass moving if you expect a ride to Dublin City."

"Oh, but I didn't," Jude burst out, flustered, and had Shawn laughing as he drew her firmly inside.

"She won't pay any mind. Can I get you some tea, then?"

"I'm fine, really." She glanced around, noting that the living room spilling off the little foyer was cluttered and comfortable.

Home, she thought again. It said home and family. And welcome.

"Aidan's down the pub seeing to deliveries." Shawn took her hand in a friendly manner and tugged her into the living room. He'd been wanting to have some time with her, to take stock of the woman who had his brother so enchanted. "So you'll have to make do with me."

"Oh. Well, that doesn't sound like a hardship."

When he laughed again she realized she'd never have flirted so easily, so harmlessly with a man a few months before. Certainly not one with a face like a wicked angel.

"My brother hasn't given me opportunity to have more than a word with you up to now." Shawn's eyes twinkled. "Keeping you to himself as he is."

"You're always in the kitchen when I come into the pub."

"Where they keep me chained. But we can make up for it now."

He was flirting right back with her, she realized, just as harmlessly. It didn't make her nervous. It didn't give her those odd and lovely liquid pulls that flirting with Aidan did. It just made her comfortable.

"Then I'll start by saying you have a lovely house."

"We're happy with it." He led her to a chair, and when she sat, made himself comfortable on the arm of it. "Darcy and I rattle about well enough."

"It's made for more people. A big family, lots of children."

"It's held that more often than it hasn't. Our father was one of ten."

"Ten? Good God!"

"We've uncles and aunts and cousins scattered all over and back again—Gallaghers and Fitzgeralds. You being one of them," he added with a grin. "I remember as a boy having packs of them coming in and out of the house from time to time, so I was always sharing me bed with some lad who was my cousin from Wicklow or Boston or Devonshire."

"Do they still come back?"

"Now and then. You did, cousin Jude." He liked the way she smiled at that, sweet and a little shy. "But it's Darcy and me in the house most times now. And will be until the first of the three of us decides to marry and start a family. The house'll go to the one who does."

"Won't the other two mind?"

"No. That's the Gallagher way."

"And you'll know you'll always be welcome here, that it'll still be home."

"That's right." He said it quietly because he read tones and nuances well, and could see she was yearning for a home of her own. "Do you have a house in Chicago?"

"No. It's a condo like a glorified flat," she added, then suddenly restless, rose. Flat, she thought again, was precisely how it seemed to her now. "This is a wonderful spot. You can watch the sea."

She started to walk to a window, then stopped by a battered old piano. The keys were yellowed, and several of them chipped, and over the scarred wood sheet music was scattered. "Who plays?"

"All of us." Shawn came up beside her, put his long fingers over the keys and played a quick series of chords.

Battered the instrument might have been, but its notes rang sweet and true. "Do you play as well?"

"A little. Not very well." She blew out a breath, reminding herself not to be such a moron. "Yes."

"Which is it?"

"Yes, I play."

"Well, then, let's hear it." He gave her a nudge, hip against hip, that surprised her into sitting down on the bench.

"I haven't played in months," she began, but he was already riffling through the sheet music, setting a piece in front of her before joining her on the bench.

"Try this one."

Because she only intended to play a few chords, she didn't bother digging her reading glasses out of her purse. Without them, she had to lean closer and squint a little. She felt the skitter of nerves, wiped damp palms on her thighs, and told herself it wasn't one of the childhood recitals that had scared her into desperate nausea.

Still, she had to take two deep breaths, which made Shawn's lips twitch before she began to play.

"Oh!" She flowed from the first bar into the second. "Oh, this is lovely." She forgot her nerves in sheer pleasure as the notes drifted out dreamily, as her throat began to ache from it. "It's heartbreaking."

"It's meant to be." He cocked his head, listening to the music as he studied her. He could see easily why she'd caught his brother's eye. The pretty face, the quiet manner, and those surprising expressive and misty eyes.

Yes, Shawn mused, the combination would draw Aidan's interest, then wind around his heart. As for her heart, it was a yearning one. That he understood well.

"You play very well indeed, Jude Frances. Why did you say you didn't?"

"I'm used to saying I don't do things well, because I usually don't." She answered absently, losing herself in the music. "Anyone could play this well. It's wonderful. What's it called?"

"I haven't named it yet."

"You wrote it?" She stopped playing to stare at him. Artists of all kinds, any kind, left her awestruck. "Really? Shawn, it's gorgeous."

"Oh, don't start flattering the man. He's irritating enough." Brenna strode into the room and stuffed her hands into the pockets of her baggy jeans.

"The O'Toole here has no appreciation for music unless it's a rebel song and she's drinking a pint."

"When you write one, I'll lift a glass to you as well."

They sneered companionably at each other.

"What are you doing here? There's nothing broken that I know of."

"Do you see my toolbox in my hand?" Would he never just *look* at her? she wondered. The bloody bat-blind moron. "I'm going to Dublin with Jude and Darcy." Brenna lifted a shoulder. "I got weary of Darcy badgering me about it, so I've surrendered." She turned and shouted up the stairs, "Darcy, for sweet Jesus' sake, what's taking you so bloody long? I've been waiting an hour."

"Now you'll have to confess that lie to Father Clooney," Shawn told her, "as you just walked in the house."

"It's only venial, and it may get her down here before next week." She dropped into a chair. "Why aren't you down to the pub helping Aidan? It's delivery day."

"Because, Mother, he asked me to stay and see to Jude until Darcy made her entrance. But since you're here, I'll be off. You'll come back and play again, Jude Frances." He smiled as he rose. "It's a pleasure to hear my tunes played by someone who appreciates music."

He started out, pausing by Brenna's chair long enough to tug the bill of her cap over her eyes. She yanked it back up as the front door slammed behind him.

"He acts as if I were still ten and kicking his ass at football." Then she gave a twinkling grin. "It's a fine ass, too, isn't it?"

Jude laughed and rose to straighten the sheet music. "The rest of him isn't bad, either. And he writes wonderful music."

"Aye, he's a rare talent in him."

Jude turned, lifted her eyebrows. "You didn't seem to think so a minute ago."

"Well, if I told him, he'd just get all puffed up about it and be more unbearable than usual."

"I suppose you've known him forever."

"Forever and a day, it seems," Brenna agreed. "There's four years between us, and he came along first."

"And you've been in this house too many times to count. You can walk into it as though it's your own, because that's the kind of house it is."

Jude rose to wander, to look at family photographs scattered here and there in frames that didn't match, an old pitcher with a chipped lip that held a brilliant array of spring flowers. The wallpaper was faded, the rug worn.

"I suppose I've run as tame here as Darcy and her brothers have in my own house," Brenna told her. "Sure, Mrs. Gallagher's laid the flat of her hand across my bottom with as much enthusiasm as she did her own children."

Jude marveled a little at that. No one had ever laid the flat of their hand across her bottom. Reason was always employed in discipline, and passive-aggressive guilt laid. "It would have been wonderful, don't you think, to grow up here, surrounded by music."

She circled the room, noting the comfortably faded cushions and old wood, the clutter and the patterns of light through the windows. It could use some sprucing, without a doubt, she mused. But it was all here. Home, family, continuity.

Yes, this was the place for family, for children, the way her cottage was the place for solitude and contemplation.

She imagined the walls in this house held the echos of too many voices raised in temper, in joy, to ever be truly quiet.

The clatter on the stairs had her turning to see Darcy race down them, her hair billowing out. "Are you just going to laze around all day?" Darcy demanded. "Or are we off to Dublin?"

It was a much different trip to Dublin than it had been from. The car was full of chatter, leaving Jude barely any room for nerves. Darcy was full of village gossip. It seemed young Douglas O'Brian had gotten Maggie Brennan in trouble and there was to be a wedding the minute the banns were called. And James Brennan had been so outraged by the idea of his daughter sneaking out to wrestle with Douglas, he'd gotten drunk as three princes and spent the night sleeping in the dooryard, as his wife locked him out of the house.

"I heard that Mr. Brennan went hunting for young Douglas, and the lad hid out in his father's hayloft—where the smart wagers are the deed was first done—until the crisis passed." Brenna stretched out like a lazy cat in the backseat, with the bill of her cap over her eyes. "Maggie's going to have second thoughts soon enough, when she finds her belly swelled and that feckless Douglas with his boots under the bed."

"The pair of them not yet twenty," Darcy added with a shake of her head. "It's a sorry way to start a life."

"Why do they have to get married?" Jude wanted to know. "They're too young."

Darcy just stared at her. "Well, they're having a baby, so what else is to be done?"

Jude opened her mouth, shut it before she could logically point out the variety of alternatives. This, she reminded herself, was Ireland. Instead, she tried another route. "Is that what you'd do?" she asked Darcy. "If you found yourself pregnant?"

"First, I'd be careful not to have sex with someone I wasn't prepared to live with should the need arise. And second," she said after some thought, "I'm twenty-four and employed, and not afraid of village gossip so much that I wouldn't raise the child on my own if I'd made a blunder."

She turned her head then, lifted a brow at Jude. "You're not pregnant, are you?"

"No!" Jude nearly swerved off the road before she recovered. "No, of course not."

"Why 'of course not' when you've been sleeping with Aidan every night for the past week? Protection's all well and good, but it's not infallible, is it?"

"No, but . . ."

"Ah, stop scaring her, Darcy. You know you're just jealous because she's having regular sex and you're not."

Darcy tossed a sneering look toward the backseat. "And neither are you, my girl."

"And more's the pity." Brenna shifted, came forward to prop her arms on the back of the front seats. "So tell us poor deprived women about sex with Aidan. There's a pal, Jude."

"No." She said it with a laugh.

"Oh, don't be a prude." Brenna poked her shoulder.

"Tell me, does he take his sweet time about it, or is he a member of the Irish Foreplay Club?"

"The Irish Foreplay Club?"

"Ah, you've not heard of it," Brenna said soberly as Darcy snickered. "Their battle cry is 'Brace yourself, Bridget.' Then they're in and out before their lager's gone warm."

Surprising herself, Jude all but screamed with laughter. "He doesn't call me Bridget unless I call him Shamus."

"She's made a joke." Darcy wiped an imaginary tear from her eye. "Our Jude. What a proud moment this is."

"And a fine one," Brenna agreed. "But tell us, Jude, does he take his time with it, sort of sliding around and nibbling in the right places, or is it all hot and fast and over with before you can call out you've seen God?"

"I can't talk about sex with Aidan with his sister in the car."

"Well, then, let's dump her out so you can tell me."

"Why can't you talk of it?" Darcy demanded, with barely a pause for a glare at Brenna. "I know he has sex. The bastard. But if it troubles you, don't think of me as his sister for the moment, but as your friend."

Exasperated, Jude blew out a breath. "All right, I'll just say it's the best I've ever had. Although with William it was like . . . a precise military march," she decided, shocking herself again. "And before him there was only Charles."

"Charles, was it? Brenna, our Jude has a past."

"And who was Charles?" Brenna prompted.

"He was in finance."

"So he was rich." Darcy pounced eagerly on the magic word.

"His family was. We met during my last year of college. I suppose the physical relationship with him was . . . Well, let's say that when it was done all the figures added up, but it was a rather tedious process. Aidan's romantic.''

Her companions made oohing noises that had her giggling helplessly. "Oh, stop. I'm not saying another word about it.''

"What a bitch to tease us that way." Brenna tugged on Jude's hair. "Sure you can give us just one little example of his romantic side as relates to good sex.''

"One?''

"Just one and we'll be satisfied, won't we, Darcy?''

"Why, of course. We wouldn't pry into her personal life, would we?''

"All right. The first time, he picked me up right off the floor at the cottage and carried me upstairs. All the way upstairs to the bedroom.''

"Like Rhett carried Scarlett?" Darcy asked. "Or over the shoulder like you were a sack of potatoes?''

"Like Rhett and Scarlett.''

"That's a good one." Brenna pillowed her cheek on her arms. "He gets high marks for that.''

"He treats me like I'm special.''

"Why shouldn't he?" Darcy demanded.

"No one ever has. And, well, since we're on the subject, and it's not exactly a secret what's going on, I don't have anything . . . well, pretty, sexy. Lingerie and that kind of thing. I thought maybe you could help me pick some out.''

"I know just the place for it." Darcy all but rubbed her hands together.

"I spent two thousand pounds on underwear.''

Dazed, Jude walked down bustling Grafton Street. There were people everywhere, swarming. Shoppers, tourists, packs of teenagers, and every few feet, it seemed, musicians playing for coins. It was dazzling, the noise and colors and shapes. But nothing was more dazzling than what she'd just done.

"Two thousand. On underwear."

"And worth every penny," Darcy said briskly. "He'll be a slave to you."

They were loaded with shopping bags, and though Jude had gone into the foray determined to buy recklessly, her idea of reckless was Darcy's notion of conservative. Somehow, within two hours she accumulated what seemed like an entire wardrobe, with accessories, all at Darcy's ruthless instigation.

"I can't carry anything else."

"Here." Stopping, Darcy snatched some of the bags from Jude and shoved them at Brenna.

"I didn't buy anything."

"So you have free hands, then, don't you? Oh! Look at those shoes." Darcy barreled through the crowd gathered around a trio of fiddlers, homing in on target. "They're darling."

"I want my tea," Brenna muttered, then scowled at the strappy black shoes with four-inch heels that Darcy was drooling over. "You'd have blisters and calf cramps before you'd walked a kilometer in those things."

"They're not for walking, you idiot. I'm having them." Darcy breezed through the door of the shop.

"I'll never get my tea," Brenna complained. "I'll die of starvation and dehydration and the pair of you won't even notice as I'll be buried under a mountain of shopping sacks, in which, I'll add, is not a single thing of my own."

"We'll have tea as soon as I try on the shoes. Here, Jude, these are for you."

"I don't need any more shoes." But she was weak and collapsed in a chair and found herself studying the pretty bronze-toned pumps. "They're lovely, but then I'd need a bag to go with them."

"A bag. Jesus." Brenna rolled her eyes back in her head and slid out of the chair in a heap.

She bought the shoes and a bag, then a wonderful jacket from the shop just down the street. Then there was a silly straw hat that she simply had to have for gardening. Because they were so overloaded, they took a vote and with Brenna the only nay hauled their purchases back to the car to lock them in the trunk before hunting up a place for a meal.

"Thank Mary and all the saints." Brenna sprawled in a booth in a tiny Italian restaurant that smelled gloriously of garlic. "I'm faint with hunger. I'll have a pint of Harp," she ordered the second the waiter shuffled over, "and a pizza with everything on it but your kitchen sink."

"No, you won't." Darcy flipped out her napkin and shot the waiter a smile that had him tumbling directly into love. "We'll get a pizza and we each pick two of the toppings. I'll have a Harps as well, but just a glass."

"Well, then, I want mushrooms and sausage for my picks."

"Fine." Darcy nodded across the booth at Brenna. "And I'll have black olives and green peppers. Jude?"

"Ah, mineral water and . . ." She caught Brenna's eye, kept her face sober as her friend desperately mouthed pepperoni and capers. "Pepperoni and capers," she ordered dutifully.

She sighed, sat back and took inventory. Her feet hurt miserably, she couldn't remember half of what she'd just bought, she had a vague headache from lack of food and presence of constant conversation, and she was joyously happy about all of it.

"It's the first day I've spent in Dublin," Jude began. "I haven't been to one museum or gallery, or taken a single picture. I didn't walk St. Stephen's Green or go to Trinity College to see the library or the Book of Kells. It's shameful."

"Why? Dublin's not going anywhere." Darcy pulled herself away from her flirtation with the waiter. "You can come back and do all that whenever you like."

"I suppose I can. It's just that normally, that's what I would have done. And I'd have planned it all out, pored over the guidebooks and made up an itinerary and a schedule, and while I would have figured in some shopping time for mementoes, that would have been at the bottom of the list."

"So you just turned the list around, didn't you?" Darcy offered the waiter another beaming smile when he served their drinks.

"Everything's turned around. Wait." She gripped Brenna's wrist before she could lift her pint.

"Jude, my throat's dry as an eighty-year-old virgin. Have pity."

"I just want to say that I've never had friends like you."

"Sure and there aren't any the likes of us." Brenna winked, then rolled her eyes as Jude held her wrist down.

"No, I mean . . . I've never had any really close women friends that I could have ridiculous conversations about sex with, or share pizza with, or who help me pick out black lace underwear."

"Oh, God, don't go misty now, there's a good girl, Jude." A little desperate, Brenna turned her hand over to pat Jude's. "I have sympathetic tear ducts, and no control over them."

"Sorry." But it was too late. Her eyes were already filled and shimmering. "I'm just so happy."

"There now." Sniffling herself, Darcy passed out paper napkins. "We're happy, too. To friendship, then."

"Yes, to friendship." Jude let out an unsteady sigh as glasses clinked. *"Slainte."*

She saw some of Dublin after all as they walked off the pizza. Jude finally dug out her camera and delighted herself with shots of the graceful arch of bridges over the grand River Liffey, and the charm of the shady greens, the lush baskets of flowers decking the pubs.

She watched a street artist paint a sunrise over the sea, then on impulse bought it for Aidan.

She had Brenna and Darcy pose a dozen times and bribed them with eclairs from a sweet shop to explore just a bit longer.

Even when they trudged back to the car park, her energy level was high. She thought she could go on endlessly. When they drove away from Dublin the western sky was splashed with the colors of sunset that seemed to last forever in the long spring evening.

And the moon rose as they approached Ardmore, to sprinkle the fields with light and to spread white swords over the sea.

Even after she'd dropped her friends at home and helped Darcy cart in her packages, she wasn't tired. She almost danced into her cottage and, hauling her own bags upstairs, called out cheerfully.

"I'm back, and I had a wonderful time."

She wasn't planning on having it end. Her toughest decision, she thought, would be to choose just what to wear under her new silk blouse.

She was going to extend the evening with a visit to Gallagher's before closing. To flirt openly and outrageously with Aidan.

FOURTEEN

HE WAS SWAMPED. There'd been a step-dance exhibition at the school that evening, and it seemed half the village had decided to drop into Gallagher's afterward to hoist a pint. Several of the young girls had changed back into their dancing shoes to reprise the show for his customers.

It made for a happy sound, and a full pub.

He was pulling pints with both hands, holding three conversations at once and manning the till. He wanted to shoot himself for giving Darcy the day off.

Shawn slipped in and out of the kitchen as time allowed and lent a hand at the bar and with the serving. But he'd get caught up in the dancing and forget to come back as often as not.

"It's not a bleeding party," Aidan reminded him, again, when Shawn strolled back behind the bar.

"Sure it sounds like one to me. Everyone's happy enough." Shawn nodded to the crowd that circled three dancers. "The Duffy girl's the best of the lot, to my thinking. She's got a way with her."

"Leave off watching them, would you, and get down to the other end of the bar."

The abrupt tone only made Shawn smile. "Missing your lady, are you? Can't blame you for it. She's a sweetheart."

Aidan sighed and passed brimming glasses into eager hands. "I haven't time to miss anything when I'm up to my ass in beer."

"Well, then, that's a pity, as she just walked in and looking fresh and pretty as a dewdrop despite the hour," Shawn added when Aidan's head whipped around.

He'd tried not to think of her. In fact, he'd made a concerted effort on it, mostly to see if he could manage it. He'd done fairly well, only finding himself distracted by thoughts of her a couple dozen times that day.

Now here she was, with her hair bound back and her smile all for him. By the time she'd squeezed her way to the bar, her smile was a laugh, and he'd forgotten about the Guinness he was building.

"What's going on?" She had to lift her voice to a near shout and lean in close, so close that he caught her scent, the mystery of it that lingered on her skin.

"A bit of a party, it seems. I'll get you some wine when I've got a free hand." He'd rather have used that free hand, both hands, to snatch her up, haul her over the bar, and gather her in.

You're well and truly hooked, Gallagher, he thought, and decided he rather enjoyed the sensation.

"Did you have a fine time in Dublin, then?"

"Yes, a wonderful time. I bought everything that wasn't nailed down. And if I started to resist, Darcy talked me into it."

"She's good at spending money," Aidan began, then caught himself. "Darcy? She's back. Oh, thank the Lord. Another pair of hands might get us through the rest of the night without a riot."

"You can have mine."

"Hmm?"

"I can take orders." The idea took root in her head and bloomed. "And serve."

"Darling, I can't ask you to do that." He shifted as someone elbowed to the bar to order pints and glasses and fizzy water.

"You're not asking. And I'd like it. If I bungle it, everyone will just think the Yank's a bit slow, then you can call Darcy."

"Have you ever waitressed before?" He gave her an indulgent smile that instantly put her back up.

"How hard can it be?" she snapped back and to prove her point, turned and muscled her way toward one of the little tables to get started.

"Didn't take a pad or a tray." Aidan looked at his customer for sympathy as he filled the order. "And if I was to call Darcy now, that one would have my head for breakfast."

"Women," he was told, "are dangerous creatures at the best of times."

"True enough, true enough, but that one is normally of a calm nature. That's five pounds eight. And," he continued as he took the money and made change, "it's the ones with the calm natures who can cut your throat the quickest when riled."

"You're a wise man, Aidan."

"Aye." Aidan took a breath in a moment's lull. "Wise enough not to call Darcy and have two females bashing at me."

Still, he figured it wouldn't take Jude more than a quarter hour to realize she was over her head. She was a practical woman, after all. And later he could smooth her feathers by saying it was a rare night in the pub in any case, and how thoughtful it had been of her to offer to help, and so on and so forth until he got her naked and in bed.

Pleased with the image, Aidan served the next cheerfully. And he had a smile waiting for Jude as she wove her way back to the bar. "I'll get you that wine now," he began.

"I don't drink on the job," she said smartly. "I need two pints of Harp and a glass of Smithwick's, two whiskeys, um, Paddy's, two Cokes, and a Baileys." She offered a smug smile. "And I could use one of those little aprons if you have one handy."

He started the order, cleared his throat. "Ah, you don't know the prices."

"You have a list of them, don't you? Put them in the apron. I can add, and quite well, too. If you have a tray, while you're filling that order, I can clear off some of the empties before they end up broken on the floor."

A quarter hour, he thought again, and dug out a menu, an apron, laid them both on a tray and passed it over. "It's kind it is of you to pitch in, Jude Frances."

She lifted her brows. "You don't think I can do it." With this, she flounced away.

"Does it hurt?" Shawn asked from behind him.

"What?"

"Shoehorning your foot in your mouth that way. I bet it cracks the jaw something fierce." He only snickered when Aidan jabbed him sharply, elbow into ribs. "She has a way with her, too," he added, watching as Jude cleared off one of the low tables and chatted with the family who sat there. "I'd be happy to take her off your hands if . . ."

He trailed off, a little daunted by the vicious look Aidan

shot at him. "Just joking," he muttered and slipped back to the other end of the bar.

Jude came back, began unloading the empties, loading the first order. "A pint and a glass of Guinness, two Orangeens, and a cup of tea with whiskey."

Before Aidan could speak, she'd hefted the tray, just unsteadily enough to make him hold his breath, and moved off to serve.

She was having the time of her life. She was in the middle of it all, part of it all. Music and movement and shouted conversation and laughter. People called her by name and asked how it was all going. No one seemed the least surprised that she was taking orders and emptying ashtrays.

She knew she didn't have Darcy's graceful efficiency and style, but she was handling it. And if she'd almost poured a pint of beer on Mr. Duffy, the operative word was "almost." He'd caught it himself with a wink and grin and said he'd sooner have it in him than on him.

She managed the money, too, and didn't think she made any important mistakes. In fact, one of her apron pockets was bulging with tips that had her glowing with pride.

When Shawn breezed by and swung her into a quick dance, she was too surprised to be embarrassed. "I don't know how."

"Sure you do. Will you come by and play my music again, Jude Frances?"

"I'd like that. But you have to let go. I'm running out of breath and stepping all over your feet."

"If you were to give me a kiss, you'd have Aidan boiling with jealousy."

"I would not. Really?" His grin was irresistible. "I'll just kiss you because you're so pretty."

When he gaped in shock at that, she kissed his cheek.

"Now, I'm supposed to be working. The boss will dock my pay if I keep dancing with you."

"Those Gallagher lads are shameless," Kathy Duffy told her as Jude cleared more glasses. "Bless them for it. A pair of good women would settle them down, but not so much they wouldn't be interesting."

"Aidan's married to the pub," Kevin Duffy said as he lit a cigarette. "And Shawn to his music. It'll be years yet before either of them's taking on a wife."

"Nothing to stop a clever lass from trying, is there?" And Kathy winked at Jude.

Jude managed a smile as she moved to another table. She managed to keep it in place as she took the orders. But her mind was whirling.

Is that what people thought? she wondered. That she was trying to wrangle Aidan into marriage? Why it had never crossed her mind. Not seriously. Hardly at all.

Did he think that was what she was aiming for?

She stole a glance at him, watched him nimbly pulling pints as he talked to two of the Riley sisters. No, of course he didn't. They were both just enjoying themselves. Enjoying each other. If the thought of marriage had crossed her mind, it was natural enough. But she hadn't dwelled on it.

The fact was, she didn't want to. She'd been down that road and had been smeared on the pavement.

Fun was better. The lack of commitment and expectations was liberating. They had mutual affection and respect, and if she was in love with him, well . . . that just made it all the more romantic.

She wasn't going to do anything to spoil it. In fact, she was going to do everything she could to enhance it, to squeeze every drop of pleasure out of the time she had.

"When you come back from your trip there, Jude, I'll have another pint before closing."

"Hmm?" Distracted, she looked down at the wide, patient face of Jack Brennan. "Oh, sorry." She picked up his empty, then frowned at him.

"I'm not pissed," he promised. "My heart's all mended. Fact is, I don't know why I got in such a state over a woman. But if you're worried, you can ask Aidan if I can stand another pint."

He was so sweet, she thought, and holding back on an urge to pat his head as she might that of a big, shaggy dog. "No urge to break his nose?"

"Well, now, I'll admit I've always half wanted to just because it's never been managed. And he broke mine some time back."

"Aidan broke your nose?" It was appalling. It was fascinating.

"Not on actual purpose," Jack qualified. "We were fifteen and playing football and one thing led to another. Aidan's never been much of a one for bloodying his mates unless . . ."

"One thing leads to another?"

"Aye." Jack beamed at her. "And I don't think he's had himself a good mix-up in months. Due for one most like, but he's too busy courting you to find time for a scuffle."

"He isn't courting me."

Jack pursed his lips on an expression caught between concern and puzzlement. "Aren't you sweet on him, then?"

"I—" How did she answer that? "I like him very much. I'd better get you that pint. It's nearly closing time."

"You've been run off your feet," Aidan said when he closed the door behind the last straggler. "Sit down now, Jude, and I'll get you a glass of wine."

"I wouldn't mind it." She had to admit it had been work.

Delightful but exhausting. Her arms ached from carting heavy trays. It was no wonder, she decided, that Darcy's arms were so beautifully toned.

And her feet, it didn't bear thinking about how much her feet were throbbing.

She sank onto a stool, rolled her shoulders.

In the kitchen Shawn was cleaning up and singing about a wild colonial boy. The air was blue with smoke, and ripe still with the smells of beer and whiskey.

She found it all very homey.

"If you decide to give up psychology," Aidan said as he set a glass in front of her. "I'm hiring."

Nothing he said could have pleased her more. "I did all right, didn't I?"

"You did brilliantly." He took her hand, kissed it. "Thanks."

"I liked it. I haven't given that many parties. They make me so nervous. The planning keeps me in a constant state of anxiety. Then the hostessing, making sure everything's running smoothly. This was like giving a party without all the nerves. And . . ." She jingled the coins in her apron pocket. "I got paid."

"Now you can sit and tell me about your day in Dublin while I clean up here."

"I'll tell you about it while I help you clean up."

He decided not to risk her good mood by arguing again, but intended to have her do nothing more complex than clearing empties and setting them on the bar. But she was quicker than he'd thought and had her sleeves rolled up while he was still dealing with behind-the-bar work and the till.

With a pail and a rag she'd gotten from Shawn, she began to mop down the tables.

He listened to her, the way her voice flowed up and down

as she described what she'd seen and what she'd done that day. The words weren't so important, Aidan thought. It was just so soothing to listen to her.

She seemed to bring such blessed quiet with her wherever she went.

He started on the floors, working around and with her. It was amazing, he mused, how smoothly she slid into his rhythm. Or was he sliding into hers? He couldn't tell. But it seemed so natural, the way she clicked into his place, his world. His life, for that matter.

He'd never pictured her carting trays or making change. Of course it wasn't what she was meant for, but she'd done it well. A lark for her, he supposed. She certainly wasn't fashioned to be wiping up spilled beer every night. But she did so with such practical ease he had an urge to cuddle her.

When he followed it, wrapping his arms around her waist and drawing her back against him, she settled right in.

"This is nice," she murmured.

"It is, yes. Though I'm keeping you up late doing dirty work."

"I like it. Now that everything's quiet, and everyone's gone home to bed, I can think about what Kathy Duffy said to me, or the joke Douglas O'Brian told, and listen to Shawn singing in the kitchen. In Chicago I'd be sleeping by now, after finishing papers and reading a chapter of a good book that received bright literary reviews."

She closed her hands over his, relaxed. "This is much better."

"And when you go back . . ." He laid his cheek on the top of her head. "Will you find a neighborhood pub and spend an evening or two there instead?"

The thought of it brought a dark, thick wall shuttering down on her future. "I have lots of time before that's an issue. I'm enjoying learning to go day by day.''

"And night by night.'' He turned her, glided her into a waltz that followed the tune Shawn was singing.

"Night by night. I'm a terrible dancer.''

"But you're not.'' Hesitant was what she was, and not yet sure of herself. "I watched you dance with Shawn, then kiss him in front of God and country.''

"He said it would make you boil with jealousy.''

"So it might have if I didn't know I could beat him senseless if need be.''

She laughed, loving the way the room revolved as he circled her. "I kissed him because he's pretty and he asked me. You're pretty, too. I might kiss you if you asked me.''

"Since you're so free with your kisses, let me have one.''

To tease—and wasn't it wonderful she'd discovered she could tease a man—she placed a chaste kiss on his cheek. Then placed another, just as soft, on his other cheek. When he smiled, when he circled her, she slid her hand from his shoulder into his hair, and keeping her eyes on his, rose to her toes to press her lips warmly to his.

This time it was his body that jerked. She ruled the kiss, taking him unawares, moving it from warm to hot, from soft to deep, sighing so that his mouth, his blood, his brain were filled with the taste of her.

Staggered, he fisted his hand at the back of her blouse and let her strip his mind clean.

"Looks as if it's past time for me to leave.''

Aidan lifted his head. "Lock up as you go, Shawn,'' he said without taking his eyes off Jude's face.

"I will. Good night to you, Jude.''

"Good night, Shawn.''

Whistling now, he clicked locks and discreetly closed the

door behind him while Aidan and Jude stood in the middle of the freshly mopped floor.

"I have a terrible need for you." He drew the hand he still held to his mouth, kissed it.

"I'm so glad."

"It makes it hard, now and again, to be gentle."

"Then don't be." Excitement spurted through her in one hot gush. Thrilled with her own boldness, she stepped back and began unbuttoning her blouse. "You can be whatever you want. Have whatever you want."

She'd never undressed in front of a man, not in a way designed to arouse. But the nerves that jumped in her belly were tangled with excitement, then swallowed by pure female delight as she saw his eyes go dark.

The black lace bra was cut low, an erotic contrast against the milky skin it was designed to showcase.

"Jesus." He let out an unsteady breath. "You're trying to kill me."

"Just seduce you." She toed off her shoes. "It's a first for me." More from inexperience than design, she slowly unhooked her trousers. "So . . . I hope you'll excuse any missteps."

His mouth went dry with anticipation of what was next. "I see nothing missing at all. Seems to me you're a natural at it."

Her fingers were a little stiff, but she pried them away and let the trousers fall. More black lace, an excuse for a triangle that veed down over the belly and rose high on the hips.

She hadn't had the nerve to try the matching garter and sheer black hose Darcy had talked her into, but seeing the expression on Aidan's face, she thought she would next time.

"I did a lot of shopping today."

He wasn't sure he could speak. She stood in the pub lights, her hair tidied back, her sea goddess eyes dreamy, wearing nothing but black lace that screamed sex.

Which part of her was a man supposed to listen to?

"I'm afraid to touch you."

Jude braced herself, then stepped out of the trousers and toward him. "Then I'll touch you." Heart hammering, she slid her arms around his neck and lifted her mouth to his.

It was so arousing to press up against him when she was all but naked and he still fully dressed. It was so powerful to feel his body quiver against hers as if he were fighting some fierce and violent urge.

It was so freeing to realize she wanted him to set that fierceness, that violence, loose.

"Take me, Aidan." She nipped his bottom lip and all but slithered against him. "Take whatever you want."

He heard his own control snap like a cannon boom inside his head. He knew he was rough and could do nothing about it as his hands bruised and his mouth feasted. Her gasp of shock was only more fuel as he dragged her to the floor.

He rolled with her, wild to have his hands on her, everywhere. Mad for more, he closed lips and teeth over the lace at her breast.

She arched up, bowed with pleasure, tingling from the nip of pain. It was power that flooded into her, the punch of the knowledge that she had pushed him beyond the civilized.

Just by being. Just by offering.

As crazed as he to touch, she tugged and tore at his shirt until she had her hands on flesh.

Then her lips, then her teeth.

Hot and frantic, with greedy hands they drove each other, pleased and pleasured. This wasn't the patient man and the shy woman, but two who had stripped down to the primitive. She gloried in it, absorbing each sharp sensation and fighting to give it back.

The first orgasm burst through her like a sun.

More was all he could think. More and still more. He wanted to eat her alive, to devour so that the suddenly wild taste of her would always be inside him. Each time her body shuddered, each time she cried out, he thought again. And again and again.

The need to mate was a fever in his blood. He plunged into her, his pace all the more frenzied when she came and called out his name. Then she was rising and falling with him, driving even as she was driven. His vision hazed so that her face, her eyes, her tumbled hair were behind a soft mist.

Then even that vanished as the animal inside him leaped out and swallowed them both.

She lay sprawled over him, exhausted, aching, smiling. He lay beneath, stunned and speechless.

Their opposing reactions had the same root.

He'd taken her on the pub floor. He hadn't been able to help himself; he'd had no control whatsoever. No finesse, no patience. It hadn't been making love but mating, just as recklessly primitive as that.

His own behavior shocked him.

Jude's thoughts ran along the same lines. But his behavior, and her own, thrilled her.

When he heard her long, windy sigh, he winced and decided he had to do whatever he could to make her comfortable.

"I'll take you upstairs."

"Mmmm." She certainly hoped so, so they could do it all over again.

"Maybe you'd like a hot bath and a cup before I see you home."

"Hmmm." She sighed again, then pursed her lips. "You want to take a bath?" The idea was intriguing.

"I thought it might make you feel a bit better."

"I don't think it's possible to feel any better, not on this plane of existence."

He shifted, and since she was limp as a noodle, found it fairly easy to turn her around so she was cradled in his arms. When she only smiled and dropped her head on his shoulder, he shook his head.

"What's come over you, Jude Frances Murray? Wearing underwear designed to drive me crazy, then letting me have my way with you on the floor?"

"I have more."

"More what?"

"More underwear," she replied. "I bought bags of it."

It was his turn to drop his head weakly on her shoulder. "Sweet Jesus. I'll be waked in a week."

"I started with the black because Darcy said it was fool-proof."

He only choked at that.

Pleased with his reaction, she snuggled closer. "You were putty in my hands. I liked it."

"She's gone shameless on me."

"I have, so I'll tell you I want you to carry me upstairs. I love when you do that because it makes me feel all female and fluttery. Then take me to your bed."

"If I must, I must." He glanced around, noting the scatter of clothes. He would come back for them, he told himself. Later.

And when he did, quite some time later, he fingered the bits of lace as he carried them back upstairs. She was full of surprises, was Jude Frances, he thought. Just as much surprising to herself, if he was any judge.

The shy rose was blooming.

Now she was sleeping, cozy as you please, in his bed. She looked right there, he decided as he sat down on the edge to watch her sleep. Just as she'd looked right serving drinks in his pub, or working in her garden, or walking the hills with the O'Tooles' dog beside her.

She had, indeed, clicked neatly into his life. And why, he wondered, shouldn't she stay a part of it? Why should she go back to Chicago when she was happy here, and he was happy with her?

It was time he had a wife, wasn't it? And started a family. He'd found no one who made the prospect of that a sunny one until Jude.

He'd been waiting for something, hadn't he? And here she had walked right into his pub one rainy night. Destiny took no more than that.

She might think otherwise, but he'd talk her around it.

It didn't mean she had to give up her work, though he'd have to puzzle on exactly how she could do what most satisfied her. She was a practical woman, after all, and would want her options spelled out.

She had strong feelings for him, he thought as he toyed with her hair. As he had for her. She had roots here, as did he. And anyone with eyes could see that now she'd found those roots she was blooming.

There was a logic to it all that he was sure would appeal to her. Maybe it made him a little jumpy in the gut, but that was natural enough when a man contemplated such a big change in his life, along with the responsibility, the permanence of a wife and children.

So if his palms were a bit sweaty, it was nothing to be

concerned about. He'd work it out in his head for her, then they'd move on from there.

Satisfied, he slipped into bed beside her, drew her against his side where he liked her best, and let his mind drift into sleep.

While he slept, Jude dreamed of Carrick, astride a white winged horse, skimming over sky and land and water. And as he flew he was gathering jewels from the sun, tears from the moon, and the heart of the sea.

FIFTEEN

It was a bold step, but she'd taken a lot of them lately. There wasn't anything wrong with it. Maybe it was foolish and impractical, but it wasn't illegal.

Still, Jude glanced around guiltily as she carried a table out to the front garden. She'd already chosen the spot, right there at the curve of the path where the verbena and cranesbill nudged against the stones. The table wobbled a little on the uneven ground, but she could compensate for it.

A little wobbling was nothing compared to the view and the air and the scents.

She went back for the chair she'd selected, arranged it precisely in back of the table. When no one came along to demand what the devil she thought she was doing, she dashed back for her laptop.

She was going to work outside, and the prospect had her giddy with delight. She'd angled her work area so that she could see the hills as well as the hedgerows, and the hedgerows were blooming wildly with fuchsia. The sun gleamed softly through the cloud layers so that the light was a delicate tangle of silver and gold. There was the most fragile of breezes to stir her flowers and bring their fragrance to her.

She made a little pot of tea, using one of Maude's prettiest pots. A complete indulgence with the little chocolate biscuits she'd arranged on a plate. It was so perfect it was almost like cheating.

Jude vowed to work twice as hard.

But she sat for just a moment, sipping her tea and dreaming out over the hills. Her little slice of heaven, she thought. Birds were singing, and she caught the bright flash of a duet of magpie, at least she thought they were magpies.

One for sorrow, she mused, two for joy. And if she saw a third it was three for . . . She could never remember, so she'd just have to stick with joy.

She laughed at herself. Yes, she'd stick with joy. It would be hard to be any happier than she was at that moment. And what was better to prolong happiness but a fairy tale?

Inspired, she got down to work.

The music of birds trilled around her. Butterflies flitted their fairy wings over the flowers. Bees hummed sleepily while she drifted into a world of witches and warriors, of elves and fair maidens.

It surprised her to realize how much she had accumulated already. More than two dozen tales and fables and stories. It had been so gradual, and so little like work. Her analysis of each was far from complete, and she would have to buckle down there. The trouble was her words seemed so dry and plain next to the music and magic of the tales.

Maybe she should try to incorporate some of that . . . lilt, she supposed . . . into her work. Why did the analysis have to be so stilted, so scientific? It wouldn't hurt to jazz it up a little, to put in some of her own thoughts and feelings, and even a few of her experiences and impressions. To describe the people who'd told her the story, how they'd told it and where.

The dim pub with music playing, the O'Tooles' busy kitchen, the hills where she'd walked with Aidan. It would make it more personal, more real.

It would be writing.

She clasped her hands together, palm pressed hard to palm. She could let herself write the way she'd always wanted to. As she thought of it, let herself touch the shining idea of it, she could almost feel that lock inside her slide open.

If she failed, what did it matter? She had been, at best, an average teacher. If she turned out to be no more than an average writer, at least she would be average at something she desperately wanted to do.

Excitement whipping through her, she placed her hands on the keys, then quickly jerked them back. Self-doubt, her oldest companion, pulled up a chair beside her.

Come now, Jude, you don't have any talent for self-expression she told herself. Just stick with what you know. No one's going to publish your paper anyway. You're already indulging yourself outrageously. At least stick with the original plan and be done with it.

Of course no one was going to publish it, she admitted on a long breath. It was already much too long for a paper or an article or a treatise. Two dozen stories was too many. The logical thing to do was pick out the best six, analyze them as planned, then hope some publication on the fringes of academia would be interested.

That was sensible.

A butterfly landed on the corner of the table, fanned

wings blue as cobalt. For a moment, it seemed to study her as curiously as she studied it.

And she heard the drift of music, pipes and flutes and the weeping rush of harp strings. It seemed to flood down the hills toward her, making her lift her gaze to all that shimmering green.

Why in such a place did she have to be sensible Jude? Magic had already touched her here. She had only to be willing to open herself to more.

She didn't want to write a damn paper. She wanted, oh, God, she wanted to write a book. She didn't want to stick with what she knew or what everyone expected of her. She wanted, finally, to reach for what she wanted to know, for what she'd never dared expect from herself. Fail or succeed, to have the freedom of the experience.

When self-doubt muttered beside her, she rudely elbowed it aside.

The rain fell and mists swirled outside the windows. A fire glowed in the little hearth in my cottage kitchen. On the counter were flowers drenched from the rain. Cups of tea steamed on the table between us as Aidan told me this tale.

He has a voice like his country, full of music and poetry. He runs the pub in the village of Ardmore that his family has owned for generations, and runs it well so that it's a warm and friendly place. I've often seen him behind the bar, listening to stories or telling them while music plays and customers drink their pints.

He has charm in abundance and a face that draws a woman's eye and that men trust. His smile is quick, his temper slow, but both are potent. When he sat in the quiet of my kitchen on that rainy afternoon, this is what he told me.

Jude lifted her hands, pressed them to her lips. Over them, her eyes were bright and shining with discovery. There, she thought. She'd begun. She'd begun and it was exhilarating. It was hers. God, she felt almost drunk on it.

Drawing another steadying breath, she tapped keys until she'd moved Aidan's tale of Lady Gwen and Prince Carrick under her introduction.

She reread the story, this time inserting how he'd spoken, what she'd thought, the way the fire had warmed the kitchen, the beam of sunlight that had come and gone in a slant over the table.

When she was done, she went back to the beginning and added more, changed some of her phrasing. Driven now, she opened a new document. She needed a prologue, didn't she? It was already rushing through her head. Without pausing to think, she wrote what pushed from her mind to her fingers.

Inside her head there was a kind of singing. And the lyrics were simple and wondrous. *I'm writing a book.*

Aidan stopped at the garden gate and just looked at her. What a picture she made, he thought, sitting there surrounded by all her flowers, banging away on the keys of that clever little machine as if her life depended on it.

She had a silly straw hat perched on her head to shade her eyes. Glasses with black wire rims were perched on her nose. A brilliant blue butterfly danced over her left shoulder as if reading the words that popped up on the screen.

Her foot was tapping, making him think there was music in her head. He wondered if she was aware of it, or if it played there as background to her thoughts.

Her lips were curved, so her thoughts must be pleasing her. He hoped she'd let him read them. Was it the influence of love, he wondered, or did she really look stunningly beautiful, somehow glowing with power?

He had no intention of disturbing her until she was done, so he simply leaned against the gate with what he'd brought her tucked in the curve of his arm.

But she stopped abruptly, snatching her hands from the keys and pressing one to her heart as her head whipped around. Her eyes met his, and even with the distance he could see the variety of sensations play in them. Surprise at seeing him, and the pleasure. Then the faint embarrassment that seemed to cloud them all too often.

"Good day to you, Jude Frances. I'm sorry to interrupt your work."

"Oh, well . . ." She'd felt him there, felt something, she thought, however ridiculous that sounded. A change in the air. Now she was caught. "It's all right." She fumbled with the keys to save and close, then took off her glasses to lay them on the table. "It's nothing important." It's everything, she wanted to shout. It's the world. My own world. "I know it's odd to be set up out here," she began as she rose.

"Why? It's a lovely day for being outside."

"Yes . . . yes, it is." She turned off the machine to save the battery. "I lost track of time."

Because she said it as if confessing a sin to a priest, Aidan laughed as he unlatched the gate with his free hand. "You seemed to be enjoying yourself, and getting things done. Why worry about the time?"

"Then I'll just say it's the perfect time for a break. I imagine the tea's cold now, but . . ."

She trailed off as she noted what he carried. Her eyes lit with delight and she hurried toward him. "Oh, you have a puppy. Isn't it sweet!"

It had been lulled to sleep during Aidan's walk from the

village, but stirred now as the voices woke it. The fierce
yawn came first, then dark brown eyes blinked open. He
was a ball of black and white fur, all floppy ears and big
feet, with a thin whip of a tail curled between his legs.

He let out an excited yip and immediately began to wriggle.

"Oh, aren't you adorable, aren't you pretty? And so
soft," she murmured when Aidan passed the puppy into
her hands. When she nuzzled his fur, he immediately covered her face with adoring licks.

"Well, now, there's no need to ask if the two of you
like each other. It's the love at first sight that our Jude
claims not to believe in."

"Who could resist him?" She lifted the pup into the air,
where he wiggled in ecstasy.

"The Clooneys' bitch had a litter a few weeks back, and
I thought this one had the most character. He's just weaned
and ready for his new home."

Jude crouched, setting the puppy down so he could climb
up and over her legs and tumble onto his back for a belly
rub. "He looks ready for anything. What will you name
him?"

"That'll be up to you."

"To me?" She glanced up, then laughed as the pup
nipped at her fingers for more attention. "Greedy, aren't
you? You want me to name him for you?"

"For yourself. I brought him to you, if you're wanting
him. I thought he could keep you company on your faerie
hill."

Her hands stilled. "You brought him to me?"

"You're fond of the O'Tooles' yellow hound, so I
thought you might like having a dog of your own, from the
ground up, so to speak."

Since she only stared, Aidan backtracked. "If you're not

inclined to dealing with one, I'll take him myself."

"You brought me a puppy?"

Aidan shifted his feet. "I suppose I should have asked you first if you were interested in one. My thought was to surprise you, and—"

He broke off when she sat abruptly on the ground, gathered the puppy into her arms, and burst into tears.

He didn't mind tears as a rule, but these had come without warning and he hadn't a clue of their direction. The more the puppy squirmed in her embrace and licked at her face, the tighter she held him and the harder she wept.

"Oh, now, darling, don't take on so. There now *a ghra*, there's no need for all this." He squatted down, digging out his handkerchief and patting at her. "Hush, now, it's all my fault entirely."

"You brought me a puppy." She all but wailed it and sent the pup into sympathetic howls.

"I know, I know. I'm sorry. I should have thought it through first. He'll be happy at the pub. It's not a problem at all."

"He's mine!" She curled herself around the pup when Aidan reached down. "You gave him to me, so he's mine."

"Aye." He said it cautiously. God above, a woman was a puzzle. "You're wanting him, then?"

"I always wanted a puppy." She sobbed it out, rocking back and forth.

Aidan dragged a hand through his hair and gave up. He sat down with her. "Have you, now? Well, then, why didn't you have one?"

Finally, she lifted her tear-drenched face. Her eyes continued to brim and spill over with tears. "My mother has cats," she managed and hiccoughed.

"I see." As much, he supposed, as he could see through

a fog of pea soup. "Well, a cat's a nice thing. We've one of our own."

"No, no, no. These are like royalty. They're gorgeous and aloof and prissy and sleek. They're purebred Siamese, and really beautiful, but they never liked me. I just wanted a silly dog that would get on the furniture and chew up my shoes and—and like me."

"I think you can depend on this one for all of that." Relieved, Aidan stroked her cheek, wet with tears and puppy kisses. "So you won't curse me when he leaves a puddle on your floor or gnaws one of the nice Italian shoes Darcy's always admiring?"

"No. It's the most wonderful present I've ever had." She reached out for Aidan, sandwiching the delighted puppy between them. "You're the most wonderful man in the world."

Much as the dog had done to her, she covered Aidan's face with adoring kisses.

Perhaps he'd brought the dog to charm her, but there was no point in feeling guilty about it because it had worked, was there? How could he have known he would be filling a deep childhood longing with a flop-eared mongrel pup?

He tucked the uneasy sensation away and managed to cover her enthusiastic mouth with his.

He wanted her happy, he reminded himself. That was the important thing.

"I need a book," she murmured.

"A book?"

"I don't know how to train a puppy. I need a book."

Because it was such a typical reaction, he grinned and drew back. "First off, I'd recommend a lot of newspapers to cut down on those puddles, and a stout hunk of rope to save your shoes."

"Rope?"

"So he'll chew on that instead."

"That's clever." She beamed now. "Oh, and he'll need food and a collar and toys and shots. And . . ." She lifted the pup into the air again. "Me. He'll need me. Nothing ever has before."

I do. The words were in his mind, struggling their way to his tongue, but she leaped up, to whirl herself and the pup in a circle.

"I have to put my things back inside and run down to the village and get him everything he needs. Can you wait and drive down with me?"

"I can, yes. I'll put the things inside. You stay out and acquaint yourself with your new friend there."

As Aidan walked to her table, he let out an unsteady breath. It was best he hadn't said it, he told himself. It was too soon for both of them to change the level of things. There was plenty of time to bring up marriage.

Plenty of time to figure how it would best be done.

She bought him a red collar and leash, and dishes of bright blue. Aidan found her some rope and tied it into a sturdy hank. Still, she filled a sack with other things she deemed essential to her puppy's happiness and well-being.

She took him for a walk around the village, or tried to. He spent most of the time trying to shake off the leash or tangling himself in it or chewing on it. She resolved to get her hands on a training manual as soon as possible.

She met Brenna as her friend was loading a toolbox into the back of her lorry outside the village bed-and-breakfast.

"Good day, Jude, and what have you there? Isn't that one of the Clooney pups?"

"Yes, isn't he wonderful? I'm calling him Finn after the great warrior."

"Great warrior, is it?" Brenna crouched down to give Finn a friendly scratch. "Aye, you're a fierce one I'll wager, mighty Finn." She laughed as he leaped up to lap at her face. "He's a lively one, isn't he? You made a nice choice. I'd say he'll be nice company for you, Jude."

"That's what Aidan thought. He gave him to me."

Lips pursed, Brenna glanced over. "Did he, now?"

"Yes, he brought him to the cottage this afternoon. It was so sweet of him to think of me. Do you think Betty will like him?"

"Sure and Betty loves company, too." After a last pat for Finn, Brenna straightened. "She'll be pleased to have the pup to play with. I was just about to stop in the pub for a pint. Do you want to join me? I'm buying."

"Thanks, but . . . No, I should get Finn home. He must be hungry by now."

The minute they parted, Brenna made a beeline for the pub. She caught Darcy's eye, gave a quick jerk of her head, then moved off to a corner table where she could have some privacy.

Darcy brought along a glass of Harp. "What are you bursting with?"

"Sit down a minute." She kept her voice low and her eye on Aidan over Darcy's shoulder when Darcy sat. "I just saw Jude walking her new puppy down the street."

"She's got a puppy, does she?"

"Shh. Keep your voice down or he'll hear we're talking of it."

"Who'll hear we're talking of what?" Darcy asked in a hissing whisper.

"Aidan'll hear we're talking of how he picked out one of the Clooney bitch's litter—handsome one, too—and took it up to Jude at her cottage for a present."

"He—" Darcy caught herself as Brenna shushed her

again, then leaned forward conspiratorially. "Aidan gave her a puppy? He didn't say a word to me about it, or anyone else as far as I know."

Since it was news both fresh and surprising, Darcy pondered over it. "He's been known to give a lass a trinket from time to time, but that's usually for an occasion."

"That's what I'm thinking as well."

"And flowers," Darcy continued. "He's always been one for taking flowers to a woman who's caught his eye, but this is different altogether."

"Exactly different." Brenna slapped the table lightly for emphasis. "This is a live and permanent thing. A sweetheart sort of thing, it is, not just the I'm-enjoying-myself-in-your-bed sort of thing." To punctuate the opinion, she lifted her glass and drank.

"Well, she gave him that painting she bought in Dublin, and he's taken with it out of all proportion if you ask me. Maybe he was after giving her something back, and just happened on the pup."

"If it was to give her something back in kind for the painting—and I thought it a lovely painting—he'd have given her a trinket or a bauble or something of the sort. A token for a token," Brenna said firmly. "A puppy is several steps up from a token."

"You're right about that." Darcy drummed her fingers, narrowing her eyes at her brother as he worked the bar. "You think he's in love with her?"

"I'd risk a wager on it that he's heading in that direction." Brenna shifted. "We ought to be able to find out, and if not us, Shawn could. And we can wheedle it out of him easy enough, for he never thinks twice about what's coming out of his mouth."

"No, but he's fierce loyal to Aidan. I'd like her for a sister," Darcy considered. "And seems to me she suits Aidan down to the ground. I've never seen him look at a woman as he does our Jude. Still, Gallagher men are notorious slow to move to marriage once the heart's engaged. My mother said she had to all but pound my father over the head with orange blossoms before he came to ask her."

"She's planning to be here more than three months more."

"We'll need to move him along faster than that. They're both the marrying kind, so it shouldn't be that hard. We'll give this some thought."

Aidan was right. Finn was good company. He walked the hills with Jude, entertaining himself when she stopped to admire wildflowers or pluck the buttercups and cowslips that flourished as May coasted to June. Summer came to Ireland on a lovely stream of warmth, and to Jude the air was like poetry.

When the weather was soft, with the rain falling like silk, she kept her wandering short so she could tuck herself cozy in the cottage.

And when days were dry, she indulged herself and Finn with those long walks in the morning so he could run wild circles around an indulgent Betty.

Whenever she did, rain or shine, she thought of the man she'd seen on the road from Dublin, walking with his dog. And how she had dreamed of doing the same whenever and wherever she wanted.

Like the dog she'd imagined, Finn slept by the hearth when she made her first attempt at soda bread. And he whimpered when he woke lonely at three in the morning.

When he dug at her flowers, they had to have a serious talk, but he made it through two full weeks without chewing on her shoes.

Except that one time they'd agreed to forget.

She let him walk and race until he was tuckered out, then when weather allowed, she set out her table and worked outdoors in the afternoons while he napped under her chair.

Her book. It was so secret, she'd yet to fully acknowledge to herself just how much she wanted to sell it, to see it with a beautiful cover, one with her name on it, on the shelf of a bookstore.

She kept that almost painful hope buried and threw herself into the work she'd discovered she loved. To add to it, she often took an hour or two in the evening to sketch out illustrations to go with the stories.

Her sketches were primitive at best, in her opinion, and awkward at worst. She'd never considered the art lessons her parents had insisted on to be particularly fruitful. But the drawing entertained her.

She made certain they were all tucked away whenever anyone came by to visit. Now and then, it took some scrambling.

She was in the kitchen going over the latest sketch of the cottage, the one she considered the best of a mediocre lot, when she heard the quick knock on her door, then the sound of it slamming.

She jumped up, sending Finn into a fit of barking, and hastily shoved the sketches into the folder she used to file them.

She barely got it closed and stuffed into a drawer before Darcy and Brenna strolled in.

"There's the fierce warrior dog." Brenna dropped down on the floor to engage in her usual wrestling match with Finn.

"Do you have something cold for a weary friend, Jude?" Darcy slid into a chair at the table.

"I have some soft drinks."

"Were you working?" Darcy asked as Jude opened the refrigerator.

"No, not really. I've finished most of what I'd planned to do this morning."

"Good, for Brenna and I have plans for you."

"Do you?" Amused, Jude set out the drinks. "You can't possibly want another shopping spree so soon."

"I'm always wanting another shopping spree, but no, that's not it. You've been with us for three months now."

"More or less," Jude agreed and tried not to think that her time was half over.

"And Brenna and I've decided it's time for a *ceili*."

Interested, Jude sat as well. She'd always enjoyed hearing her grandmother talk of the *ceilis* she'd been to as a girl. Food and music and dancing all spilling out of the house. People crowded into the kitchen, flooding out into the dooryard. "You're going to have a *ceili*?"

"No." Darcy grinned. "You're having it."

"Me." With something akin to terror, Jude gaped. "I couldn't. I don't know how."

"There's nothing to it," Brenna assured her. "Old Maude used to have one every year at this time, before she took poorly. The Gallaghers will give you the music, and there are plenty more who'll be more than happy to play. Everyone brings food and drink."

"All you have to do is open the door and enjoy," Darcy assured her. "We'll all help you put things together and make sure the word gets out. We thought a week from Saturday, as that's the solstice. Midsummer's Eve's a fine night for a *ceili*."

"A week?" Jude croaked it out. "But that's not enough time. It can't be enough time."

"More than enough." Darcy winked at her. "We'll help you with everything, so don't worry a bit. Do you think I can borrow that blue dress of yours? The one with the little straps and the jacket.''

"Yes, of course, but I really can't—"

"You're not to fret.'' Brenna climbed into a chair. "My mother's all set to lend a hand as well. She's been looking for distractions since Maureen's making her crazy about the wedding. Now my advice would be to have the music in the parlor, the main of it anyway, and the kegs and that outside the back door. That gives you a nice flow from one to the other.''

"We'll need to move some of the furniture for dancing,'' Darcy put in. "And if it's a fine night, we could set some chairs outside as well.''

"The moon will just be coming full. My mother had the thought of setting candles about outdoors, to make it festive and to keep people from tripping over things.''

"But I—"

"Can you get Shawn to make colcannon, Darcy?'' Brenna interrupted before Jude could get the protest out.

"Sure he'll make plenty, and the pub will donate a keg and some bottles. Maybe your mother would make some of her stew pies. No one has a finer hand at it.''

"It'll please her to do it.''

"Really.'' Jude felt as if she were going under for the third time, and her friends were smiling indulgently after tossing her an anchor instead of a rope. "I couldn't ask—"

"Aidan'll close the pub for the night, so I'll be able to come along early and help with anything that needs it.'' Darcy let out a satisfied breath. "There, we're all but done with it.''

All Jude could do was lay her head on the table.

"I think that went well,'' Darcy said as she and Brenna climbed back in the lorry.

"I feel a bit guilty, running over her that way."

"It's for Jude herself we're doing it."

"We've left her stuttering and pale, but it went well enough." With a laugh, Brenna started the engine. "I'm glad I recalled how my father proposed to my mother at a *ceili* right here in this cottage. It's a fine omen."

"Friends look out for friends." Some might have called her flighty, but there was no firmer friend once made than Darcy Gallagher. "She's mad in love with him and too shy to push him where she wants him. We'll see they have the night and the music, and I'll come around early enough to hold her down and work on her until she's so lovely Aidan's eyes will fall out on his boots. If that doesn't do the trick, well, then, he's hopeless."

"As far as I've been able to judge, Gallagher men are as hopeless as they come."

SIXTEEN

"AND HOW," JUDE asked, "am I supposed to give a party when I don't know how many people are coming? When I have no menu, no time schedule? No plan?"

Since Finn was the only one within earshot, and he didn't appear to have the answer, Jude dropped into a chair in her now spotless living room and shut her eyes. She'd been cleaning for days. Aidan had laughed at her and told her not to take on so. No one was going to hunt up dust in the corners and have her deported for the shame of it.

He didn't understand. He was, after all, only a man.

How the cottage looked was the only aspect of the entire business she could control.

"It's my house," she muttered. "And a woman's house reflects the woman. I don't care what millennium we're in, it just does."

She'd entertained before, and she'd managed to hold reasonably satisfactory parties. But they'd been weeks, if not months, in the planning. She'd had lists and themes and caterers and carefully selected hors d'oeuvres and music.

And gallons of antacids.

Now she was expected to simply throw open her doors to friend and stranger alike.

At least a half a dozen people she'd never laid eyes on had stopped her in the village to mention the *ceili*. She hoped she'd looked pleased and said the appropriate thing, but she'd all but felt her eyes wheeling in her head.

This was her first *ceili*. It was the first real party she'd given in her cottage. The first time she'd entertained in Ireland.

She was on a different continent, for God's sake. How was she supposed to know what she was doing?

She needed an aspirin the size of Ardmore Bay.

Trying to calm herself again, to put things into perspective, she laid her head back and closed her eyes. It was supposed to be informal. People were bringing buckets and platters and mountains of food. She was only responsible for the setting, and the cottage was lovely.

And who was she trying to fool? The entire thing was headed straight for disaster.

The cottage was too small for a party. If it rained she could hardly expect people to stand outside under umbrellas while she passed them plates of food out the window. There simply wasn't room to stuff everyone inside if even half the people who'd spoken to her showed up.

There wasn't enough floor space or seating space. There wasn't enough air in the house to provide everyone with oxygen, and there certainly wasn't enough of Jude F. Murray to go around as hostess.

Worse, she'd gotten lost in the writing of her book several times over the last few days and had neglected to keep the party preparation list she'd made up on schedule. She'd meant, really she had, to stop writing at one o'clock. She'd even set a timer after the first time she ran over. Then she turned it off, intending only to finish that one paragraph. And the next time she surfaced it was after three, and neither of her bathrooms had been scrubbed as planned.

Despite all that, in a matter of hours, people she didn't know would be swarming into her house expecting to be entertained and fed.

She wasn't to worry about a thing. She'd been told that over and over again. But *of course* she had to worry about everything. It was her job. She had to think about the food, didn't she? It was her house, and damn it, she was neurotic, so what did people expect?

She'd attempted tarts that had come out hard as rock. Even Finn wouldn't touch them. The second effort was an improvement—at least the dog had nibbled on them before spitting them out. But she was forced to admit that she would never win gold stars for her pastry baking.

She had managed to put together a couple of simple casseroles following a recipe in one of Old Maude's cookbooks. They looked and smelled good enough. Now she could only hope no one came down with food poisoning.

She had a ham in the oven. She'd already called her grandmother three times to check and recheck the process of baking it. It was so big, how could she possibly be sure it was done? It would probably be raw in the center and she'd end up giving her guests food poisoning. But at least she'd serve it in a clean house.

Thank God it didn't take any talent to scrub a floor or wash windows. That, at least, she knew was well done.

It had rained during the night, and fog had slithered in from the sea. But the air had cleared that morning to bright sun and summer warmth that lured out the birds and the blossoms.

All she could do now was hope the weather held.

She had those sparkling windows open wide to keep the house airy and welcome. The scents of Old Maude's roses and sweet peas tangled together and slipped through the screens. The fragrance smoothed out Jude's stretched nerves.

Flowers! She bolted out of the chair. She hadn't cut any flowers to arrange in the house. She raced into the kitchen for the shears, and Finn raced after her. He lost purchase on the newly waxed floor, skidded, and ran headfirst into the cabinets.

Of course then he needed to be cuddled and comforted. Murmuring reassurances, Jude carried him outside. "Now, there'll be no digging in the flower beds, will there?"

He gave her an adoring look, as if the thought never crossed his mind.

"And no chasing butterflies through the cornflowers," she added and set him down with a little pat on the butt.

She picked up a basket and began to select the best flowers for cutting.

It was a task that relaxed her, always. The shapes, the scents, the colors, finding the most interesting mix. Wandering through the banks and flows on the narrow rock path with the hills stretched to forever and the country quiet sweet as the air.

If she were to make her home here, permanently, she thought, she would extend the gardens in the back. She'd have a little rock wall built on the east side and cover it with rambling roses or maybe a hedge of lavender. And in front of that, she'd plant a whole river of dahlias. And maybe she'd put an arbor on the west side and let some sweet-smelling vine climb and climb until it arched like a tunnel.

She'd have a path through it, so that she could walk there—with camomile and thyme and nodding columbine scattered nearby. She would wind her way through flowers, under them, around them, whenever she set out to walk the hills and fields.

There'd be a stone bench for sitting. And in the evenings, when work was done, she'd relax there and just listen to the world she'd made.

She'd be the expatriate American writer, living in the little cottage on the faerie hill with her flowers and her faithful dog. And her lover.

Of course, that was fantasy, she reminded herself. Her time was already half gone. In the fall she'd go back to Chicago. Even if she had the courage to pursue the idea of actually submitting the book to a publisher, she would have to get a job. She could hardly live off her savings forever. It was . . . wrong.

Wasn't it?

It would have to be teaching, she supposed. The idea of private practice was too daunting, so teaching was the only option. Even as depression threatened at the thought, she shook it off. Maybe she could look for a position in a small private school. Someplace where she could feel some connection with her students. It would give her time to continue writing. She simply couldn't give that up now that she'd found it.

She could move to the suburbs, buy a small house. There was nothing forcing her to stay in the condo in Chicago. She'd have a studio there. A little space just for her writing, and she would have the courage to submit the book. She wouldn't allow herself to be a coward about something that important. Not ever again.

And she could come back to Ireland. A couple of weeks every summer. She could come back, visit her friends, rejuvenate her spirit.

See Aidan.

No, it was best not to think about that, she warned her-self. To think of next summer or the summer after and Aidan. This time, this . . . window she'd opened was magic, and it needed to be cherished for what it was. All the more precious, she told herself, because it was temporary.

They would both move on. It was inevitable.

Or he would move on, and she would go back. But she had the pleasure of knowing she'd never go back to just how things had been. She wasn't the same person anymore. She knew she could build a life now. Even if it wasn't one of her fantasies, it could be satisfying and productive.

She could be happy, she thought. She could be fulfilled. The last three months had shown her she had potential. She could, would, finish what she'd started.

She was mentally patting herself on the back when Finn barked joyfully and dashed to the garden gate right through her pansies.

"Good day to you, Jude." Mollie O'Toole let herself in, and Finn out so that he could leap on Betty. The two dogs dashed happily toward the hills. "I thought I'd stop by and see if I could do anything for you."

"Since I don't know what I'm doing, your guess is as good as mine." She glanced down at her basket and sighed. "I've already cut too many flowers."

"You can never have too many."

Mollie, Jude thought with gratitude and admiration, al-ways said just the right thing. "I'm so glad you're here."

Mollie waved that off even as her cheek pinkened with pleasure. "Well, isn't that nice of you to say?"

"I mean it. I always feel calmer around you, like nothing can go too terribly wrong when you're nearby."

"Well, I'm flattered. Is there something you're afraid's gone terribly wrong?"

"Only everything." But Jude smiled as she said it.

"Would you like to come inside while I put them in water? Then you can point out the six dozen things I've forgotten to do."

"I'm sure you've forgotten nothing at all, but I'd love to come in and help you with the flowers."

"I thought I'd scatter them through the house in different bottles and bowls. Maude didn't have a proper vase."

"She liked to do the same. Put little bits of them everywhere. You're more like her than you realize."

"I am?" Odd, Jude thought, how the idea of being like a woman she'd never met pleased her.

"Indeed. You pamper your flowers, and take long walks, nest down in your little house here, and keep the door open for company. You've her hands," she added. "As I told you before, and something of her heart as well."

"She lived alone." Jude glanced around the tidy little house. "Always."

"It was what suited her. But alone she wasn't lonely. There was no man she loved after her Johnny, or as Maude used to say, there was no man she loved in this life once he was gone. Ah." Mollie took a sniff of the air as they went inside. "You've a ham in the oven. It smells lovely."

"Does it?" Jude sniffed experimentally as they started toward the kitchen. "I guess it does. Would you take a look at it, Mollie? I've never made one and I'm nervous."

"Sure, I'll take a peek."

She opened the oven, did her inspection while Jude set down her basket and stood gnawing her lip.

"It's fine. Nearly done, too," she pronounced after a quick check to see how easily the skin tugged free. "From the smell of it, you won't have a scrap left for your lunch tomorrow. My Mick's fond of baked ham, and will likely make more of a pig of himself than where this one came from."

"Really?"

With a shake of her head, Molly closed the oven. "Jude, never have I known a woman who's always so surprised at a compliment."

"I'm neurotic." But she said it with a smile rather than an apology.

"Well, you'd know, I suppose. You've shined this cottage up like a penny, too, haven't you now? And left not a thing for a neighbor to do but give you a bit of advice."

"I'll take it."

"When you finish with your flowers and take your ham out to cool, put it up high enough that your pup can't climb up and sample it. I've had that experience, and it's not a pretty one."

"Good point."

"After that, go on up and give yourself the pleasure of a long, hot bath. Put bubbles in it. The solstice is a fine time for a *ceili*, and it's a finer time for romance."

In a maternal gesture, Molly patted Jude's cheek. "Put a pretty dress on for tonight and dance with Aidan in the moonlight. The rest, I promise you, will take care of itself."

"I don't even know how many people are coming."

"What difference does it make? Ten or a hundred and ten?"

"A hundred and ten?" Jude choked out and went pale.

"Every one of them is coming to enjoy themselves." Mollie got down a bottle. "And that's what they'll do. A *ceili*'s just hospitality, after all. The Irish know how to give it and how to take it."

"What if there isn't enough food?"

"Oh, that's the least of your worries."

"What if—"

"What if a frog jumps over the moon and lands on your shoulder." With amused exasperation, Mollie lifted her hands. "You've made your home pretty and welcoming. Do the same with yourself, and the rest, as I told you, will take care of itself."

It was good advice, Jude decided. Even if she didn't believe a word of it. Since a bubble bath was a fail-safe method of relaxation, she took one in her beloved claw-foot tub, indulging herself until her skin was pink and glowing, her eyes drooping, and the water going cold.

Then she opened the cream she'd bought in Dublin and slathered herself in it. It never failed to make her feel female.

Totally relaxed, she toyed with the idea of a short preparty nap. Then walked into the bedroom and shrieked.

"Finn! Oh, God!"

He was in the middle of her bed, waging a fierce and violent war with her pillows. Feathers flew everywhere. He turned to her, tail thumping triumphantly as he held the vanquished pillow in his teeth.

"That's bad. Bad dog!" She waved feathers away and rushed to the bed. Sensing fun, he leaped down, tearing off with the pillow. Feathers leaked out and left a downy trail in his wake.

"No, no, no! Stop. Wait. Finn, you come back here this minute!"

She rushed after him, robe flapping as she tried to scoop up feathers. He made it all the way downstairs before she caught up, then she made the mistake of grabbing the pillow instead of the pup.

His eyes went bright with the notion of tug-of-war. Snarling playfully, teeth dug in, he shook his head and sent more feathers billowing.

"Let go! Damn it, look what you're doing." She made a grab, and between the wax and the feathers on the floor, went skidding. She managed one short scream as she sailed, belly-first, across the living room.

She heard the door open behind her, glanced over her shoulder, and thought, *Perfect. Absolutely perfect.*

"What are you up to there, Jude Frances?" Aidan leaned on the jamb while Shawn peeked in over his shoulder.

"Oh, nothing." She blew hair and feathers out of her eyes. "Nothing at all."

"Here I thought you'd be slaving away polishing the polish and scrubbing the scrubbing as you've been every day for a week, and I find you're lazing about playing with the dog."

"Ha ha." She untangled herself into a sitting position, rubbing the elbow that had banged against the floor. Finn bounced over and generously spit the pillow at Aidan's feet.

"Oh, that's right. Give it to him."

"Well, you've killed it, haven't you, boy-o? Deader than Moses." After giving Finn a congratulatory pat, Aidan crossed the room to offer Jude a hand. "Have you hurt yourself, darling?"

"No." She sent him a sulky look. "It's not a laughing matter." She slapped his hand aside, spreading the glare out to Shawn as he began to chuckle. "There are feathers everywhere. It'll take me days to find them all."

"You could start with your hair." Aidan reached down, gripped her by the waist, and hauled her up. "It's covered with them."

"Fine. Thanks for the help. Now I have work to do."

"We've brought some kegs from the pub. We'll set them around back for you." He blew a feather off her cheek, then leaned in to sniff her neck. "You smell perfect," he murmured as she shoved at him. "Go away, Shawn."

"No, don't you dare. I don't have time for this."

"And close the door behind you," Aidan finished and pulled Jude closer.

"I'll just take the dog, too, since he's finished here. Come on, you terrible beast." Shawn clucked to the dog and dutifully shut the door behind them.

"I have to clean up this mess," Jude began.

"There's time for that." Slowly, Aidan walked her backward.

"I'm not dressed."

"That's something I noticed." When he had her back to the wall, he ran his hands down her body, and up again. "Give us a kiss, Jude Frances. One that will hold me through the longest day."

It seemed a perfectly reasonable request, at least when his eyes were holding hers so intimately, and his body was so hard and warm and close. To answer it she lifted her arms to wrap them around his neck. Then, on impulse, she moved quickly, yanking him around until it was his back to the wall and her body pressed firm to his, her mouth crushed hard and hot to his.

The sound he made was like a man drowning, and drowning willingly. His hands gripped her hips, fingers digging in to remind her of the night he'd lost all patience and control. The thrill of it whipped through her, potent and strong with a snap of the possessive.

He was hers, as long as it lasted. To touch, to take, to taste. It was her he wanted. Her he reached for. She was the one who made his heart thunder.

It was, she realized, the truest power in the world.

The door opened, slammed. Jude kept her mouth fused to his. She didn't care if every man, woman, and child in the village trooped in.

"Jesus Mary and holy Joseph," Brenna complained. "Can't the pair of you think of something else to do? Every time a body turns around, you two are locked at the lip.''

"She's just jealous," Jude said, nuzzling at Aidan's neck.

"I've better things to be jealous of than some softheaded woman kissing a Gallagher."

"She must be mad at Shawn again." Aidan buried his face in Jude's hair. He wasn't sure he was breathing. He knew he didn't want to move for another ten years or so.

"Men are all boneheads, and your worthless brother's bonier than most."

"Oh, leave off complaining about Shawn," Darcy ordered as she breezed in. "What happened in here? The place is full of feathers. Jude, let go of that man, you have to get dressed, don't you? And so do I. Aidan, get out there and help Shawn with the kegs. You can't be expecting him to deal with all that himself."

Aidan merely turned his head to lay his cheek on Jude's hair. The look on his face gave his sister such a jolt, she stared a full ten seconds, then began to shove Brenna toward the kitchen. "We'll just put these dishes in the kitchen and fetch a broom."

"Stop pushing. Bloody hell, I've had it to the ears with Gallaghers for the day."

"Quiet, quiet. I have to think." Flustered, Darcy dropped the dishes she carried onto the counter and paced. "He's in love with her."

"Who?"

"Aidan, with Jude."

"Well for pity sake, Darcy, so you already thought. Isn't that why we're fussing here for a *ceili*?"

"But he's really in love with her. Didn't you see his face? I think I should sit down." She did so abruptly, then blew out a breath. "I didn't realize, not really. It was all more of a kind of game. But just now, when he was holding her. I never thought to see him look like that, Brenna. A man looks like that over a woman, she could hurt him, slice right into the heart.''

''Jude wouldn't hurt a fly.''

''She wouldn't mean to.'' Darcy's stomach was fluttering with worry. Aidan was her rock, and she'd never thought to see him defenseless. ''I'm sure she cares for him, too, and she's all caught up in the romance of it.''

''Then what would the problem be? It's just as we said.''

''No, it's nothing of what we said.'' Hadn't she avoided the desperation of love long enough to recognize it when it bashed her own brother on top of the head? ''Brenna, she's got that fancy education with initials after her name, and a life in Chicago. Her family is there, and her work, and her fine home. Aidan's life is here.'' Genuine distress poured out of her heart and into her eyes. ''Don't you see? How can he go, and why would she stay? What was I thinking, putting them together like this?''

''You didn't put them together. They were together.'' Because what Darcy was saying was beginning to trouble her as well, Brenna got out the broom. She thought better when her hands were busy. ''Whatever happens happens. We've done nothing more than push her into giving a party.''

''On the solstice,'' Darcy reminded her. ''Midsummer's Eve. We're tempting the fates, and if it blows wrong, we're to blame.''

''If we've tempted the fates, then it's up to the fates. There's nothing else to be done,'' Brenna announced and began to sweep.

Jude decided on the blue dress, another Dublin acquisition she'd never have bought if Darcy hadn't badgered her. The minute she slipped it on, she blessed Darcy and her own lack of will.

It was a long sweep of a dress, very simple, without a frill or a flounce as it dropped square at the bodice from thin straps and fell with just the most subtle of flares to the ankles. The color, a silvery blue, echoed the hue of midsummer moonlight. She wore small pearl drops at her ears. More moon symbols, she thought.

She very much wanted to take the rest of Mollie's advice and dance with Aidan under the glow of the full moon.

But on this, the longest day of the year, just as evening drifted in, the sky remained light and lovely. Color shimmered outside the cottage window, blues and greens achingly vivid. The air seemed painted with fragrance.

Nature had decided Midsummer's Eve would be one of her triumphs.

All Jude could think as she watched and listened and absorbed was that there was music playing in her living room, bouncing in it. Soaring through it. There were people crowded together in her house, dancing and laughing.

Nature's triumph, she thought, was nothing against her own.

Already more than half of her ham had been devoured.

No one seemed to show any ill effects because of it. She'd managed a bite or two herself, but for the most part was too excited to do more than nibble, or sip now and then from her glass of wine.

Couples were dancing in her hallway, in the kitchen, or out in the yard. Others juggled babies or just cozied in for a gossip. She'd tried to play hostess for the first hour, moving from group to group to make certain everyone had a glass or a plate. But no one seemed to need her to do anything in particular. They all helped themselves to the banquet of dishes jammed into the kitchen or set out on the board stretched across sawhorses that some clever soul had set up in the side yard.

There were children racing around or tucked onto laps. A baby might fuss for some milk or attention, and both were cheerfully provided. More than half the faces that passed through were strange to her.

She finally did what she realized she'd never tried at one of her own parties. She sat down and enjoyed it.

She was jammed up between Mollie and Kathy Duffy, half listening to the conversation and forgetting the slice of cake on a plate in her lap.

Shawn was playing a fiddle, bright, hot licks that made her wish desperately she knew how to dance. Darcy, radiant in the borrowed red dress, teased out notes on a flute while Aidan pumped music from a small accordion. Every now and again, they switched instruments, or brought out another. Pennywhistles, a bodham drum, a knee harp, slipping from hand to hand without a break in rhythm.

She liked it best when they added their voices, producing such intricate, intimate harmony it made her heart ache.

When Aidan sang of young Willie MacBride being forever nineteen, Jude thought of Maude's lost Johnnie, and didn't care that she shed tears in public.

They moved from the heartbreaking to the foot-stomping, never letting the pace flag. Each time Aidan would catch her eye or send her that slow smile, she was as starstruck as a teenager.

When Brenna settled down at Jude's feet and rested her head against her mother's leg, Jude passed her down the plate of cake.

"He's a way with him when he's into his music," Brenna murmured. "Makes you forget—nearly—he's a bonehead."

"They're wonderful. They should record. They should

be doing this onstage, not in a living room.''

"Shawn plays for his own pleasure. If ambition came up and knocked him on the head with a hammer, it wouldn't make a dent.''

"Not everyone wants to do everything at one time," Mollie said mildly. But she stroked Brenna's hair. "Like you and your father.''

"The more you do, the more gets done.''

"Ah, you're Mick through and through. Why aren't you dancing like your sisters instead of brooding? Lord, girl, you're O'Toole to the bone.''

"Oh, I've some Logan in me.'' Brightening, Brenna leaped up and grabbed her mother's hand. "Come on, then, Ma, unless you're feeling too old and feeble.''

"I can dance you breathless.''

A cheer went up as Mollie began a quick, complicated series of steps. Other dancers gave way with claps and whistles.

"Mollie was a champion step dancer in her day," Kathy told Jude. "And she passed it along to her daughters. They're a pretty lot, aren't they?''

"Yes. Oh, just look at them!''

One by one, Mollie's girls joined in until they were three by three facing each other. They were six small women, a mix of the fair-haired and the bright, with hands sassily on hips and legs flying. The faster the music, the faster their feet until Jude was out of breath just from watching.

It wasn't just the skill and the dazzle, Jude thought, that caught at her throat with both envy and admiration. It was the connection. Female to female, sister to sister, mother to daughter. The music was just one more bond.

It wasn't only legends and myths that made up the traditions of a culture. Aidan had been right, she realized. She couldn't forget the music when she wrote of Ireland.

War drums and pub songs, ballads and great, whirling reels. She would have to research them as well, their sources, their irony, their humor and despair.

She hugged the new inspiration to her, and let the music sweep her away.

By the time they were done, the room was crammed with those who'd wandered in from other areas of the house or outside. And the last note, the last sharp stomp of feet were greeted by wild applause.

Brenna staggered over and dropped at Jude's feet again. "Ma's right, I can't keep up with her. The woman's a wonder." Swiping an arm over her brow, she sighed. "Someone have mercy and get me a beer."

"I'll get it. You earned it." Jude got to her feet and tried to squeeze her way through to the kitchen. She received several requests for a dance that she laughingly declined, compliments on her ham that gave her a dazzled glow and on her looks that made her think several of her guests had been enjoying the kegs quite a bit.

When she finally reached the kitchen, she was surprised that Aidan was behind her and already had her hand caught in his. "Come outside for a breath of air."

"Oh, but I told Brenna I'd get her a beer."

"Jack, take our Brenna a pint, will you?" he called it out as he pulled Jude through the back door.

"I love listening to you play, but you must be tired of it by now."

"I never mind making a few hours of music. It's the Gallagher way." He continued to pull her along, past the pack of men huddled near the back door, toward the curving path of candles nestled in the grass and garden. "But it hasn't given me time to be with you, or to tell you how lovely you're looking tonight. You left your hair down," he said, tangling his fingers in the tips of it.

"It seemed to go better with the dress." She shook it back and lifted her face to the sky. It was a deep, deep blue now, the color of a night that would never fully become night because of the white ball of moon.

A magic night of shadows and light when the faeries came out to dance.

"I can't believe what a state I got myself into over this. Everyone was right. They said it would just happen, and it did. I guess the best things do."

She turned when they reached the spot where she'd imagined putting an arbor. Behind them the house—her house, she thought with warm pride—was lit up bright as Christmas. The music continued to pour out, tangled with voices and laughter.

"This is how it should be," she murmured. "A house should have music."

"I'll give you music in it whenever you like." When she smiled and slipped into his arms, he guided her into a dance, just as she'd dreamed he would.

It was perfect, she thought. Magic and music and moonlight. One long night where the darkness was only a brief flicker.

"If you came to America and played one song, you'd have a recording contract before you'd finished it."

"That's not for me. I'm for here."

"Yes, you are." She leaned back to smile at him. Indeed, she couldn't imagine him anywhere else. "You're for here."

And it was the magic and the music and the moonlight that pushed him before he had the words ready. "And so are you. There's no reason for you to go back." He eased her away. "You're happy here."

"I've been very happy here. But—"

"That's enough right there to keep you. What's wrong with just being happy?"

His abrupt tone had her smile turning puzzled. "Nothing, of course, but I need to work. I have to support myself."

"You can find work to content you here."

She had, she thought. She'd found her life's work in writing. But old habits die hard. "There doesn't seem to be much call for psychology professors in Ardmore at the moment."

"You didn't like doing that."

He was starting to make her nervous. A chill slid up her arms and made her wish for a jacket. "It's what I do. What I know how to do."

"So you'll figure out how to do something else. I want you here with me, Jude." Even as her heart gave one wild leap at the words, he continued on. "I need a wife."

She wasn't sure if the thud was her heart dropping again, or just simple shock. "Excuse me?"

"I need a wife," he repeated. "I think you should marry me, then we'll figure out the rest of the business later."

SEVENTEEN

"YOU NEED A wife," she repeated, keeping her voice calm, spacing the words evenly.

"I do, yes." It wasn't precisely how he'd meant to put it, but it was too late now. "We need each other. We mesh well, Jude. There's no point in you going back to a life that didn't satisfy you, when you can have one here that does."

"I see." No, she didn't see, she thought. It was like trying to look through dark, murky water. But she was trying to see. "So, you think I should stay here and marry you because you need a wife and I need . . . a life?"

"Yes. No." There was something wrong with how she'd phrased that. Something not quite right about the tone of it. But he was too flustered to figure it out. "I'm saying I could support you well enough until you find the kind of work you enjoy doing, or if you'd just rather work at making a home instead, that's fine as well. The pub does well enough. I'm not a pauper, and though it may not be the style of living you're accustomed to, we'd manage it all right."

"We'd manage it. While you . . . support me in the style I'm not quite accustomed to. Support me, until I bumble around and find what I might be good at doing?"

"Look." Why couldn't he get the words to line up the right way? "You have a life here, is what I'm saying. You have one with me."

"Do I?" She turned away as she struggled to hold back something dark and bubbling that wanted to spew out of her. She didn't recognize it, wasn't sure she wanted to, but she sensed it was dangerous. The Irish, she mused, were supposed to be poets, to have the most charming of words flow right off the tongue.

And here, for the second time in her life, she was being told she should marry a man because it would be good for her.

William had needed a wife, too, she remembered. To help cement his position, to entertain, to look presentable. And of course, she'd needed a man to tell her what to do and when and how to do it. A wife for one, a life for the other. What could be more logical?

The first time she'd been told that, she'd obeyed. Quietly, almost meekly. It infuriated and it shamed to remember that. It infuriated and it shamed to realize how much a part of her wanted to do the same with Aidan.

But there was more to her now. More than she'd realized. She was making something of herself, and by God, she intended to finish. Without being guided gently along because she was so inept at finding her own way.

"I've had time here, Aidan." Face composed, voice level, she turned back to study his face in the silvered light of the swimming moon. "I've had time with you. These months don't make a life, and it's my life I'm trying to figure out, so I can build on it, make something of it. And of myself."

"Make it with me." The quick jolt of desperation stunned him, left him floundering. "You care for me, Jude."

"Of course I do." Somehow she managed to keep her voice pleasant when she said it, though that dark and bubbling brew was still churning inside her. "Marriage is a serious business, Aidan. I've been there, and you haven't. It isn't a commitment I intend to make again."

"That's ridiculous."

"I haven't finished." Her voice was chilly now, ice over steel. "It isn't a commitment I intend to make again," she repeated, "until I trust myself, and the man, and the circumstances enough to believe it's forever. I won't be cast aside again."

"Do you think I would do such a thing as that?" Angry now, he gripped her arms, held tight. "You'd stand here and compare me to that bastard who broke his vows to you?"

"I have nothing else to compare you to, or this to. I'm sorry that annoys you. But the fact is, marriage isn't in my plans at this time. I thank you for the thought. Now I really should go back inside. I'm neglecting my guests."

"The hell with them. We'll settle this."

"We have settled it." Keeping that same rigid smile on her face, she shoved his hands away. "If I didn't make myself clear, I'll try again. No, I won't marry you, Aidan, but thank you for asking."

As she said it, thunder boomed over the hills and a lance of lightning exploded, shooting a flash of thin white cracks across the bowl of the sky. She turned to walk into the house while the wind reared up to slap the air and send her chimes into a wild and bitter song.

Odd, she thought, that her heart felt just the same. Wild and bitter.

Aidan only stared after her. She'd said no. He simply hadn't prepared himself for the possibility she would say no. He'd made up his mind that they would marry. She was the one. For him there would only ever be one.

The sudden fury of the wind streamed through his hair, and the air stung with ozone from the next hurled spear of lightning. He stood in the midst of the oncoming storm struggling to clear his head.

She just needed a bit more time and persuading. That was it. Had to be it, he thought as he rubbed the heel of his hand over his heart. The ache in it was a new and panicky feeling he didn't care for. She'd come around, of course she would. Any fool could see they needed to be together.

He just had to make her see she'd be happy here, that he would take good care of her. That he wouldn't let her down as she'd been let down before. She was just being cautious, that was all. He'd taken her by surprise, but now that she knew his intentions, she'd grow used to them. He'd see to it.

A Gallagher didn't retire the field at the first volley, he reminded himself. They stuck. And Jude Frances Murray was about to find out just how hard and how long a Gallagher could stick.

Face set, he strode back to the house. If he'd glanced up, he might have seen the figure in the window above. The woman stood, her pale hair around her shoulders, and a single tear, bright as a diamond, sliding down her cheek.

• • •

Jude managed to get through the rest of the party. She laughed and she danced and she chatted. It took no effort to keep herself surrounded by people and avoid another confrontation with Aidan. It took more to nudge him out the door when people began to leave, to make smiling excuses to him about being exhausted. She needed to sleep, she told him.

Of course she didn't. The minute her house was empty, she rolled up her sleeves. She didn't want to think, not yet, and the best way to avoid it was good, solid work.

She gathered up plates and glasses from all over the house, then washed and dried and put away every one of them. It took hours, and her body was as exhausted as she'd claimed. But her mind refused to rest, so she continued to push herself, wiping, scrubbing, tidying.

Once she thought she heard the sound of a woman's weeping drift down the stairs, but she ignored it. The despair in it made her own eyes sting, and that wouldn't do. Her own tears wouldn't help Lady Gwen. They wouldn't help anyone.

She dragged furniture back into place, then hauled out the sweeper and vacuumed the floors. Her face was pale with fatigue, her eyes dark with it by the time she climbed the stairs to her bedroom.

But she hadn't wept, and the sheer manual labor had burned off everything but a reeling physical exhaustion. Still fully dressed, she lay down on the bed, turned her face into the pillow, and willed herself to sleep.

Dreaming of dancing with Aidan under the silver light of a magic moon with flowers sweeping out, colorful and gay as faeries, and the air charmed by their scents.

Riding with him, on the broad back of a white winged horse, over glistening green fields, stormy seas, and placid lakes of impossible blue.

This is what he offered her. She heard him tell her. This, a country that fascinates and calms. A home waiting to be built. A family waiting to be made.

Take them, and me.

But the answer was no, had to be no. It was not her country. Not her home. Not her family. Couldn't be until there was strength in her, trust in them, love from him.

Then she was alone in the dream, standing at the window while the rain washed the glass, because in all the promises he'd made, there had not been a single word of love.

When she awoke, the sun was streaming bright, and the sound of the woman's weeping was her own.

Her mind was fuzzy from lack of sleep, and her body felt frail, as if she'd awakened old and ill. Self-pity, Jude thought, recognizing the symptoms all too well. Encroaching depression. After her marriage had been yanked out from under her feet, she'd fallen into that pattern for weeks.

Restless nights, endless unhappy days, clouds of misery and embarrassment.

Not this time, she promised herself. She was in control now, making her own decisions. And the first was not to wallow, not even for an hour.

She gathered up flowers, tied a pretty ribbon around their stems, and with Finn and Betty for company set out on the walk to Maude's grave.

The storm that had threatened the night before had never struck. Though there were still some clouds brooding in the southwest, the air was beautifully warm. The sea sang out its song, and on the hills, the buttercups sunned their faces. She spotted a white-tailed rabbit seconds before the yellow hound scented it. Betty took off, a sleek bullet after the bounding white blur, only to romp back moments later. Her tongue lolled in a sheepish expression as if she was embarrassed to have once again been lured into the chase.

Five minutes of watching the puppy race around Betty, tumble, and yip put Jude in a better mood.

By the time she reached the grave site, she was soothed, and sat down as was now her habit to tell Maude the latest news.

"We had a wonderful *ceili* last night. Everyone said it was good to have music in the cottage again, and people. Two of Brenna O'Toole's sisters came with their young men. They look so happy, all four of them, and Mollie just beams when she looks at them. Oh, and I danced with Mr. Riley. He seems so old and frail I was afraid I'd just shatter him, but I could barely keep up."

Laughing, she shook her hair back, then settled down on her heels for the visit. "Then he asked me to marry him, so I know I'm accepted here. I baked a ham. It was the very first time I ever did, and it worked. I didn't even have scraps left for the dogs. Late in the evening Shawn Gallagher sang 'Four Green Fields.' There wasn't a dry eye. I've never given a party where people laughed and cried and sang and danced. Now I don't know why anyone gives any other kind."

"Why don't you tell her about Aidan?"

Jude looked up slowly. It didn't surprise her to see Carrick standing on the other side of Maude's grave. Another wonder, she supposed, that such a thing didn't seem the least odd to her now. But she raised her brows because there was temper glittering in his eyes and a snarl on his mouth.

"Aidan was there," she said calmly. "He played and sang beautifully, and brought enough beer from the pub to float a battleship."

"And the man took you out in the moonlight and asked you to be his wife."

"Well, more or less. He took me out in the moonlight and said he needed a wife and I would fill the bill." Jude glanced down as her puppy sniffed around Carrick's soft brown boots.

"And what was your answer?"

Jude folded her hands on her knee. "If you know that much, you know the rest."

"No!" The word exploded out of him, and the grass shivered and lay flat. "You tell him no because you haven't the sense of a carrot." He jabbed a finger at her, and though they were feet apart she still felt the impatient stab of it against her shoulder. "I took you for a bright woman, one with a fine mind and manner, with a good strong heart as well. Now I see you're fickle and fainthearted and mulish."

"Since you think so little of me, I won't subject you to my company." She got to her feet, jerked up her chin, then gasped when she turned and rapped straight into him.

"You'll stay where you are, madam, until you're given leave otherwise."

For the first time, she heard royalty in his tone, the threat and power of it. Because she wanted to tremble, she stood her ground. "Leave? I'm free to come and go as I please. This is my world."

As his eyes flashed with fury, the skies shuddered and went storm-dark. "It's been mine since your kind still huddled in caves. It will be mine long after you're dust. Have a care and remember that."

"Why am I arguing with you? You're an illusion. A myth."

"And as real as you." He gripped her hand, and his flesh was firm and warm. "I've waited for you, a hundred years times three. If I'm wrong, and must wait for another to begin it, I'll know why. You'll tell me now why you said no when the man asked you to wife."

"Because that was my choice."

"Choice." He let out a half laugh and turned away from her. "Oh, you mortals and your blessed choices. They're always such a matter to you. Fate will have you in the end anyway."

"Maybe, but we'll choose our own direction in the meantime."

"Even if it's the wrong direction."

She smiled a little as he turned back to her. His handsome face was such a study in honest puzzlement. "Yes, even if it's wrong. It's our nature, Carrick. We can't change our nature."

"Do you love him?" When she hesitated, it was his turn to smile. "Would you bother to lie, colleen, to an illusion and a myth?"

"No, I won't lie. I love him."

He threw up his hands and groaned. "But you won't belong to him?"

"I won't be anyone's convenience ever again." Her voice rose, snapped with a different kind of power. "The belonging, if it ever happens, will be on both sides, and be complete. I gave myself once to a man who didn't love me, because it seemed the sensible thing to do and because . . ."

She closed her eyes a moment, realizing she'd never admitted it, never once even to herself. "Because I was afraid no one ever would. I was afraid I'd always be alone. Nothing seemed more frightening to me than being alone. That's just not true anymore. I'm learning how to be alone, and to like myself, to respect who I am."

"So the fact that you can be alone means you must be?"

"No." She threw up her hands this time, whirled around to pace. "Men," she muttered. "Why does everything have to be explained step by step to men? I don't *have* to be married to be happy. And I'm certainly not going to change the life I've just started, risk marriage again and throw myself into someone else's vision unless I damn well want to. Until I know *I* come first for a change. Me, Jude Frances Murray.''

Her voice rose as she jabbed a hand at her own heart. And Carrick's eyes went narrow and thoughtful.

"I'm not settling for one inch less than all. Just because I'm in love with Aidan, just because we're lovers, doesn't mean I'm going to swoon from the thrill of being told he's decided he needs a goddamn wife and I'm the one he's picked out. I'll do the picking out this time, thank you very much.''

Flushed and out of breath, she glared at Carrick. And there, she realized, was everything she hadn't put into words before. Hadn't understood was inside her to be put into words. She would never, never again settle for less than everything.

"I thought it was mortals I didn't understand," Carrick said after a moment. "But I'm thinking now it's just female mortals I don't understand. So explain this to me, would you, Jude Frances? Why isn't love enough?''

She let out a quiet sigh. "It is, when it is.''

"Why are you speaking in riddles?''

"Because until you solve it yourself, it doesn't do any good to be told. And when you do solve it, you don't need to be told.''

He muttered something in Gaelic, shook his head. "Heed this—a single choice can build destinies or destroy them. Choose well.'' Then, flicking his wrists, he vanished in a ripple on the air.

Aidan was no less frustrated with women than Carrick at that moment. If someone had told him his ego was badly bruised, he would have laughed at them. If someone had told him that was panic that kept sneaking up to tickle the back of his throat, he would have cursed them as a lying fool. If they'd mentioned that the clutching around his heart was hurt, he'd have snarled them out of the pub.

But it was all those things he felt, and confusion along with them.

He'd been so certain that he understood Jude. Her mind and heart as well as her body. It was lowering to realize he'd missed a step somewhere. It was true enough he'd jumped his fences, so to speak. But he hadn't expected her to be so cool and casual in her response to his proposal.

For Christ's sake, he'd proposed marriage to a woman, to *the* woman, and she'd smiled and said no thank you as pretty as you please, then gone back to the *ceili*.

His sweet and shy Jude Frances hadn't stammered and blushed, but had eyed him with cool consideration, then had turned him down flat. It didn't make a bit of sense when any fool could see they belonged together.

Like two links in a long and complicated chain. It was a chain he could envision perfectly, one of sturdy continuity and tradition. Man to woman, generation to generation. She was the one he was meant to be with, so that together they could forge the next links on that long chain.

A different approach altogether was needed, he told himself as he paced his rooms instead of finishing up the day's paperwork. He knew how to woo and win a woman, didn't he? He'd wooed and he'd won plenty before.

Of course that had been for entirely different purposes, he thought and began to worry again. But not so much he admitted to himself—not yet—that he was a babe in the woods in the matter of wooing a woman into a wife.

He heard footsteps on the stairs minutes before Darcy, as was her habit, breezed in without knocking. "Shawn's down the kitchen and, considering me his errand girl, sent me up to see if you've ordered potatoes and carrots, and if we've any more whitefish coming in from Patty Ryan by week's end as he's plans for it.''

''Patty promised us fresh fish tomorrow, and the rest will be coming by middle week. He hasn't starting cooking tonight's menu already, has he? It's barely half one.''

''No, but he's fussing about, studying some recipe one of the ladies gave him last night at the *ceili*, and leaving the bulk of the serving to me. Are you coming down to man the bar or are you just going to sit around up here and stare at the walls?''

''I was working,'' he said, more than a little put out, for he'd been spending considerable time staring at the walls. ''Anytime you want to take over the paperwork here, sweetheart, you just say the word.''

The tone of his voice had her wondering. Knowing she was leaving Shawn and their afternoon help in the lurch, she flopped down in a chair and tossed her legs over the arm. ''I leave the figuring to you, since you're so wise and clever.''

''Then leave me to it and go down and do your part.''

''I've a ten-minute break coming, and since I find myself here, here I'm taking it.'' She smiled at him, much too sweetly to be trusted. ''What are you brooding about, then?''

''I'm not brooding.''

She only lifted a hand and casually examined her nails. He paced to the window, back to the desk and to the window again when the silence did the job. ''You've gotten close to Jude the past couple of months.''

''I have, yes.'' Her smile sharpened. ''Not as close as you, in a manner of speaking. Did you have a spat? Is that what's got you pacing about up here and scowling?''

''No, we didn't have a spat. Exactly.'' He jammed his

hands in his pockets. Oh, it was humiliating, but what choice did he have? "What does she say about me?"

Darcy didn't snicker out loud, but her head filled with laughter as she batted her eyelashes at her brother. "That would be telling. I'm no blabbermouth."

"An extra hour off Saturday next."

Instantly Darcy sat up, and her eyes were crafty. "Well, why didn't you say so? What do you want to know?"

"What does she think of me?"

"Oh, she thinks you're handsome and charming, and nothing I can say will turn her mind to the truth of it. You've swept her off her feet with the romance of it. That carrying her up the stairs was a fine move." She did laugh when she saw his pained expression. "Don't ask what women talk of together if you don't want to know."

He managed one careful breath. "She didn't go on about . . . the after of it."

"Oh, every sigh and murmur." Unable to stop herself, she jumped up, grabbed his face and kissed him. "Of course not, you pea-brain. She's too discreet for that, though Brenna and I did pump her a bit. What's worrying you? As far as I can tell, Jude thinks you're the greatest lover since Solomon took Sheba."

"Is that all it is, then? Sex and romance and being swept along for a few months. Nothing but that?"

The amusement faded from her eyes as she looked into his. "I'm sorry, darling. You're truly upset. What happened?"

"I asked her to marry me last night."

"You did?" Instantly she leaped on him, wrapping her legs around his waist, her arms around his neck, squeezing like a delighted boa constrictor. "Oh, but this is wonderful! I couldn't be happier for you!" Laughing, she gave him smacking kisses on both cheeks. "Let's go down to the kitchen and tell Shawn, and call Ma and Dad.''

"She said no.''

"They'll want to come back and meet her before the wedding. And then we'll all . . . What?''

His heart sank deeper in his chest as Darcy gaped at him. "She said no.''

Guilt all but swallowed her. "She couldn't have. She didn't mean it.''

"She said it clear enough and was polite and added a thank you.'' Oh, and that thank you was a bitter pill.

"Well, what the devil's wrong with her?'' Abruptly furious, Darcy wiggled down and planted fists on her hips. Rage, as she knew well, was always a more comfortable fit than guilt. "Of course she wants to marry you.''

"She said she didn't. She said she didn't want marriage at all. It's the fault of that bloody bastard who left her. Compared me to him, and when I called her there, she said how she had nothing else to compare to. Well, compare me to no one, by Christ. I'm who I am.''

"Of course you are, and ten times the man that William is.'' Her fault, she thought again. She'd seen the fun of it, but hadn't counted on the pain. "It wasn't—it wasn't just that she didn't want to leave her life in America, then?''

"We never got that far. And why wouldn't she when she's happy here as she never was there?''

"Well . . .'' Darcy huffed out her breath and tried to think it through. "It hadn't occurred to me that she wouldn't want marriage.''

"She's just not thinking beyond what happened before. I know it hurt her, and I'd like to wring the man's neck for it.'' Emotions swirled into his eyes. "But I won't hurt her.''

No, he would treasure and tend, as he did all the things he loved, Darcy thought, aching for him.

"Maybe it is, in part, a wound that isn't quite healed.

But the fact is, not all women want a ring and a baby under the apron.''

She wanted to get up and stroke and hug him into some comfort, but could see there was too much temper in his eyes yet for him to accept petting. ''I understand her feelings on that, Aidan. On the borders of it, the finality.''

''It's not an end but a beginning.''

''For you it would be, but it isn't for everyone.'' Darcy sat back, drummed her fingers. ''Well, I'm a good judge, and I'm saying our Jude's the marrying kind, whether she believes it or not at the moment. A nester she is who's never had a chance to make that nest if you're asking me, before she came here on her own. Maybe we moved a bit faster than we should.''

''We?''

''You, I mean,'' Darcy corrected as she thought of the plotting she'd done with Brenna. No need to mention that, she decided, since it seemed the mess made wasn't her fault—entirely. ''But it's too late to change that, so you'll just have to move forward. Persuade her.'' She smiled again. ''Take some time on it, but let her see what she'd be giving up if she didn't grab what you're offering. You're a Gallagher, Aidan. Gallaghers get what they want sooner or later.''

''You're right.'' Pieces of his shattered ego began to slide back into place. ''There's no moving back now. I'll just have to help her get used to the idea.''

Relieved to see the gleam back in his eyes, Darcy patted his cheek. ''My wager's on you.''

EIGHTEEN

SHE WOULDN'T BE expecting him, not so early in any case. But since Darcy was being so cooperative, Aidan had taken off a couple of hours before closing to walk the road to Jude's cottage.

The night was balmy with the breeze from the sea. Clouds sailed briskly over the sky so that patches of stars winked out, glimmered, then vanished. The moon was round and fat, its light gentle.

A fine night, Aidan thought, for romancing the woman you intended to marry.

He'd brought her a clutch of fairy roses in delicate pink that he'd stolen from Kathy Duffy's garden. He didn't think the woman would mind the loss when it was going to such a good cause.

There were lights glowing in her windows, a warm and welcome sight to him. He imagined that in years to come, when they were married and settled, it would be the same. He'd walk home after work and she'd be waiting with the lights burning to guide his step. It no longer surprised him how much he wanted that, or how clearly he could see it all. Night following night, year following year, toward a lifetime.

He didn't knock. Such formalities had already slipped away between them. He noted that she'd already tidied from the party. It was so like her, he thought with affection. Everything was neat and orderly and just as it should be.

He heard music drifting down the stairs and walked up toward it.

She was in her little office with the radio playing soft and the pup snoring at her feet under the table. Her hair was bound back, her fingers moving briskly over computer keys.

He had an urge to scoop her into his arms and gobble her whole. But he didn't think that was the right move under the circumstances.

Persuasion, he reminded himself, didn't come from the fast and the hot, but the slow and the warm.

He crossed to her, moving quietly, then bent down to brush a soft kiss on the nape of her neck.

She jolted, but he'd anticipated that and, chuckling, wrapped his arms around her so the flowers were under her chin and his mouth was at her ear.

"You look so pretty sitting here, *a ghra*, working away into the night. What tale are you spinning out?"

"Oh, I . . ." Her heart was in her throat. He was right that she hadn't expected him. Not just so early, but at all. She knew she'd been abrupt and rude, and even cold, and had convinced herself that what had been between them was done. She'd even begun to mourn for it.

Yet here he was, bringing her flowers and speaking softly in her ear.

"It's, ah, the story of the pooka and Paddy McNee that

Mr. Riley told me. These are lovely, Aidan.'' Since she was far from ready for anyone to see her work, she tipped the top of the computer down, then sniffed the roses.

''I'm glad you like them as they're stolen goods and the *garda* may come by at any moment to arrest me.''

''I'll pay your bail.'' She turned in the chair to look at him. He wasn't angry, she noted with puzzled relief. A man couldn't smile like that if he was angry. ''I'll go put them in water, and make you some tea.''

When she rose the pup turned over with a grumble and a groan and recurled himself.

''As a guard dog he's a pure failure,'' Aidan commented.

''He's just a baby.'' She took the flowers as they walked downstairs. ''And I've nothing to guard anyway.''

It was such a pleasure to slide back into routine, the friendliness and flirtation. Part of her wanted to bring up what happened the night before, but she tucked it away. Why mention something that put them at odds?

He was probably regretting that he'd asked her, and relieved that she'd said no. For some reason that line of thinking had that dark, nasty brew bubbling inside her again. She ordered herself to settle down and tucked the pink roses into a pale blue bottle.

As she did, she noticed the time and frowned. ''It's barely ten o'clock. Did you close the pub?''

''No, I took a couple hours. I'm entitled now and then. And I missed you,'' he added, laying his hands on her waist. ''For you didn't come see me.''

''I was working.'' *I didn't think you'd want to see me. Weren't we angry with each other?* she wondered even as he bent down to brush his lips over hers.

''And I've interrupted. But since that deed is done . . .'' He drew back. ''Come walking with me, won't you, Jude Frances?''

"Walking? Now?"

"Aye." He was already circling her toward the back door. "A lovely night it is for walking."

"It's dark," she said, but she was out the door.

"There's light. Moon and stars. The best kind of light. I'll tell you a story of the faerie queen who only came out from her palace at night, when there was a moon to guide her steps. For even faeries can have spells cast on them, and hers was that she was cursed to take the form of a white bird during the day."

As they walked, her hand linked with his, he spun it out for her, painting the picture of the lonely queen wandering by night and the black wolf she found wounded at the base of the cliffs.

"He had eyes of emerald green that watched her warily, but her heart couldn't resist and overcame any fear. She tended to him, using her art and her skill to heal his hurts. From that night he became her companion, walking the hills and the rock with her night after night until as dawn shimmered over the sea she left him with a flutter of white wings and a sorrowful call that came from her broken heart."

"Was there no way to break the spell?"

"Oh, there's always a way, isn't there?" He lifted their joined hands to his lips, kissed her knuckles, then drew her along toward the cliff path where the sea began to roar and the wind fly.

Moonlight splattered on the high, wild grass, and the path cut between it, turned pebbles into silver coins and weathered stone into hunched elves. She let Aidan guide her up while she waited for him to start the story again.

"One morning, a young man was hunting in the fields, for he was hungry and had no more than his quiver of arrows and his bow to feed him. Game had been scarce for many days, and that day, as others, the rabbits and deer eluded him until it came to afternoon and his hunger was great. It was then he saw the white bird soaring, and thinking only of his belly, he notched his arrow in his bow, loosed the arrow, and brought her down. Mind your step here, darling. That's the way.''

"But he can't have killed her."

"I've not finished yet, have I?" He turned to pull her up. Then he held her there a moment, just held her as she fit so well against him.

"She let out a cry, filled with pain and despair that ripped at his heart even as his head reeled from lack of food. He raced to her, and found her watching him with eyes blue as a lake. His hands trembled, as they were eyes he knew, and he began to understand."

Turning Jude, tucking her under his arm, he began to walk again under the splattering light of star and moon. "Though he was half starved, he did what he could to heal the wound he'd made and took the bird to the shelter of these cliffs. And building a fire to warm her, he sat guarding her and waited for sunset."

When they reached the top, Aidan slipped an arm around her so they could look out at the dark sea together. Water rolled in, then back, then in again, a rhythm constant, primitive, sexual.

And understanding that Aidan's stories had their rhythm too, Jude lifted a hand to cover his. "What happened next?"

"What happened was this. As the sun dipped, and night reached out for day, she began to change, as did he. So woman became bird and man wolf, and for one instant they reached for each other. But hand passed through hand, and the change was complete. So it went through the night, with her too feverish and weak to heal herself. And the wolf never left her side, but stayed to warm her with his body and guard her with his life if need be. Are you cold?'' he asked, as she shivered.

''No,'' she whispered. ''Touched.''

''There's more yet. Night passed into day again, and again day into night, and each time they had only that instant to reach for each other and be denied. He never left her side to eat, as man or as wolf, and so was near to dying himself. Sensing it, she used what power she had left to strengthen him, to save him rather than herself. For the love she felt for him meant more than her life. Once again dawn shimmered in the sky, and the change began. Once again they reached for each other, knowing it was hopeless, and her knowing she would never see another sunrise. But this time, the sacrifice they'd both made was rewarded. Hands met, fingers clasped, and they looked on each other, finally, man to woman, woman to man. And the first words they spoke were of love.''

''Happy-ever-after?''

''Better. He who had been a king in his own right of a far-off land took his faerie queen to wife. Never did they spend a single sunset or a single sunrise apart for the rest of their days.''

''That was lovely.'' She laid her head on his shoulder. ''And so is this.''

''It's my place. Or so I thought of it when I was a boy and would come clambering up here to look out at the world and dream of where I'd go in it.''

''Where did you want to go?''

''Everywhere.'' He turned his face into her hair and thought that now, here was everywhere enough for him. But for her, it was different. ''Where do you want to go, Jude?''

"I don't know. I've never really thought about it."

"Think now, then." He shifted her, then settled down with her on a rock. "Of all the places there are, what do you want to see?"

"Venice." She didn't know where that had come from, and laughed at herself to realize it had been in her mind ready to pop out. "I think I'd like to see Venice with its wonderful buildings and grand cathedrals and mysterious canals. And the wine country in France, all those acres of vineyards with grapes ripening, the old farmhouses and gardens. And England. London, of course, for the museums, the history, but the countryside more. Cornwall, the hills and the cliffs, to breathe the air where Arthur was born."

No tropical islands and baking beaches or exotic ports of call for his Jude Frances now, Aidan noted. It was romance and again tradition with the hint of legend that she wanted.

"None of those places is so very far from where we're sitting now. Why don't you come away with me, Jude, and we'll see them?"

"Oh, sure, we'll just fly off to Venice tonight and wend our way back through France and England."

"Well, now, tonight might be a bit of a problem, but the rest is what I had in mind. Would you mind waiting till September?"

"What are you talking about?"

A honeymoon was what he nearly said, but he thought it best to be cautious for the time being. "About you coming away with me." He had her hand again, nibbling along her fingers as he smiled at her over them. "About you flying off with me to places of romance and mystery and legend. I'll show you Tintagal, where Arthur was conceived the night Merlin worked his magic on Uther so Ygraine thought she was greeting her own husband. And we'll stay in one of those farmhouses in France and drink their wine and make love in a big feather bed. Then we'll stroll along the canal in Venice and wonder at the grand cathedrals. Wouldn't you like that, sweetheart?''

"Yes, of course." It sounded glorious, magical. Like another of his stories. "It's just impossible."

"Why would that be?"

"Because . . . I have work, and so do you."

He chuckled, then switched his attentions from her fingers to the side of her jaw. "And do you think my pub would crumble or your work vanish? What's two weeks or so in the grand scheme of things, after all?"

"Yes, that's true, but—"

"I've seen those places you spoke of." He moved to her mouth to quietly seduce. "Now I want to see them with you." His hands skimmed over her face, and he began to lose himself in her, the tastes and textures of her. "Come away with me, *a ghra*." He murmured it, drawing her closer when she shivered.

"I . . . I'm supposed to go back to Chicago."

"Don't." His mouth grew hotter, more possessive. "Be with me."

"Well . . ." Her thoughts wouldn't line up. Every time she tried to align one, it tumbled down, scattering others. "Yes, I suppose . . ." What was a couple of weeks, after all? "In September. If you're sure—"

"I'm sure." He got to his feet, then plucked her off the rock, grinning when she gave a gasp and locked her arms around his neck. "Are you thinking I'd be dropping you, now that I've got you? I take better care of what's mine than that."

Of what was his? The phrase worried her a bit, but before she could think of how to respond, she saw the figure behind them.

"Aidan." Her voice was barely more than a breath.

He tensed, tucked her under his arm to defend, then turning, relaxed again.

The lady barely made a ripple on the air as she walked. But her pale hair gleamed in the moonlight, as did the tears.

"Lady Gwen, out looking for the love she lost." Pity stirred in his heart when he saw the tears glittering on her cheeks.

"As he does. I saw him again today. I spoke with him."

"You're becoming right chummy with faeries, Jude Frances."

She felt the wind on her face, could smell the sea. Aidan's arm was strong and warm around her. Yet it seemed like an illusion that would vanish the moment she blinked. "I keep thinking I'll wake up in my own bed in Chicago, and this, all of this, would have been some long, complex dream. I think it would break my heart."

"Then your heart's safe." He bent his head to kiss her. "This is no dream, and you've my word on it."

"It must hurt her to see lovers here." She looked back. The lady's gilded hair was flying, and her cheeks were wet. "They don't have even that instant at dawn or sunset to reach out."

"A single choice can build destinies, or destroy them."

When she looked up at him, startled to hear him echo Carrick's words to her, he stroked her hair. "Come, let's go back. She makes you sad."

"Yes, she does." Jude clung to Aidan's hand now, for going down was trickier than going up. "I wish I could talk to her, and I can't believe I'm casually saying I wish I could talk to a ghost. But I do. I'd like to ask her what she feels and thinks and wishes, and what she would change."

"Her tears tell me she would change everything."

"No, women cry for all manner of reasons. To change everything, she'd have to give up the children she'd carried inside her, raised and loved. I don't think she could do that. Would do that. Carrick asked too much of her, and he doesn't understand that. Maybe one day he will, then they'll find each other."

"He only asked what he needed, and would have given all he had."

"You're thinking like a man."

"Well, it's a man I am, so how else would I think?"

It made her laugh, that hint of irritated pride in his voice. "Exactly as you do. And because a woman thinks like a woman, it explains why the two species are as often at odds as they are in sync."

"I don't mind being at odds off and on, as it keeps things more interesting. And since I'm thinking like a man right now . . ." He swept her up into his arms and muffled her surprised gasp with his mouth.

How could a kiss be gentle and searing at the same time? she wondered. So gentle it had tears swimming to her eyes, so hot it liquefied the bones. She let herself slide into it, a warm pool with flames licking at the edges.

"Do you want me, Jude? Tell me you want me."

"Yes, I want you. I always want you." She was already neck-deep in that pool, and slipping under.

"Make love with me here." He chewed restlessly on her bottom lip. "Here in the moonlight."

"Mmmm." She started to consent, then surfaced with a shot, an incautious diver clawing into the air. "Here? Outside?"

He would have been amused by her reaction, but the seduction he'd begun had circled around to claim him. "Here, on the grass, with the night breathing around us."

Still holding her, he knelt. And with his mouth roaming

her face, murmured to her, "Give yourself to me."

"But what if someone comes by?"

"There's no one but us, in the whole world, no one else." His hands moved over her, and his mouth. Even as she opened her own to protest, he spoke again. "I've such a need for you. Let me show you. Let me have you."

The grass was so soft, and he was so warm. To be needed was such a miracle, so much more important than sense and modesty. There was a tenderness in his hands as he stroked her, slowly, slowly, heating her blood. His mouth brushed over hers, whispering of promises.

And suddenly there was no one else in the world, and no need for there to be.

Lazily, she lifted her arms as he drew off her sweater. when he trailed his fingertips down her body, her eyes grew heavy, her body slumberous. He slipped off her shoes, her slacks, undressing her without hurry and letting his hands touch and linger where they liked until it seemed her skin hummed.

She lay naked in the grass, moonlight sprinkling over her. When she reached for him, he drew her up.

"I want to unbind your hair, to watch it tumble down." He kept his eyes on hers as he freed it. "Do you remember the first time?"

"Yes, I remember."

"Now I know what pleases you." He pressed his lips to her shoulder, then let her hair riot down to curtain his face and smother him with silk and scent. "Lie back on the grass and let me pleasure you." His teeth scraped lightly down the side of her neck as he lowered her again. "I'll give you all I have."

He could have feasted, but instead he only sipped. Long, luxurious kisses that shuddered into the soul and drew soft moans from it. And at each moan he went deeper.

He could have ravished, but instead he seduced. Slow, tender caresses that slid over the skin and sent it quivering. And at each quiver, he lingered.

She lost herself in him, in the delightfully dizzy mix of senses and sensations. Cool grass and warm flesh, fragrant breezes and husky whispers, strong hands and patient lips.

She watched the moon soar overhead, a gleaming white ball against a deep blue sky, chased by tattered wisps of clouds. She heard the call of an owl, a deep, demanding cry, and felt the echo of it leap into her blood as he urged her up and up to that first rippling crest.

She sang out his name, floating as the high, warm wave cascaded through her.

"Go higher." He was desperate to watch her fly, to know that he could send her up until her eyes were wild and blind and her body quaking. "Go higher," he demanded again, and drove her there more ruthlessly than he'd intended.

Heat flashed into her, a star exploding. The shock of pleasure was so intense, so unexpected after the tenderness, her body reared up, half in protest, half in delight. This time it wasn't a moan that escaped her, but a scream.

"Aidan." She gripped him for balance as her world went mad and they rolled over. "I can't."

"Again." He dragged her head back by the hair and savaged her mouth. "Again, until we're both empty." The hands that had been so gentle dug into her hips, lifted her. "Tell me you want me inside you. Me and no one else."

"Yes." She was frantic, all but weeping as her body bowed back. "You and no one else."

"Then take me."

He drew her down until she was filled with him, until the glory of it burst through her. Her breath tore from his throat as she arched back, her body silvered by the moonlight. Her hair rained back in a dark tangle. She lifted her arms, a gesture of abandon, tangling her own fingers in those tumbling curls.

Then her body began to rock, to move, to seek.

The power was hers now, the control of each whip of pleasure. As his body rose and fell to her pace, she let herself take. His muscles trembled as she stroked her hands over him. His eyes seemed dark as the night as she leaned close to torment his mouth as he had hers. The low groan she ripped from him had her laughing in triumph.

"Higher." She braced herself over him. "This time I'll take you higher." Boldly she took his hands, closed them over her breasts. "Touch me. Touch me everywhere while I take you."

She guided his hands where she wanted them, reveling in the feel of them over her slickened skin as she rode him closer and closer to the edge.

She felt his body plunge helplessly under her, heard his breath strangle in a gasp, and thrilled with what she'd done to him, let herself leap after.

It was he who shuddered, he whose hands slid limply away when she lowered to nuzzle her mouth to his. When she pressed her lips to his throat, she felt the wild beat of his pulse.

Then with a sound of triumph, she drew back and threw her arms high. "Oh, God, I feel wonderful! People should always make love outside. It's so . . . liberating."

"You look like a faerie queen yourself."

"I feel like one." She shook her hair back, then looked down to smile at him. "Full of magic and marvelous secrets. I'm so glad you're not angry with me. I was sure you would be."

"Angry? How could I be?" He gathered enough energy

to sit up so he could hold her, torso to torso. "Everything about you delights me."

She snuggled closer, still flying on the pleasure of the moment. "You weren't delighted with me last night."

"No, I can't say I was, but since we've straightened it all out, it's nothing to worry us."

"Straightened it out?"

"Aye. Here, let's get you back into your jumper before you get cold."

"What do you mean—" She broke off as he dragged her sweater over her head.

"There, that's all you'll need, as I'm going to get it off you again as soon as we get inside." He began to gather clothes and bundle them into her arms.

"Aidan, what do you mean we've straightened it all out?"

"Just that we have." Smiling easily, he picked her up and carried her toward the cottage. "We'll be married in September."

"What? Wait."

"I am, till September." He nudged open her garden gate.

"We're not getting married in September."

"Oh, we are, yes. Then we'll go off to the places you want to see."

"Aidan, that's not what I meant."

"It was what I meant." He smiled at her again, pleased he'd found just the way to handle the situation. "I don't mind if you need to wiggle around it for a while, darling. Not when we both know it's what's meant."

"Put me down."

"No, not quite yet." He carried her inside and started up the stairs.

"I'm not marrying you in September."

"Well, it's only a few months away, so we won't have long to see who's right in the matter."

"It's insulting, and it's infuriating that you simply assume I'll fall in line with your plans. And that I'm too stupid to know what I want for myself."

"I don't think you're stupid at all." He walked down to the bathroom. "Fact is, darling, I believe you're one of the smartest people I know. A bit stubborn is all, but I don't mind that." He hitched her up a bit, so he could reach out and turn on the shower.

"You don't mind that," she repeated.

"Not at all. Just as I don't mind having your eyes shoot darts at me as they are at the moment. I find it . . . stimulating."

"Put me down, Aidan."

"All right." He obliged by setting her in the tub, right under the stream from the shower.

"Damn it!"

"Don't worry about the jumper, I'll take care of it." And laughing while she shoved and wiggled, he stripped it off and tossed it with a wet plop onto the floor.

"Keep your hands off me. I want to settle this."

"You've settled it in your mind just as I have in mine. I say I want my way more than you want what you're thinking is yours. But . . ." He brushed the wet hair out of her face. "If you're so sure of yourself, you've nothing to worry about, and we can just enjoy the time we spend together."

"That isn't the point—"

"Are you saying you don't enjoy being with me?"

"Yes, of course I do, but—"

"Or that you don't know your own mind?"

"I certainly know my own mind."

He pressed still curved lips to her brow, her temples.

"Well then, what's wrong with giving me at least the chance to change it?"

"I don't know." But there had to be something wrong with it. Didn't there? Reason, she decided. Cool reason. Even if she was standing naked in the shower. "We're not talking about a whim here, Aidan. I take all of this very seriously, and I don't intend to change my mind."

"All right, then, in the fine Irish tradition, we'll wager on it. A hundred pounds says you will."

"I'm not betting on such a thing."

He lifted a shoulder carelessly, then picked up the soap. "If you're afraid to risk your money . . ."

"I'm not." She hissed out at him, trying to see exactly where he'd turned things around and trapped her. "Make it two hundred pounds."

"Done." He kissed the tip of her nose to seal it.

NINETEEN

IT WAS RIDICULOUS. She had actually bet money on whether or not she would marry Aidan. It was laughable. And annoying. And not a little embarrassing.

Temper had pushed her into it, which was odd in itself. She usually had such a mild and easily controllable temper.

She would forget the bet entirely, of course, when the time came. What point would there be in making herself or Aidan feel foolish by bringing it up?

For now she had chores and work to concentrate on. She needed to take Finn for a walk, and return the dishes that Mollie O'Toole had brought to her party. It was time to call home and check in with her family. Then, if the weather held, she'd set up her outside work area.

She wanted to write down the story Aidan had told her the night before. Already she had the rhythm of it in her head, and the images of the white bird and the black wolf. She doubted she would do them justice, but she needed to try.

She gathered the dishes, along with a container of sugar cookies she'd baked. Ready to set out, she glanced around for the dog just in time to see him squat under the kitchen table and pee. Naturally he'd missed the paper by two feet.

"Couldn't have waited one more minute, could you?" She only chuckled when he cheerfully thumped his tail, then she set the dishes down again to deal with the puddle.

He had to leap and lick at her face and make growling sounds while she scrubbed it up, which made her forget to scold him. Since cuddling him made her as happy as it made him, she spent ten minutes nuzzling, wrestling, and scratching his belly.

She'd spoil him, of course, Jude admitted. But who could have known she had all this love inside her she needed to give?

"I'm nearly thirty," she murmured as she stroked Finn's long, silky ears. "I want a home. I want a family. I want them with a man who loves me outrageously." She cuddled as Finn wiggled around to lick her hand. "I can't settle again. I can't take a life in pieces just because it looks like the best I can get. So . . ."

She picked Finn up to rub her nose against his. "For right now, it's just you and me, pal."

The minute she opened the back door, he was off like a spotted arrow. It delighted her to see him race even if his first sprint was directly toward her flowers. He stopped, skidding and tumbling, when she called his name sharply. She considered it progress that he flattened only one row of ageratum.

Finn darted ahead of her, darted back, raced in circles around her feet, then zigged and zagged off to sniff at everything of interest. She imagined how he'd look when he grew into his feet, a big, handsome dog with a whipcord tail who loved to run the hills.

What in God's name was she going to do with him in Chicago?

Shaking her head, she pushed that worry aside. There was no point in thinking of something that would spoil the pleasure of her walk.

The air was crystal, with the sun sliding and streaming through clouds on their way to England. She caught glimpses of Ardmore Bay, rolling dark green toward shore. If she stopped, concentrated, she could almost hear its music in the shimmering silence. Tourists would flock to the beaches today, and some of the locals as well if they had an hour or two to spare.

Young mothers, she thought, letting their toddlers dip their toes in the surf, or fill their red plastic buckets with sand. Castles would be built today, then washed away by the sea.

The hedgerows that lined the road were ripe with summer blossoms, and the grass beneath her feet was springy and sparkled with morning dew. To the north, the mountains hulked under the clouds that covered their peaks. And between them and Jude, it seemed the green, glorious hills rolled forever.

She loved the look of them, the simple and sheer beauty of land, the tumble of old castles that had been swamped not by sea but by time and enemy. They made her think of knights and maidens, of kings both petty and grand, of merry servants and clever spies. And of course of magic and witchcraft and the songs of faeries.

More tales to be told, she mused, of sacrifices for love and glory, of the triumph of the heart and of honor, of spells cast and broken.

In a place like this, a storyteller could spend years collecting them, creating them, and passing them on. She could spend silvery mornings like this one roaming and imagining, rainy afternoons writing and compiling. Evenings would be for curling up after a satisfying day and finding pictures in the turf fire, or wandering into the pub for noise and company and music.

It would be such a lovely life, full of interest and beauty and dreams.

She stopped short, startled by the thought, more startled yet that the thought had been in her head at all. She could stay, not just for three more months but forever. She could write stories. The ones that were told to her and the ones that seemed always forming in her head.

No, of course she couldn't. What was she thinking of? She let out a laugh, but it was edgy and weak. She had to go back to Chicago as planned, to find work in some area of the field she knew to support her sensibly while she pursued the dream. To consider anything else was completely irresponsible.

Why?

She'd only taken two more steps when that question struck out.

"Why?" She said it out loud, flustered. "Of course there's a reason why. A dozen reasons why. I live in Chicago. I've always lived in Chicago."

There was no law that said she *had* to live in Chicago. She wouldn't be chained in a dungeon for relocating.

"Of course not, but . . . I have to work."

And what have you been doing these past three months?

"That's not work, not really." Her stomach began to jitter, her heart to flutter toward her throat. "It's more of an indulgence."

Why?

She closed her eyes. "Because I love it. I love everything about it, so that must make it an indulgence. And that is incredibly stupid."

It might have been an odd place for an epiphany, on a shaggy hill in the middle of the morning. But she decided it was the perfect place for hers.

"Why can't I do something I love without putting restrictions on it? Why can't I live somewhere that's so much more home than anywhere else? Who's in charge of my life," she said on a baffled laugh, "if I'm not?"

With her knees a little shaky, she began to walk again. She could do it; if she could dig down and find the courage. She could sell her condo. She could do what she'd been avoiding out of fear of failure and send a sample of her work to an agent.

She could finally stick, win or lose, with something she wanted for herself.

She would think about it, seriously, carefully. Walking faster, she ignored the voice in her head that urged her to act now, right away, before she could find excuses. It would be a big move, she reasoned, an enormous step. A sensible person thought through big moves and enormous steps.

Jude was grateful when she saw the O'Toole cottage over the hill. She needed the distraction, something to take her mind off herself for a while.

Clothes were already drying on the line, making her wonder if Mollie did laundry twenty-four hours a day. The gardens were in glorious bloom and the little shed as stuffed and jumbled as ever. Betty rose from her morning nap in the yard and gave a welcoming woof that sent Finn into devoted yips as he streaked down the hill toward her.

Jude started after and had just reached the edge of the yard when the kitchen door opened.

"Well, good morning to you, Jude." Mollie sent her a wave. "You're up and about early today."

"Not as early as you, from the looks of things."

"You have yourself a houseful of chattering girls and a

man who likes his tea before his eyes are open, you don't have much chance to stay in bed. Come in, have some tea and visit with me while I make my bread.''

''I brought your dishes back, and some of the sugar cookies I made yesterday. I think they're better than the last batch.''

''We'll sample them with the tea and see.''

She held the door open wide, and Jude walked into the warmth and the scents and the clatter of Brenna wielding tools under the kitchen sink.

''I've about got it now, Ma.''

''So you'd better.'' Mollie moved to the stove. ''I tell you, Jude, I'm the shoemaker's wife in this house. Off himself goes, as does this girl here, fixing and fiddling with everyone else's matter, while I live with drips and rattles day and night.''

''Well, you don't pay a body a living wage, now do you?'' Brenna said and earned a light kick from her mother.

''A living wage, is it? And who ate a mountain of eggs and a tower of toast and jam just this morning?''

''I only did so I'd have my mouth full and not tell Maureen to stop her harping on the wedding plans. The girl's driving us all batty, Jude, fussing and whining and bursting into tears for no reason at all.''

''Getting married's plenty of reason for all of the above.'' Mollie set out the tea and cookies, nodded for Jude to sit, then plunged her hands back into the ball of dough she was kneading. ''And when your time comes you'll be worse yet.''

''Ha. If I was thinking of marriage, I'd haul the man before the priest, say the words and be done with it,'' Brenna declared. ''All this fancy work—dresses and flowers and just which song needs to be played just when. Months in the making for one single day, for a dress that will never be worn again, flowers that will fade and wither, and songs you could sing any damn time.''

She scooted out from under the sink and gestured with her wrench. ''And the cost of it all is sinful.''

''Ah, Brenna, you romantic fool.'' Mollie sprinkled more flour onto her dough and turned it. ''That one single day is the start of a life, and worth every minute of time and every penny that goes into it.'' But she sighed a little. ''Still, it does get wearying, dealing with her nerves.''

''Exactly.'' Brenna put the wrench in her dented toolbox and rose to snatch one of the cookies. ''Look at our Jude here. Calm as you please. You don't hear her blathering on about whether she'll have white roses or pink in her bouquet.'' Brenna bit into the cookie and dropped into a chair. ''You're a sensible woman.''

''Thank you. I try. But what are you talking about?''

''The difference between you and my flighty sister. The both of you have weddings coming up, but are you pacing around the room wringing your hands and changing your mind about the flavor of the cake every two minutes? Of course not.''

''No,'' Jude said slowly. ''I'm not, because I don't have a wedding coming up.''

''Even if you and Aidan have a small ceremony—though how you'd pull that off when he knows every second soul for a hundred kilometers—it's still a wedding.''

Jude had to take a breath, then another. ''Where did you get the idea that I'm marrying Aidan?''

''From Darcy.'' Brenna leaned forward for another cookie. ''She had it straight from the horse's mouth.''

''The horse's ass is more apt.''

At the snap of her tone, Brenna blinked and Mollie paused in her kneading. Before Brenna could speak, Mollie shot out a warning look. ''Fill your mouth with that biscuit, lass, before you put the rest of your foot in it.''

"But Darcy said—''

"Perhaps Darcy misunderstood.''

"No, I don't imagine she did.'' Temper leaped into Jude's throat. When she couldn't choke it down again, she shoved away from the table and got to her feet. "Where does a man get that kind of nerve, that much arrogance?''

"Most are born with it,'' Brenna said, then ducked her head and winced at her mother's hiss.

"I have to say, Jude, that I myself thought that's where the two of you were heading, seeing the way you are with each other.'' Mollie kept her voice soothing, and her eyes keen on Jude's face. "When Brenna told us at dinner last night, not one of us was surprised, but we were pleased.''

"Told you . . . at dinner.'' Jude stopped at the table, braced her palms on it and leaned into Brenna's face. "You told your whole family?''

"Well, I didn't see how—''

"Who else? How many people have you told this ridiculous story to?''

"I . . .'' Brenna cleared her throat. Having a rare temper herself, she recognized the danger signs when they were stuck in her face. "I can't recall, precisely. Not many. A few. Hardly anyone at all. We were so pleased, you see, Darcy and myself. As we're so fond of you and Aidan, and knowing how Aidan can plod about before he gets to the center of things, hoped that the *ceili* might give him a bit of a boost.''

"The *ceili*?''

"Aye, Midsummer's Eve and the moon and such. You remember, Ma?'' She turned to Mollie with a desperate look in her eye. "Remember how you told us the way Dad proposed to you when you were dancing in the moonlight at a *ceili*? And at Old Maude's cottage, too.''

"I do, yes." And she began to see. With a quiet smile, she patted her daughter's shoulder. "You meant well, didn't you?"

"Yes, we—ow!" Wincing, Brenna grabbed the nose her mother had just twisted.

"That's to remind you to keep that nose of yours out of other people's business however well meant."

"It's not her fault." Jude lifted her hands to her hair and barely resisted pulling it out. "It's Aidan's fault. What is he thinking of, telling his sister we're getting married? I said no, didn't I? Very plainly and several times."

"You said no," Brenna and Mollie said together, with mirror looks of shock.

"I see what he's doing, I see what he's up to." She whirled away to stalk around the room again. "He needs a wife and I'm available, so that's it. I'm just to fall in line because, after all, I obviously have no backbone. Well, he's wrong about that. I've got one. Maybe I haven't used it much, but it's there. I'm not marrying him or anyone. I'm never going to be told what to do again, or where to live or how to live or what to be. Not ever, ever again."

Mollie studied the flushed face, the fisted hands and nodded slowly. "Well, now, good for you. Why don't you take a bit of a breath now, darling, and sit down here, drink your tea and tell us, as we're all friends, exactly what happened."

"I'll tell you what happened. Then you," she added, jabbing a finger at Brenna. "You can go down to the village and tell everyone just what a brainless fool Aidan Gallagher is and that Jude Murray wouldn't have him on a platter."

"I can do that," Brenna agreed with a cautious smile.

"Fine." Jude took that breath, then sat down to tell the tale.

•   •   •

It helped a great deal to vent to friends. It took the sharpest edge off her temper, strengthened her resolve, and gave her the satisfaction of having two other women outraged at Aidan's behavior.

By the time she left, she'd been given pats and hugs and congratulations on her stand against a bully. Of course she had no way of knowing that the minute she left, mother and daughter dug out twenty pounds each to lay on Aidan.

It wasn't that they didn't sympathize with Jude, or believe she had sense enough to know what she wanted. It was simply that they believed in destiny—and a good wager.

With the stake in her pocket, Brenna drove into town to tell Darcy what a great boob her brother was—and to start the pool.

Fortunately ignorant of this, Jude walked back to her house feeling lighter of heart and stronger in the spine. She wasn't going to bother confronting Aidan. She told herself it wasn't worth the time or effort. She would be calm, she would remain firm, and this time he would be the one humiliated.

Pleased with herself, she went directly to the phone in her kitchen and took the next step without a moment's hesitation.

Thirty minutes later, she sat at the table and laid her head on her arms.

She'd done it. She'd actually done it.

Her condo was going on the market. As the couple Jude had rented to had already made inquiries about the possibility of buying it, the realtor was optimistic that it would sell quickly and with a minimum of fuss. She'd booked a flight for the end of the month so that she could go through her possessions, ship or store what she wanted to keep, and sell or give away the rest.

So much, she thought, for a life she'd built on other people's expectations. She stayed as she was, holding her breath to see what reaction would set in.

Panic? Regret? Depression?

But it was none of those. It was done, so easily, too, and there was a huge weight off her shoulders at the idea of it. Relief was what she felt. Relief, anticipation, and a wicked little thrill of accomplishment.

She no longer lived in Chicago. She lived in Faerie Hill Cottage, County Waterford, Ireland.

Her parents were going to faint.

At the thought of that, she sat up, pressed both hands to her mouth to hold back the wild laughter. They'd think she'd lost her mind. And would never, ever understand that what she'd done was found it. She'd found her mind, and her heart and her home.

And, she thought, a little dizzy herself, her purpose.

"Gran, I found me. I found Jude F. Murray in six months or less. How about that?"

The call to New York was harder. Because it was more important, Jude realized. Beyond the symbolism of the sale of the condo. That only meant money. The call to New York equaled her future, the future she was giving herself.

She wasn't certain whether her acquaintance from college had remembered her or had simply pretended to out of politeness. But she'd taken the call, and she'd listened. Jude couldn't quite remember what she'd said, or what Holly had said back. Except that Holly Carter Fry, literary agent, told Jude F. Murray she very much liked the sound of her book and instructed Jude to send a sample of her work in progress.

Because the thought of doing so made her stomach pitch

crazily, Jude made herself get up, walk up the stairs. Her fingers might have trembled as she sat down to type the cover letter. But she clicked her mind over to logical and wrote what she thought was both polite and professional.

She only had to stop to put her head between her knees once.

She gathered the first three stories, and the prologue, words she'd labored over, poured her heart into. She could feel herself getting weepy as she slid the drawings into a folder, packaged everything in a padded envelope.

She was sending her heart across the ocean, risking having it shattered. Easier not to, she thought, stepping away to rub her chilled arms and stare out the window. Easier to just go on pretending she meant to, one day. Easier still to go back to convincing herself it was just an indulgence, an experiment she had no real stake in.

Because once she mailed that envelope, there was no going back, no more pretending, no more safety net.

That was it, had been it all along, she realized. It was easier to tell herself she wasn't very good at something. Safer to believe she wasn't clever or quick. Because if you had confidence enough to try something, you had to have courage enough to fail.

She'd failed with her marriage, and ultimately with her teaching—two things she'd been certain she was suited for.

But there were so many other things she'd wanted, dreamed of, that she'd locked away. Always telling herself to be sensible because people expected her to be.

But more, deep down more, the knowing if she failed, she'd have to live with it. And she hadn't had the courage for it.

She glanced back at the envelope, squared her shoulders. She had it now. This time, with this dream, if she didn't try, she *couldn't* live with it.

"Wish me luck," she murmured to whatever drifted through her house, and grabbed the envelope.

She didn't let herself think on the drive to town. She was going to mail it, then forget it, she told herself. She would not spend every day agonizing, fretting, projecting. She would know when she knew, and if it wasn't good enough . . . somehow she'd make it better.

While she was waiting, she would finish the book. She would polish it until it gleamed like a diamond. Then, well, she'd start another. Stories that came out of her head this time. Mermaids and shape-changers and magic bottles. She had a feeling that now that she'd popped the cork on her imagination, things would spurt out so quickly she wouldn't be able to keep up.

There was a roaring in her ears as she parked in front of the post office. Her heart was beating so fast and so thick her chest hurt. Her knees wanted to buckle, but she made herself cross the sidewalk and open the door.

The postmistress had snowy white hair and skin as dewy as a girl's. She sent Jude a cheery smile. "Hello, there, Miss Murray. How's it all going, then?"

"Very well, thank you." *Liar, liar, liar* chanted in her head. Any second she would lose the battle with nausea and humiliate herself.

"To be sure it's a lovely day. The finest summer we've had in many a year. Maybe you've brought us luck."

"I like to think so." With a smile that felt like a death grimace on her face, Jude set the envelope on the counter.

"Are you sending something to a friend in America, then?"

"Yes." Jude kept the smile in place while the woman read the address. "An old college friend of mine. She lives in New York now."

"My grandson Dennis and his wife and family live in

New York City. Dennis, he works in a fancy hotel and makes a good wage hauling people's luggage up and down the elevator. He says some of the rooms are like palaces.''

Jude was afraid her face might crack, but she continued to smile. She'd learned enough in three months to know one didn't just scoot in and out of the post office, or anywhere else in Ardmore, without a bit of conversation.

''Does he enjoy his work?''

''Aye, that he does, and his pretty wife worked doing hair and such until the second baby came along.''

''That's nice. I'd like this to get to New York as soon as possible.''

''If you're wanting to send it special that way, it'll be a bit dear.''

''That's all right.'' She felt as if she were moving through clear syrup as she reached into her bag for her wallet. In a daze she watched the weight and cost calculated, passed over the pounds and took the coins in change.

''Thank you.''

''It's not a problem. No problem at all. Will your friend from New York be coming in for the wedding?''

''What?''

''No doubt your family will, but it's nice to have old friends as well, isn't it?''

The roaring in her head became a harsh buzzing. Nerves were so quickly smothered by blank fury, she could only stare.

''My John and I've been married near fifty years now, and still I remember so clear the day we wed. It rained a torrent, but it didn't matter in the least to me. All my family was there, and John's as well, packed into the little church so the smell of wet wool fought with the scent of the flowers. And me da, rest him, wept like a baby when he walked me down the aisle, for I was his only daughter.''

"That's lovely," Jude managed when she had her breath back. "But I'm not getting married."

"Oh, now, did you and Aidan have a lovers' spat already?" The postmistress tut-tutted kindly. "Don't take on about that, darling, it's natural as the rain."

"We didn't have a spat." But she had a feeling they were going to have the world's champion of spats very soon. "I'm just not getting married."

"You make him work for it," she said with a wink. "Doesn't hurt them a bit, and makes for a better husband in the end. Oh, and you should talk to Kathy Duffy about the wedding cake. She makes a fine one, pretty as a picture."

"I don't need a cake," Jude said between her teeth.

"Now, then, just because it's your second time doesn't mean you don't deserve a cake. Every bride does. And for the dress you should talk to Mollie O'Toole, as she found a lovely shop in Waterford City for her daughter's."

"I don't need a cake or a dress," Jude said, waging a vicious war for patience, "because I'm not getting married. Thank you."

She turned on her heel and marched to the door.

When she stepped out on the sidewalk, sucked in air, she glared at the sign for Gallagher's.

She couldn't go in now, couldn't possibly. She'd kill him if she did.

And why the hell shouldn't she? He deserved to die.

Long, purposeful strides ate up the ground until she reached the pub. And flung the door open.

"Aidan Gallagher!"

The room filled to bursting with locals and the tourists who'd stopped in for a bite to eat or a drink went dead quiet at her outburst.

At the bar Aidan paused in the draft he was drawing.

When she stalked to the bar, the gleam in her eye laser-bright, he set the pint aside. She didn't look a thing like the soft, sleepy woman he'd left shortly after dawn. That woman had looked silky and satisfied.

And this one looked murderous.

"I want a word with you," she told him.

He didn't think it was going to be a good word. "All right, then, give me a minute here and we'll go upstairs where we can be private."

"Oh, now he wants privacy. Well, forget it." She turned to the room. The stares and interested faces didn't embarrass her this time, didn't give her that hollow feeling in the belly. This time they fueled an already black temper.

"You're all welcome to listen to what I have to say, since every one of you who lives in the village is already discussing my business by now. Let me make it very clear. I am not marrying this baboon disguised as a man."

There were a few snickers, and when she saw the kitchen door slit open, she spun back again. "Don't stand behind the door, Shawn, come right on out. It's not you I'm after."

"And thank God for it," he muttered, but being a loyal brother he came out to stand beside Aidan.

"Pretty as a picture, the pair of you. And you, too," she said, pointing at Darcy. "I hope you both have more brains than your brother, who seems to think because he's got a handsome face women are going to swoon at his feet at the first sign of attention."

"Now, Jude darling."

"Don't you darling me." She reared up over the bar to rap a fist on his chest. "And don't call me Jude in that patient, infuriatingly placating tone, you . . . bloody moron."

His own eyes flashed and temper threatened. He jerked

his thumb at Shawn to take over the taps and nodded to Jude. "We'll go upstairs and finish this."

"I'm going nowhere with you." She rapped her fist on his chest again, enjoying the violence of it. "I will not be bullied."

"Bullied? Who's bullying you, I'd like to know, when you're the one pounding on me?"

"I can do worse." She was suddenly, thrillingly, sure of it. "If you think that by telling everyone who'll listen I'm going to marry you, you'll pressure me into it, or embarrass me into it, or just wear me down, you're in for a surprise. I have no intention of being told what to do with my life, not by you, not by anyone."

She spun around again. "And everyone here better understand that. Just because I'm sleeping with him doesn't mean I'm shopping for a wedding cake when he snaps his fingers. I'll sleep with whomever I please."

"I'm available," someone called out and brought on hoots of laughter.

"That's enough." Aidan slammed a hand on the bar, and the glasses jumped. "This is private business." He shoved past Shawn to flip up the pass-through. "Upstairs, Jude Frances."

"No." She kept her chin up. "And since that appears to be a word you have trouble with, I'll ask which part of no you don't understand."

"Upstairs," he said again, and took a firm grip on her arm. "This isn't the place."

"It's *your* place," she reminded him. "And it's your doing. Take your hand off me."

"We'll discuss this in private."

"I'm done discussing it." When she tried to yank her arm free, he simply started hauling her toward the back. The fact that he could, that people parted way for them, that he was strong enough to drag her wherever he chose snapped something inside her. And the last lock of that dark, bubbling brew broke clean.

"I said take your hand off me, you son of a bitch." She couldn't quite remember doing it, not with the red haze coating her vision, but she felt the impact sing up her free arm as her fist connected with his face.

"Holy Christ." Stars exploded in his head, and the pain was as awesome as the sheer shock of what she'd done. Instinctively he pressed a hand under his nose as blood began to pour.

"And keep them off," she said with great dignity, as the pub once again fell silent. She turned and walked out seconds before the applause erupted.

"Here, try this." Shawn passed him over a rag. "That's a hell of a right jab our Jude has."

"Aye." He had to sit down and did so as Darcy pulled him toward a vacated stool. "What hell got into her?" He ignored the new bets being laid in the marriage pool, and took, with gratitude, the ice Shawn brought him.

He stared at the bloody rag with both amazement and disgust. "The woman's managed what hasn't been done in thirty-one years. She's broke my goddamn nose."

TWENTY

"I'M NOT GOING after her, chasing her like a puppy."

Shawn continued to fry up fish and chips while Aidan iced down his abused nose in the kitchen. "So you've said, ten or twelve times in the last twenty minutes."

"Well, I'm not."

"Fine. Be a bloody brick-headed idiot."

"Don't you start on me." Aidan lowered the ice pack. "I can hit you back."

"And so you have, more times than I care to count. Doesn't make you less of an idiot."

"Why am I an idiot? She's the one who comes swaggering in here, peak hour, too, looking for trouble, badgering me, poking at me, and breaking me fucking nose."

"That's got you, doesn't it?" Shawn slid the golden hunks of fish and servings of chips onto plates, added a scoop of slaw, and garnished them with a bit of parsley. "That after all these years and all the fine battles, it's a woman half your size who did the deed."

" 'Twas a lucky punch," Aidan muttered as his pride throbbed in time with his nose.

"Sucker punch, more like," Shawn corrected. "And you're the sucker," he added as he swung out the door with the orders.

"So much for family loyalty." Disgusted, Aidan got up to root through cupboards for some aspirin. His face ached like a bitch in heat.

Under other circumstances, he supposed he'd have admired Jude for her fine show of temper, and her aim. But he couldn't find it in him at the moment.

She'd hurt him, face, pride, and heart. He'd never had a woman break his heart before, and didn't know what the devil to do about it. He'd understood, at least in part, that he'd bungled things the night of the *ceili*. But he'd been so sure, so confident, that he had fixed all that the night before.

Romance and teasing, perseverance and persuasion. What else did the damn woman want, damn it to the devil and back again? They fit together, anyone could see that.

Everyone, it seemed, but Jude Frances Murray herself.

How could she not want him when he wanted her so much he could barely breathe? How could she not see the life they'd make together when he could see it clear as glass?

It was all to do with that first marriage of hers, he thought darkly. Well, he'd gotten over it, why couldn't she?

"She's just being stubborn," he said to Shawn when his brother came back in.

"That makes her a perfect match for you, then."

"It's not being stubborn to go after what you know is right."

Shawn shook his head and began to build the sandwiches needed out in the pub. The place was a madhouse, he mused, with people staying long past their usual time, and others coming in as they got word of the situation. They'd asked Michael O'Toole and Kathy Duffy to lend a hand at the bar, and Brenna was on her way. He didn't think Aidan would be in the mood for pulling pints and making conversation for a bit longer yet.

"No, I suppose it's not," he said after a moment. "But there are ways and ways of going about it with a woman."

"A lot you know about women."

"More than you, I wager, as I've never had one plant her fist in my face."

"Neither have I up till now." Even half frozen from the ice, his nose was pounding like a kettledrum. "It's not the reaction a man expects when he asks a woman to marry him."

"It wasn't the asking, I'd say, but the way of asking."

"How many ways do you ask?" Aidan demanded. "And why is this my fault, I'd like to know?"

"Because it's pitiful obvious that she loves you, and needs love in return. So if you hadn't made a mess of it, she wouldn't have said no and broken your nose."

While Aidan gaped at him, Shawn strode out to deliver the next order. He started to leap up and follow, then calculated he'd spread enough of his personal business out into the pub and village that day. So he paced impatiently and waited for Shawn to come back in.

He carried empty plates this time and slid them into the sink. "Make yourself useful and wash up, would you? I've more fish and chips wanted."

"Maybe I made a mess of it the first time," Aidan began. "I admit that. I even talked it over with Darcy."

"Darcy?" All Shawn could do was roll his eyes to heaven. "Now I can say without a doubt you are an idiot."

"She's Jude's friend, and a woman."

"Without a single romantic bone in her body. Forget the

washing, I'll tend to it later," he continued as he dredged fish in flour. "Sit down and tell me how you went about it."

He wasn't used to his younger brother issuing directions, and he wasn't sure how it sat with him. But he was a desperate man ready to take desperate measures. "Which time?"

"However many there were, starting with the first." Shawn slid the fish and potatoes into the oil and began to make a fresh batch of slaw.

He listened without a word while he worked. When the order was finished before his brother was, he held up a finger, surprising Aidan into silence, and went out again to serve it.

"Now, then." When he came back, he sat, folded his arms on the table, and gave Aidan a level look. "I'm taking ten minutes here to tell you what I think. But first I have a question. In all this telling her what you wanted and how it would be and what should be done, did you happen to mention that you love her?"

"Of course I did." Hadn't he? Aidan shifted in his chair, moved his shoulder. "She knows I love her. A man doesn't ask a woman to be his wife unless he loves her."

"First off, Aidan, you didn't ask her at all, but told her, and that's a different matter entirely. Plus it seems to me the one who asked her before didn't love her, else he wouldn't have broken his vows to her before a year was up. Certainly she'd have no reason to think he loved her, would she?"

"No, but—"

"Did you tell her or not?"

"Maybe I didn't. It's not so easy just to blurt such a thing out."

"Why?"

"It just isn't," Aidan muttered. "And I'm not some bloody Yank who'd leave her that way. I'm an Irishman who keeps his word, a Catholic who thinks of marriage as a sacrament."

"Oh, well, then, that'll convince her. If she marries you it'll be a matter of your honor and your religion that keeps you with her."

"That's not what I meant." His head was starting to spin. "I'm just saying she should trust me not to hurt her the way she's been hurt."

"Better, Aidan, she trusts you to love her as she's never been loved."

Aidan opened his mouth, shut it again. "When did you get so smart?"

"Nearly thirty years of watching people, and avoiding the situation you find yourself in. I don't think she's a woman who's been given love and respect in equal measure. And she needs them."

"I have both for her."

"I know you do." Sympathy stirred and Shawn gave Aidan's arm a squeeze. "But she doesn't. It's time to humble yourself. That's the hardest thing for you, I know. She'll know it, too."

"You're saying I have to grovel."

Now Shawn flashed a grin. "Your knees'll take it."

"I suppose they will. Can't be more painful than a broken nose."

"Do you want her?"

"More than anything."

"If you don't tell her just that, if you don't give her your heart, Aidan, if you don't bare it for her and give her the time to trust what she sees there, you'll never have her."

"She might turn me away again."

"She might." Shawn rose, laid a hand on Aidan's shoulder. "It's a risk. I don't recall you ever being afraid of taking a chance."

"Then here's another first for you." Aidan reached up, laid his hand on his brother's. "I'm terrified." A little shaky in the gut, he rose. "I'll take a walk if you can hold things here. Get my mind clear before I go see her." Then he touched his fingers gingerly to his nose. "How bad is it?"

"Oh," Shawn said cheerfully. "It's bad. And it'll get worse."

Her hand hurt like six devils. If she hadn't been so busy cursing, she would have worried she'd broken something in it. But as she could still make a fist, she assumed it was only jarred from ramming into the concrete block that disguised itself as Aidan Gallagher's head.

The first thing she did was grab the phone and change her airline reservations. She was leaving the very next day. Not that Aidan was running her off—oh, no indeed. She just wanted to get to Chicago, handle what needed to be handled quickly, efficiently, and personally before she came back.

Then she would plant herself in Faerie Hill Cottage and live a long and happy life doing as she chose, when she chose, and with whom she chose. And the single person who was not on that list of choices was Aidan Gallagher.

She called Mollie and arranged for her to dog-sit Finn.

Already missing him and riddled with guilt for leaving him behind, she picked him up and hugged him.

"You'll have a wonderful time at the O'Tooles'. You'll see. And I'll be back before you know I'm gone. I'll bring you a present." She kissed his nose.

Since she was in no mood to work, she went upstairs to pack. She wouldn't need much. Even if the business of relocating took a week or two, she had clothes in Chicago. She'd make do with no more than her carry-on and her laptop and feel very cosmopolitan.

Once she was on the plane, she'd settle back with a glass of celebratory champagne and make a list of all that needed to be done.

She'd persuade her grandmother to come back with her, to spend the rest of the summer. She would even try to convince her parents that they should come visit so they could see that she was settled and happy.

Everything else was just practical. Selling her car, the furniture, shipping the few things she loved. It was surprising how little of what she'd collected in the past few years she really loved.

Closing bank accounts, she mused as she set her carry-on beside the closet door. Finalizing paperwork. Arranging for a permanent change of address. A week, she calculated. Ten days at most, and it would be behind her.

The sale of the condo could be completed by mail and by phone.

It was all arranged, she thought. She'd take Finn and the keys to the cottage to Mollie in the morning, then drive to Dublin. Then she looked around and wondered what she would do with herself until morning.

She would work in the garden for now, so she could leave it in absolutely perfect shape, without a single weed or faded bloom. Then she'd go visit Maude one more time just to let her know she was going away for a few days.

Pleased with the idea, Jude gathered her gardening tools and gloves, slapped her hat on her head, and went out to work.

Aidan hadn't intended to walk by Maude's grave; but he usually followed impulse. When his feet took him there, he loitered, hoping, he supposed, to find inspiration—or at least a bit of sympathy for his situation.

He crouched down to trail his fingers over the flowers Jude had left there.

"She comes to see you often. She has a warm heart, and a generous one. I have to hope it's warm enough, generous enough, to spare a bit for me. She's your blood," he added. "And though I didn't know you as a young woman, I've heard tales that tell me you had a quick temper and a hard head—begging your pardon. I've come to see she takes after you, and I have to admire her for it. I'm going to see her now, and ask her again."

"Then don't make the same mistakes I did."

Aidan looked up, and into sharp green eyes. He straightened slowly. "So, you're real as well."

"As real as the day," Carrick assured him. "Twice she's said no. If she says so again, you're of no use to me, and I've wasted my time."

"I'm not asking her to be of use to you."

"Still and all, I've only one chance left. So have a care, Gallagher. I can't weave a spell here. It's forbidden, even to me. But I've a word of advice."

"I've had plenty of that today, thanks."

"Take this as well. Love, even when pledged, isn't enough."

Annoyed, Aidan dragged a hand through his hair. "Then what the devil is?"

Carrick smiled. "It's a word that still sticks a bit in my throat. It's called compromise. Go now while she's being charmed by her own flowers. It might give you an edge." The smile widened into a grin. "The way you're looking right now, you'll need all the help you can come by."

"Thanks very much," Aidan muttered even as his visitor vanished in a silver shimmer of air.

Shoulders hunched, he started toward the cottage. "My own brother calling me a brickhead. Sneering faeries insulting me. Women punching me in the face. How much more am I to swallow in one bloody day?"

As he spoke, the sky darkened, and thunder rumbled ominously. "Oh, go ahead, then." Aidan glanced up with a scowl. "Shake your fist. This is my life I'm dealing with here."

He jammed his hands in his pockets and tried to forget that his face ached like one huge bad tooth.

He came around the back, had nearly knocked on the kitchen door when he remembered Carrick had said she was with her flowers. Since she wasn't at the ones there, it meant she was in the front.

Breathing slow to steady his nerves, he circled the house.

She was singing. In all the time he'd known her, he'd never heard her sing. And though she'd claimed to do so only when nervous, he didn't think that was what brought her voice out.

She was singing to her flowers, and it stirred his heart. She had a sweet and a tentative voice that told him she didn't trust it, not even when she thought no one could hear.

It was a pretty sight she made, kneeling by her blossoms, singing quietly of being alone in a festive hall, with her foolish straw hat tipped over her face and the pup curled sleeping on the path behind her.

She didn't seem to notice the dark clouds brewing overhead, the threat of storms grumbling. She was a steady and bright spot in a magic little world, and if he hadn't already loved her, he would have tumbled at that moment. But he didn't know how to explain to either of them the why of it.

His heart was simply hers. He knew stepping forward

with nothing to guard it was the greatest risk a man could take.

He stepped forward, and said her name.

Her head whipped up, her eyes met his. He was sorry to see that soft and content expression vanish from her face, to be replaced by a cold and steely anger. But it wasn't entirely unexpected.

"I've finished talking to you."

"I know it."

Finn woke and with a joyful bark, scrambled to greet him. That's what he'd expected of her, he realized. That she would always be happy to see him, that she would rush forward eager for his attention.

It was hardly a wonder, he thought, she'd given him the boot when he'd treated her a bit like a puppy.

"I have a few things to say to you. The first of them being I'm sorry."

That threw her off, but not enough to soften her. It might have taken her years to learn how to use her spine, but she knew now. "Fine. Then I'll apologize for hitting you."

His nose was swollen, and bruising was already spreading under his eyes. Had she actually done that? She found the fact horrifying and shamefully thrilling.

"You broke my nose."

"I did?" Shock struck first, and she took a step toward him before she snapped herself back. "Well, you deserved it."

"I did, yes." He tried a smile. "You'll be the talk of the village for years."

Because she discovered a dark place inside her that found delight in that, she spoke primly. "I'm sure everyone will find something more interesting to talk about soon. Now, if that's all, you'll have to excuse me. I need to finish this and see to a number of other things before I leave tomorrow.''

''Leave?'' He recognized panic now when it grabbed him by the throat. ''Where are you going?''

''I'm going back to Chicago in the morning.''

''Jude—'' He started forward, stopped short, warned back by the flash in her eye. He wanted to kneel, to beg and plead, imagined he would before it was done. ''Is your mind set on it?''

''Yes, it is. I've made the arrangements.''

He turned away to gather himself. He looked out over the hills, and toward the village, the sea. Home. ''Would you tell me if you're going because of me, or because it's what you want?''

''It's what I want. I'm just—''

''All right, then.'' Shawn had said he'd be humbled, and so he was. He turned back, walked toward her slowly. ''I've things to say, things to tell you. I'm only asking you to listen.''

''I am listening.''

''I'm getting to it,'' he muttered. ''You could give a man a moment when he's changing his life right in front of your eyes. I'm asking for another chance, even if I don't deserve it. I'm asking you to forget the way I put things twice before and listen to how I put them now. You're a strong woman. That's something you're just finding out, but you're not a hard one. So I'm asking you to put aside your anger for just a moment so you can see . . .''

When he trailed off, looking perplexed and flustered, she only shook her head. ''I don't know what you're talking about. I accepted your apology, you accepted mine.''

''Jude.'' He grabbed her hand, squeezed hard enough to have her eyes widen in surprise. ''I don't know how to do this. My stomach's in knots over it. It never mattered before, don't you see? I've got words. I've barrels of words, but I don't know the ones to use with you, because my life's in the balance.''

She'd hurt him, Jude realized. Not just physically. She'd slapped his ego, humiliated him in front of his friends and family. And still he was sorry. Part of her did soften now. ''You've already said it, Aidan. We'll put it aside, just as you said, and forget it happened.''

''I've never said it, and that's the problem.'' There was temper in his eyes again, and the edge of it in his voice. Overhead, thunder crashed like balls of lead. ''Words have magic. Spells and curses. Some of them, the best of them, once said change everything. So I haven't said them, hoping, in a cowardly way, that you would change first, and I'd just tend to you after. I'm sorry for that, too. I do want to take care of you.'' He lifted a hand to her cheek. ''I can't help it. I want to give you things and show you places, and to see you happy.''

''You're a kind man, Aidan,'' she began.

''It has nothing to do with kindness. I love you, Jude.''

He saw her eyes change, and the fact that it was shock and wariness that came into them only showed him how far he'd gone wrong. There was nothing left to do but bare his heart. ''I'm lost in love with you. I think I was the moment I saw you, maybe somehow before I ever did. You're it for me. There was never one before, there'll never be another after.''

She felt a desperate need to sit down, but there was only the ground and it seemed much too far away. ''I'm not sure . . . I don't know. Oh, God.''

''I won't rush you the way I did before. I'll give you all the time you need. I'm only asking you to give me the chance. I'll settle things here, then come to Chicago. I can open a pub there.''

She had to press a hand to her head to make certain it stayed on her shoulders. "What?"

"If that's where you need to be, that's fine."

"Chicago?" It didn't matter about her head now. Nothing mattered but the man gripping her hand and looking into her eyes as if everything in the world he wanted was centered there. "You'd leave Ardmore and come to Chicago?"

"I'd go anywhere to be with you."

"I need a minute." She tugged her hand free to walk to the garden gate, lean on it while she caught her breath.

He loved her. And because of it he would give up his home, his legacy, his country to follow her. Not asking her to be what he wanted, what he expected. Because she was enough just as she was.

And more, he was offering to be what she wanted. What she expected.

A miracle.

No, no, she wouldn't think of loving and being loved in return just as strongly, just as deeply, just as desperately as a miracle. They deserved each other, and the life they would make.

So she would just consider it right.

She'd found Jude Murray, all right. And a great deal more.

Her heart was steady when she turned back. Steady and quiet and calm. He didn't quite know what to make of the little smile on her face.

"You said you needed a wife."

"And I do, so long as she's you. I'll wait as long as you need me to wait."

"A year?" She lifted her brows. "Five, ten?"

The knots in his stomach twisted like snakes. "Well, I'll hope I can persuade you sooner."

Dreams took risks, she thought. And courage. Her deepest dream was standing, waiting for her answer.

"Tell me again that you love me."

"With all my heart, with everything I am or will be, I love you, Jude Frances."

"That's very persuasive." With her eyes on his, she walked back down the garden path. "When I realized you were attracted to me, I thought I would have an affair, something hot and reckless and daring. I'd never had one before, and here was this big, gorgeous Irishman more than willing to cooperate. Isn't that what you wanted, too?"

"I did—thought I did." Panic snuck back up on him. "Damn it, it isn't enough."

"That's convenient, because the trouble was—is—" she corrected, "I'm just not built for reckless affairs, not in the long run. So even before that first night, when you carried me upstairs, I was in love with you."

"*A ghra.*" But when he reached for her, she shook her head and stepped back.

"No, there's more. I'm going back to Chicago, not to leave but to sell my condo and settle my business so that I can move here permanently. It wasn't for you, and it still isn't for you that I've chosen to do this. It's for me. I want to write. I *am* writing," she corrected. "A book."

"A book?" Everything in his face went brilliant, with a pride, she realized, that astonished her. And sealed everything. "That's wonderful. Oh, it's what you're meant to do."

"How do you know?"

"Because just saying it makes you happy. It shows. And you've a lovely way of telling a story. I said so before."

"Yes," she said quietly. "Yes, you did. You said it before I could."

"I'm so pleased for you."

"I've always wanted to, but I didn't have the courage to do it, to even consider it. Now I do." Now, she understood, she had the courage for anything. For everything. "I want to write, and I'm going to be good at it. I want to write here. This is my place now. This is my home."

"You weren't leaving?"

"Not for long, but I was determined not to come back to you. I found my place here. *My* place, Aidan. It had to be mine first. And I found a purpose. That had to be mine, too."

"I understand that." He reached out, just touched the ends of her hair. "I do, for I was the same. Can you accept that I know that, and want all of that for you, and still want the rest?"

"I can accept that I found my place, my purpose, and now I've found you. So it's you I'll come back to. And I'm going to be good, very good, at all of it." This time she reached out, took his hand. "You've given me the words, Aidan, and the magic of them. I'll give them back to you. Because what we start here, today, we start on even ground."

She paused, waiting for the fears and the doubts, but all that came into her was joy. "There was never one before," she said quietly. "Though I wanted there to be, tried to make myself into someone so that there would be, because I was afraid to be alone. Now I've learned how to be alone, and trust myself, to like myself. I won't be coming to you weak and malleable and willing to always do what I'm told so as not to make trouble."

With his heart humming, he touched a finger lightly to his battered nose. "I think I've got that part, darling."

She laughed, and wasn't the least bit sorry. "Once I take you, there'll never be one after." She held out her other hand. "Forever, Aidan, or never."

"Forever." He took her hands, bringing first one, then the other to his lips, then on a deep breath, he knelt at her feet.

"What are you doing?"

"Doing it proper, finally. There's no pride here," he told her, and his heart was in his eyes for her. "I don't have a bag of jewels taken from the sun to pour at your feet. I've only this."

He reached into his pocket to take out a ring. The band was thin, and old. The little diamond in its center caught a stray beam of light and sparkled between them, a promise once kept, waiting to be given and kept again.

"It was my mother's mother's, and the stone is small, the setting simple. But it's lasted. I'll ask you to take it, and me, for my love for you is beyond measure. Belong to me, Jude, as I belong to you. Build a life with me, on even ground. Whatever that life is, wherever it is, is ours."

She promised herself she wouldn't cry. At such a moment she wanted her eyes clear. The man she loved was kneeling at her feet, and offering her . . . everything.

She knelt with him. "I'll take it, and you, and treasure both. I'll belong to you, Aidan, as you belong to me." She held out her hand so he could slip the ring on, a circling promise to the heart. "And the life we build starts now."

As he slid the ring on her finger, the clouds whisked away and the sun poured out light bright as jewels.

And kneeling there among the flowers, they didn't notice the figure watching from the window, or the wistful way she watched them.

They reached for each other. Lips met. And as fresh pain exploded, Aidan sucked in his breath.

"Oh! It hurts." Jude eased back, struggling not to laugh as she stroked his cheek. "Come inside, we'll put some ice on it."

"I've a better cure than that." He rose and scooped her up into his arms. "Just have a bit of a care, and we'll be fine."

"Are you sure it's broken?"

He slanted her a look. "Aye, since it happens to be attached to my face, I'm sure. And there's no need to look so pleased about it." He pressed a kiss to her forehead as he paused at the front door. "And I'm thinking, since you are, this might be just the time to remind you, Jude Frances, you're owing me two hundred pounds."

"And *I'm* thinking you'll make it worth my while."

She lifted her hand, watched the way the little diamond sparkled in the sun. Then reaching out, reaching forward, she opened the door herself.

Turn the page for a preview of

TEARS OF THE MOON

**The second book in Nora Roberts's
all-new Irish trilogy of the Gallagher siblings**

Coming soon from Jove Books!

ONE

IRELAND IS A land of poets and legends, of dreamers and rebels. All of these have music woven through and around them. Tunes for dancing or for weeping, for battle or for love. In ancient times, the harpists would travel from place to place, playing their tunes for a meal and a bed and the loose coins that might come with them.

The harpists and the *seanachais*—the storytellers—were welcome where they wandered, be it cottage or inn or campfire. Their gift was carried inside them, and was valued even in the faerie rafts beneath the green hills.

And it is still.

Once, not so long ago, a storyteller had come to this quiet village by the sea, and had been made welcome. There, she found her heart and her home.

A harpist lived among them, and had his home where he was content. But he had yet to find his heart.

There was music playing in his head. Sometimes it came to him soft and dreamy, like a lover's whisper. Other times it was with a shout and a laugh. An old friend calling you into the pub to stand you for a pint. It could be sweet or fierce or full of desperate tears. But it was music that ran through his mind. And it was his pleasure to hear it.

Shawn Gallagher was a man comfortable with his life. Now there were some who would say he was comfortable because he rarely came out of his dreaming to see what was happening in the world. He didn't mind agreeing with them.

His world was his music and his family, his home and the friends who counted. Why should he be bothered over-much beyond that?

His family had lived in the village of Ardmore in the county of Waterford, in the country of Ireland for generations. And there, the Gallaghers had run their pub, offering pints and glasses, a decent meal and a fine place for conversation as long as most cared to remember.

Since his parents had settled in Boston some time before, it was up to Shawn's older brother, Aidan, to head the business. That was more than fine with Shawn Gallagher as he didn't quibble to admit he had no head for business whatsoever, or the desire to get one. He was happy enough to man the kitchen, for cooking relaxed him.

The music would play for him, out in the pub, or inside his head, as he filled orders or tweaked with the menu of the day.

Of course there were times his sister, Darcy—who had more than her share of the family energy and ambition— would come in where he was working up a stew or building some sandwiches and start a row.

But that only livened things up.

He had no problem lending a hand with the serving, especially if there was a bit of music or dancing going on. And he cleaned up without complaint after closing, for the Gallaghers ran a tidy place.

Life in Ardmore suited him, the slow pace of it, the sweep of sea and cliffs, the roll of green hills that went shimmering toward shadowed mountains. The wanderlust the Gallaghers were famed for had skipped over him, and Shawn was well rooted in Ardmore's sandy soil.

He had no desire to travel as his brother, Aidan, had done, or as Darcy spoke of doing. All that he needed was right at his fingertips. He saw no point in changing his view.

Though he supposed he had, in a way.

All of his life he'd looked out his bedroom window toward the sea. It had been there, just there, foaming against the sand, dotted with boats, rough or calm and every mood in between. The scent of it was the first thing he'd drink as he leaned out his window in the morning.

But when his brother had married the pretty Yank, Jude Frances Murray, the previous fall, it seemed right to make a few adjustments.

In the Gallagher way, the first to marry took over the family home. And so Jude and Aidan had moved into the rambling house at the edge of the village when they'd returned from honeymooning in Venice.

Given the choice between the rooms above the pub and the little cottage that belonged to the Fitzgerald side of Jude's family, Darcy had opted for the rooms. She'd browbeat Shawn, and whoever else she'd twisted around her beautiful finger, into painting and hauling until she'd turned Aidan's once sparse rooms into her own little palace.

That was fine with Shawn.

He preferred the little cottage on the faerie hill with its view of the cliffs and the gardens, and its blessed quiet.

Nor did he mind the ghost who walked there.

He'd yet to see her, but he knew she was there. Lady Gwen, who wept for the faerie lover she'd cast away, and waited for the spell to run its circle and free them both. Shawn knew the story of the young maid who'd lived three hundred years before in that very same cottage on that very same hill.

Carrick, prince of the faeries, had fallen in love with her, but instead of giving her the words, offering his heart, he had shown her the grandeur of the life he would give her. Three times he brought her a silver bag of jewels, first diamonds cast from the fire of the sun, then pearls formed from tears dripped from the moon, and finally sapphires wrung from the heart of the sea.

But doubting his heart, and her own destiny, she refused him. And the jewels he poured at her feet, so legend had it, became the very flowers that thrived in the dooryard of the cottage.

Most of the flowers slept now, Shawn thought, bedded down as winter blew over the coast. The cliffs where it was said the lady often walked were stark and barren under a brooding sky.

A storm wanted to happen, and was biding its time.

The morning was a raw one, with the wind knocking at the windows and sneaking in to chill the cottage. He had a fire going in the kitchen hearth, and his tea was hot so he didn't mind the wind. He liked the arrogant music it made, and sat at the kitchen table, nibbling on biscuits and toying with lyrics for a tune he'd written.

He didn't have to be at the pub for an hour yet. But to make sure he got there at all, he'd set the timer on the stove, and as a backup, the alarm clock in his bedroom. With no one there to shake him out of dreams and tell him to get his ass moving, he tended to forget the time altogether.

Since it irritated Aidan, and gave Darcy an excuse to hammer at him, he did his best to keep on schedule. The trouble was, there were times he was deep enough in his music that the buzzing and beeping of the timers didn't register and he was late in any case.

He was swimming in it now, in a song of love that was young and sure of itself. The sort, to Shawn's thinking, that was as fickle as the wind, but fun while it lasted. A dancing tune, he decided, that would require fast feet and flirting.

He'd try it out at the pub sometime, once it was polished a bit, and if he could convince Darcy to sing it. Her voice was just right for the mood of it.

Too comfortable to bother going into the parlor where he'd jammed the old piano he'd bought when he'd moved in, he tapped his foot for time and refined lyrics.

He didn't hear the banging at the front door, the clomp of boot steps down the hallway, or the muttered and annoyed curse.

Typical, Brenna thought. Lost in some dream world again while life went on around him. She didn't know why she'd bothered to knock in the first place—he rarely heard it and they'd been running tame in each other's houses since childhood.

Well, they weren't children anymore, and she'd as soon knock as walk in on something she shouldn't.

He could have had a woman in here for all she knew. The man attracted them like sugar water attracted bees. Not that he was sweet, necessarily. Though he could be.

God, he was pretty. The errant thought popped into her head, and she immediately hated herself for it. But it was hard not to notice, after all.

All that fine black hair looking just a bit shabby as he

never remembered when it was time for a trim. Eyes of a quiet and dreamy blue—unless he was roused by something, and then, she recalled, they could fire hot and cold with equal measure. He had long, dark lashes each of her four sisters would have sold souls for and a full, firm mouth that was meant, she supposed, for long kisses and soft words.

Not that she knew of either firsthand. But she'd heard tell.

His nose was long and just slightly crooked from a line drive she'd hit herself, smartly, when they'd been playing American baseball over ten years before.

All in all he had the face of some fairy tale prince come to life. Some gallant knight on quest. Or a slightly tattered angel. Add that to a long, lanky body, wonderfully wide-palmed hands with the fingers of an artist, a voice like whiskey warmed by a turf fire, and he made quite the package.

Not that she was interested, particularly. It was just that she appreciated things that were made well.

And what a liar she was, even to herself.

She'd had a yen for him even before she'd beaned him with a baseball and she'd been fourteen to his nineteen at the time. And a yen tended to grow into something hotter, something nervier in a woman of twenty-four.

Not that he ever looked at her like she was a woman.

Just as well, she assured herself, and shifted her stance. She didn't have time to stand around mooning over the likes of Shawn Gallagher. Some people had work to do.

Fixing a thin sneer on her face, she deliberately lowered her toolbox, then let it fall with a terrible clatter. That he jumped like a rabbit under the gun pleased her.

"Christ Jesus!" He scraped his chair around, thumped a

hand to his heart as if to get it pumping again. "What's the matter?"

"Nothing." She continued to sneer. "Butterfingers," she said sweetly, and picked up her dented toolbox again. "Give you a start, did I?"

"You damn near killed me."

"Well, I knocked, but you didn't bother to come to the door."

"I didn't hear you." He blew out a breath, scooped his hair back and frowned at her. "Well, here's the O'Toole come to call. Is something broken then?"

"You've a mind like a rusty bucket." She shrugged out of her jacket, tossed it over the back of a chair. "Your oven there hasn't worked for a week," she reminded him, with a nod toward the stove. "The part I ordered for it just came in. Do you want me to fix it or not?"

He made a sound of assent and waved his hand toward it.

"Biscuits?" she said as she walked by the table. "What kind of breakfast is that for a man grown?"

"They were here." He smiled at her in a way that made her want to cuddle him. "It's a bother to cook just for myself most mornings, but if you're hungry I'll fix something up for the both of us."

"No, I've eaten." She set her toolbox down, opened it, started to rummage through. "You know Ma always fixes more than enough. She'd be happy to have you wander down any morning you like and have a decent meal."

"You could send up a flare when she makes her griddle cakes. Will you have some tea in any case? The pot's still warm."

"I wouldn't mind it." As she chose her tools, got out the new part, she watched his feet moving around the kitchen. "What were you doing? Writing music?"

"Fiddling with words for a tune," he said absently. His eye had caught the flight of a single bird, black and glossy against the dull pewter sky. "Looks bitter out today."

" 'Tis, and damp with it. Winter's barely started and I'm wishing it over."

"Warm your bones a bit." He crouched down with a thick mug of tea, fixed as he knew she liked it, strong and heavy on sugar.

"Thanks." The heat from the mug seeped into her hands as she cupped them around it.

He stayed where he was, sipping his own tea. Their knees bumped companionably. "So, what will you do about this heap?"

"What do you care as long as it works again?"

He lifted a brow. "If I knew what you did, I might fix it next time."

This made her laugh so hard she had to sit her butt down on the floor to keep from tilting over. "You? Shawn, you can't even fix your own broken fingernail."

"Sure I can." Grinning, he mimed just biting one off and made her laugh again.

"Don't you concern yourself with what I do with the innards of the thing, and I won't concern myself with the next cake you bake in it. We each have our strengths after all."

"It's not as if I've never used a screwdriver," he said and plucked one out of her kit.

"And I've used a stirring spoon. But I know which fits my hand better."

She took the tool from him, then shifting, stuck her head in the oven to get to work.

She had little hands, Shawn thought. A man might think of them as delicate if he didn't know what they were capable of doing. He'd watched her swing a hammer, grip a drill, haul lumber, cinch pipes. More often than not, those little fairy hands of hers were nicked and scratched or bruised around the knuckles.

She was such a small woman for the work she'd chosen, or the work that had chosen her, he thought as he straightened. He knew how that was. Brenna's father was a man of all work, and his eldest daughter took straight after him. Just as it was said Shawn took after his mother's mother, who had often forgotten the wash or the dinner while she played her music.

As he started to step back, she shifted, her butt wriggling as she loosened a bolt. His eyebrows lifted again, in what he considered the automatic interest of a male in an attractive portion of the female form.

She did, after all, have a trim and tidy little body. The sort a man could scoop up one-handed if he had a mind to. And if a man tried, Shawn imagined Brenna O'Toole would lay him out flat.

The idea made him grin.

Still he'd rather look at her face any day. It was such a study. Her eyes were lively and of a sharp, glass green under elegant brows just slightly darker than her bright red hair. Her mouth was mobile and quick to smile or sneer or scowl. She rarely painted it, or the rest of her face come to that, though she was thick as thieves with Darcy who wouldn't step a foot from the house until she was polished to a gleam.

She had a sharp little nose, like a pixie's, that tended to wrinkle in disapproval or disdain. Most times she bundled her hair under a cap where she pinned the little fairy he'd given her years before for some occasion or other. But when she took the cap off, there seemed miles of hair, a rich bright red that sprang out in little curls as it pleased.

It suited her that way.

Because he wanted to see her face again before he took himself off to the pub, Shawn leaned back casually on the counter, then tucked his tongue in his cheek.

"So you're walking out with Jack Brennan these days, I'm hearing."

When her head came up swiftly, connected with the top of the oven with a resounding crack, Shawn winced, and wisely swallowed the chuckle.

"I'm not!" As he'd hoped, she popped out of the oven. There was a bit of soot on her nose, and as she rubbed her sore head, she knocked her cap askew. "Who said I am?"

"Oh." Innocent as three lambs, Shawn merely shrugged and finished his tea. "I thought I heard it somewhere, round and about as such things go."

"You've a head full of cider and never hear a bloody thing. I'm not walking out with anyone. I've no time for that nonsense." Annoyed, she stuck her head back in the oven.

"Well then, I'm mistaken, easy enough to be when the village is full of romance these days. Engagements and weddings and babies on the way."

"That's the proper order anyway."

He chuckled and came back to crouch beside her again. In a friendly way, he laid a hand on her bottom, and didn't notice when she went very still. "Aidan and Jude are already picking out names, and she's barely two months along yet. They're lovely together, aren't they?"

"Aye." Her mouth had gone dry with that yen that was perilously close to need. "I like seeing them happy. Jude likes to think the cottage is magic. She fell in love with Aidan here, and started her new life, wrote her book, all the things she says she was afraid even to dream of once happened right here."

"That's lovely, too. There's something about this place,"

he said half to himself. "You feel it at odd moments. When you're drifting off to sleep, or just waking. It's a . . . a waiting."

With the new part in place, she eased out. His hand slid up her back lazily, then fell away. "Have you seen her? Lady Gwen?"

"No. Sometimes there's a kind of movement on the air, just at the edge of your vision, but then nothing." He pulled himself back, smiled carelessly then got to his feet. "Maybe she's not for me."

"I'd think you the perfect candidate for a heartbroken ghost," Brenna said and turned away from his surprised glance. "She should work fine now," she added, giving the dial a switch. "We'll just see if she heats up."

"You'll see to that for me, won't you, darling?" The oven timer buzzed, startling them both. "I've got to be going," Shawn said, reaching over to shut it off.

"Is that your warning system then?"

"One of them." He lifted a finger, and on cue came the cheerful bell from the clock by his bed. "That's the second round, but it'll go off on its own in a minute as it's a windup. Otherwise, I found I'd be having to run in and slap it off every bloody time."

"Clever enough when it suits you, aren't you?"

"I have my moments. The cat's out," he continued as he took his own jacket from the hook. "Take no pity on him should he come scratching at the door. Bub knew what he was after when he insisted on moving out here with me."

"Did you remember to feed him?"

"I'm not a complete moron." Unoffended, he wrapped a scarf around his neck. "He's food enough, and if he didn't, he'd go begging at your kitchen door. He'd do that anyway, just to shame me.'' He found his cap, dragged it on. "See you at the pub then?"

"More than likely.'' She didn't sigh until she'd heard the front door close behind him.

Yearnings in the direction of Shawn Gallagher were foolishness, she told herself. For he'd never have the same aimed her way. He thought of her as a sister or worse, she realized, a kind of honorary brother.

And that was her fault as well, she admitted, glancing down at her scruffy work pants and scarred boots. Shawn liked the girlie type, and she was anything but. She could flounce herself up, she supposed. Between Darcy and her own sisters, and Jude for that matter, she'd have no limit of consultants on beautifying Brenna O'Toole.

But beyond the fact that she hated all that fuss and bother, what would be the point in it? If she polished and painted and cinched and laced to attract a man, he wouldn't be attracted to what she was in any case.

Besides, if she put on lipstick and baubles and some slinky little dress, Shawn would likely laugh his lungs out, then say something stupid that would leave her no choice but to punch him.

There was hardly a point in that.

She'd leave the fancy work to Darcy, who was the champion of being female. And to her sisters, Brenna thought, who enjoyed such things. She'd stick with her tools.

She went back to the oven, running it at different temperatures and checking the broiler for good measure. When she was satisfied it was in good working order, she turned it off, then packed up her tools.

She meant to go straight out. There was no reason to linger, after all. But the cottage was so cozy. She'd always felt at home there. When old Maude Fitzgerald had lived, for more years than Brenna could count, in Faerie Hill Cottage, Brenna had often stopped in for a visit.

Then Maude had died, and Jude had come to stay awhile. They'd become friends, so it had been easy to fall back into the routine of stopping in now and then on her way home, or into the village.

She ignored the urge to stop in more often than not now that Shawn was living there. But it was hard to resist. She liked the quiet of the place, and all the pretty little things Maude had collected and left sitting about. Jude had left them there, and Shawn seemed content to do the same, so the little parlor was cheery with bits of glass and charming statues of faeries and wizards, homey with books and an old faded rug.

Of course, now that Shawn had stuffed the secondhand spinet piano in the doll house space, there was barely room to turn around. But Brenna thought it only added to the charm. And Old Maude had enjoyed music.

She'd be pleased, Brenna thought as she skimmed her finger over the scarred black wood, that someone was making it in her house again.

Idly, she scanned the sheet music Shawn forever left scattered over the top of the piano. He was always writing a new tune, or taking out an old one to change something. Her brows knit as she studied the squiggles and dots. She wasn't particularly musical. Oh, she could sing out a rebel song without making the dog howl in response, but playing was a different kettle of fish altogether.

Since she was alone, she decided to satisfy her curiosity. Setting her toolbox down again, she chose one of the sheets and sitting, gnawing her lip, found middle C on the keyboard and slowly, painstakingly picked out the written notes, one finger at a time.

It was lovely, of course. Everything he wrote was lovely,

and even her pitiful playing couldn't kill the beauty of it completely.

He'd added words to this one, as he often did. Brenna cleared her throat, scowled in concentration and attempted to match her voice to the proper note.

"When I'm alone in the night, and the moon sheds its tears, I know my world would come right if only you were here. Without you, my heart is empty of all but the memories it keeps. You, only you, stay inside me in the night while the moon weeps."

She stopped, sighed a little as there was no one to hear. It touched her, as his songs always did, but a little deeper this time. A little truer.

Moon tears, she thought. Pearls for Lady Gwen. A love that asked, but couldn't be answered.

"It's so sad, Shawn. What's inside you that makes such lonely music?"

As well as she knew him, she didn't know the answer to that. And she wanted to, had always wanted to know the key to him. But he wasn't a motor or machine she could take apart to find the workings. Men were more complicated and frustrating puzzles.

It was his secret, and his talent, she supposed. All so internal and mysterious. While her skills were . . . She looked down at her small, capable hands. Hers were as simple as they came.

At least she put hers to good use, and made a proper living from them. What did Shawn Gallagher do with his great gift but sit and dream? If he had a lick of ambition, or true pride in his work, he'd sell his tunes instead of just writing them and piling them up in boxes.

The man needed a good kick in the ass for wasting something God had given him.

But that, she thought, was an annoyance for another day. She had work of her own to do.

She started to get up, to reach for her toolbox again when a movement caught the corner of her eye. She straightened like a spike, mortified at the thought of Shawn coming back—the man was always forgetting something—and catching her playing with his music.

But it wasn't Shawn who stood in the doorway.

The woman had pale gold hair that tumbled around the shoulders of a plain gray dress that swept down to the floor. Her eyes were a soft green, her smile so sad it broke the heart at first glance.

Recognition, shock, and a giddy excitement showered through Brenna all at once. She opened her mouth, but whatever she intended to say came out in a wheeze as her pulse pounded.

She tried again, faintly embarrassed that her knees were shaking. "Lady Gwen," she managed. She thought it was admirable to be able to get out that much when faced with a three-hundred-year-old ghost.

As she watched, a single tear, shiny as silver, trailed down the lady's cheek. "His heart's in his song." Her voice was soft as rose petals and still had Brenna trembling. "Listen."

"What do you—" But before Brenna could get the question out, she was alone, with only the faintest scent of wild roses drifting in the air.

"Well then. Well." She had to sit, there was no help for it, and let herself drop back down to the piano bench. "Well," she said again and blew out several strong breaths until her heart stopped thundering against her rib cage.

When she thought her legs would hold her again, she

decided it was best to tell the tale to someone wise and sensible and understanding. She knew no one who fit those requirements so well as her own mother.

She calmed considerably on the short drive home. The O'Toole house stood back off the road, a rambling jigsaw puzzle of a place she herself had helped make so. When her father got an idea for a room into his head, she was more than pleased to dive into the ripping out and nailing up. Some of her happiest memories were of working side by side with Michael O'Toole and listening to him whistle the chore away.

She pulled in behind her mother's ancient car. They really did need to paint the old heap, Brenna thought absently, as she always did. Smoke was pumping from the chimneys.

Inside, it was welcome and warmth. It smelled of the morning's baking. She found her mother in the kitchen where Molly was just pulling out fresh loaves of brown bread.

"Ma."

"Oh, sweet Mary, girl, you gave me a start." With a laugh, Molly put the pans on the stovetop and turned with a smile. She had a pretty face, still young and smooth, with the red hair she'd passed on to her daughter bundled on top of her head for convenience.

"Sorry, you've the music up again."

"It's company." But Molly reached over to turn the radio down. Beneath the table, Betty, their yellow dog, rolled over and groaned. "What are you doing back here so soon? I thought you had work."

"I did. I do. I've got to go into the village yet to help Dad, but I stopped by Faerie Hill to fix the oven for Shawn."

"Mmm-hmm." Molly turned back to pop the loaves

from the pan and set them on the rack to cool.

"He left before I was done, so I was there by myself for a bit." When Molly made the same absent sound, Brenna shifted her feet. "Then, ah, when I was leaving . . . well, there was Lady Gwen."

"Mmm-hmm. What?" Tuning in, Molly looked over her shoulder.

"I saw her. I was just fiddling for a minute at the piano, and I looked up and there she was in the parlor doorway."

"Well then, that must've given you a start."

Brenna's breath whooshed out. Sensible, that was Molly O'Toole, bless her. "I all but swallowed me tongue then and there. She's lovely, just as Old Maude used to say. And sad. It just breaks your heart how sad."

"I always hoped to see her myself." A practical woman, Molly poured two cups of tea, and carried them to the table. "But I never did."

"I know Aidan's talked of seeing her for years. And then Jude when she moved into the cottage." Relaxed again, Brenna settled at the table. "But I was just talking to Shawn of her, and he says he's not seen her—sensed her, but never seen. And then, there she was, for me. Why do you think that is?"

"I can't say, darling. What did you feel?"

"Other than a hard knock of surprise, sympathy, I guess. Then puzzlement because I don't know what she meant by what she said to me."

"She spoke to you?" Molly's eyes widened. "Why, I've never heard of her speaking to anyone, not even Maude. She'd have told me. What did she say to you?"

"She said his heart's in his song, then she just told me to listen. And when I got back my wits enough to ask her what she meant, she was gone."

"Since it's Shawn who lives there now, and his piano

you were playing with, I'd say the message was clear enough.''

''But I listen to his music all the time. You can't be around him five minutes without it.''

Molly started to speak, then thought better of it, and only covered her daughter's hand with hers. Her darling Mary Brenna, she thought, had such a hard time recognizing anything she couldn't pick apart and put together again. "I'd say when it's time for you to understand, you will.''

''She makes you want to help her,'' Brenna murmured.

''You're a good lass, Mary Brenna. Perhaps before it's done, help her is just what you'll do.''